Sally Newton

Virri feels she is alone in all the world. Always an outsider in her community and now widowed, she is unjustly blamed for her settlement's troubles and cast out into the wild. But Virri has a skill that might save her - the ability to work copper, something that few people know how to do. Can she find her surviving kin? Can she learn to trust her step-daughter? Will she ever, truly, belong anywhere?

Coppersmith
ISBN 978-1-909936-60-7

Published 2025
Pendown publishing
Cornwall, United Kingdom

Set in 11pt Gentium BB
Printed by Amazon KDP
Cover design by PenguinBoy

Other books by Sally Newton:
The Defiant Prince - book 1 of the Caradoc Trilogy
The Druid Heir - book 2 of the Caradoc Trilogy
The Rebel King - book 3 of the Caradoc Trilogy

Author's note

Coppersmith is a work of fiction inspired by real archaeology. As the story is set in the place now called Britain, 4125 years ago, I had no historical records to go on, but a wealth of archaeological material is available and, as time progressed, quite a lot of DNA evidence too. Readers familiar with the archaeology of the British Isles may recognise the places Virri goes to, most of which are based on real sites and locations. Although Virri and Huerin are fictional characters their fathers are based on famous skeletons - both of whom could, potentially, have had children. Objects in the story are also often based on artefacts, and the ancient copper smelting process depicted is as accurate as I could get it.

In some areas, however, there is no definitive theory or consensus, and I had to indulge in a bit of speculation. Archaeologists understand from the evidence, for example, that the sacred sites were built by large groups of people in episodic bursts, but how these projects were organised is unknown. For the story I have therefore invented the 'stint', that all people do before marriage, or at re-marriage, either at a local sacred site or at one of the bigger ones, as a sort of working pilgrimage. Just my theory, but plausible, I hope.

The collapse of the indigenous population in the British Isles and large-scale replacement by incomers at the beginning of the Bronze Age is widely believed, now, and DNA research backs it up, but disease is just one possible cause. Which disease is a matter of ongoing research, so I have gone for a respiratory infection. Pneumonic plague is one of the diseases suggested, with traces of *Yersinia pestis* found in Early Bronze Age skeletons from the European mainland: www.nature.com/articles/nature.2015.18633,
but it could have been something more akin to influenza, or multiple diseases.

The worship of the moon and particularly the sun during this period seems clear from the evidence available. The fabulous exhibition 'The World of StoneHenge' at the British Museum (17/02/22 to 17/07/22) certainly came to that conclusion. I would also recommend a visit to Stonehenge itself, the surrounding landscape and the excellent visitor centre:

www.english-heritage.org.uk/visit/places/stonehenge/
www.nationaltrust.org.uk/visit/wiltshire/stonehenge-landscape

The nearby Wiltshire Museum in the town of Devizes: www.wiltshiremuseum.org.uk
also has interesting permanent displays on the local archaeology.

Exactly what form the religious practices took, however, is a matter of speculation, so I have covered a variety of rituals here.

I hope you enjoy Coppersmith and, if you are interested in the period depicted, I am planning a sequel. Keep an eye out on social media. You can find me on Twitter, Bluesky, Facebook and Goodreads.

Places in Coppersmith with their current names

The Great Circle Stonehenge
The Mother Circle Avebury Circle
Duck Camp Peacock's Farm, Shippea Hill
Crane Camp Plantation Farm, Littleport
Tomb Camp Therfield Heath
The Holes Grimes Graves
Chalk Hill Camp Whiteleaf Hill
The Old Moonspeaker Tomb West Kennet Long Barrow
Maiden Rock Spinster's Rock, Dartmoor
Pink Flint Camp Blick Mead
Huerin's sacred site Knowlton Circle
The stone animals beach Charmouth Beach

Within The Great Circle complex:

The Ancestor Forest Woodhenge
Old Camp Durrington Walls
The First stones The Heel Stone [They were a pair]
The Wait Stone The Slaughter Stone
The Stone on Its Own The Cuckoo Stone

Places mentioned:

Moonspeak Hill Silbury Hill
The Winter Isles The Orkney Isles
Axe Lake Camp Great Langdale, Lake District
The West Isle Ireland
Ox Ring Camp's sacred site The Rollright Stones

Virri's journey,
4125 years ago.
The West Isle
The Holes
Duck Camp
Tomb Camp
Chalk Hill Camp
The Mother Circle
The Great Circle
Huerin's sacred site
Maiden Rock

1.

The woman kept her chin up and her back straight as her kin and neighbours circled her.

Fight, she told herself. *Fight this, or you'll be dead by sundown.*

'They came to trade! Trade – that's all! Your father invited them back, last summer. It's you who sees the ill in all – *I* didn't insult them.'

There might have been a ripple of agreement among the people at that but the house behind them, which had been disappearing into a plume of acrid smoke, chose then, just then, to crumble in a burst of sparks. Frandi, her stepson's wife, started to howl.

'See! See what you have done?' Elyc spat, jabbing out his right hand, and Virri flinched, despite herself.

Fight.

Virri looked her stepson in the eyes. 'Blaming me is very easy, isn't it? I didn't invite them here! I didn't treat them rudely – '

'They're your people!'

Virri stalled. It was true. For ten years the camp had never missed a chance to point out the differences: her "watery" eyes, "sick-pale" face and hair "like grass on fire". Even her skill with the metal was watched with both awe and fear. Her husband had tried to make her laugh about it – when he was alive.

'They look like me, but they're not my kin,' she insisted. 'I never met them until las–'

Elyc hit her, right across the face, making her stumble backwards. 'Don't *lie!*'

She crouched down, holding her cheek.

From the back of the circle she heard old Gerna, in a warning tone, say, 'You've no proof she knew them, Elyc.'

'Anyone who supports her can share her fate!' Elyc snapped back.

There was a gasp. Virri straightened up again and looked about the circle, but everyone shifted their gaze, even the old man.

How surprising . . .

'Your father would be ashamed of what you are doing to me,' Virri said.

'He was blind to any lies from you. Don't think I don't know.'

'Just go!' Frandi yelled, through sobs and snot. 'No-one wants you here.'

Virri's heart jolted. *Better than death – at least!* A clod of earth struck her. She whirled. *But I could still end up dead.* She ducked down, sheltering her head, scrambling for the weakest point in the circle. Elyc tried to grab her back, but she twisted out of it.

'Oh just let her go!' someone shouted, and it was echoed by others.

'We don't want her ancestors angry with us.'

'Let the wilderness kill her.'

Virri felt a chill slip up her spine.

Elyc threw out his hands. 'If she runs she might catch up with the raiders – '

Gerna sneered, 'They're halfway down the river by now.'

They froze as sudden movement among the reeds made his words seem foolish, but it was Maka, Elyc's younger sister, who emerged. She was panting, holding her knees, her bow and quiver over one shoulder and a brace of ducks over the other.

'I saw the smoke,' she said, scanning the scene. 'What's going on?'

'She's out-shone herself this time,' Elyc said, rolling his eyes.

Virri felt the danger of that bow and quiver. *Speak fast.* 'I am being falsely blamed for your brother's mista-'

'They took everything!' Frandi cut in. 'The calf! The wean-pigs! They may as well have killed us outright.'

'Then why aren't we going after them?!' Maka snapped.

Virri watched her stepdaughter's sharp face gather mood as the excuses rolled: the raiders were too many, their weapons too good, the speed it happened so fast. *There were nine*, Virri thought, *and the weapons were no better than I could make if I had the ore . . .*

Maka had thrown down the ducks and was looking about the circle with the ire of the young and righteous. 'What are we going to do then?'

'It was decided, just before you got here, that Virri would be banished,' Gerna said.

Maka snorted. 'How will that help?'

'It's fair, Maka – there's no real proof she is to blame,' the old man added.

'One less mouth to feed,' Frandi said, with a side-eye to Elyc, and there was a grim murmur of assent from those around. Virri felt her stomach turn. *Ten years I've lived here*! *Ten years of quiet living. I never hurt a little finger on anyone. While Elo was alive none of you would have touched me*. She fought down the sudden tightness in her nose and eyes. *No tears. No tears, by Father Sun*. Virri thought of the journey she had made as a young woman, happy in her new love. Vast, vast lands stretched between her and any kin who might still be living. *What am I going to do*?

'Fine then,' Maka barked. 'I'll go with her.'

'What?' Elyc's face dropped open like a fish for a moment, but then the scowl was back. 'No. *No!*'

'You did say that any who supported her would share her fate. . .'

Elyc turned on the old man, again with the jabbing finger. 'You! You can shut your mouth.'

There was a whistle through the teeth from everyone at this disrespect and a woman muttered, 'He was protecting this camp when you were still pissing the bed at night.' Elyc whipped round to Virri – but in truth it was not her. Virri was staring open-mouthed at the 'daughter' she'd first met as a hard-eyed, bitter seven-year-old – and who hadn't warmed up that much since. *Of all the people to speak up for me . . .*

'Maka, you do not need to do this . . . I do not ask it of you.'

The girl scowled. 'You don't want my help? You're useless with a bow. You'll die without me.'

'There's no argument,' Elyc said. 'You're not going.'

'You have no right to stop me, brother,' Maka whipped an arrow from her quiver and notched it. She went no further, but there was still a gasp. The circle shrank back. 'Virri – leave.'

A gap opened up, on the scrubland side, where the dark alder woodland lay beyond. The two women backed out of the circle, their gaze never leaving the accusers.

A few steps . . . and they were out.

2.

Virri was the taller of the two, but Maka's youth gave her stride stretch and Virri found herself struggling to keep up. As soon as they were across the graze-patch and into the woods she made an excuse to slow.

'Easy – the mires!' Virri warned.

'I know the ways, just follow me.'

It was true, but the wood had soaked wetter and wetter every winter for five years and although it was now late summer, and about as dry as it got, they soon bogged down and were forced to slow. They reached a dry patch ringed by bull-rushes, an old crane nest by the looks of things, and Maka raised her hand for halt.

'We should decide where we're going before we go any further,' she said.

Virri nodded. 'We should.'

'Have you a plan?'

Virri plonked herself down on the soft rushes, avoiding her stepdaughter's gaze. *Honestly . . . no. I got up this morning expecting to end it with fewer baskets and a bit more copper, that's all.*

'It went through my mind, when they banished me, that I should try to get back to my kin.'

Maka blinked. 'Are there any?'

'My father, mother and foster-brother were all dead when your father wed me, but my uncle and elder sister could still be living.' Virri shrugged. 'At least, I don't know they're dead.'

'Where are they?'

'I don't know for certain. My sister was in the far north when we left her.'

'Alone?'

'No, with her new husband and their baby. I planned to go back, if my foster-brother was healed at the Circle – or even if he wasn't, to be honest – but then I met Elo, and he helped me bury my brother, and I came here with him instead. My sister would understand.'

Maka took off her left shoe and slapped a grit out of it. 'You say north – where? Near The Holes?'

'No, no – much further than that, where this isle has its skinny waist and flares out again.' She looked at the younger woman and realised this description was meaningless to her. 'At least two moons' walk, even if we had supplies, and I might not find my sister living at the end of it.'

'And the baby wouldn't remember you.'

'No. He would be eleven now, if he's alive, but he won't remember my face.'

'You said an uncle, too? Wouldn't he be really old?'

Virri's face twisted into a smile. 'Five-and-forty or so, no older than Gerna. He could still be alive.'

'Where would he be?'

'He was at the Great Circle, the last time I saw him, but he was thinking of leaving.'

'To row back to where you all came from?'

Virri smarted inside, but let it go. 'No, to journey south-west, to look for ore – that had been my father and Uncle Charn's original plan, before everything else.'

Maka sighed. 'It's a good two moons walk whichever way we go, then.'

'And that's if we'd prepared and had supplies.' Virri looked beyond the alder branches to the sky. 'It will be dark soon enough and we don't even have fire-stones.'

'Oh I'll get a fire going, don't worry about that.'

'But we need stuff, we can't journey across the Isle naked as we were born.'

Maka sucked in a breath. 'Well you can go back and pack a bag if you like! I thought you needed to get out of there, before it got worse . . .'

Virri raised her hands. 'I did, you're right.'

'And look at all we *do* have.'

In the silence they both took stock of what they did have. Maka had her bow, quiver and arrows – just seven, she'd not intended to be out long – and a short flint knife with ash-wood haft tucked in her belt. Her deep-brown hair, wavy to her waist if loose, was braided with, and strapped up in, a long leather thong. So, with her woven-wool belt, they had two long fastenings if they needed any. Virri's skirt was made of hundreds of twisted nettle-string cords she'd made for herself, when her original mother-made string skirt fell apart, so they had plenty of cordage.

'We'll be cold, come night-fall, even with a fire,' she commented, waving a hand at her own legs, bare below the knee, and Maka's dress was no better. Maka lived in that brown ox-skin dress all summer, but she'd never spent a night in it outdoors without a blanket before. It had no sleeves and ended at her knees. Virri's deer-skin blouse at least had sleeves.

'If we could get to Beach Camp, tomorrow, or the next day, we could trade your hair-glinters for supplies,' Maka said, and Virri's hand flew to the gold toggles on her left-side braid.

'No. No, my father made these for me. Besides, they might not welcome us – and they had the lung-fever there, last I heard. We shouldn't go anywhere near.'

Maka raised her eyebrows but didn't argue. 'We could go to our own Crane Camp, pick up some things . . . '

Virri thought of the day they'd packed up and moved, cattle, pigs and house-poles, earlier in the summer. 'We didn't leave anything worth taking.'

Maka knew the truth of it, and they were silent a good while as the sun sank in the sky. 'What are we going to do then?' she said at last.

What indeed? 'You mentioned The Holes. Last summer, when your father and I went there, Tayoc of The Holes made it clear he wanted to learn how to make the copper, but Elo wouldn't let me teach him.'

'Father was right – Tayoc already has enough.'

Virri shrugged. 'Well, yes, but I don't owe Elyc and the others anything . . . not now. And Tayoc would give us food, blankets, anything, for the journey, for this knowledge.'

'Elyc won't like it . . .'

'I know, but I'm never going back. You, you still could, if you want.'

'Are you trying to get rid of me?'

'I'm giving you a chance to get out of it, before I make it worse.'

Maka looked to her feet. 'I'm not going back there.'

Why? Why is that? You've always been close with your brother, not me.

'Besides,' Maka went on, 'how are you going to show Tayoc how to do the copper if you don't have any ore?'

Virri's eyebrows twitched. 'Well, that's another thing. I'm going to have to get it.'

'You mean catch up with the Pales?'

'No! I mean go back to camp and steal my own things back.'

Maka was, for once, lost for words. 'Are you mad?' she asked at last.

Virri almost smiled. 'Possibly. But we won't get far if we start out with empty hands.'

She felt less confident come dawn. The fire Maka rubbed into life before dusk offered them some comfort but neither slept much, with twigs and stones digging in their flesh and cool breezes on whichever side they didn't turn to the hearth. Each time they began to doze a squawk or grunt out in the dark got hearts racing again. By midnight their stomachs started to rumble. The 'plan', such as it was, must have changed five times in their hushed conversations of the night. It was with that strange, brittle, hollowed out feeling that they emerged from the woods in Father Sun's first rays.

There was no point in going back during the night. With their own house burnt Elyc and Frandi would have moved into her own, for sure, and her things would be well guarded, if not intentionally so. Maka believed fear of the Pales coming back for a second raid might even lead them to set a guard overnight and, though Virri was not so sure about that, in her forthright stepdaughter's absence, it was plausible they could have a watcher awake. The camp's dogs would be alive to any footfall out of place. There was a fear, too, that the others could pack up and move, to Crane Camp, or north and east onto the heath, rather than risk laying open-bellied to a return raid.

'I'll never get my tools back if we don't act fast,' Virri had said, 'It has to be the morning, when they are busy,' but now, watching from the reeds south of camp, all was quiet.

'They are up late this morning,' Virri commented, with a wry smile sideways to Maka, crouched beside her.

'They'll have been arguing well into the night.'

I think you're right.

Her stomach gurgled yet again and Virri felt a flush of blood to her face.

'I saw a stand of blackberries when we came out of the wood,' Maka said. 'I'll nip back and get some.'

She was off before Virri could argue. *If I see my chance I'll just have to take it without her*, she thought, but as it was Maka was back, the skirt of her dress loaded with plump berries, before so much as a dog stirred ahead of them. Virri let the strengthening sun warm her aching back, the deerskin shirt heating up like a baking stone. The berries felt good too. She crushed the next two against her palate, letting the sweet juice run down her parched throat. All the while her mind turned over: *Have they already gone? Have we missed them?*

No – there!

The door flap opened and Frandi emerged, just to throw the night-piss urn out, first, but soon followed by Elyc. He thumped on the side of his friends' house and the three of them set off west, bows in hand and dogs at heel, driving the cattle out into the margins to forage. Other people came out of their houses, stretching and yawning, to go for firewood or water, none of them going off alone. They saw old Gerna and his grand-daughter heading with a bowl of scraps towards the sow pen. Even Gerna had his bow and a quiver of arrows at his back.

Virri passed Maka a look. 'Everyone's a bit jumpy this morning, it seems.'

'Just what we need. What do we do if Frandi doesn't go out?'

I have no idea. Virri popped a few more blackberries into her mouth, for lack of anything else to do, for now. *If she doesn't come out soon the others will start coming back.*

At last, Frandi appeared at the doorway, clutching a basket under her left arm and what looked like a piece of firewood in her right hand. She cast a good look around.

'What's she going to do with that club?' Maka huffed. 'I've seen more muscles on a whelk.'

'Shh!'

Frandi did look their way, peering out, and they both froze.

Go on. Go. I don't want to hurt you.

Frandi tucked the basket further under her arm, cast another glance around, and scuttled off, east.

Yes. 'She's going to the veg patch. Now's our chance.'

Virri shot across the clearing, Maka right behind her.

'Stay by the door, keep watch,' Virri hissed.

It was dark inside the house after the bright clearing, especially with the door flap closed, but Maka could only have it open a crack. Virri let her eyes adjust a moment. There was some light, from the tiny gaps in the willow-wattle walls. It would be enough.

She could tell straight away the house was not as she'd left it. Sure enough Elyc and Frandi had moved across anything of their own they'd managed to salvage. The tang of burnt wood in the air hit her first. She saw the baskets she'd had out to trade yesterday morning had been piled up to one side, maybe to make room for the dog to sleep. Her tall, striped ferment-milk pot that she'd treasured for years was out of its position and, she found, nigh on empty.

Thieving swine. Hope it makes you sick.

Virri picked it up, pulled the leather top off and drained the last, setting it back in pride of place.

'Come on, don't hang about,' Maka urged.

You're right.

Virri went to the biggest basket, on the west side of the house. *Thank Sun, they haven't touched it.* Her bellows were there. She'd spent a good moon preparing the leather and making those. There was what remained of her greenstone too, in its little bead bag. She would need something bigger to carry everything in. Virri looked to her baskets. No, not for a journey like this. She went to her old goatskin bag, hung on its peg, and slung it over her shoulder. In went the bellows, the ore, her best crucible, her father's second-best polishing stone, the smallest mould.

This is going to be heavy.

'Looks like Gerna's finished up – he's just giving the old sow a scratch,' Maka warned.

Virri cast another frantic look around the house.

My oak ear-discs! Elo made them for me.

In they went to the bag. Hazelnuts by the handful. A lump of salt pork. A strip of dried beef. *Fire-stones!* In they went. The copper knife her foster-brother had left her, in its rawhide sheath. *There's Maka's wrist-guard – I keep reminding her.*

'Come on!'

'All right, all right.'

Virri went to the door. She could see why Maka was worried – Gerna wasn't over by the pigs anymore. He was out of sight entirely. 'Right, let's go.'

'Back to the reeds?'

Virri shook her head. 'No, straight to the wood, like we did yesterday – we don't know where he is now, we need to get out of sight fast.'

Maka agreed and they set off at a dash – until a shout stopped them in their tracks.

'You!'

Gerna was there, arrow notched and bow drawn, tucked behind the calf pen, waiting for them to come out.

3.

They both stopped dead. There was no time for Maka to draw her own bow and Virri was willing her not to try it. Her mouth dried as her heart rate galloped up. Gerna had the bow taut. He hadn't shot yet but he could – maybe even by mistake. She could see the strain he had the bow string under, the sweat beading on his forehead.

'Where's little Andar, Gerna?' she asked.

'Run to get Elyc.'

Oh no.

'Please, I was just getting my things. I only took my own things.'

Gerna's gaze swung from Virri's face to Maka's. A droplet of sweat ran down the side of his nose.

'Please, Gerna. . .'

They could see the bow string shaking under the strain. Virri felt herself wince, turning away.

The old man raised his bow and discharged the arrow to the sky.

'Go. I'll tell them I missed,' he said. 'Just go. Run.'

Maka looked like she was going to be sick. Virri grabbed a handful of her dress and dragged her. Running to the woods was out of the question now – it was too close to where Elyc and the others had gone with the cattle. Virri chose north, striding out as fast as her legs would let her, the goatskin bag banging on her left hip. She kept glancing at Maka. The girl was following but there was something strange about her. 'Run,' Virri urged. 'They won't have gone far.'

A yell behind proved her point. Virri whipped round. She saw Elyc running out from the wood, his two friends and the dogs following. Elyc raised his bow.

'Come on!' Virri yelled.

Before them the 'high' ground of the camp had run out. They were heading into flat fen, with no more cover than reeds and rushes could give, stretching as far as the eye could see. *What can I do*?

A flurry of yells and whoops behind them seemed to wake Maka up. 'This way!' she said, twisting off to the right, striding out faster than Virri now. Virri glanced round. The men were gaining on them.

'What are you doing?! We can't let them get in range!'

Maka shook her head. 'Just hurry.'

She wove between stands of reeds, splashing through water. They reached the northern bend of the river and Maka splashed straight through it. A heron flew off with a start as Virri charged on behind her. She was starting to see the girl's logic. Above them the funeral platforms loomed. The smell of burning clung to the air. They scrambled up the bank and Maka gripped Virri's arm. She hauled her up onto the middle platform with her.

'They'll be here in a blink,' Maka said, taking the bow from her shoulder and notching her first arrow. Her hands were shaking. 'Get behind me.' Virri obeyed. She saw Elyc's dog first, crashing through the reeds, then the man himself, his two companions close behind. All of them pulled up sharp at the river. The dogs were spinning, whining with excitement, wanting to press on with the hunt, but the men had their eyes fixed on Maka's arrow. Could she take all three of them? And the dogs? Virri looked at her stepdaughter's trembling flesh and doubted it. She'd get one, maybe two, before the remaining man or men could shoot back.

Sun and Moon protect us.

'By the spirits of our mother and our father don't you put one toe further forward brother!'

Virri peeked out and saw Elyc smirk. 'You won't kill me.'

Maka's body tensed as she drew the bow string back. 'I could put one through your bollocks though. Try me.'

The other men laughed. A nervous titter of a laugh like the dogs' whining. Elyc drew back his own bow.

'It's not you we want,' he said. 'It's her. Well you know it.'

Virri shrank in, so close to the girl she could smell the ox-hide dress.

'Well you can't have her. Back off.'

'What's it to you?' Elyc yelled back.

Virri cringed. *What indeed*? As Maka hesitated her heart fell further.

'Father still watches us, Elyc.'

There was silence. Virri held her breath. She snuck a look out again and saw Elyc's face contorted with malice. He did look like his father, but his father on a bad day. A bad day every day. She could remember moments of decency from him but not once out of the company or sight of Elo.

Oh Elo. Why did you have to go before me?

Elyc eased his tension on the bow and lowered it, and Virri pulled in a good breath, but Elyc wasn't finished yet. He pointed with one end of the bow at Maka. 'You. You won't ever be welcome here again. Your ancestors' tombs will never see your shadow. The sun will rise and set on this land and the crops will grow without you.' He spat at the ground and then stabbed the spit through with the arrow. 'Home is closed to you. By the twentieth winter from now no-one will even know you existed.'

He clucked his tongue at his dog and the three men and dogs withdrew, melting back into the reeds, like the spirits he had invoked.

4.

Maka was still shaking and Virri now got the distinct impression she had wet herself. The girl's brown eyes were sparkling with tears. 'Come, come away from here,' Virri said, taking Maka by the shoulders and steering her down from the platform. She headed upriver a little, out of sight of the ancestor place, and urged the girl to wash, washing her own face and hands of the sweat and dirt of the last days. All the while the girl was meek and quiet as a cow at cud. It chilled her.

'Don't let his words cut you deep,' she said. 'He is no Sun-Speaker or Moon-Speaker or even a wise old one. He was a spiteful boy and he's turned into a vindictive man. His curse is just words on the wind.'

'You don't know that. You don't even believe the same things as us.'

'Well, it isn't so very different when it comes down to it.' Virri scooped another handful of water over her hot face. 'And I never knew your mother, but I know your father would never shun you, not if a knife was held to his throat.'

Maka went quiet. 'I – I'm not so sure,' she said at last.

'Why? Why is that?'

The girl pursed her lips. 'I don't want to talk about it.'

Virri sighed. 'Fine. Let's get going then.'

It was possible to walk to the Holes in one day, Virri had done it before at her husband's side, but that was setting off at dawn, and on a full stomach. They didn't get far before they stopped and built a fire and munched down upon the thin, dry nibbles she'd thrown into the bag. At least they were out of the fen and onto drier land.

Virri took a good look around. Open, coarse grassland surrounded them, studded with an occasional tree spared the axe. Their own cattle had grazed here for a good chunk of the autumn and sheltered beneath the oaks in the rain. She remembered nights cuddled up to Elo under the hide-tent listening to distant howls while he snored away.

'There could be wolves here, at night, don't you think?'

Maka shrugged. 'The fire will keep them off.'

Virri added another few sticks to the flames, studying the scowl on her stepdaughter's face.

I'm going to have to ask her outright, sooner or later.

'So, what was going on back there? That wasn't all about me.'

Maka shrank further upon herself, hugging her knees. 'I said I don't want to talk about it.'

'Well, if we are to journey on to The Holes and then south and west across the Isle together, I deserve to know, don't you think?'

Silence.

The sun was starting its descent by the time they got near The Holes. Tayoc didn't have a guard set up, as such, but they were spotted long west of the village and escorted in. Virri expected nothing less. The boy ordered his dog to guard his sheep and set off at a lick of a pace towards home.

'Is all well with your father?' she asked the boy, for she had recognised him as one of Tayoc's own. The lad beamed back with gleaming white teeth.

'Never better. Father says the seam of flint we found this summer is the best ever.'

Virri suspected Tayoc would have trained his offspring in what best to say from the moment they talked, but smiled, nonetheless. 'We have come with something precious of our own to trade.'

Now it was the boy's eyes that gleamed. 'What is that?'

'Oh I'll tell your father when we see him later.'

It worked, they were taken straight to him, but first they had to cross through the busy village and Virri – despite having visited before - was still an exotic amongst them. Men and women stopped their work and stared, and children swarmed around her, trying to touch her straw-like hair, pale skin and most of all the hair-glinters. She did not mind, happy to see a flock of healthy children and feel the calm easiness of the settlement. It boded well for the trade she wished to make.

Maka was a stranger too but nothing much out of the ordinary to them and Virri could see she was content to be ignored, taking it all in. It was an odd place. Everywhere pits and hollows marked the land. Some were the open holes that gave the place its name, with ladders poking out of them. Youngsters were emerging, baskets of flint upon their backs. Adults took it from them and over to shaded shelters to sort and work and it was to one of these willow-woven awnings that the boy led them.

Tayoc looked up with a smile as they approached. He didn't look surprised. *Did he know we were coming? How?*

'What news from Duck Bill Hill?' he said, and there was laughter, but it wasn't mocking laughter. Virri knew it for an old joke. She, too, had seen real hills that took more than three steps to get up them.

'More news than I can tell stood here with no cup of water in my hand.'

Tayoc laughed again, flashing his own moonbeam teeth. He was entering the latter half of life now but still looked good, strong of muscle and just the odd grey streak in his black curls. 'A good answer,' he said. He wiped his dusty hands upon his sheepskin kilt. 'Tano, go to the east pit and tell your sister to come up for her meal. I will take our guests now.'

They followed him to the largest house. His wife looked up with her habitual frown as they entered. The medicine-tattoo between her brows she'd got for migraines in recent years didn't help that look. There was now also a new baby in a sling on her left side, gurgling and smiling as he played with his mother's wolf-fang necklace.

Virri smiled. 'Greetings Savti. I am pleased to see you safely delivered – he was four moons off when I was last here.'

Savti nodded back. 'Greetings to you. We were all sorry to hear of the death of your husband.'

Virri's head fell and Tayoc put his arm around her shoulders. 'He was a good man,' he said. 'May his ancestors welcome him.'

'Was it lung-fever?' Savti continued. 'We lost three of our own last winter.'

Maka had been quiet until that point but now flicked Virri a glance. 'No, Father had it, but he recovered – then he cut himself working on a fence for our pigs and the fever came back like fire.'

Virri felt stung. *I tried my best. It wasn't my fault.* She willed herself to keep her head up, knowing Tayoc would be watching everything they did.

Tayoc ushered them to the rush mats by the hearthside and they both sat cross-legged while Savti set about serving cups of water and bowls of mutton stew. As Savti offered round the barley bread Virri forced herself to take only a modest chunk. She began to practice the words she would use to trade what she wanted when the trade-talk began, but the arrival of Tayoc's smiling daughter initiated another delay. The girl had an antler pick tucked into her belt and was coated in chalk dust so she had to put it down and go and wash before she could sit down to eat. Virri tried to remember if she had met the lass before.

'Is this your eldest?' she asked Savti, but it was Tayoc who answered.

'No, no, Sawa will get wed in the Spring, they are both down at the Circle doing their stint. This is Jaya, the second.'

'You've grown!' Virri said, with a smile, clawing back, and the girl herself grinned, at least.

She wondered if Tayoc deliberately chose that moment to start the bargain talk. He had sat upon a stool on the north side of the hearth as if he was going to eat too but so far had not touched a crumb. 'So,' he began, 'What is it that brings you both here?'

He didn't actually say 'alone', 'without Elyc' or 'in such a state' but Virri felt she could see it in his eyes. She chose to be honest.

'Elyc has banished me, following a trade-talk with boat-comers that went badly wrong. I have come simply seeking the supplies for the two of us to travel safely south-west. In return I have something of my own I am willing to trade.'

Tayoc's eyes glittered but again he chose not to pursue the bargain talk at that stage and she could not let it throw her. He looked to Maka.

'Did Elyc banish you too?'

She nodded.

'What happened?'

Maka looked to Virri and it was Virri who answered. 'The boat-comers had been invited, by my husband, after their first visit last year. They brought the ore we had asked for, and Elyc knew all about it – he knew they were coming, and what we'd agreed to pay. When they arrived, he changed the goods he was prepared to trade, and when they objected, he insulted them.'

'Already enough beer-swilling Pales over here, throwing their weight about?'

'That sort of thing, yes. He even said that the lung-fever comes from them.'

Tayoc and Savti's eyebrows raised a little at that.

'They then stole everything they could carry and burnt the house down,' Maka finished, and Virri had to nod in assent.

'Where are these boat-comers now?!' Savti asked.

Virri could only raise her hands. 'I don't know. They could be back across the sea for all I know or heading up the coast.' She looked to Tayoc. 'They did not mean any harm, at first. It was Elyc who poked the bear.'

Tayoc nodded, resting his hands upon his knees. 'If they come here, I will trade with them as if I know nothing, but thank you for the warning.' His left eyebrow twitched. 'They would not be the first Pales to come here trading for flint.'

No indeed. Virri smiled. 'That is why I am here. I am what you call a Pale too, am I not? I will give you what none of the others will. Not just the metal tools, the shiny axes, or the ornaments at a blown-up price – no. *I* will give you the knowledge of how to make them.'

5.

Tayoc had a greedy look in his eyes now. 'Are you sure supplies for a journey are all you want? For this knowledge, if it's true, you could both stay here if you need. I'm not afraid of Elyc.'

Virri was sure, but the sharp look she saw in Savti's eyes did nothing to dissuade her. 'It's no small thing I ask for – we aim to reach my kin, the other side of the isle. We need food, clothes, more weapons. Do we have a trade?'

'We have a trade, as long as you can do as you have said.'

Virri shrugged. 'It will take most of tomorrow, because I'm starting from scratch, but by sundown you shall have what you want. I will need some help from your people.'

'Go on.'

'Fire-wood – the driest you have. Part-burnt is ideal. And clay and grog as if making a coarse pot.'

'That's easy enough,' said Savti. 'I make as good a pot as anyone here.'

'Good.' Virri licked her dry lips. 'Also . . . somewhere to do all this. I mean . . . do you want *everyone* to know? Or just you and your family?'

Tayoc smiled. 'We are all family here. Do it in the heart of the yard if you want.'

Virri raised her hands. 'All right. Fine with me. It's just not everyone would want every last villager to know how to work the copper. It's quite a sight.'

'It is that kind of thinking that's led Elyc to banish two kin for the theft of three pigs. I would rather sleep easy at night.'

Virri admired his thinking but was still a little surprised.

Later, when the sun was starting to set and Tayoc had returned to the mines to oversee the end of the day's work, Virri took her leave. Savti was busy cooking the evening meal and Maka seemed content enough, sharing tales of strife with Jaya as they compared tools. Virri said she would take a turn about the village, to choose a good site for the smelting. Her second purpose she kept to herself.

It was the end of a hot, clear day and the village glowed in warm pink light. The children who flocked to her once again as soon as she crossed the threshold were, thank Sun, called in to dinner one by one. As soon as she was alone again Virri doubled back to somewhere she had seen on her first turn, a lone pine tree a little above the most northern of the holes. It was tall, taking its strength from the earth, gnawed at the base by sheep and goats but strong enough to take it, spared the axe for its welcome shade. She sat now, cross-legged, at its base, facing west. There was a good view of the setting sun.

Virri took her father's second-best polishing stone from her bag and clasped it between her palms, keeping both hands in her lap. Closing her eyes, she took in a good breath through her nose and let it out through her mouth.

One.

'Sky-God, if you hear me, send my Father to me in the sun's last rays.'

Six more times. As she opened her eyes the sunlight seemed to have grown redder, the golden glowing red of molten copper in its crucible.

'Father, this is the first time I have spoken to you since my husband's death. You see the straits I am in now. Please, you who were loved by everyone, please support me tomorrow. Don't let this smelting go wrong. Don't let me mess this up.'

Virri was up before anyone else the next morning. She washed, combed her hair as best she could through her fingers and re-braided it, tight. The hair-glinters went back on, but her oak ear-discs too. Finding plentiful chalk dust everywhere she put a stripe of it over her nose and cheek bones, aware of how red she would go in the heat of the smelting even if it wasn't another baking-hot late summer day. The spot she had chosen, on her walk the night before, would offer some shade, from noon onward, thanks to a high fence to corral the settlement's goats. More importantly it also offered a break from the prevailing wind. It wasn't far from where Savti made her pots, either. Ideal.

She was there when the others started to gather round. The most unimpressive part of the whole process, the digging and smoothing of the small shallow pit, was already done. All her tools and bits she needed were by her side but for now under an upturned basket. She had rolled up her sleeves.

'Are you ready for the clay and grog?' Savti asked, handing her a bowl of plumped-wheat and a horn spoon.

'Yes please.'

She wanted to gulp down the breakfast, but aware eyes were on her she ate it with studious calm, staring out across the village as if in deep thought.

Tano and Jaya brought the clay and grog, followed by Maka with a crock of water.

'You will need my help, I think,' Maka whispered as she set it down.

'If you're willing, yes, help would be useful.'

'Of course.'

'Stay here now, then.'

Virri set to mixing up the clay and grog with the water. She added dried cow-dung and shredded bits of straw, sprinkling on both with large ostentatious gestures and then crushing and squeezing the mixture between her fists as if to throttle it. The grog itself was good, small pieces of crushed old pots, nothing bigger than a barley grain and most a lot smaller. It boded well.

Other people arrived, finishing their breakfasts, watching her with guarded curiosity. Tayoc was among them, but he was not eating. She felt he had tidied himself up too. He had on a boar-tusk pendant, shining white against the brown of his proud chest muscles. She remembered it had been among the trade items she and Elo had brought last year for their flints.

'Do you have everything you need?' he asked.

'Yes, for now. It will be the part-burnt wood next.'

Tayoc nodded to two of his men. 'Pile it there, in her reach.'

She began balling the clay mixture, big balls like bull testicles, and then placed two on the base of the small pit. She pounded and flattened them to form a solid base, smoothing it over with a slick of water, manipulating the edges with her fingers. The next set of clay balls she placed in a ring around the edge of the base. Once the ring was complete she smoothed it out, inside and outside, to form a thick steady wall, and as soon as that layer was finished she started a new ring of clay balls above it. She smoothed them out as before, taking care not to leave a single air bubble. The one breach was a small stick, a pine stick she had picked up after her prayer the day before, that now lay sticking through the base layer, near where the clay met the earth.

'What type of wood is that?' Tayoc asked.

'Pine, from your tree up north of the camp, but it doesn't matter. It's just to leave a hole.' She smoothed out the last imperfection of the clay wall. 'The key thing is to have it the same width as your bellows pipe. I happen to know mine is the width of my thumb.'

'Bellows?'

'You will see them later. It's too soon for those.'

'All right.'

Savti had been nursing the baby but now her attention was back. 'That looks like a lot of grog and bits to clay in that mixture. It will crumble to bits in heavy rain.'

'It will, unless you stick a roof over it. But the main thing is that it will stand the heat. This will be no ordinary fire we are starting.'

That piqued their interest.

'Fire now Maka, please.'

The speed and skill with which Maka started a fire in the clay ring was impressive in itself, at least to the youngest ones. Once the tinder was well ablaze and Maka had begun to place the charcoal Virri gently removed the pine stick to leave a hole. She let Maka continue to fill the ring with charcoal until the pieces were about her thumb's length from the top. A little smoke was rising but not much, thanks to the dryness of the fuel. The flames, for now, were normal but good. She took her little crucible from beneath the upturned basket.

'This is called a crucible. It's just a small, tough, pot, with a thick bottom and tall sides. You place it directly into the furnace, making sure it stays upright.'

Virri put it in the centre, making sure it felt solid beneath, building more charcoal up around it. The sun was well high by now. She could feel sweat moistening her forehead but resisted the urge to wipe it off with her filthy hands. The crud on her hands was drying and falling off so that was good. She brushed it off a little more and then carefully, almost reverently, took the bellows out from beneath the basket.

'These are “bellows”. They are made from cow-leather, but any strong leather will do. Sew them like you would a bag, but a bag with wooden handles and a second small opening.' She tapped the pipe. 'This I made from clay, it is the width of my thumb and goes into the hole where the stick was.'

Virri eased the pipe into the blow hole, seeing a few amused looks on the adults' faces. 'Yep, easy as that,' she said, with a smile. 'You don't want to break it.' She nodded to Maka and the girl sat back a little from the furnace. 'Keep the young children well back now.'

Virri depressed the bag of the bellows once and the flames leapt. The whole furnace seemed to breathe.

'It's just like blowing on a fire, but there's more air and you can keep it up for longer. You need a *lot* of heat.'

She looked to Maka. 'You start, I'll show them the greenstone.'

As the flames rose and fell Virri removed her beaded bag from under the basket. She un-pursed it and rolled the top back a couple of folds. 'This,' she said, 'is greenstone. Copper ore. It comes from the ground, like your flint, but only in a few places. Father said mountains are always worth a look.' She got up and took it round for everyone to have a look, keeping tight hold of the edges. 'Take a good look at the colour – it's not the green of leaves. More like a stormy sea, or the sky when it's about to thunder.'

Savti frowned. 'It's powder?'

'It's powder because I powdered it. Just like grinding grain – but use separate stones to grind, not your flour ones.'

Tayoc had ventured his finger into the bag and now looked up. 'It's poisonous?'

'Not in small amounts – just don't lick your finger.'

Everyone laughed, even Tayoc. She returned to Maka and knelt beside her. 'Ease off the flames a moment,' she whispered, 'Just a moment.' Virri took a handful of the copper powder and cast it into the furnace. The flames flashed green. There was a satisfying 'ooh!' from the crowd and Virri grinned.

'The rest of the powder I will put inside the crucible.'

Again, Maka eased off the flames while Virri pinched the rim of the bag into a soft spout and poured copper into the crucible. She was careful about how much she used.

Not much left . . . but it has to be impressive.

'Now we melt it. This will be hard work with the bellows and may take a while. If you need to get on with something else, now's the time. You can come back; we'll still be here.'

A few people did drift off, to tend to animals or infants, but the majority stayed. Virri and Maka took turns with the bellows, swapping over once their arms grew painful, never letting the heat slide back. Again it was like breathing. Hot, heavy breathing which made the adults smirk and swap knowing looks. The sun peaked in its height. Virri felt grimy with sweat and filth and was conscious of two dozen eyes focussed on her, Tayoc's included – but it was working. The powder wasn't green anymore . . . and it wasn't powder. It started to glow.

'You see how it turns like the glowing sun? That's what you want. But we keep going a bit longer, to make sure it is all melted. It needs to be fully liquid – no lumps.'

'Is gold done in the same way as this?' Tayoc asked.

'Similar, very similar. It's a bit quicker, because it doesn't need to be quite so hot. And you don't get the green fire with gold.' She screwed up her nose. 'It's a bit boring.'

Tayoc laughed again and Virri felt the barb of one of Savti's dagger looks.

'You carry on with the bellows a moment,' Virri whispered to Maka. 'I'll get the mould.'

She delved under the basket again and brought out her little stone mould. It fitted into the flat of her hand, but only just, and she took it round to show everyone as she had the bag of copper.

'This I carved out of stone – it took the best part of a moon, but it's lasted me for years, and I can carry it about. Father said you can make moulds out of other things – clay, tightly packed sand, even bee-wax with clay round it to leave a hole when it melts - but I like the stone. You can't go wrong with stone.'

There were murmurs of agreement with that, as she had expected. 'Is that an axe?' someone asked.

'Yes, this will be an axe – the shape is not the same as when you make a flint one.'

'Can I have a look?' Tayoc asked. 'At the mould?'

Virri handed it over.

'It's limestone?' he said.

'Yes, limestone works well. Don't use river pebbles – they're too hard. Sandstone is good if it isn't the really crumbly kind.'

He showed it to the man next to him and she worried they were about to pick fault with her carving, but the man just asked if chalk would be any good.

I don't know. I've never tried.

'Chalk might work, worth a try.'

They seemed to accept that and handed it back. She put the mould down, near the furnace but not too near, making sure it was stable. The next item to be brought out was – on the face of it – the dullest. A simple hazel stick. She dipped it in the crock of water.

'This is the trickiest bit of the whole thing – make sure you keep the little ones back. I have to get the crucible out and pour the copper, and it is hot enough to burn a hole right through my hand. The burns from this could kill. The tongs stick – ' she brandished it, 'needs to be springy, strong, flexible. Willow is ideal, hazel good. Father said spend as much time choosing your tongs stick as you do anything else.'

Maka passed her a look. 'Ready?'

Ready.

6.

Virri dipped the stick in the crock again, for good measure, and then bent it in two to form tongs, with a curving bend at her hand end. She tried them in the air a moment then motioned for everyone, Maka too, to keep back. They obeyed.

Sky-God, Father, watch over me now.

She put the tongs into the furnace, hearing the sizzle of the wet wood, and clamped the ends either side of the crucible. She remembered her father's reassuring words, the first time she had done this, as a girl of twelve: 'One swift move. Don't rush. Don't dally.'

Virri tested a lift of the glowing crucible, just a heartbeat, to make sure it wasn't caught on anything, and it wasn't. Right. She lifted the tongs, feeling the weight, smelling the burn as they charred, but ignoring it, and swung the pot over to the mould. Using the earth to steady the base she poured the molten copper in one smooth manoeuvre. It glowed as it flowed and there was a pronounced 'aah!' from everyone watching but for now she ignored it. She poured until the crucible was empty, making sure every corner of the mould recess was full and even. Little flames licked from the copper and the tongs, for a moment. She ignored them. A flake of char was stuck to the glowing surface of the axe – that she removed, with a deft flick of the tongs. All the watchers were rapt as the axe changed from white to pinky gold to pink to red.

Thank you Sun, thank you Father.

'One swift, move,' she said. 'Don't rush. Don't dally. My father's words to me, and it works.'

Tano had wriggled to the front to get a better look. 'It's still burning hot, don't touch it,' she warned.

'I can see that,' he said, and Virri smiled.

'Yes, I know, but never rely upon an absence of idiots.'

Tayoc grinned. 'Is that another saying of your father?'

'No, that one came from Mam.'

Everyone laughed and Virri took the opportunity to knock the crucible a bit further away. It was still hot, but returning to a normal colour, and the axe was changing too. It had gone a dark red, with black patches forming on the surface. Good. She tested the tongs. Still strong – a bit charred – but still strong. Good. She scooped up the axe in its mould and plunged the whole lot into the crock of water. There was a sharp hiss and instant bubbles from the water, and a gasp of concern from the crowd.

'It's all right, it's just to cool it. You'll see.'

There was a satisfying clunk as the mould hit the bottom of the crock. Using the tongs she fished around, turning the mould over, and heard another clunk as the axe fell out. Virri's heart leapt. She remembered she usually warmed the mould.

Oh I hope that's just the axe and not my mould cracking in two . . .

'The hissing and bubbling are fine, it's normal, but it's a hot day and the mould, the basket it was under, even the water, are warm. If it's a cold day, or even just a normal day, warm the mould. You can put it on the edge of the furnace as long as you've built the walls thick enough.'

She scanned their faces and felt she got away with that.

Virri peered into the crock and let out a breath. The axe was fine and so was the mould. She brought the copper axe out, with the tongs at first, but it was wet and unwieldy and only warm by that point, so she did a quick touch test and then transferred it to her hand.

Not perfect . . . but close.

'It doesn't look much at the moment, but I'll spend the rest of the afternoon polishing it up. It'll shine as well as gold by sundown.'

Everyone was looking back at her incredulous. 'What are you talking about?' Tayoc said. 'It's astounding.'

'That was amazing,' Jaya gushed. 'I mean, it went in like – like liquid sunlight and now, now, well you could never tell.'

Virri felt her face redden but couldn't help but smile. 'Liquid sunlight. I like that.'

Savti shifted the baby's weight a little and held out her hand for the axe. She turned it over in her palm, feeling the weight, running her thumb along the edge. 'This, this will be the end of us,' she said.

Virri shook her head. 'No, no I don't think so. Copper is hard to find – there's none round here, I've looked. I have to rely on traders for it, and at a high price.' *This is the first smelting I've done in six moons*, she thought, but didn't voice it. 'People will still need flint.'

She threw a look to Maka and was glad to see the girl nodding along.

The axe had been passed around and now made it to Tayoc. The man was admiring the colour, holding it up to catch the light, testing the edge.

'It can be sharpened, the edge can be improved,' she said. 'And like I was saying the polishing will bring up the colour.'

'It's incredible. . . And yet . . . the boat-comers try to sell us these at a huge price, but you've just achieved it in less than one day, mostly with things we could find around, with no real strength.'

She shrugged. 'Skill, though. And preparation. Patience.'

'Oh I agree. I'm not knocking you.'

Virri felt a frown forming on her face and forced it away. 'The real beauty of it is that if it does go wrong – and it can then you can just melt it down and start again. You can melt two or three small pieces in together and make something bigger. You remember that handful of powder I cast in for the green flames? That will be there, as a nugget, or a sliver, at the bottom of the furnace, and it can be melted and it can be melted and formed again.' She rose to her feet, relieving her sore knees, and held out her hand for the axe. 'Do we have a trade?'

Tayoc handed her the axe, brown eyes glittering. His lips turned up in a smile. 'We have a trade.'

Virri spent the rest of the afternoon polishing up the axe as she had said. Only the most ardent of observers stayed the whole day, Jaya among them, watching with absorbed attention. The rest, including Tayoc, were called away to other demands, but he got in another hint that she was welcome to stay before he went.

Jaya helped her to fix the gleaming axe onto a pine haft using nettle-string cords from Virri's own skirt.

'Father will like that,' the girl said. 'A bit too much – don't tell him, or Mother.'

Oh I won't.

Virri's sense of caution climbed higher through the evening. The whole camp gathered in a circle and cheered when she presented Tayoc with the finished axe – she could not help but be pleased about that – but the feast seemed to be going too far. Tayoc ordered a boiling trough dug in one of the incipient mine pits and had a sheep slaughtered. There was venison and juniper stew besides, bread and fruit while they waited, mead made from wild honey, music, dancing. Each time he got too close to her in the dancing she got out of it in as subtle a way as possible – but subtle can't be subtle forever. As soon as Tayoc absented himself for a moment she fled.

Virri was sat with her feet in the stream, north of the lone pine, when Maka found her. She looked up with a start when she saw someone coming.

'Are you all right?' the girl asked.

'Me, yes – just cooling my feet.'

'I thought you were enjoying yourself.'

Virri felt the accusative edge to that and sighed. 'I'm pleased we were successful, but that's as far as it goes.' She tipped her head back towards the drumming. 'All this – it's a bit much, isn't it?'

'Tayoc said we are honoured guests – and they'd already started that boiling pit, us being here just gave them the poke to finish it.'

Virri was not convinced. Maka sat down beside her and scooped a handful of water. 'Are you sure you don't want to stay? I mean . . . they clearly like you.'

'Are you sure *you* don't want to stay? The lad with the armband seemed keen.'

Maka looked back at her in utter horror. 'Eh?'

'The one you were dancing beside – with the chevron tattoo on the other arm.'

'Oh *him*. He's gone down a ladder with one of the others so you're way off there.'

'Seriously, though, don't you want to stay here? It's a good place, on the whole.'

The girl stared out over the water. 'Me, no. No, it's not far enough from Elyc for me.'

Fair enough. Me neither.

'Any way, you're changing the subject,' Maka said. 'It's you who's had the offer to stay, really. They like *you*.'

Virri raised her eyebrows. *More than the rest of you ever did at home, do you mean*? She picked at the strings of her skirt, choosing her words. 'Well, I like them – both of them, to be honest, but I'm not sure it would last if I actually lived here. I don't want to become his new pet to show off, or hers to eventually abuse.'

Maka nodded. 'Did you see her earlier? Chopping vegetables like she was slitting the throats of her enemies?'

Virri snorted a laugh, checking behind her into the darkness. 'You're not wrong,' she whispered.

'Shall we head off in the morning then? First light?'

'That's the plan.' She got up, sorting out her skirt and straightening her blouse so that it covered her midriff. 'Let's just hope we get all we asked for.'

It was more like mid-morning by the time they got away. Virri could not complain, though. They were given a deerskin cape apiece, Virri's trimmed with wolf fur, Maka's with otter, big enough to roll up and sleep in. It was decided easier to do this than to carry a tent. Maka's quiver was filled with arrows tipped with the Holes' glossy black flint and Virri was given a fine fur sheath for her knife. She had been tucking it into her skirt waistband, but Tayoc and Savti convinced her this would prove uncomfortable on a long journey and insisted she took a sheath and belt for it. There was dried meat, nuts and grain, a loaf of good bread to get them through the next day, a smallish pot to cook with and a leather bag for Maka to carry it all in. Their shoes were strengthened and padded; their stomachs filled with a hearty breakfast. All in all, considering everyone seemed hungover and Tayoc's desire had been thwarted, it was as good a send-off as Virri could hope for.

'Remember all I showed you!' she called out as they were waved off. 'And trade for ore – only ore!'

'Do you think they will do as you've said?' Maka asked, in a low voice, once they were leaving earshot.

'Yes, I think so. I am more hopeful for this village if boat-comers come trading than our own.'

Maka raised her eyebrows. 'We'll need to skirt round our old territory if we're to keep safe on the next leg . . . easier said than done.'

'We can do it. But we need to head south-west and we'll come close, so we need to be careful.' She shifted the bag upon her shoulder to get more comfortable. 'There's a sort of ridge that runs south-west, like a spine of the land. We need to pick that up in the next couple of days and it will take us most of the way.'

Maka nodded. 'Father spoke of it.'

'The only thing is we'll be pretty close to Tomb Camp and the southern territory . . .' She glanced aside to check her stepdaughter's face. 'But . . . I don't know about you, but I for one would like to visit Elo's bones before we leave this place forever.'

The girl took in a good breath. 'So would I,' she said. 'I think we should risk it.'

7.

It was another shimmer hot day and what with the increased load they both carried their pace was slow. At noon they sheltered beneath the shade of a juniper thicket and had a nap, making up for the uneasy sleep of the night before. They covered more ground in the late afternoon.

Thunder was starting to rumble as they set up camp. Maka chose the site. It was near a stand of hawthorn, beside a creek, where the soil had fallen away in a winter flood leaving a sort of beach.

'If there's lightning, we won't be the tallest thing,' Maka said.

'What if it floods out though?'

Maka went to check the wall of the bank. 'I don't think it will, not in summer.'

Virri decided not to argue. If it came to it, they could always scramble up onto the plain. She began gathering up hawthorn sticks and twigs for a fire, wandering up-creek to get more, checking under every shrub she found. It felt good to be free of the heavy bag and rolled-up cape. She took off her throbbing sweaty shoes and paddled in the water a while.

In the distance Maka seemed to be hunting something. Virri saw the arrow poised at the slate grey sky. A bird squawked as it fled upwards and then fell like a stone.

She is good.

Virri put the wood down and congratulated her with a cheery wave.

'May as well stretch the stores if we can!' Maka yelled.

'Yes!'

She has been better to me the last few days . . . should I ask her again? Virri wiped the sweat from her brow and picked up her wood pile. *Is it really my business*? Virri thought of her husband, telling her all about his son and daughter as they walked this journey in reverse, ten years before, so eager for her to meet them. *Yes, it is, whether I want it or no.*

Virri smiled as she went up to her stepdaughter. 'I'll get the fire going and we'll try to roast it before it rains,' she said. 'Is it a snipe?'

Maka nodded, removing the arrow. There wasn't much to the bird to be honest, but Virri did not mention it. 'I don't think I've ever eaten snipe before,' she said then realised, too late, that this comment could be considered snarky as well.

Maka's right eyebrow twitched. 'Could be delicious.'

'Could be.'

The girl laughed. 'It's all right – I'm not going to bite your head off.'

Virri chuckled back. 'Well there's a first . . . Are you ready to tell me what the feud between you and Elyc was about?'

Maka side-eyed to nothing. 'No.'

'We'll be skirting north of our old territory tomorrow. I think your father would want me to know – I might be able to help you.'

'No. I don't think so.'

'What can it be then? You and Elyc were always close, your whole lives. Is it just you don't like Frandi?'

Maka snorted. 'No.'

'What then?'

The girl looked to her feet. 'It's personal . . . and icky.'

Icky? Virri's eyes widened. 'Well,' she said. 'I have been walking this land these thirty years, mud, blood and all. I'm not a spirit of the woods. I helped you yourself, by Sun, when your moon-times started, even though you didn't want me to.'

'Not like that.'

'Like what then?'

Maka sat down with a thump and started cleaning the arrow tip on a tuft of grass. 'He . . . he tried to get me wed.'

Virri sat down too. 'Is that all?' was her first thought but she was glad she stifled saying it. 'He never discussed it with me.'

'He said it was nothing to do with you.'

'Hmm . . . well I suppose it isn't clear.'

'It *isn't* anything to do with you! I should be able to wed who I like!'

Virri sighed. 'Well that's honey and sunshine but real life can be cruel. My own grandmother was taken in a raid and spent the next twenty years of her life used like a dog by a man she hated. Why do you not like this man? Is it someone I know?'

Maka shivered, her face sour like sucking a sloe. 'Why didn't she just kill him? I would have done.'

'Then the others would have killed her children. They had done nothing; it wasn't their fault.'

Maka looked away.

'What of this man then? Is it one of Elyc's friends?'

'No.' Maka picked at a scab on her knee. 'You remember when Frandi's brother visited from Beach Camp, after Father died?' Virri nodded. 'He said his cousin's wife died the past winter and he was looking for a new wife. He lives up the coast and Elyc thought it would be good for us, for the grazing in winter.'

Virri sighed. 'It's not the stuff of hearth-side song . . . but he might be all right, you know. I was second wife to your father and happy all these years.'

'That's not the point – I haven't even met him. Elyc just agreed it! Like I was one of the cows.'

Virri frowned. *You could have held it off until later, till you'd got to know him – insisted on both doing your stint in sacred lands first. That would be what anyone would suggest, if you asked. What else was going on here*? Virri's heart jolted. It felt like the mist blew away from her eyes. The girl's boyish ways, her forthright tongue. The way she'd sloughed off that flirty lad up at The Holes. She took a deep breath. 'Is it that you don't like men at all and would rather wed another girl? There's nothing wrong in that if it's the way the gods made you – my own Uncle Charn is flighty as a goose-down feather and it never stopped him fr– '

'Are you *kidding* me?!!'

Maka's eyes looked fit to bust out of her skull.

Virri felt a chasm would be welcome beneath her now. There was no clawing back out of this. She looked at her stepdaughter with mouth open and a stomach of pure water.

Oh gods. Oh Sun and Moon forgive me.

Maka's mouth crinkled, her eyes glistened. Out burst a laugh harsh as a rutting deer. They both fell into a fit of laughter, great snorting laughter, piercing the eerie calm air, drowning out the thunder. A flash of lightning made them both flinch and then set them off again.

'And *you* have the cheek to say *I* have a loose tongue?' Maka said, laughter tears streaking down her face, as they calmed.

Virri raised her hands. 'That's fair.'

'So now you know why I ran away with you, you'll stop going on about it?'

'Fair point.'

'And if I choose to wed you'll not stick your nose in and tell me who I can and can't?'

Virri laughed. 'Absolutely. That's the beauty of having a stepmother. You can marry a horse for all I care.'

Maka grinned. She started to build the forgotten fire, chuckling away while the thunder grumbled. She had brought the flame into life, plucked, gutted and spatchcocked the snipe upon a green stick when she suddenly looked back to Virri.

'What's a horse?' she said.

Virri smiled and began to explain.

The night was more comfortable than it might have been, since they had laughed it out. The thunder and lightning dwindled and was replaced with torrential rain as predicted. They just about managed to roast the snipe and eat it before the clouds burst open and spent the wet spell cramped up underneath their capes, crushed as far under the nearest hawthorn's shelter as the small tree could offer them, chewing on the last hunk of the bread. The rain did not persist the whole night but felt like it did. All their stuff was soaked. They did not sleep a moment. Virri hoped for a scorching hot morning to dry them out and send steam rising from their clothes but the weather broke cool. She went to the creek side to fill their little pot with water to drink but found the once clear stream now nut-brown with silt and decided against.

'Let's just get going. The walking will warm our bodies and we'll find better water somewhere else.'

Maka nodded, swinging her bag and quiver upon her back with a weary sigh. Even her tanned, youthful face was pallid and drawn. 'Perhaps we should visit Tomb Camp properly and get a good night's rest,' she said. 'Elyc might not have got word to them yet about the banishment.'

Virri pursed her lips. 'Maybe. But I don't think we should risk it. What if he turns up whilst we are there?' She swung on her own bag and felt the weight hit her hip like a punch. *This is going to be a long day . . .* 'We should just check there's no-one at the actual tomb, say our farewells, and leave.'

'You look tired . . .'

'So do you.'

'Well I'm not old as the rock.'

Virri was about to snap 'Neither am I just yet' but saw the amusement in her stepdaughter's eyes and laughed.

Noon found them back in fenland and – thank the Sun – the weather had warmed up again. Their shoes became wet anew as they trudged on through it but at least their clothes and loads dried out. They stopped on a flattened nook of rushes where a deer had once bedded down and ate some stores, surrounded by dragonflies and the scent of hot greenery. 'We should take off our shoes, let them dry out, and have a nap, like we did yesterday,' Virri suggested. 'Maybe even camp here tonight. Arriving at the tomb at dusk tomorrow is no bad thing.'

Maka cast a wary look to the bull-rushes around them. 'You don't think Elyc could be this far west?'

Virri shook her head. 'Even if they moved to Crane Camp as we thought they would he will not be out after dark.'

'No fire until after night-fall then – they could see the smoke.'

Virri agreed. It took them what was left of the day to gather wood in any case, once they'd had their restorative nap, because there were few willows or alder around. Maka brought down a garganey but lost both it and the arrow in dense sedge. 'Oh for a dog,' she moaned, but did find it at last. Virri prepared and spatchcocked the bird in near darkness. Thank Moon the night was cloudless, in one way, but on the other hand all the wood they had was green.

'They still might see the smoke,' Maka warned. 'This is going to go up like a stripe.'

Virri shrugged. 'We can't eat the bird raw . . . and we'll have another night without a blink of sleep if we're not careful . . . With all the animals out here . . .'

'I can *deal* with the animals.'

Virri stood and, for the first time in years, dared to give her stepdaughter a hug. 'Elyc will be sound asleep by the time we've got this going – when was the last time you knew him to be out after dark?'

'Eel fishing, last summer.'

She could kick herself. 'But we know the spot, and it's not here,' she said with a sigh. 'Calm down.'

She got away with that, Maka relented.

They reached sight of the tomb of their territory just as the sun was setting the next day, as planned. Caution had got them this far and they took no chances. Virri took off her hair-glinters and hid them in her bag, in case the moonlight caught them. They took shelter behind some gorse to check no-one was about before they ventured any further in. Smoke was rising from the camp itself, over the crest of the slope, and they could hear sheep.

'I can see someone,' Maka whispered. 'Down at the tomb.'

Virri stared hard and caught what she meant as the figure turned. Some beads or something on the person's front caught the light. They knelt or crouched and disappeared for a moment before getting up again with a pot or such in their hands.

'A woman I think,' she said.

Maka nodded. 'Looks like old Brae, Kalo's ma.'

Elo's elder sister didn't seem much of a threat, she'd always been nicer than most, but they waited it out. Brae finished her respects and walked back towards camp as the last rays of the sun slipped below the horizon. Virri and Maka scurried forth once she was out of sight.

The forecourt of the tomb was muddy, which was a surprise. Virri slipped but righted herself before she went down. *Perhaps the storm was worse here.*

Maka had found stew in the bowl Brae had left. 'Someone must have died recently,' she whispered. She set it back down.

There was a definite whiff of fresh soil in the air, behind the smell of stew. Virri wasn't sure in the darkness, but it looked like there was more than one fresh-dug place in the side of the mound. She whipped round to look at the smoke again.

Just one. One plume of smoke for a camp of eighteen people.

'Let's say our prayers and get out of here.'

Maka looked back at her in terror. 'What? What is it?'

'I'm not sure, but something's not right.'

Virri knelt and felt around in her bag for the chunk of dried meat they'd reserved. *Sorry it's not more, Elo.* She leant it beside the bowl of stew. There was a little twist of flowers too, beginning to rot. Maka knelt beside her. They did not hold hands but when Virri began the prayer their voices whispered in unison.

'Ancestors in the west may the setting Sun warm you,
As the warmth of the Sun sustains us.
We who remember you, remember us,
Until we too are one with the land and rock.
Accept our gift, given – '

Behind them a third voice rang out: 'What are you doing here?! Who are you?!'

8.

The two women scrambled to their feet, Maka making a grab for her bow, but if he had meant harm it would have been too late. Thank Sun he did not. The man who towered above them jumped backwards as soon as they moved.

'Virri? Maka?'

A drifting cloud unveiled the moon and now Virri recognised him: Kalo, Elo's nephew. Young, skinny Kalo, with his hair in a top knot to make himself taller, a kestrel feather speared through it for extra effect. His brown face broke in a grin as his cousin dropped her bow and threw her arms about him.

'Sorry, I didn't see who it was from way over there,' he said, waving west, where his flock of sheep now waited under the steady stare of his dog. 'Did I make you jump?'

They followed him over the grass, not towards the camp, but towards his flock and few possessions, out in the breezy open pasture.

'I was just about to bed down, then I saw you,' he said.

'Aren't you heading home?' Virri asked.

'Oh no.'

Virri passed Maka a look. 'What's up, Kalo?' the girl asked.

He had crouched down to gather his things but looked up, sad brown eyes shining. 'Too much to tell in one breath. Let's move down the slope and get a fire going and I'll tell you everything.'

Kalo was good to his word. He built a fire at the base of one of the gentle slopes, near a crooked elder, spared the axe for its berries and flowers. He had smelly wind-dried mutton to share and water in a leather bottle to soften it up with. Virri established early on that he knew nothing of Elyc's banishment of them and, in a moment of rash honesty, Maka told him everything.

'You're all right,' Kalo said, 'I'm not going to tell anyone you were here.' He looked to the sky. 'As Mother Moon is my witness.'

'Have you been banished, Kalo?' Maka blurted.

The lad's face lifted but he didn't quite laugh. 'Not as such. If I have, I've done it to myself.'

Virri frowned. 'What happened?'

'Nothing I could have foreseen. You remember at Uncle Elo's funeral I said I was thinking of going to the sacred lands for the summer?' Virri nodded. 'Well, I did go, but I didn't get very far. I got sick with lung-fever within four days of leaving camp.' He sighed. 'I did the most stupid thing – but what most people would do, I think. I came home. My elder sister, her husband, her little son, her new baby, my little sister, my little brother . . .'

His eyes filled with tears and Virri almost reached for his shoulder then stopped herself.

What are you thinking? He has been over this for moons.

She gripped his left shoulder and the lad looked up with a sad smile.

'It wasn't necessarily your fault,' she said. 'They might have all had it anyway and your sickness just came out after you'd left.'

Kalo shook his head. 'No, it was definitely me.'

'Did you meet any boat-comers on the journey Kalo?' Maka asked.

Virri raised her eyebrows but did not protest the question – how could she, when the answer came back yes?

'I camped a night with two boat-comers – they were nice. They shared their meal with me.'

Maka flicked Virri a look. 'Were they sick?'

He shrugged. 'One was a bit grass-time-snotty, that's all.'

Virri's heart stalled. *It's no proof.*

'It would be safe to go back now,' Virri said, gently. 'You survived it; you must be all right. Your mother must miss you.'

'Oh we see each other. We keep an eye on each other. I leave her meat and wool and she leaves things for me.' He tapped the ram horn that hung at his left hip from his belt. 'I have this to blow in case of trouble.' He sighed. 'Maybe we will be all right. We've survived this far.'

They were sombre as they left in the morning, waving goodbye to lone Kalo as he watched them from the crest of the hill.

'Go to the sacred lands next summer!' Virri called as they walked away. 'Find a good girl, start afresh!'

She saw him wobble his right hand. 'Maybe!'

'Try the Mother Circle! The Moon-Speaker is good, better than the Sun-Speaker!'

Maka cast her a quizzical glance as they got out of earshot. 'You talk as if you knew them personally.'

'Well, I do.'

'Really?'

Virri laughed. 'Yes, *really*.'

'How?'

Virri laughed again. *Well ten years ago I was not the widowed second wife of a fen-dwelling cattle-herder . . . much as I loved you, my Elo.* 'Ten years ago I was the daughter of the man who had brought copper and gold to the Great Circle. He was loved by everyone, mourned like a chief when he passed. The old Sun-Speaker was his closest friend, like an uncle to me. My actual uncle, Charn, had a hope of becoming Sun-Speaker when the time came . . . I knew them all.'

Maka frowned. 'I know you met Father at the Great Circle, but didn't you grow up in the north?'

'I spent some of my girlhood in the north – but Mother only moved us up there because my elder sister was getting wed . . . and because of the way we'd been treated, to a certain extent.'

'Treated? How?'

'Well, for being "Pales". I mean, Father was given a lavish burial, but the mound was away from the actual Circle – Mother hated that. And then when Uncle Charn lost out on the Sun-Speakership...'

Maka swooped down with the limbs of the young and swiped a strand of yellow-rattle to stick in her hair. 'It doesn't sound *that* bad. If you're such a big egg at the Circle, why don't we just head there?'

Virri smiled. 'Are you thinking of doing your stint to wed after all?'

'No.' Maka rolled her eyes. 'But seriously . . . we need a new place to live. Why not there?'

'Because the latest Sun-Speaker is a stretched up little shit and he always was.'

The girl cast a glance at the sun. 'Careful.'

'The Sun knows I have no disrespect for the Sun, nor any god of Sky or Earth. I don't need any gold-grabbing self-lover to speak for me, not with the gods nor anyone.'

'Said like a true Pale.'

Virri wiped the sweat from her brow. 'Weird we might be, doesn't mean we're wrong.'

They had climbed to the top of the next hill and now looked upon the chalk downlands stretching out in the sunlight, their flowers rippling in the welcome breeze. The prospect of a downhill spurt cheered her.

'What do you reckon then? Crest the next hill then stop for a bite?'

The next day could not have been more different. Grey, humid, misty, torrential, misty again, sodden, windy, torrential again. By late afternoon they were so soaked their eyes stung from the water pouring into them. Not a tree to be seen. Pretty little chalk streams churned into puking flumes.

They reached a valley bottom as the day's gloom darkened. Every step was a squelching trudge.

'Can you smell smoke in the air?' Maka said.

'Yes. I thought I heard a cow lowing just then, too.'

'That might have been my stomach.'

They ducked below the bows of a spreading oak as they picked their way across another brook-turned-torrent, using it to steady themselves. As they emerged onto the other side there were definite cow pats among the mud.

'Whose territory are we in now?' Maka asked.

'I'm not sure – probably the Chalk Hill people, by now.'

'Do you know them?'

Virri shook her head, feeling the rivulets slide down her neck. 'Your father used to trade with them sometimes. I never went.'

'Why?'

'It wasn't friendly – or skim-level-friendly – like with Tayoc. They'd just do the trade-talk, swap and be done with it.' She shrugged. 'No point making a proper visit.'

Maka swept the latest pool of water from her eyes. 'We could do with a proper visit now though, couldn't we? Dunno about you but I'm getting cold.'

Yes, me too. We haven't a hope of starting a fire out here and all our stuff is soaked. We'll be lucky to survive the night, summer or no . . .

'We can try to find the camp – which way do you think the smoke is coming from?'

'That way I think.'

They scrambled up a bank for a better look. The visibility was so poor it didn't do much good but what was before them was clear enough – a field of wheat stubble, rimmed with weeds. Dead centre were two posts with a cord strung between them, festooned with dead crows, hanging upside down by their left leg. The smell was powerful despite the saturated air.

'We can't be far,' Virri whispered.

'Why are you whispering?' Maka whispered back.

Virri couldn't help but laugh. They skirted left of the field, trudging downhill. The scent of woodsmoke was getting stronger. A row of hawthorn obscured their vision much further forward but Virri hoped the camp was just beyond them. The prospect of warmth and shelter sped her feet. *They might not be friendly, but they wouldn't leave us out here to die . . . would they?*

'Virri.'

'What?'

'Look.'

Maka gripped her shoulder and pointed right. In the bottom corner of the field, under the darkness of a spreading yew, two hooded figures had bows trained upon them.

Well, I said they weren't too friendly.

'Keep going,' Virri said. 'But we should put our hands up, so they know we're not a threat.'

They did as she said and, as they got to the bottom, the two men came out of their shelter towards them. They still had their bows poised. One was fat, wearing a thick wrap of fox fur around his neck that made him look fatter still. The other, thinner one, had a row of dots tattooed over his nose and a sun swirl on the back of his left hand. Both wore a scowl fit to curdle milk.

'Who are you? What do you want?' the fat one asked.

Virri felt a scowl start on her own face but suppressed it. 'I am Virri, widow of Elo of Duck Camp, whom you have traded with before. This is Maka, his daughter.'

The gaze of both men flicked from her to the girl and back again.

'You've come to trade?'

No. Should I tell them no? I haven't really got anything. Not even enough ore for another show. 'Not on this occasion, no. We journey south-west and would appreciate your hospitality for a night.'

The two men looked to each other. She thought she saw a glimmer of sarcasm in their eyes. *Maybe that was a bit too direct . . . but who would really say no? On a night like this?*

The tattooed one was looking her up and down. 'You are a boat-comer,' he stated.

'Well, it's been a while . . . but yes.'

The men exchanged glances again.

'Laracida will want to see you,' the fat one said. 'Come with us.'

9.

They continued down the hill, one of the men in front and the other behind. Virri's instinct was burning to run, but her head knew it was pointless. She wondered if Maka felt the same. They were in single file, picking their way down the sodden path, so she could not see her face. The men had not taken Maka's bow and knife, or her own knife, yet, but if she and Maka did run the men could shoot them down within a heartbeat. There was no cover, to speak of, for Maka to shoot back from.

Laracida . . . Laracida. The name was not familiar but there was something about it. A woman's name, she would say; a boat-comer name, it sounded like.

'Come on, keep up,' the fat man barked.

They turned along the valley bottom to where the path widened. The settlement crouched at the base of the looming chalk hill, greasy smoke curling into the mist. There was a fence of thorn-bush prunings around the few houses and another hooded man stood within the narrow entrance.

'Have you been raided?' Maka asked. 'Our camp was raided, recently.'

Neither man answered. Virri felt her heart rate rising.

'We don't mean any harm,' she said.

The fat one laughed. 'We know.'

The entrance guard stood aside and they swept in towards the turf-topped roundhouses. All the houses were normal bar one. It was bigger than the rest, with sun swirls up the door posts in white pigment and an ox skull over the lintel. A strange smell seeped through the wattle.

The tattooed, thinner man knocked twice on the right doorpost. 'Laracida, Laracida. Visitors.'

'Let them enter.'

It was a female voice. Young, Virri would say. A hint of strange accent.

He made no attempt to draw back the drape. He leaned in closer to the doorpost. 'But they're all wet,' he said.

'It's all right, Jayon, they can dry out here.'

Definitely a boat-comer accent. Like Mother? This is so weird.

'In you go then.' The fat one gave her a "friendly" shove and she found herself in the warmth. The smoke was sharp in her nose but the warmth was welcome. The hearth glowed at the centre and, behind it, a beaming woman stood peering back at them. She was young, no more than twenty, with a slight but plump frame. She looked almost unnaturally clean, wearing a sleeveless pale-wool dress, right down to her ankles, her light blond hair piled up on her head, like a flame in the darkness.

'You're women!' the woman said.

'Yes! We are!' Maka returned.

Laracida squealed in delight, clapping her palms and actually jumping up and down.

What by Sun have we got here..?

'Come, come, sit by the fire. You look like you've been drowned,' Laracida said, laughing. She ushered them to the cow-hide rugs by the hearth. Her own seat, padded with hay or such like, was a little higher. 'You must tell me your names and all about yourselves – I am so curious! But first food. Are you hungry? I'm hungry.' Another gale of laughter. She got up again and went towards a basket, stumbling into a little pot where resin or such like burned. 'Oh by Sun! I should be more careful.'

Virri took the chance to look to Maka as soon as the woman's back was turned. Maka mouthed "She's mad".

You're not wrong . . . but they were already starting to dry out, she had offered them food. It was getting dark outside by now and still pouring with rain.

"Harmless though," she mouthed back.

Maka's eyebrows leapt further up her brow.

Fair enough – I suppose that remains to be seen.

Laracida was coming back, her arms laden with food. There was a chasm between the way she dumped it all on the rug nearest her seat and then served it to them with great delicacy, taking her own good time to choose the right crocks from her wicker dresser. Virri could not help but admire the crocks, despite the rumbling of her stomach.

'You have fine pots,' Virri said, by way of conversation.

Laracida turned with a radiant smile. 'Thank you. I made these three myself – the rest Father left with me. They left everything heavy with me.'

All right . . . that could be important. 'When is your father coming back?'

Laracida returned and sat back down on the seat with a thump. 'Oh I suppose they might eventually.' She offered the two of them some cheese, now unwrapped from its nettles, upon a fine dish. 'Father and my brothers went west, to look for gold. They said they might even try the far isles. More cheese?'

'Why did they leave you behind?' Maka asked. 'Were you sick?'

Laracida laughed. 'No! No, this is my home now. I am betrothed to the chief.'

Virri's concern was back. 'Where is the chief now?'

'Heryc went to the Great Circle, to do “his stint”, like they do here.' She rolled her eyes. 'It's been four moons – but that's good, really. I've got used to everyone now. They've all been so nice.'

Maka frowned. 'Why didn't you go with him? To the sacred lands?'

Laracida looked back at the girl as if she'd said something beyond stupid. 'But then who would look after Mama Kwi?' She turned to the gloom at the back of the house. 'Do you want some *cheese,* Mama Kwi?!' she yelled into the darkness.

For a heartbeat Virri thought Laracida was, indeed, mad as a badger in a bag – but then the pile of blankets at the back of the house moved.

'Cheese Mama Kwi!'

Virri made the mistake of flicking a look at her stepdaughter and saw the girl's face spilling over with laughter, both her hands clamped over her mouth.

Oh Gods. . .

The evening continued swinging from disquiet to embarrassed laughter and back again until late. They found out a lot, Laracida more than willing to talk. 'Mama Kwi' was near silent, even when she was awake, sat at the edge of the hearth like a giant ball of dough wrapped in blankets. The older woman punctured her silence with an occasional glare, not always at them, but the younger was consistently accommodating to her, to the point of cutting up her food. Mama Kwi, it turned out, was not Laracida's mother. She was widow to the previous chief, the one Elo used to sometimes trade with, and mother to both the current one, Heryc, Laracida's intended, and the two men they had met so far. Gryc, the fat one, was Heryc's twin, younger by a few pushes, while slender tattooed Jayon was two years younger, closer to Laracida in age.

'Father said it had to be Heryc I married, eh Mama Kwi?' Laracida said at one point. 'To make the trade. No eldest son no swap, eh?'

Maka frowned. 'Swap for *what*?'

Laracida chucked another log on the fire and giggled. 'Enough food and flint to continue their journey. Me, and a little gold, for that – things were getting tight, by then. They couldn't have carried on west without a trade.'

'We have just had to trade for a similar purpose ourselves,' Virri admitted. 'My copper working skills for food.' Then she regretted her honesty, seeing Maka aghast, but it was not her unguarded honesty that had the girl riled up.

'How did you feel, being bargained over like a bag of wheat?' Maka asked.

Blunt as ever, Virri thought, but Laracida laughed it off.

'Oh I don't mind. Heryc will be a good husband, and everyone has been so nice. I'm well looked after, aren't I Mama Kwi? Your boys take good care of me.' She beamed at the old woman and got nowt but a blank stare back. Laracida turned back to Virri. 'Did you say you worked copper?'

Virri took a deep breath. *I shouldn't have said anything, I don't have much ore . . . but then maybe she has ore.* 'Yes,' she admitted.

Laracida looked dumbstruck. 'Yourself?'

'Yes.'

'That's so funny! I never met a woman who worked metal before – not even one of us.'

Virri shifted in her seat, throwing an uncomfortable look at her stepdaughter. 'It's not that strange, really. Father couldn't really teach my foster-brother without teaching my sister and me too.'

'*My* father managed it. He said working metal isn't good for girls. Is that why you don't have any children of your own?'

Virri sucked in a sharp breath. 'Father always said to learn everything you can. Doesn't matter, man or woman, watch and learn, listen and learn. You never know what will be useful.' *Learn to think before you speak.* She thought it, but didn't say it.

Later, as they bedded down in the guest place by the hearth and Kwi snored away at the west of the house, Maka turned to her with eyes wide. Laracida had nipped out to relieve herself, but Maka still whispered. 'I don't like her,' she said. 'Let's go at first light.'

Virri sighed. *Well I don't like her much either but let's look at the full view.* They couldn't fault Laracida's hospitality. Their bellies were full, their belongings dried out. Everything would smell of the strange burn-resin, but so be it. Virri's aching legs felt better for a night in a softer bed, too, wrapped up in furs. 'It's still raining,' she said.

'I don't care. She's off her head – they both are.'

Virri threw a look at the old woman. 'Shh – she might not really be asleep.'

'Eh? She's out like a rock. Besides, it's not her I'm worried about, it's Laracida. She's dangerous.'

Dangerous? 'I think she's just lonely.'

Maka shifted, propping herself up on her elbow, but kept her voice low. 'That's another thing – why aren't the boys over here? It's the middle of the night. What are they up to?'

'That's their way. She and Heryc aren't wed yet. They'll be bedded down somewhere else.'

'But she's the only boat-comer here, apart from you. Why are they all treating her like she's the best pig to fatten up?'

Virri sighed. 'Well she's new, she's brought gold, new pots, this crazy burn-resin. They are fascinated by her.'

Maka made a face. 'I'm not. I say we get out of here at first light. While we still can.'

'Let's just see how it goes tomorrow. We could do with a rest while the bad weather passes. Calm down.'

'Calm down? You won't be saying that when we're in pieces in a mound.'

'Shhh! She's coming back.'

Maka relented, in terms of being quiet, but Virri could only guess the wild thoughts riding through her mind. Both of them settled down to sleep, Virri grateful for the soft bed for her aching bones, the warmth of the house and shelter from the pouring rain. Her own thoughts, nevertheless, kept her awake long into the night.

10.

The day dawned wet. As far as Virri was concerned there was no question of leaving then, but she did have a good deal of sympathy with Maka's discomfort. The weirdness continued through the day.

Gryc came knocking at the doorpost as soon as the light broke. Kwi was still asleep and Laracida not far from it, splashing water on her face, so Virri went to the door. He was close but Jayon hung back, out in the pouring rain, his gaze down in his shoes.

'Milk,' Gryc said, presenting her with a pot.

'You still have a cow milking? This late in the year?'

'Goat,' he said.

Virri flicked a glance over her shoulder. 'Are you both coming in to have breakfast with us? Everyone is dressed.'

'No.'

Jayon was still immoveable, but she thought she saw him wince.

Is that embarrassment at his brother's rudeness? Or something I said?

'Right, thanks for the milk then.'

She let the door flap go but watched them retreat, through the crack, out of sight.

As Virri turned she saw Laracida's gaze upon her. The dozy resin-haze appeared to have gone. She looked curious as a bird . . . and a little hostile.

'Still raining,' Virri said, by way of cover. 'Looks like it's set in for all day.'

There was a pause, as if Laracida was deciding whether she believed her or not. 'Yes,' she said at last. 'There's no question of you being able to leave today.'

Well . . . that's not menacing at all.

Maka was right behind Laracida, wiping a cloth over her own hands, but Virri dared not look into her face.

'It's a good job you got the wheat cut before the rain set in,' Virri said, scrambling.

Laracida smiled, with her mouth at least. There remained something hostile about her eyes. 'Yes, isn't it just?'

Sky-God help me. Is she about to erupt?

'Is there anything I could help you with today? Whilst we wait? To thank you for your hospitality? Perhaps some new baskets? I'm a dab hand with baskets.'

'I don't have any rushes, or any willow prepared.'

Of course. Shit.

Laracida raised her eyebrows. 'I suppose you could have helped with the beer for the ceremony, but I made all that days ago.'

'What ceremony?' Maka asked.

Laracida turned to her with another weasel smile.

'Why, the harvest thanks, of course. You can't possibly leave before the harvest thanks.'

Virri felt the shiver that ran up her spine was visible to all.

Virri and Maka were never alone together through the day. They had to go out to relieve themselves, of course, but couldn't very well go together, and neither did Laracida or Kwi. Mama Kwi was pretty much silent, as before, but she stayed irritatingly awake. Every time Virri went out she saw one or both of the men hanging around. Other people came and went, leading animals or carrying tools, but Gwyc and Jayon were always there, rain or no.

They were kept 'busy', despite never leaving the small house, eating the food they were given and answering Laracida's endless questions. Laracida managed to extract their full family names and lineages, through the front of friendly conversation, but Virri did not reveal too much of her father's status at the Great Circle, or her uncle's, in the past. The subject of gold came up – a lot – and Virri suspected Laracida was doing a little prospecting of her own, though her kin had left her here in the east. She was glad she had left her hair-glinters out of sight in her bag.

Each time Virri left the house to go for a pee she tried to get the lie of the land. She wondered if Maka did the same. The rain eased off a bit in the afternoon and the 'Windy Chalk Hill' that gave the settlement its name became more visible. There seemed to be tomb mounds at the top. No cover beyond the odd shrub. There must be a copse or woodland somewhere for all the wood they were burning but she couldn't see it. To the south-west were more hills – the ridge way they had been aiming for.

Maybe we should have kept going.

But no. Cold and wet could have killed them just as well as this young madwoman might. Besides, perhaps they misjudged her. She could be lonely, like she'd said. There was nothing certain . . . just that odd feeling in your guts. They could be jumping at shadows.

Then she saw young Jayon, staring at Laracida's door like a deer about to be shot, and her uneasiness came back tenfold.

Sometime in the deepest darkness of the night Virri worked it out.

She was wide awake, staring at the ember glow of the hearth, but she could hear the sleepy breathing of the others around her. Could she wake Maka without waking the other two? Maybe – but what good would it do? If she was right, then it wasn't the two of them who were in danger here . . . unless by misadventure.

We should leave, but it will have to wait for morning.

Virri waited until the first gleams of sunlight crept through the gaps in the wattle. Sunlight! That was a good sign. Time to go. She listened. Kwi was still snoring at the west of the house. Laracida's gentle breathing could be heard just to her left. Back and forth like bellows. If she wasn't truly asleep then it was a spot-on fake.

Virri placed her hand over her stepdaughter's mouth then gave her the gentlest of pokes in her shoulder. Maka woke with a start, but the resulting yelp was stifled, as intended. The girl's eyes were wild, for a heartbeat, until

Virri cast a glance at the other two women and shook her head.

'I think I've worked it out,' she whispered as she released her hand.

'They're going to sacrifice us, aren't they? At this ceremony. I told you we should have got out of here.'

'No! Nothing like that.'

She had whispered but it was a sort of shouting whisper and she threw another nervous look towards the two others.

'What then?'

'I think the younger brother hankers for Laracida, despite her being his brother's betrothed, and *she* knows it. That's why they don't mingle, even in daylight. She can't do anything that puts her home here at risk. And the other brother knows too and is trying to keep everything from bubbling over.'

Maka turned up her nose. 'Really? That's all?'

'Well it won't be nothing if the brothers start killing each other while we're still here. We need to leave.'

'You don't need to tell *me* that – let's grab our stuff and get out.'

'I don't mean right now. It would be rude to leave before the harvest thanks.'

Maka rolled her eyes. 'Are you joking? What if *you're* wrong and I'm right?'

'Look, it's more likely I'm right – and we can't leave a trail of enemies everywhere we go. Let's pack up and be ready but leave with good grace.'

Maka was about to answer but Laracida gave out a little groan and flexed her shoulders as if about to stretch. She started to push herself up.

Oh Sun and Moon . . . she heard. She might have heard everything. Virri felt her mouth run dry. *But she might just have heard us talking. That might be all – think.*

'Morning Laracida,' she said, forcing cheer into her voice. 'Look – sunshine! We were just saying it will be good for our journey later.'

Laracida turned to look at her, bleary eyed but with a slight crease of frown. 'You will help me with the ceremony though, won't you? You said you would.'

Virri took a deep breath. It was true. Her suspicion that Laracida might simply be lonely came back, a moment, alongside a pang of guilt. As the morning wore on, though, another suspicion floated to the fore – did she just want servants? Some preparing of the feast did occur, but Laracida spent far longer preening herself. The long sleeveless woollen dress was replaced by one almost identical but in pale linen, clinging even closer to her body. She cinched in her waist with a sash of linen kept in place with a shiny jet slider, combed her hair a good dozen times and piled it up with bone pins, added an amber bead necklace across her cleavage and a gold ring at the top of her plump right arm. All the while Virri fed Mama Kwi milk-soak-wheat, spoon by spoon.

Maka was kept busy carrying crocks of beer to the yard, seething like a tethered wolf, until she cracked. 'Are you going to be much longer? Only we were hoping to leave today.'

Virri winced, inside. *So rude.*

Laracida stopped dead, eyes livid. 'I thought *you* might tidy yourself up a little. It is a festival – the Sky-God will be watching us.'

'God watches us every day – covered in filth or not. Given the choice the Sun would probably have us all naked.'

Laracida clucked her tongue. 'You can go out there naked if you want, no-one's stopping you.'

'Well I might. It isn't me who's got the local youths' tongues lagging out like a dog in heat.'

Virri sucked in a breath. *Oh by Sun.*

Laracida swung round towards her. 'You might have taught her the guest laws, since you know them.'

'Laracida, I'm so sorry. We'll – we'll just go.'

The young woman bit her lip, head well down now. 'Please stay until the end of the ceremony,' she said. 'Don't shame me in front of the others.'

Virri felt her cheeks blushing hot. She nodded and – within a heartbeat – Laracida turned to her intended's mother.

'Almost eaten your plumpy, Mama Kwi?' she said. Another empty smile. 'It's almost time – we'll get him out, shall we?'

Oh by Sun what now? Virri had wild thoughts as to what 'him' referred to and, from the look of abject horror on Maka's face, so did she. The memory of one of Mother's tales came back to her, of her first days on the Isle, when someone had brought out the skull of their ancestor between courses at a feast. Mother had laughed about it in later life but at the time it scared her half to death. Virri's panic rose as Laracida delved into the darkness at the back of the house and drew out a long basket, almost like a fish trap. *A leg bone*? But no, what Laracida brought out was a long, tapering wooden god, dark from age and use, naked and staring.

'Actually, do you think I should keep him covered until the time?' Laracida asked. 'What's the done thing here?'

Virri had no idea. She tried to gauge Mama Kwi's face for clues. Nothing. 'I doubt it matters. It's the ceremony day, after all.'

They left the house, Laracida leading the way with the god held aloft, Mama Kwi shuffling with difficulty behind her. Maka made a point of removing their bags and her quiver and bow and leaving them to the left of the door, but Virri chose not to comment and risk riling her up again. It was good to smell fresh clean air and the scent of wet earth. Jayon, Gwyc and the other villagers were there, circled around the pots of beer, but everyone was quiet for now, and Virri felt reassured. Laracida sank the god into a notch at the centre of the yard, among the beer vessels. 'Help me get the covers off, will you?' she whispered and Virri obliged, even under the gaze of Maka's scorn.

'Almost time! Get in a circle!' Laracida announced. They were already more or less in a circle, but it formed up now, integrating Virri, Maka and Mama Kwi into the ring. Only

Laracida stayed centre, close to the god. She took a glance at the sky, checking the god's shadow on the ground. 'Noon!' she said, with a smile, clap and jump. She took up one of the biggest crocks of beer, using both hands, and took from it a delicate sip. 'Sky-God we thank you, now and always.' Laracida passed the crock now to Kwi, but the poor woman had not the strength in her arms to hold it herself, so Laracida did it for her, letting her take a sip and then saying the words, before passing it on to Gwyc. From that point she returned to the centre, careful – Virri felt – not to look at Jayon. He watched her, though, all the time. She started casting handfuls of grain about, onto the onlookers as they passed the beer, onto the god and the ground, chanting prayers, her movements sinuous and fluid. Every time she got within Jayon's reach, or the grains hit the phallus of the god, it looked to Virri as if he was collapsing in on himself with lust, like dry leaves cast on a fire.

Everyone was so focussed on Laracida that no-one saw the man approaching from the west. By the point Virri saw him he was coming through the gap in the thorns. He looked like Gwyc, but in different clothes. He was carrying a heavy bag. Everything about him looked heavy, in fact – his tired, red eyes, his drooping shoulders and jowly face. The first most knew of his presence was when he sneezed into his hand.

Laracida stopped what she was doing and turned. Her face lit up with a genuine smile.

'Heryc!'

11.

Heryc opened his mouth to respond but all that came out was another powerful sneeze. He waved them away as if to apologize. 'Thank Sun I'm home,' he said.

Maka was looking from him to the rest and back again with eyes wide. 'Don't come near!' she shouted.

Heryc's weary face clouded. 'What are you talking about? This is *my* village. Who are you?'

Maka's gaze swung to Virri. 'We've got to leave. Now. He's got lung-fever.'

There was a gasp from everyone at that – Virri included – but whether horror at lung-fever or her rudeness was difficult to tell.

Laracida held out her hands. 'Come, Heryc, come inside and rest. You look terrible.'

'Don't let him near you!' Maka shrieked. 'It's lung-fever!'

Laracida rounded on her. 'Enough! Enough from you for a lifetime! Get out of the way!'

Gwyc and Jayon had stood stunned and silent, but her words now woke them up. Neither had their bows on them but as soon as they moved towards Maka Virri's heart jumped.

'Maka – let's go. Let's just go.'

The girl slapped her own head with her hand. 'Look, I want to go too! But we can't let them do this! Remember Kalo?' She threw out a hand towards Heryc. 'He's going to kill them all!'

'It's their village – it's not our right to interfere.'

Everyone had shrunk back at Maka's words, but Laracida now grabbed Heryc by the arm. 'Absolutely it's not your right to interfere!' she yelled. 'You've done nothing but carp and moan since you got here!'

'I'm trying to help you, you dumb cow!'

Virri's stomach fell another level. *Maka shut up, shut up now.*

Laracida's eyes were on fire by this point. 'I have never, in all my life, met such a rough, oafish woman as you. You'll be lucky to ever get a husband – '

'Well at least I'll only have one not one and a half!'

The whole village gasped. Even so Laracida might have got away with it if Jayon had not thrown Heryc such a wide-eyed look of desperation, like a child caught with a hand in the honey pot, that he revealed all. Gwyc cast Jayon a frantic 'don't' look and made it worse. Heryc's jaw fell.

'That's it, we're going.' Virri grabbed Maka by the arm with one hand, throwing both their bags over her other shoulder. She tried to throw on the bow and quiver too, but they slipped and Maka took them from her. There was another worried yelp from the villagers at that.

'It's all right, I'm not going to hurt any of you,' Maka snapped. 'Virri, let's go.'

They walked, fast, through the gap in the thorns, Virri wincing the whole way, expecting to feel the thud of an arrow in her back any moment, but it did not come. They could hear the shouting and screeching long into the distance.

The two of them were high on the nearest hill, still walking at speed, before Virri broached the subject of what had just happened. Maka remained red with fury, and she thought twice about it, but concluded she had to.

'You were right to warn them about lung-fever,' she began. '. . . But don't you feel that you could have paddled round that a bit better?'

'Oh here we go.'

Great.

'They could have killed us, Maka.'

'Oh *they* could kill us, the wolves could kill us, the cold, the wet. Sometimes, you know, you have to make a stand.'

'Don't make this about me.'

'Well I'm too old by now to get a telling off from you. Drop it.'

Virri took in a long breath. 'I'm not telling you off. I'm just saying that it's quite possible to be right and to be wrong at the same time.'

They walked in silence for the rest of the day, Virri churning the last events in her mind. The increased closeness she had thought was growing with Maka as they journeyed now felt smashed to pieces. She tried to find solace in the warm sunlight, the easy – if hilly – walking on the close-cropped grass, the strength in every step that she'd got from two days rest. It had been a mental strain at Laracida's but not a physical one. Her eyes felt a bit heavy from the poor sleep, but that was all.

It was only late in the afternoon, when they started to camp, that Maka began talking again. They had come down off the path to camp among trees, near a brook, and the girl had started to build a fire.

'You know, we didn't actually touch him, or get near him, but he did sneeze near us,' she said. 'Do you think he could have passed it to us?'

Virri had been unpacking the fire-stones but now looked up in surprise. 'I don't know, to be honest – I'm not sure anyone does. What's wrong? Do you feel ill?'

The pause chilled Virri's heart.

'No,' Maka said at last.

'You're sure? No sore throat, fuzzy head?'

Maka shook her head, frowning. 'No, nothing like that. I was just thinking.'

You're scared. So brash, in so many ways, but scared to the bone of this.

'Well, we can try to get a good night's sleep, keep warm, and in the morning if neither of us feels it coming on, I'd say we're probably out of the woods.' Virri took their ceramic pot out of her bag and scooped up some water from the brook. 'If there is lung-fever at the Great Circle, though, that's another good reason to avoid it.'

'We're way off yet though, aren't we?'

'Not really – if the weather stays good now and we don't have any problems the ridge path will take us all the way to the Mother Circle, probably five days walk, then the Great Circle is another couple of days walk due south of that.' She remembered the trek with Elo all those years ago. 'Like I say, assuming we don't have any problems and we've got enough food. There's a big river to ford tomorrow or the next day, so that could be tricky.'

'Tricky' proved the wrong word. As they bounced down off the hills, the day after next, they could see two jetties either side of the river crossing, four small rafts spread between both and a selection of poles. Virri remembered having to swim the middle section, ten years before, holding her bag above her head, fighting with her legs to keep her head above water and trying not to swallow any of it.

'This is a lot better. Your father and I swam this before.'

Maka actually smiled, the first time in days. 'He said you were so worried about your stuff getting wet you almost let yourself drown.'

Did he? *Really*? She remembered him rubbing her hair dry with his knapping cloth and fretting she'd catch a chill, so rare and precious was she then.

'Whose territory are we in now?' Maka went on. 'It isn't still Windy Chalk Hill, is it?'

Virri shook her head. 'No, not for a while. I think the Ox Ring people by now. Strange that there's no-one here to watch the crossing.'

'There's someone over there,' Maka said, tipping her head to the far shore. Virri tried to focus – the bright sunlight on the water and the dark of the wooded far shore did not make it any easier, but she did see movement. A man, a woman and a dog, it looked like, coming down through the trees and approaching the opposite jetty. 'The man has a bow I think.'

Maka nodded. 'So do I.' She put her bag down, making her own bow and quiver more visible. The man and woman duly stopped, though the dog carried on scampering around.

'Easy,' Virri warned, 'they could just be travellers, like us.' She stepped up onto the platform and waved. 'Don't be afraid!' she yelled across the water. 'We're just travelling!'

'So are we!' came back the call.

'Do you have lung-fever?!' Maka yelled.

'No! Do you?!'

Oh by Sun . . . she's off again. 'No, we're all right.'

On the other side of the river it looked as if the woman was shading her eyes with her hand. 'Virri? From Duck Camp? Is that you?'

'Yes!'

Even from this distance it looked like the woman smiled. 'It's Sawa! Tayoc's daughter. Come over and we'll share our meal.'

Sawa and her man were good to their word. They'd shot a juvenile boar the previous evening and had leftover roast meat to share, plus cheese-patties the south-side Ox people had given them. There were dozens of well-coppiced hazels near the far jetty too, so there was plenty to eat. On the face of it both seemed happy enough. Sawa was good-looking and healthy, as Virri remembered – as she would expect of Tayoc's daughter – and the two of them were very much in love, passing little looks and finishing each-others words. There was something amiss, though. Cam, Sawa's betrothed, had an old bruise going yellow beneath his left eye and Sawa herself had bruises on her arms. She had leant down to unpack the meat and her sleeves rode up.

'We left a moon early,' Sawa admitted. 'We've done our stint and then some at the Great Circle. I just want to go home and get wed and be done with it.'

'Was it that bad? It's always been hard work – I'm sure your parents would say the same – but most people have fun too.'

Sawa screwed up her nose. 'Not these days. The residents were all like "Aw, come back for the Solstice Festival" and we just thought "no way".'

'Was it the Sun-Speaker being unreasonable? I remember him from when I was young, and I didn't like him then.'

Sawa laughed, glancing to Cam. 'Yes. Unreasonable is one word for it.'

Cam snorted. 'Not the one I'd use.'

'Yes,' she continued. 'It was weird though – we didn't even see him at all for the first three days. They just took our "tribute" and set us to work – dawn to dusk – and then from the fourth day on he was everywhere, shouting, throwing himself about, telling everyone we were getting it wrong. Start again, not like that, bigger, taller, deeper . . .' Sawa side-eyed her betrothed again. 'Great fun.'

Cam sighed. 'Aye. I mean I can move rocks around all day long, but I don't expect to get treated like shit.'

'It felt more like we were there to work for him than the ancestors,' Sawa added. 'The tasks were getting more and more ridiculous by the day.'

Virri exchanged looks with Maka. 'We were thinking of avoiding the Great Circle anyway,' Virri said, 'but that seals it.'

Sawa nodded. 'Do your stint at the Mother Circle instead,' she said to Maka. 'That's what I'll be telling everyone when I get home.'

Maka reddened. 'Um, I'm not actually going to do my stint. Neither of us are. We're moving south-west, because of Elyc.'

They then had to tell them everything, but it was all right. Sawa was glad to hear good news of her family. When the conversation turned back to the Circle, though, her face clouded over.

'I'm sorry to hear about Heryc,' she said. 'He was all right, not one of the arse-lickers. He left before we did.'

Cam shook his head. 'He should've taken the lass with him. Must be mad.'

'Well, there's a lot going on there,' Virri said, trying to be fair. 'Best give them a miss, though, on the next leg.'

Their dog pressed his nose into the food bag and Sawa batted him away with a playful swipe. 'The Ox people are fine, stay with them tonight. We'll show you the path, it's not far off the main.' She passed them some more of the roast boar in its wrapping of docks. 'Did you know the Moon-Speaker too, when you were younger?'

Virri nodded. 'Yes, very well. She was not Moon-Speaker then, not yet. Is she well? Did you see her?'

'Yes, we stayed with her when we'd had enough of it and left.'

'We weren't the first to do that,' Cam added, with a raise of his brows.

'Was there a man with her? Called Charn? He would be quite old now, older than me. About her age? He's my uncle.'

Sawa pursed her lips, thinking. 'No, sorry. There were lots of people there, even a few Pales, but no-one called Charn.'

Virri's heart sank but Cam was frowning. 'Charn, Charn,' he said. 'The name's familiar though – I heard some of the men talking about him. Did he work gold? In the old days?'

Virri smiled. 'Yes – he was a master.'

It was something . . . he was remembered, at least, but she still didn't know whether he was living or dead.

12.

Five days walk to the Mother Circle turned into seven, thanks to Virri slipping on some loose soil and spraining the tendons in her left ankle, but it could have been worse. They rested up a couple of days with a cattle-herding family and then carried on. The weather stayed fine and dry, though a distinct nip crept into the air morning and evening. The leaves were starting to turn.

'We'll have to slow down, once we get past,' Maka commented as they breakfasted that seventh morning. 'The days will be shorter.'

'And I won't know where I'm going, from here on in. I've never been west of the sacred lands.'

Maka shrugged. 'There'll be people going that way, if we wait long enough. We could tag along with them if they'll let us. The Moon-Speaker would let us stay, wouldn't she? If we did some work?'

'Oh yes – even if we didn't do any work. It should be a willing gift to the ancestors, from what everyone says. She's never been a tyrant, not like Sulo – the Sun-Speaker.'

'Tyrant?' Maka rolled her eyes. 'Is that what you call it? It didn't sound that bad – I think they were just itching to get home and get wed.'

'Hmm . . . well I don't think so.'

They finished the rest of the meal in silence and got walking.

As the sun sank towards the horizon it was fitting that the ancestors' sacred lands came into view. The sight of the Mother Circle stones bathed in gold brought a smile even to Maka's face. The white chalk in the ring ditches glowed.

'Impressed?' Virri asked.

'How could anyone not be?'

Virri laughed. 'I'm sure there is someone somewhere who isn't. Do you think I should try to comb my hair and put my hair-glinters back on, before we go down? I feel very drab.'

Maka was pointing beyond the stones themselves. 'That hill – that isn't natural. Is that Moon Speak Hill?'

'It is. You should see it when the river floods, it looks like an island then. The Moon-Speaker climbs to the top and talks to the goddess in the reflection in the water. It's very beautiful.'

Maka nodded. 'Father said he found the ceremony here more moving even than the Solstice at the Great Circle.'

'Well a naked woman bathed in moonlight will do that to a man.'

Maka gave her a light punch in the top of her arm. 'Hey! You're being coarse, now, not me. I think he meant it. Anyway, isn't the Moon-Speaker usually really old?'

'They become old, if they are lucky to live that long, but no, not to start with. Not *really* old.'

Old to the young sapling is a full-grown tree, they do not even see the mountain. When they are the tree themselves, they will know the mountain is ancient.

'What's that over there?'

Virri followed Maka's point south to a round building with a pointy, layered roof, adorned with strips of linen so they fluttered in the breeze. 'That's the rest house, where they take the bodies before the ceremony. Your Father's Father put the new roof on that, before he wed, Elo told me.'

Another smile from Maka, which pleased her. They had started the final descent off the ridge when she realised Maka never had answered her question. 'Should I comb my hair do you think? Do I look a hay pile?'

'Oh you look all right. I'm more worried about getting there before everyone's eaten – I'm starving. I'm surprised we haven't seen anyone yet to be honest.'

She was right. There was no-one anywhere to be seen. Tools lay in the ditches, chalk was piled high in the baskets, but no-one was at work.

'We'll head straight for the camp. This way.'

The huge stones that made up the Mother Circle were jaw-drop impressive up close. They were walking fast, a late day spurt on the promise of food and rest, but they slowed a moment to admire the nearest stones before speeding on up the path, parallel to the ancestor way. The 'camp', by contrast, was a ramshackle bundle of lean-to shelters and tents that looked like it had been slung up in one morning. Virri remembered it looking much the same in her youth, although every single building had been replaced a dozen times since then. Only one thing was absolutely the same – the Moon-Speaker's 'tent', a shelter of hazel overlaid with hides of deer and wild ox, bristling with antlers and bones. They could hear the clack-clack-clack of the strings of bones as they swung in the cool evening breeze.

'Everyone is very quiet,' Virri whispered. 'They could be praying – we should check before we go charging in.'

Maka smirked. 'Point taken.'

Virri could smell food by this point and had to slow her own pace. She dragged her fingers through her hair and tried to sweep it back from her forehead. *I should have washed it at the last river and braided it again.* That morning had been cold, though. *The Moon-Speaker won't care. She will remember me; she was always friendly to me and mine.* She shifted the weight of the bag on her shoulder.

The door flap opened and Virri smiled, expecting a welcome, but the woman who stood before them was no-one she knew. Virri's smile faltered. This was a woman but as tall as most men and muscular with it. Virri had never seen anyone like her – neither a boat-comer like herself nor one of The People either. She was as brown of skin as Maka or anyone but with startling blue eyes, sky blue, staring out with fierce intensity like a bird. Her hair was as black and straight as the crow feathers that adorned it. There was a copper knife at her belt and another, it looked like, tucked into a sheath strapped to her thigh.

'Welcome, ' the woman said.

'Um, thank you.' Virri felt her palms sweating. *This is madness – calm down.* 'Can we see the Moon-Speaker straight away? Is she praying? We can wait.'

There was a smile, if you could call it that. More like a baring of teeth.

'The Moon-Speaker is not here. She is at the Great Circle. I am Babca, the Sun-Speaker's chief-of-guard.'

The woman had not asked but Maka nevertheless volunteered their own names. Virri thought she saw a spark of recognition when Virri's name was mentioned, though she couldn't be sure.

'Is the Moon-Speaker well?' Virri asked, trying to make it sound like a reasonable question, not an accusation. She wasn't sure she succeeded.

'Yes,' Babca said. 'Tomorrow, I will take you to her. Come inside.'

Babca was not alone. There were three other 'guards' inside, all men, as relaxed and easy together as a pack of wolves. None of them were boat-comers, in looks, but they had a good deal of boat-comer stuff: copper knives, stone wrist-guards, long flared heads to their arrows. One man had a strip of gold twisted around one of the braids in his long black hair, different to her own hair-glinters in actual form but striving for the same effect. They were even passing a striped and curvy beer crock round, sun-wise, as if they had each robbed the corpse of a boat-comer's very soul.

They cheered when Virri and Maka entered.

'Come, sit, share our food!' the gold braid one said, and they made room for them in the circle about the hearth. Virri hesitated but Maka was down in a heartbeat, leaving her no option but the other slim space. As she sat Virri saw the path she and Maka had taken, through the gap in the door flap, clear as day.

They saw us coming – long before we got to the door. They sent the woman to meet us so we did not run.

'Come, eat,' Gold-Braid insisted, thrusting a dish of meat towards Maka.

Maka's smile spread across her whole face. 'Thank you! I'm starved. We've walked all the way from the far east of the Isle.'

'What, today?' Babca quipped.

Everyone laughed – everyone but Virri. It was noticed, she was sure of it.

'Virri, Virri,' Babca said, the slightest of frowns between her brows. 'That name is so familiar. There was a Virri at the Great Circle in the past, in the old Sun-Speaker's time. Was that you?'

Should I lie? No... I'll only cast a snare for myself.

'I have been to the Great Circle before, yes, in my younger days.'

'Did you see the great stones going up?'

By Sun – I'm not that old. My parents didn't even.

'After that.'

Maka was casting her a puzzled look. 'She knew the old Sun-Speaker, and the current one, and the Moon-Speaker. Her family lived there.'

Oh well done.

Babca's eyes widened. She started to open her mouth to speak but Virri got in first.

'Why is the Moon-Speaker at the Great Circle? And her attendants? All the pilgrims? What has happened here?'

'The Sun-Speaker called on everyone to help. The build must be completed before Solstice,' Babca said.

Thin lips, hard eyes. Virri did not believe her. She tried to judge how old this woman was. From her skin she would say not much older than Maka but that hardness in the eyes . . . and since when did the Sun-Speaker have guards anyway? Let alone a young woman?

'Who are your parents?' Virri asked. 'Perhaps I knew them, when I was at the Circle before?'

Another baring of teeth. 'My parents are the sun and the wind,' Babca said. 'The wind brought me to the Sun-Speaker like a prayer.'

Virri darted a look to the men. No-one contradicted her or commented at all at such a strange statement. She looked back to Babca. *Sulo's daughter*? No, she was not *that* young, and there was nothing of his face about hers.

'You should eat,' Babca went on. 'It will be a long day tomorrow.'

Gold-Braid shoved the beer crock into Virri's hands while another offered the meat.

'Her hands are full, give it to me,' Maka said, with a grin.

Now was she helping me or was that a jibe?

The other man laughed. He slapped Maka on the back with his greasy hand, but the girl did not seem to mind. This one had a bright scar across his stubbly chin, as if someone had swiped him with a blade and missed his throat.

'You have a fine bow,' he said, to Maka. 'Do you hunt?'

Maka was tucking into the joint and had to just nod.

'I thought you did, when you walked in. You've got the legs for it.'

Maka snorted a chortle through the fat and the other men emitted a sort of 'ooh-er' but Scar's face – and Babca's, Virri noticed – stayed dead straight.

Steady Maka, he's twice your age.

'So, what's the relationship between you two?' Babca asked all of a sudden. 'Not mother and daughter I think.'

'Not by blood.'

They both said it, at the same time, and inside Virri cringed.

Babca raised her eyebrows. 'I can see that.'

Virri felt the blood rushing to her face. 'My husband was her father.'

'Elo, of Duck Camp, in the far east,' Maka added. 'He made the bow for me.'

Virri watched their faces as Maka said Elo's name but saw no recognition. Elo had helped her with her foster-brother's burial, helped her to keep it quiet and helped her get away east with him on the quiet too, but clearly his name had not stayed notorious down through the years . . . *Doesn't bode well for me.*

'You should both rest,' Babca said. 'It will be an early start tomorrow.'

Virri took in a good breath, looking round at the crowded tent. There wasn't much room even with all six of them sat upright. *Should I say something? They're never going to let us sleep elsewhere . . . but I must do something. Elo would never forgive me.*

'Maka and I must be together,' she said. 'She is my husband's daughter and unmarried, my responsibility.'

Babca's eyebrows crept up again – not least at the look of shock on Maka's face. 'Don't fret yourself, we'll make room,' she purred. She jabbed a thumb towards the third man, the one who had said least so far. 'Aric – move your junk.' He looked up with just his eyes, brown eyes cold, like a bear about to roar. 'You can sleep outside, ' she said, 'you smell like a sheep.'

The quiet man stood, smirking. He started to bundle his bedroll and belongings into his arms. As he stood his deerskin over-tunic slipped to the side and Virri saw that he, too, bore a copper weapon slung through his belt. It was an axe, fine work, with an ash haft once richly decorated but now showing its age. Virri would have known those stripes and zigzags anywhere. Her sister had done the pattern and got it wrong, with one chevron going the wrong way, so the next stripe had a false gap, but Father had loved it anyway. She was only eleven and his eldest, after all.

The last time Virri saw that axe her sister was laying it in Father's grave.

13.

Virri would have loved a good night's sleep that night. No chance. The fears rolling round her head would have kept her awake on their own, let alone the snoring of three men – Aric was only outside the door – and the thick smelll of cold meat, sweat and leather. She positioned herself between Maka and the rest, with Babca on her left and the wall on Maka's right, but 'who am I kidding?' flew through her mind. Her fighting talk to protect Maka's youth and innocence might have been a goad to them, for all she knew. To be fair none of them did touch the girl . . . yet.

They were up and out at dawn, bolting down a cold breakfast with no time to wash. Gold-Braid and Scar were left behind, on Babca's orders, while Babca and Aric would 'escort' Virri and Maka to the Circle. Virri got the impression Scar was none too happy about it, as Babca barked 'Back in a few, be good' and strode away. He watched them leave, from the doorway, arms folded across his chest, his gaze lingering on Maka most of all.

She did that on purpose – why? To keep his attention on herself? It didn't seem like that, but as far as Virri could tell she had needed two to go and two to stay, to keep an eye out for any other pilgrims, it did not matter which two. Is she protecting Maka? Actually respecting me? Virri berated herself as a trusting fool.

Babca led the way, striding out, quiver on her back and crow-feather hair ornaments flying. All her arrows were fletched with crow-feathers too, Virri noticed, and the sun-swirl markings across the back of her cape were charcoal black. *Well it's one way to make yourself look older*. What made all these men follow her like pups? Every single one was older and, big as she was, they were still bigger than her. If she was not the Sun-Speaker's own kin then there must be something . . . what was it she said last night? 'The wind brought me to the Sun-Speaker like a prayer'. His lover? It didn't seem like the Sulo she remembered, but it had been ten years.

'Pick up a bit of speed!' Babca called from the front. 'We'll get there before dark if we're lucky.'

Everyone duly picked up the pace. Maka kept up with ease, youthful legs striding out almost as fast as the young chief-of-guard. Aric had begun the walk at the rear – keeping an eye on them, so Virri thought – but now he lengthened his strides too. Virri was soon well to the back. She had been long-range walking pretty much every day since being banished, but at her own pace – this was different. Her bad ankle started to hurt early on. By mid-morning both ankles were killing her. The goatskin bag banged on her hip so much she thought it would bruise. Sweat streamed into her eyes.

As the others disappeared into the distance, Maka too, 'stuff this' went through her mind. What was to stop her turning due west and leaving? But she was still within bow range. All three of them kept turning to check she was still following. The landscape was open grassland as far as the eye could see.

At noon Maka raised her hand. Virri heard her call out but could not make out what she said, from where she was. They were climbing a hill at that point, the three others nearing the top and Virri near the bottom. She saw them stop and gather under the shade of a lone oak. They sat and watched as Virri wound her painful way up.

Babca held out her leather water bottle. 'Maka said we should stop for water. She was worried about you.'

Did she now? Virri took a long draught of the water, looking towards her stepdaughter. She wasn't sure if Maka was frowning or just squinting into the sun. It could be true. There was something fishy, though, about the way Babca and Aric looked so pleased with themselves, smirking like polecats. *This was a test . . . they were seeing how far they could push her before she would speak up for me.*

Too far.

'Is it necessary to walk to the Great Circle from the Mother Circle in one day?' Virri asked. 'Most people split it into two. What's the hurry?'

Babca's eyes hardened as she took the bottle back. 'I thought you wanted to see the Moon-Speaker? Besides, we do this walk all the time.'

Oh I bet you do.

There was a glimmer of concern in Maka's eyes now. 'We should ease up the pace a bit,' she said. 'Virri did her ankle in, only days ago. We risk having to carry her.'

The other two nodded along, as if they were completely reasonable, but Virri felt sick.

They are trying to recruit her.

The pace did slow, in the afternoon, from lung-crushing fast to ground-eating fast. Virri continued suffering . . . but, small comfort, she didn't feel like she was going to die. She tried to judge the distance left as she remembered landmarks, to encourage herself on with a 'nearly there', but there had been a few changes in the last ten years. They had been alongside the Sacred River for a while as the sun slipped downwards and she thought they were drawing near the camp but suddenly they were inside a birch woodland. That wasn't there before. The trees were slim, flimsy, but there were hundreds of them. It was ten times darker and now – despite her grim thoughts all day – she was desperate to keep the others in sight, picking up her feet in fear of being left behind.

Babca stopped, so abrupt it was like a cord pulled tight at her back. She pointed to the right, nodding to Aric.

'Over there, remember the place,' she said.

He looked the same way and nodded, and they set off again, fast as wolves.

What was that about?

As Virri passed the spot herself she took a few heartbeats to peer into the murk. More birch trees, moss, bracken, toadstools. Was it the toadstools? They were the red, white-spotty kind, though most were the young white bulbous buds more like infant puffballs.

Poison. They are after poison.

Again her mouth ran dry, but she strove to keep up with them nonetheless, trudge-trudge-trudge through the dark wood.

As the moon rose they emerged from the wood and Old Camp came into view. The surface normality of it brought a sting of tears to her eyes. Smoke was rising from the houses; a shepherd was driving a small flock into a pen. She could smell the wood-smoke and a whiff of stew. Babca and Aric let out a little cheer themselves, and she saw Maka's teeth bright in a grin.

Babca raised her bow in a horizontal grip of her right hand, holding it high above her head. 'Guard home!' she called, and a dozen people came dashing out, most of them men. Virri did not see Sulo among them, but it still caused her to stop, heart rate flying up again.

'Virri, is that you?'

She turned. At the doorway of the left side house an old woman was smiling. Grey curls framed a brown, lined face. Her rounded figure and mound-like bosom were barely contained by the buck-skin tunic she wore.

It was ever thus, but she had gained even more girth in the ten years that had passed.

'Good to see you, Kenna.'

Kenna, the Moon-Speaker, grinned. She held out her hands in welcome.

Virri saw the rope burns at her wrists.

14.

Kenna followed the line of Virri's gaze and pulled down her sleeves. 'You look terrible,' she said, to Virri. 'Come inside, rest. Let me look after you.'

Both of them cast a wary glance towards Babca but the woman shrugged, with a wisp of a sneer. 'Go ahead, don't mind us. I've got things to do.' She turned to Maka, who was eyeing up the settlement, hands on her hips. 'Actually, you've never been to the Great Circle before, have you?'

Maka shook her head. 'No, never.'

Babca slapped her on the back. 'Then we must show you round – introduce you!'

Aric shot a sly smile towards Virri as Maka's face lit up.

Oh I saw you . . . but what choice do I really have?

'Go on,' she said, to Maka. 'It's quite a sight. I'll be here, see you later.'

She put a slight emphasis on 'later', without intending to, and kicked herself.

Virri watched Maka out of sight, going down the slope between the other two, past the ancestor place, towards the moonlit stones.

Be careful.

Maka didn't look back once.

'Come, come inside,' Kenna said, drawing her by the elbow. As soon as they had dipped below the door lintel Kenna released the heavy door flap. The 'guards' and whoever the others were had started to drift back to their own houses and no-one had been taking any notice of them, as far as Virri could tell, but Kenna tied the door flap in place and stuffed a cloth into a persistent gap besides.

'Tell me everything,' she said, waving Virri to a seat by the hearth, 'But keep your voice low.'

Virri sank to the seat. 'You first I think.' She gestured to Kenna's rope-burned wrists. 'What's happened to you? Are you a prisoner here?'

Kenna did a so-so gesture with her left hand. She fetched a cup and a crock of water and slumped herself by the hearth. '*Openly,* I'm a guest. They brought me here saying that there was lung-fever among the healers – which was true – and that they needed my help, which was probably true as well, only, when I got here, well, it all turned nasty quite quick.' She met Virri's gaze with a wry smile. ' . . . I haven't been allowed to leave.'

She handed over a cup of water and turned back to the hearth, putting on pebbles to warm. 'You can take those shoes off before your feet explode – I've both seen and smelled everything in this life, don't worry! I'll start some washing water going.'

Virri eased the shoes off and cast them into a corner with relief. It felt like her feet were glowing. There were red patches at the heels and on both little toes, but it would have been worse if she had not already walked across the Isle.

'Could be worse,' Kenna said.

Virri nodded. 'I felt exhausted, like I'd been hollowed out. I'm feeling my age a bit, I think.'

Kenna laughed. 'You're a spring lamb compared to me – I've seen forty-six winters, forty-seven come this one, and by Sun and Moon it feels like it. Every bone crunches like old bread. I didn't think I would be fighting young bucks and attempting escapes this year of all years.'

'Did they tie you up?'

'Yes, when I protested – out of sight of the pilgrims, of course.'

'Are there lots of pilgrims still here?'

Kenna shook her head. 'Not that many. Lots had left. Those they think are most loyal to me have been encouraged to leave, if anything.'

'We met Sawa and Cam on the path, they told us things were bad here – we'd planned to visit you at the Mother Circle and then go on west. We weren't planning to come to the Great Circle at all.'

'That girl, who went off with Babca – is that Elo's daughter?'

Virri sighed. 'Yes. Maka, his younger child. She saved my life, a moon or so ago. I thought she had finally warmed to me, but I think we're back to sour acquaintance by now.'

'Has Elo passed, Virri?'

'Yes. Not that long ago, really – this spring just gone. He survived the lung-fever, just, then cut himself and came down with fever again.'

'May his ancestors welcome him. He was a fine man.' Kenna protected her hand with a cloth and added three of the hot pebbles from the hearth edge to the crock of water. 'You were happy together, since I saw you last?'

Virri nodded. 'Yes, all these years. It was only his children who always put the sting into it . . . and still do, to be honest.'

Kenna crumbled some dried herbs into the warming water, dipped in a cloth and wrung it out. 'Here you go. Do your face first, you'll feel a bit better.' She sighed. 'She is just the type Sulo will try to draw into his web, you'd better watch it.'

'Oh I know, I've been seeing it all day. What is it with this Babca? What is she to him? I don't remember the old Sun-Speaker – or Moon-Speaker, come to that – ever even having "guards".'

Kenna chuckled. 'Quite. Guarding from what? His own night terrors? His own plots coming back to bite him in the arse? I think the truth is it started because he was always off somewhere, off his head for days on end, so he needed people to lead the builds for him, in his absence.' She rolled her eyes. 'But they soon turned to something more aggressive than that. I don't think the Circle has ever seen anything quite like it.'

'And this Babca?'

'I wasn't here at the time, but the word is that she just turned up here one day, about seven years ago now. She was a young girl then, perhaps twelve, thirteen. Sulo took her in, raised her like an orphaned cub.'

Virri raised her eyebrows. '*Just* that? Surely people are suspicious he misused her?'

Kenna tipped her head to one side. 'Well, yes. People have been suspicious all along, me included, but to be fair there's no evidence for that and never has been. They sleep in separate houses; I've never seen them touch in all these years.' She let out a worried breath. 'But there's a hold between them, like an invisible rope. Sometimes it's as if they think with the one mind.'

Virri felt herself shiver and then her stomach rumbled. Kenna laughed. She got up and took some food down from the dresser. 'When was the last time you ate?'

'A bit of cold meat at dawn.'

Kenna passed Virri a bowl and started to break the bread and cut the dried meat. 'Sorry I've not got more. There are hazelnuts too, after. Here, have some of the sour sorrel too, it will do you good.'

Virri ate without talking. As she finished, though, she built up the courage to ask Kenna the question that had lurked in her mind, dreading the answer. 'Do you know anything of my Uncle Charn, Kenna? Do – do you know if he is still alive?'

The older woman sighed, dropping her gaze back to the hearth. 'I can't say I do know that Virri, sorry. He was alive the last time I saw him, but that was nearly eight years ago by now. He left not that long after you did, really.'

'He went west, as he planned?'

'Yes, but it was so sudden – more fleeing than leaving. I didn't get to see him. And hundreds of pilgrims have come from the west over the years, but no-one has ever mentioned him. Perhaps he changed his name.'

Virri's heart sank. 'I don't know. He has quite a distinctive "look".'

Kenna shrugged. 'Yes . . . but there's plenty of so-called Pales around these days, especially men – and the people he's with could be helping him hide. He always had charm. He could coax the meat from a wolf's jaws.'

'Not with Sulo, Sulo always hated him.'

'Sulo was jealous, he always was. Like a child whose brother gets the better treats. That's why he wanted all your gold – your family were always a threat to him. Charn knew he would either be forced to work gold under Sulo's whip for the rest of his life or end up murdered, that's why he fled.'

Virri felt tears fill her eyes. 'Uncle Charn didn't deserve that.'

. . . And neither do I. Is that what Sulo will do with me?

Kenna shook her head. 'No, no he didn't, and there was a lot of sympathy for him, among most of us folk, but in a way what came after was even worse.'

'What?'

Kenna's eyes were bleak. 'The word is that days after Charn went missing a different boat-comer was found here – younger than Charn, but not by much, fit, tall, handsome. Everything Sulo is not. I don't know what the man was at the Circle for – probably a pilgrim, like anyone else, completely innocent, but Sulo cooked up some allegations.' She snorted. 'Sacrilege, so he said, and Sulo had him murdered, shot with arrows, killed like a pig, right in the centre of the Circle, with the ancestors' spirits looking on in horror. What's more sacrilege than that?'

Virri shivered. 'Did no-one protest?'

'I did, when I found out about it, but it was hushed up, the man was buried quick, not that many people knew. When rumours started floating it was emphasised how the man had transgressed, disrespecting the Sun, and paid for it.'

'Elo's eldest, the son, Elyc, was here to do his stint not two years ago. He said to us that no-one but the Sun-Speaker and his attendants are allowed into the centre of the Circle anymore, but he didn't seem to see anything wrong in it. None of us thought anything of it, at the time.'

Kenna shrugged. 'That's the rub – most pilgrims come, they do their stint, they've only been here the once, so they don't see the downhill slide. They might gripe a bit to their mother or father when they get home, if they have a parent living, but nothing much will ever change while pilgrims still come here. The Sun-Speaker has been an honoured position, for generations, stretching back. . . Sulo can do much as he wants.'

Virri shook her head. 'Did no-one come to avenge this boat-comer? No brothers, kin?'

Our people might be few on this isle, but we are strong . . .

'No, no-one.' Kenna raised her eyebrows. 'People say his ghost is seen, sometimes, in the shadows, near the Circle, drawing a bow in the dark of the woods. They call him "The Hunter". The real man has been forgotten and it has become a hearth-side tale.'

A knock on the doorpost lurched them both out of their skins.

Maka wrenched back the door flap and poked her head round. 'Just me,' she said. 'The others have given me food and said I can stay in the guest lodge tonight, so I didn't want you to be worried.'

Virri's stomach leapt. *Well, I am worried.*

'I met the Sun-Speaker,' Maka went on, with broadening smile. 'He remembers you. He said he'll talk with you in the morning, to catch up on the many years. He'll send someone to fetch you.'

15.

Virri cast the Moon-Speaker a frantic glance but now was not the time to discuss it.

First things first.

'The guest lodge – will there be other women there, not just you, the guards and this Babca?'

Maka frowned. 'Oh yes – men, women, children. A good dozen people. You needn't concern yourself.'

Again, Virri looked to Kenna and Kenna nodded. 'It's bigger than the old one.'

'See you tomorrow then,' Maka said, jaunty as you like, and she was gone, as quickly as she had appeared. Virri turned to her old friend.

'Do I try to flee? Tonight? . . . Do you think I'd get anywhere?'

Kenna shook her head. 'No. Don't even try it,' she whispered. 'Why do you think he's left the meeting until the morning? He's inviting you to run. There'll be someone watching this house all night, they'll take turns. Any move from you and the rest will be woken with one blast of a horn.'

Virri sighed. 'I am disappointed in Maka. How can she be taken in like this? I know I'm not her greatest favourite, but she does usually have more sense – she's too suspicious, if anything.'

She told the Moon-Speaker of all that had happened during their journey so far.

Kenna looked to her with a sad smile as she finished up. 'She's young, and she needs a new home, to find a new place in this world. Don't be too hard on her.'

Virri threw up her hands. 'Well so do I, I need a new home too, but I don't want to spend the rest of my days smelting gold to make trinkets for Sulo, under threat of death. Does he even have gold to smelt? Does he steal it from our graves? Did I tell you that this Aric of the guard has my father's axe?'

The Moon-Speaker looked to the hearth. 'That isn't all, Virri . . . '

'What?!'

'When they disturbed the grave, they didn't find the gold, but they brought the axe out and one of your father's bones as well, a rib. Charn told me, the last time I saw him. He didn't like it and stopped them going further . . . but it is our people's way to pray with the bones of ancestors. Charn couldn't protest about it too much.'

Virri felt sick.

Father . . . loved by most . . . envied by some. We did right to hide my foster brother's hair-glinters in his mouth when we buried him.

'He has enough gold for me to work, then? If that's what he forces me to do?'

Kenna laughed a bitter laugh. 'Oh yes. Quite apart from what he's stolen from boat-comers over the years there's all the "tribute" from the pilgrims. It's not just a few piglets or a sack of wheat or whatever if you've sent your son or daughter from the west – he wants gold, or ore itself.'

Virri put her head into her heads. 'We should have gone north. Sought out my sister, if she's still living.'

Kenna shuffled herself round the hearth and put her arm about Virri's shoulders. 'I've sometimes thought the same. You remember my little daughter? She's not so little now, she married and moved up to the Winter Isles. I thought perhaps I could go to her . . . but that journey is hard even for a youngster, I think it would kill me . . . and, let's face it, I have the Moon Stone, my place is here. It wouldn't be right for me to flee with my tail between my legs.' She sighed. 'Come, it's late, we should sleep. I'll make you up a bed.'

Exhaustion gave Virri deep, dreamless sleep despite her worries but she was awake with the first slivers of light through the wattle. She determined, in a spirit of gratitude and generosity, to relight the fire and make her friend a mint tea, but when she delved into her bag to get the fire-stones she found her hair-glinters had been squashed, from all the banging about the day before, and it brought tears to her eyes, a moment.

Come on . . . I can fix this.

She put the ornaments aside, got on with lighting the fire, made the tea and turned back to them. It didn't take long to soften them by the side of the hearth and re-curl them about the wooden handle of a spoon. Kenna watched with a smile as she sipped her tea.

'What do you think?' Virri asked. 'Should I wear them today, to be true to myself and my kin? Or bury them?'

Kenna laughed. 'Wear them. Wear any finery you've got. Go out there with your chin held high and show everyone you're equal to Sulo – the Sun-Speaker won't be the only one watching you.'

Virri raised her eyebrows. 'I should wash my hair then.'

Virri had been in two minds about washing her hair, in truth, much as she wanted to, wary of being bent double with a crock of water over her head when the guards came for her, so she dithered. The morning wore on while she wrung her hands and watched from the doorway. The camp was quiet, with the pilgrims gone to work. Eerie quiet, it seemed to her. She resolved to go ahead, with Kenna's help, having a full-on wash in the end, combing out her bramble-briar hair and scrubbing the grass stains off her knees. They mended and re-padded her shoes, trimmed off knotted cords from her skirt that had come loose, scraped the dirt from under her nails . . . still no-one came. She was sat on the threshold of Kenna's prison, letting the late-morning sun shed the last dampness from her hair, wearing her oak ear-discs and restored hair-glinters, when at last someone approached.

Aric. *Why did it have to be Aric?*

He had his bow and was still wearing her father's axe slung through his belt, but it was his sly cold-eyed face that put the shiver up her spine.

I should have run.

'It's late in the morning,' she said, forcing a boldness she did not feel. 'Is the Sun-Speaker quite well?'

Aric's eyes glittered. 'Very well. He will see you now. It's quite a walk – do you want a cup of water?'

Don't rise to it.

'No thank you.'

They walked south, out of the camp, seeing no-one. The first of the ancestor places in the sacred area was dead ahead of them. Circular 'forests' of tree trunks, shaped and carved, pointed up at the sky, casting short shadows at this time. Virri could smell rotting fruit and burnt meat where offerings around some of the poles were dwindling away.

Instead of skirting around the ancestor place Aric headed straight in.

'The Sun-Speaker said you could stop to pay your respects to your people,' he said. 'I can wait.'

She threw him a look. *My people? Is this some sort of test?*

'No, no. It's all right. I can do that another time.'

'I insist.'

'I – I don't have any offerings with me.'

Aric reached down the front of his shirt and brought out a twist of wheat-heads, hitherto invisible. 'There you go. I'll wait.'

Shit.

She stepped into the 'forest', heart racing. *What by Sun am I supposed to do now?* There must have been a dozen-by-dozen poles there, over a hundred. Each was the work of a people who had visited the sacred lands. Most poles were dark with age. There was the odd new pole, pale and smelling of fresh carved wood, but in all the time her family lived there they had never raised one. 'Leave the people their sacred places untouched,' her father had said. She could see the sense in that. Had some other boat-comers bucked that tradition? She peered at the poles around her.

The carvings were on every side, top to bottom – sun swirls, animals, zigzags, curls, boats, birds, fish, moon curves, dots, rings . . . *How will I know it belongs to my people*? She wandered a bit further in. It would be newer, one of the fresher ones . . . and the symbols on it, maybe axes?

She could not see him by this point, but Aric's voice rang out. 'I said I'll wait, but let's not be all day.'

His shout had made her flinch and she saw two grains of wheat drop to the ground as her fist clenched. *What's to stop me just putting it by any of the newer ones*? But no, he would check. It would get back to Sulo.

'Sorry, it's been ten years since I've been here,' she called back, then regretted it. *Don't show weakness*, she told herself – but the thought had thrust her a clue. Ten years. Ten years ago, she had left here with Elo. Duck Camp – Duck Camp was the pole she was looking for.

'Here, I'll help you,' Aric said.

'Don't worry, I'm getting there.'

She looked to the poles again. She'd been to the Duck Camp pole before. Which one had Elo left the joint of pork by, the evening before they left? Near the middle, if she remembered it right, east of the centre. Virri passed forward, zigzagging between the uprights fast now, ignoring the fresh new ones, heading for the sunlit centre.

As she reached it, she saw a pit had been dug, longer than it was wide. Its fresh chalky soil stood out stark among the mat of picked-over offerings.

A grave. This is a grave.

'Any closer?' Aric called.

Virri dug her nails into her palms. *Come on*. The grave was small, far too small for her. She crossed to the east side. There were a good half-dozen poles that could be the one. She couldn't remember which one . . . her eyes had only been on Elo then. She would have to go on the carvings, but at first glance they all seemed much alike. More than one had symbols for birds and reeds and fish –

There!

One symbol stood out. A reed-flanked squiggle for the home river. The same as a tattoo old Gerna had, she remembered, on hotter days when his chest was bare.

Virri placed the wheat at the base of the pole for Duck Camp.

Aric appeared behind her. As she turned, she felt she saw a flash of disappointment cross his face, but he soon masked it.

'Who is the grave for?' she asked.

'One of the orphan children, died of lung-fever.'

Really? Kenna's tale of ghosts and murder from the night before shot back to her mind.

'Come on, let's go,' Aric snapped.

They strode out of the circle, out into the open grass, he leading and she following, but the little dismay and pique he had let slip made her smile.

If that was a test . . . I just passed it.

They left the camp, the river and the ancestor poles behind them, walking south-west towards the stone circle itself. The path through the grass went parallel to another path a while, one she didn't remember from before. There were pilgrims kneeling and crouching either side of this new path, scraping out the chalk with great care, watched over by a tall, long-faced boy with a bow. Three young women were singing a work-song as they loaded up the baskets. All of them stopped as Virri and Aric approached. People greeted Aric – and stared at her – as they walked but Aric ignored them, making a bell-line for the Circle. They were not parallel to the new pathway anymore. The new path headed for the stones too, but not before it did a massive kink to the right. She could see Babca up there, at the bend of the new path, bow over her shoulder, with Maka beside her. It looked like they were practising shots – practising shots at the First Stones. Surely that couldn't be true?

Ahead of them, among the Circle stones themselves, she thought she could see the figure of a man moving about. *Is that him*? He looked too thin, from here at least. Thinner than the Sulo she remembered.

Maka saw her and waved.

'You can talk at the evening meal,' Aric snapped. 'The Sun-Speaker is waiting.'

I didn't say anything! Virri bit her tongue. Some battles weren't worth it.

They skirted past the pair of First Stones, walking on to the next. Now she was nearer Virri could see Babca and her stepdaughter were firing at a side of pork leant up against the right-hand First Stone, not the stone itself, but she was still shocked.

'Wait here.'

Aric pointed to the next stone – the Wait Stone, appropriately enough. She recalled being told to wait here, years ago, shoulder to shoulder with her mother and siblings, at the old Sun-Speaker's funeral, even though he had treated them like family. Mother had been seething. Sulo wasn't the only one to exclude them, but his voice had been sharpest in the mob.

Aric loped forward, casting a glare over his shoulder. Was he checking she wouldn't run? There was nothing but sacred stones and flat, sunlit grassland around, she knew an arrow would bring her down with ease. Besides, the dread at meeting Sulo was mixed with a little curiosity. She could see him, in glimpses, as he moved among the inner stones. He was wearing some sort of full-length cape, in linen by the looks of it, as pale as the sun-bright stones. It had arm holes – she could see him pointing to something. He wasn't alone. There were at least two children in there. She remembered what Aric had said about the grave being for one of the 'orphan children' – what was that about? There had never been orphan children living at the Great Circle before, never many children here at all, in her memories. Not surprising, given the nature of the 'stints' the people do. She and her siblings had been indulged like favourites, so rare were they.

Aric reached the outer edge of the circle and stopped. Sulo saw him, his posture as if he had only *just* seen him, but Virri didn't believe it. The two of them shared some words, too low for her to hear. Sulo turned and said something to those behind him and now the children left the Circle, walking out with heads down. There were two, a boy and a girl, holding something in their cupped hands. Both looked to be about nine or ten. They didn't look at her at all.

'Stay there! The Sun-Speaker will approach!'

She had been observing the children and Aric's shout made her jump. Aric had withdrawn a few paces away from the Sun-Speaker to create an illusion of privacy but, she suspected, close enough to protect him if necessary. No-one had taken her knife but in truth it hadn't crossed her mind for a moment to attack. She stayed dead still, like a terrified animal, as he walked forward, feeling Sulo's gaze boring through her. He had changed – changed so much she might not have recognised him. The thinness struck her most. He had been a young lad when she left, chubby-cheeked if bitter of heart – there was nothing rounded about him now. His bones were visible in his face. His hair, as long and dark as Maka's when he was younger, had been shaven off so just a shadow remained, making him look all the thinner. The linen cape was his main clothing, but she could see his chest and legs – see the bones. At his waist was an ochre-red leather knife belt, pulled tight, with a sort of flap or apron to cover his loins. It was adorned with teeth – pig teeth? She wasn't sure. The long earring that hung down from his left, almost to his shoulder, was a bone too, sharpened to a point at the far end, but the knobbly bit, the bit carved to go through his ear lobe, looked like a rib –

Virri's stomach turned.

No . . . it couldn't be. Could it?

She felt like the blood was draining from her.

The Sun-Speaker smiled.

16.

'Virri! Welcome back. It's been too long.'

Sulo's words threw her, a moment, unsure whether to play along with the fake friendliness or not.

No.

'I wouldn't be back here at all, given the choice. I've been brought here against my will.'

His lips thinned. 'You wished to visit the Moon-Speaker. The Moon-Speaker is here.'

'*Also* held against her will.'

Sulo swung his bony hand out towards the open grasslands. 'You've both had ample opportunities to leave.'

True, she couldn't argue that – but how long would either of them had lived? His swinging gesture had taken in both Aric and Babca, with their bows. She looked past him, into the stones, thinking of the boat-comer man Kenna had told her about, murdered within this circle.

'I might add,' Sulo continued, 'That I have known where you were, these last ten years. If I had ordered it, you could have been brought back here at any time.' His eyes narrowed. 'You are seeing poison where there is none.'

Am I now? She took a bold step forward. 'Then why did my uncle have to flee for his life? Why did you murder another boat-comer in his stead?'

'*I* have never murdered anyone.' The Sun-Speaker had held his ground, kept his voice low. Virri felt like stepping back but resisted it. '*Your* people, on the other hand, are responsible for the death of thousands.'

Lung-fever. He's talking about lung-fever. Oh by Sun...

'Our people get lung-fever too – I had it myself as a ch – '

'Yet only *our* people die from it.' He advanced, jabbing out his right hand. 'What do you have, that the Gods love you so much?'

Well, there it is. She didn't know what to say. In getting closer she could see how bloodshot his eyes were. It whipped through her mind to remark on his own sickness, but she bit her tongue.

'We'll leave,' she said. 'We'll go far from here. You'll never see me again.'

Sulo's left brow shot up. 'We?'

'My – my stepdaughter, and I.'

'She is not your blood kin. You have no right to take her if she doesn't want to go.'

True. That was true. 'I'll leave, then.'

He sneered. 'Not before you've done your tribute. You're here now. You can do your tribute, like anyone else.'

'I have no desire to marry again.'

'Doubtless. Given how fruitless it was before I doubt anyone would want to marry you, either, but tribute is largely for the ancestors and the gods, not for ourselves.'

You little shit.

Sulo raised his hand, gesturing to Aric. 'You can take her back to camp now!' He looked back to her, looking down his skinny nose. 'Excuse me, but I must start the noon prayers. Sun's blessings on you, daughter.'

Aric escorted her back to camp, as instructed. She was fuming but silent. The 'daughter' bit at the end had been the final barb to stick in her craw. They were of an age, no more than a year or two between them. And how *dare* he wear her father's rib as an ornament?! She played out a vision in her mind of ripping it from his lobe and spearing him through the eye with it, imagination granting her a violence – and courage – she felt no crumb of in reality.

I am sorry Father . . . I will avenge you, some other way.

As they passed the workers on the new path, she risked a look over her shoulder. Maka was still practising shots, but Babca was over at the Circle talking with the Sun-Speaker. She saw them both stare in her direction.

What are you cooking up now?

Kenna was in her doorway when they got back, pounding seeds and watching. Aric addressed them both.

'You are both expected at the evening meal,' he said. 'Be there, be on time, be nothing to remark upon.'

Virri and Kenna exchanged a look but said nothing until he had gone.

They did turn up to the evening meal, but Sulo did not, not until the end. 'Evening meal' was under-pricing it a bit. There was indeed food and plenty of it but still more drink – honey mead and beer in giant boat-comer crocks, handed round sun-wise with prayers and flounce but having the usual effects besides. A fire was built out in the open and there was singing loud and long around it. Someone brought out a drum. Two of the women pilgrims started dancing, to the cheers and whoops of the guards. When the sun went down the huge beer crocks were refilled and passed round all the quicker. It was like the evenings at the Circle Virri remembered . . . and yet not. She recalled the old Sun-Speaker being at the heart of the gatherings, joking, telling stories, praising everyone for their good work during the day. This just seemed so . . . rotten. His devoted followers were sodden drunk and getting clumsy by the time Sulo showed up. There were cheers and genuine warmth in the welcome he received, but it didn't feel the same.

Maybe I'm just getting old.

'Cheer up! We could still be out in the rain, with blisters on our feet.' Maka slapped her on the back and sat down with a plonk beside her.

'I would rather that, than be here,' Virri muttered and Maka laughed.

'I bet you would – until the weather turns.' She swung her hand out, sloshing beer. 'Can you imagine us still being without a home when winter starts?'

'We would have been far west by then. We would have found somewhere.'

'You don't know that. You were only hoping.'

Virri sighed. 'Yes, but that was still better. Can't you see what's going on here? How they are trying to twist you?

When we were with poor Laracida you could see murderers in every corner, yet you think everyone here is fine.'

Maka snorted. 'Well they *are* fine. Everyone's been really kind – the Sun-Speaker himself welcomed me.'

Virri snorted in her turn. 'Well so he should – this place is his responsibility, he is host here, not his hangers-on. It doesn't mean he's not up to no good. Do you know he wears my father's rib as an earring? That your friend Aric carries my father's axe, robbed from his grave?'

She saw Maka's jaw drop – just for a blink – then the girl reddened. 'That's just respect. You said your father was well loved here.'

'Not by them.' She jabbed a thumb at Sulo, sat flanked by guards, backed by the distant stones. 'Not by him.'

'Ugh! You have got such a thorn in your arse!' Maka got up, as if to leave. 'Maybe he wears it to protect himself from lung-fever – did you think of that?! It's well known here that *our* people die from it more than yours.'

Virri felt the sting of tears in her eyes as the girl stomped away. Back to her friends.

'You are young, and foolish,' she whispered to Maka's departing back. 'Sooner or later you will open your eyes.'

Will I live long enough to see it?

Babca came to fetch Virri the next morning. Kenna had gone out to collect a pot of water from the river and Virri got the distinct impression Babca had waited for her to come back before approaching the threshold. She appeared, black clad and scowling as ever, the moment Kenna returned. Her bow was slung across her back, but her right hand was never far from the blade at her belt.

'The Sun-Speaker has a task for you,' she said to Virri. 'You'll be out all day. Bring your things.'

Kenna frowned. 'And if she refuses?'

'Then you will suffer. If you refuse to do what is required of you, she will suffer. The Sun-Speaker knows you both show disrespect, you have both shown dissent.' A dismissive shrug. 'Your fates are therefore twined, like ivy round the tree.'

Virri went to pick up her bag, but Kenna argued on.

'The Sun and Moon know *we* mean no harm to anyone! It is we who have been wronged.'

Babca pursed her lips. 'Don't bring the gods' names into this. Blame only yourselves.'

As soon as Virri had passed the threshold Babca let the door-flap go. 'Someone will be along for you later,' she called back over her shoulder.

They walked north, out of camp, Virri's heart pounding more with every step. It didn't help that they were soon in the wood. The sounds of camp, the pilgrims at work on the path, faded as they disappeared among the birch trees. The sunshine of the day dimmed.

Babca was careful, Virri noticed, to always keep somewhat behind, urging her onward.

This is how people disappear. I should not have gone so quiet.

'Where are we going?' Virri demanded.

'You'll see. Left a bit now.'

The river was on her left. They walked north up its right bank a bit further and skirted round the meander. Virri smelt smoke.

A pyre? Are they going to burn me?

'Go on,' Babca ordered. 'Through that thicket.'

Virri clutched on to her bag with one hand, pushing through the birch fronds with the other. She could feel sweat trickling down her forehead.

'Go on.'

She emerged, into a copse. There was no pyre, but a fire burnt, underneath a simple lean-to built with birch poles and roofed with skins. A boy crouched beside the fire, poking at it with a blackened stick. He sprang to his feet as they appeared. It was the boy she had seen at the Circle the day before, wide-eyed and skinny like a fawn.

'This is Ruc,' Babca announced. 'The Sun-Speaker wishes him to learn the art of gold-working. Here, out of sight, he will learn. You will teach him.'

17.

Virri's heart rate was still soaring but this time from swift-seen opportunity. She scented freedom. Whole days, out here in the wood, with just a scrawny little kid? Really? Her gaze shot to the lean-to for tools. Tools could be weapons.

Babca dragged her down soon enough.

'Don't think you can hare it out of here,' Babca said. 'One of us will always be here, watching.'

Think! Lie.

'I – I need space and peace to work metal, it's – it's a sacred experience. I can't have you or anyone else interfering.'

'I didn't say interfering, I said watching,' Babca said, blue eyes icy, but she did withdraw. She went to sit on a tree stump beside the river, within arrow range but, perhaps, not earshot. Virri couldn't be sure.

She turned to the boy, 'Ruc', who had observed this whole exchange without a word. He looked tired, with dark rings beneath his brown eyes and sallow, almost yellow skin. His brown hair was further browned with filth. She noticed, being so close to him now, that there were a good dozen little cuts and burns on both arms, up to his elbows, even a nasty looking burn on his left foot.

'How long have they had you out here, trying to work metal?' she asked, keeping her voice low.

'Almost two moons now.'

By Sun and Moon . . .

'Why you?' she said. 'Why did they pick you?'

The lad ran his left hand through his filthy thatch of hair. 'They – they thought I might know what to do. After Father died Ma took up with a boat-comer, so I'd lived with them, until she died . . .'

'But did he work metal?'

'No. Never.' His voice came out a squeak. 'He built boats. We were on the coast, that's what he did. I don't know any more than anyone else.'

Virri cast a glance over the charred chunks of ore and twists of misshapen slag that littered the ground and knew the truth of it.

'I'll show you what to do, don't worry. Were you threatened with harm if you failed?'

He blinked. 'No. No, I was just to keep trying.'

Virri picked up one of the charred nuggets. *You'd have been here all year.*

'How long have you been captive here at the Circle?' she asked.

The boy's jaw dropped. 'Captive? I'm not captive – I would have been starved and dead years ago if the Sun-Speaker hadn't taken me in. I don't have a living relative anywhere. The Sun-Speaker is Father to me in all but bones.'

He was so indignant his voice tangled into an awkward croak again. She had thought him very young, being so small – but there was fluency in his words, squeaky voice or no.

'How old are you, Ruc?'

'Thirteen next moon,' he said, defensive as a little robin.

Thirteen, but the height and build of a ten-year-old . . . oh yes, the Sun-Speaker loves you as a father all right.

Virri sighed.

She worked at the lean-to all day, as instructed. Babca was relieved at about noon by the guard Virri had nicknamed Gold-Braid, days ago, who arrived with a small loaf of bread to toss in their direction. She hadn't seen him or Scar arrive, but she had seen two guards setting off north the day before, so it made sense. He, too, left them to it, to be fair, content to sit or stand by the river, picking his scabs, picking his nose, scratching his balls, scratching his arse. She tried to ignore him and get on with the task to be done.

There was plenty to do. Ruc had separated the raw ore into two piles, copper and gold, but there was useless rock and unidentified rock among the heaps too, so she started with sorting it out and separating out the best ore from the hardest to smelt. Ruc hadn't known to grind the copper ore into powder, so they searched the riverside for some good grinding pebbles. By the time Gold-Braid turned up with the bread she felt they had got somewhere.

'Has the Sun-Speaker told you what he wants you to make, once we've got gold and copper to work with?' Virri asked Ruc as they ground up copper ore that afternoon.

The boy nodded. 'Things to honour the Sun, most of all. You know the collar he wears, during the festivals?'

She scanned her mind for the outfits she had seen on him so far, and the festival finery of the previous Sun-Speaker too. 'No. I don't think I've seen that.'

'Well it's a funeral tonight, so you will, but anyway he dreams of having that re-made, in gold . . .' He looked up at her with naked fear in his eyes. 'But for now smaller things, to practice. Knives, hair ornaments.'

'Gold knives? That would be daft.'

He shook his head. 'Decoration for the handles.'

Fair enough.

She brushed the ore she had ground so far into her beaded bag. 'You said it's a funeral feast tonight. Do you know what the person died of?'

Ruc nodded. 'Oh yes. Lung-fever. Both of them – it's two people tonight.'

'Did you know either of them?'

'Not very well. The Elder is one of the healers, old Firon. I'd not been around her much, and the other one, the little girl, she'd only just arrived.'

Virri remembered the small grave in the ancestor 'forest'. 'She definitely died of lung-fever?'

He shrugged, picking at a scab on his knee. 'Yeah. Both her parents probably died of it before she was brought here – she probably had it already.'

His head stayed down, and she started to regret this turn of conversation but all the same felt compelled to ask. 'Was it lung-fever that took your parents, Ruc?'

He nodded. 'Definitely Ma, maybe Pa too.'

. . . And his mother had taken up with a boat-comer. . . Oh by Sun.

She took another chunk of ore from the pile and carried on grinding, letting the matter drop.

As the sun sank towards the horizon Gold-Braid woke from his torpor and escorted them back to camp. It was one of those sun-drenched early autumn evenings dappling the light among the birch and with half her heart Virri wished she could stay out there among the trees . . . but if Ruc wasn't trusted to sleep out there, then there was no way she would be. She rolled excuses around, thinking of lies she could spin about smelting work which needed overnight effort, but dismissed the ideas as too unbelievable. She flicked a look at the guard. Just how intelligent were they, though? He'd been bored as a stone all afternoon, 'guarding' them with the lightest of touches. At night there was every chance he'd nod off. She could be halfway to the coast before anyone knew . . .

But Kenna – maybe even Maka, they'd be dead. Dead because of me.

They reached camp and Ruc peeled off to wherever the orphans were housed, while Gold-Braid escorted her the whole way back to Kenna's. As the scent of woodsmoke hit her nose another thought shot to her. *Charcoal.* Charcoal burning could take all night. She'd *need* charcoal. It was the very best type of devious excuse – the type that's true.

She saw Kenna watching from the doorway and threw the thought from her mind.

The Moon-Speaker smiled as Virri crossed the threshold, but she looked weary, too, her curly hair hanging limp over her brow. Her eyes were as red as Sulo's, but from tears, not sickness.

'What did they have you doing?' Virri asked. She dumped her bag by her bed place and slumped while Kenna scooped them both a cup of water.

'Oh I've been working with the dead and dying all day.'

Kenna's sarcastic tone came as a surprise. As Moon-Speaker she had been healing people for years – and easing their passage to the ancestors when she failed, come to that. Virri chose to keep quiet but the look on her face must have betrayed her.

'You think I should be used to it?' Kenna asked, with a grim smile.

Virri sighed. 'Well . . . the Great Circle has always been a place for healing, no? My own father would not have limped the whole way up here – '

'It's not like that anymore. There's no healing only dying.'

Kenna's head dropped at Virri's sharp intake of breath.

'You don't blame me for lung-fever too, do you?' Virri asked.

'What? No – that's not what I meant.' Kenna kept her chin well down, swiping a tear rolling down her face. 'It's – it's just it's all prayers and offerings now, not the healing I was taught. No herbs, no salves, just endless prattle – and only ever to the Sun, not to Mother Moon.' She shook her head. 'It's like offering someone a meal and giving them the bowl but not the soup.' Kenna drained back her cup and scooped another. 'What did you end up doing?'

Virri started to go through her day but a slap on the doorpost jolted them out of it. Aric's voice followed.

'Funeral feast! Show your respect!'

The two women looked to each other, rolling their eyes, but they filed out all the same.

Old Firon's pyre had been built, with great care and reverence, at the heart of the camp's gathering place during the afternoon – Kenna said she had been one of those building it – but for now the stack lay empty. The little girl Virri had seen with Sulo at the stones was circling the pyre, inserting yarrow blossoms into the faggots and singing a prayer in a sweet, high voice.

'Is she a grand-daughter of Firon?' Virri asked. 'Or another orphan?'

'Orphan,' Kenna said, throwing a look over her shoulder. 'And be careful what you say out here.'

A crowd was building around the eastern edge of the circle but Virri could not see Maka yet, nor Babca, nor Sulo. Some of the female pilgrims were bringing out pots of food while the guards flexed their bows and showed off. The long-faced boy guard was helping a woman carry a roast pig on a greenwood stake.

'If we want any food tonight,' Virri murmured, 'I think we have to go over there, whether we want to or not.'

Kenna nodded and they crossed the circle to join the throng. The sun was setting. To the south Babca now appeared, leaving the rest-house with a lit torch. She held it aloft, leading a small procession to the pyre, four men bearing the litter with Firon's wrapped body atop. The Sun-Speaker himself was still nowhere to be seen.

'Does Sulo not even turn up to funerals anymore?' Virri muttered, aside to Kenna. Kenna had been tearing off a chunk of bread but leaned in again for her reply.

'He's in the Ancestor Forest, praying. He has been since noon.'

Sulo did appear, but not until the sun was down and Firon was on her pyre, well ablaze. The hum of music and feasting fell quiet as he emerged from the forest of poles. He had to be helped to walk, held up on either side by Maka and Scar. *Real weakness or feigned?* Virri wasn't sure. They walked him to the heart of the gather-circle and sat him, with his back to the flames, onto a stool Aric brought. Sulo's head remained bowed, his chin on the collar Ruc had told her about. It was ochre-reddened leather, ornamented with teeth like the loin-cloth, and came halfway down his shoulders. He was still wearing the abhorrent earring. It showed up bright against the red.

Babca next approached, her crow feathers bobbing as she swept down to kneel in front of him, holding out a small pot.

Sulo drank it down . . . and now his head rose.

'What was in *that*?' Virri whispered – but not low enough.

'Honey,' a wide-eyed pilgrim woman answered. 'The Sun's own food. Sacred honey and the sacred mushrooms, the Moon's own food, those are the only foods that pass his lips,' she gushed.

Kenna snorted. 'And *that's* why he looks like he's starving to death.'

There was a sharp breath from all around. Virri's heart rate sprinted up. She could see Scar moving towards them both. Maka had turned, a frown on her face.

'Thank you for telling me,' Virri said to the female pilgrim, with a nod. *Should I risk pushing forward my foreign ways*? For once it seemed prudent. 'Forgive me, I'm still getting used to the traditions here.'

There were a few gentle smiles, the odd nod, but the guards remained stone-faced. She resisted the urge to cast Kenna a look.

You were telling me *to watch what I said*!

'Virri, come and have some mead. You're red enough already, won't hurt.'

Maka's voice. There were a few titters. Virri looked up and saw Maka was watching her, from over by the crocks. *Was that a barb*? Somehow, despite the titters, Maka's face told her no, it wasn't. She walked forward, accepting the cup Maka handed her.

'Thanks.'

'It's nothing.' Maka checked behind her – Scar wasn't far away. 'You need to be careful, though. Stay away from the Moon-Speaker.'

'What? What do you mean? Do you know what they are planning for her?'

Maka recoiled. 'No – no I don't know much more than you, but open your eyes, for Sun's sake. She is on the slide; her time of power is over. Don't go down the pit with her.'

“Her time of power is over”. Virri knew the truth of it. She cast Kenna, still down by the food, a guilty look. By going towards her stepdaughter Virri had left her all alone.

'She's my friend.'

Maka shrugged. 'Fine, but make sure she's not your only one. Come, the Sun-Speaker is about to talk to us all. Keep near to me.'

Virri obeyed. Against her conscience, she obeyed. They walked forward to stand before the Sun-Speaker, side by side.

The look of betrayal on Kenna's face burned through her like molten ore.

18.

Virri could not help but think of the old Sun-Speaker again as they lined up waiting for Sulo's great oration. The old one would tell his stories of Sun and Moon, the beginnings of all life and people, with old and young sat rapt at his feet. She remembered his sparkling eyes, the way he would flap his arms about as he was getting to the heart of the stories. Sulo, by contrast, could not even be seen at this point. He was still sat on his stool with the pyre at his back, but a great sheet of fine linen had been placed over him, forming a sort of tent. From the movements beneath it appeared he was eating.

Mushrooms. "Sacred mushrooms", that's what the pilgrim woman had said. The significance of the red leather pieces he wore, with their decoration of white bones, became clear. Virri recalled being warned off so much as touching that type of mushroom as a child, yet here he was using them as his main solid food. *Well, this is new . . . no wonder he looks like shit.* Perhaps it wasn't true, just tales to suck in the gullible – but everything she'd seen so far since arriving pointed towards it being true.

Once Sulo had finished eating a drumbeat started from somewhere behind and two attendants now removed the linen cloth, careful not to touch the Sun-Speaker himself or to allow any part of the cloth to touch him apart from the top of his head. The little girl from earlier approached and took the empty dish from his hands. Sulo's eyes were closed. A strange hum emanated from his tight-pressed lips. Babca now stepped forward, the white linen cloth cast around her shoulders, smothering her usual black. She held a different pot in her hands.

'All afternoon our Sun-Speaker has communed with the Sun! The Sun speaks through our Sun-Speaker! Keep well back!'

Babca flicked liquid from the pot towards him and there was a hiss as if it turned to steam. The crowd oohed. *Some trick. How are they pulling that one off?* Virri guessed there was someone behind the pyre with another pot of water. She cast a look around, but the rest of the back-shuffling crowd looked awe-struck, Maka included. *Careful – don't show the doubt on my face.* She dared not look at Kenna. Sulo was the first 'Sun-Speaker', as far as she knew, to take the title as far as this.

Sulo stood, throwing out his arms. His eyes were now open, but he cast them upwards to the sky.

'Father Sun! Your voice burns! Ease the passage of your words through your vessel!'

Babca kept flicking on the water and there were more hisses. This time Virri felt sure she heard the difference in the sound, the way it did seem to come from behind the pyre. Didn't anyone else notice this? She dared a glance towards Maka, Kenna, young Ruc, but no, no-one else, as far as she could tell.

The drumbeat grew louder and faster. Sulo swayed his weight, such as it was, from foot to foot.

'Two spirits,' he mumbled. 'Two walk to join the ancestors tonight. The Sun sees them. Bright! Follow, follow.'

He set off, fast, but lurching and unsteady like someone drunk. Babca relit her torch at the pyre and walked after him, a good ten paces behind. Aric now appeared from the back of the pyre with his drum and got behind her, continuing the beat. As the rest of the crowd filed onward Virri threw a quick look back at the pyre. She could see a small pot pushed into the embers.

'What is it?' Maka asked.

'Oh nothing. Just curious – the ceremony has changed a bit.'

The Sun-Speaker had made it to the river and clambered into one of the waiting boats. Babca, with the torch, got into the first barge with him, as did Aric, but Scar barred the way to more.

'No-one else on this one!'

Scar and two other guards stayed to divide the party onto the remaining boats, releasing the one at the front of its ropes as soon as it was full and starting to fill the next. Virri and Maka made it onto the fourth barge. This, at least, was tradition – the symbolic journey of the spirits on the sacred river. Virri recalled floating in the front barge with her mother and siblings, the old Sun-Speaker and the spirit torch before they buried her father. In the past it was always nearest kin at the front. Perhaps Firon had no kin . . . *but who knows, these days?*

'It's beautiful, isn't it?' Maka said.

She turned to Maka. The girl had tears in her eyes, watching the boats float downriver.

'I suppose it is, with the spirit torch and starlit sky.'

The boat journey was short, but the river had a strong meander and, as Virri remembered, there came a point where everyone at the edges of the boat had to paddle hard. Not long after they had to pull up. Gold-Braid was stationed by the river, ready to catch each rope as thrown and guide each barge to the mooring posts. Virri wasn't sure but she had the feeling they were getting off at a different place from before, a bit further downstream, and when they joined the processional way – the new one – it became clear. Sulo was darting about at the front, touching the chalky ground and the side stones.

'Not fast enough! The Sun is displeased the work is so slow.'

There were shocked gasps but, as Virri glanced about, subtly as she could, she didn't see anyone roll their eyes. *Doesn't anyone else see through all this shit?* Fast as the thought came it was followed by guilt. Kenna did, Kenna her friend, somewhere at the back. Virri turned to look for her but was recalled to eyes front by a sharp cry from the Sun-Speaker.

'Too many! Too many joining the ancestors – Father Sun weeps for us!'

Sulo threw his hands over his head and doubled up. He had gone beyond the Wait Stone himself but at this point Aric and Scar held everyone else back. Only Babca, bearing the Spirit Torch, went further but Virri noticed even she kept a wary distance as he thrashed about, slapping the stones, thumping the ground. It reminded her of dog-bite fever. There was a visible weave, though, in the things he said, a chilling, common thread, so much so that she began to suspect Sulo's mania was faked.

'These Stones! These stones were raised by our people! Our people respect the Sun above all. Why O Sun? Why does the lung-fever take so many? Old, young – so young! Why? Is it because we are *more* worthy?' he threw himself up against one of the mighty load-bearing stones, spreading out his arms as if to hug it. As he lurched away the torch threw his shadow, enormous, like a great bird. 'More loved! Yes, Sun, I hear you. More loved, we are more loved. The pale ones are held away from your embrace. Held away. Yes, yes.'

Virri saw Maka's gaze turn to her.

Oh I hear it.

Sulo disappeared into the Circle a moment, reappearing at a different trio-gate, throwing out his arms once more.

'I see! I see your path!'

He vomited. He actually vomited right in front of one of the stones. Virri recoiled without thinking and someone behind her in the crowd tutted.

'O Sun! If I am worthy to be your vessel send me more of your words.'

The Sun-Speaker crouched, covering his head with his arms. Babca circled him, with the Spirit Torch, speaking prayers in a low tone. Sulo began to groan, rocking back and forth. Perhaps this was the poison taking hold? But then he sprang up again, flapping his arms like a bird, spinning, circling, before going rod straight, fast as hot copper plunged into water.

'People hear me. People of the Sun.'

His voice is actually deeper. How is he doing that?!

'People you have been patient for too long. The boat-comers brought the disease, the sickness is their weapon, more than any blade or arrow. I call the faithful to me, the weak and innocent, but the strong must stay strong. They must make the Pales pay for what they have done.'

His eyes now fixed on Virri, those red eyes burning. She felt everyone turn to her.

'If they will not pay in gold then the payment will be in blood.'

Virri was unsurprised to find herself alone on the walk back to camp. Scar engaged Maka in conversation early on, drawing her away pace by pace. Kenna, having lagged at the back, was now way out in front. Virri kept her chin up, her gait a nonchalant stroll, drinking in the pleasant night-scent of grass and soil. She could hear the whispers. She felt the gaze of dozens drilling into her. Where to sleep that night? Even if she had not burned her bridge with Kenna earlier the Moon-Speaker might not want her. Who was more shunned than who right now? It must be close.

The temptation to run off into the night grew strong, but she was never able to lag back too far, not with Babca and Aric following. Babca was now without the linen cape or the Spirit Torch and looked very much a guard again. Aric's gaze was on her every time Virri threw a look back in their direction. His eyes looked more filled with hate than anyone else's.

Sulo was not with them. He appeared content to spend what remained of the night out at the Circle, among the stones, without light, fire, shelter, company.

If I'm right about the mushrooms, then one of these days they'll find him dead out here.

Can I just wait it out?

His words earlier argued no.

As the pilgrims entered Old Camp the sound of a hacking cough reverberated from a house at the southern edge. The pace of walking had quickened at the last, in expectation of rest and bed, but now the group paused. Virri felt their stares strafe her once again.

'Father Sun bless another poor soul,' someone said.

Virri turned but could not see who. There were murmurs all around. She felt the trembles start, her knees turn to curd cheese.

No. No, don't let them get to you – lung-fever is not my fault.

'The Sun and Moon protect all those sick,' she said. 'The gods know I never wished sickness on anyone.'

A few people looked embarrassed, Maka among them, but there were scowls too, that slight curl to the lips as if a bad smell is under the nose.

'Virri.'

Virri turned. Kenna had reached the threshold of the house they had so far shared. The Moon-Speaker stopped and faced her at the doorway.

Virri took in a good breath and held it. *Forgive me, Kenna.*

'Are you coming in then?' the older woman said.

19.

When the guards came for them in the morning it was almost a relief. Scar had come for Virri and Aric for Kenna. The men slapped hard on the doorpost but both women had long since been awake. Virri stepped outside first and welcomed the fresh dawn air, the breeze on her sore, tired face. The morning had begun cool and cloudy.

'What do you order me to do today?' Kenna asked, from within the house. She slipped on her cape and shoes, taking her own good time.

'The other healer isn't expected to make it through the night,' Aric said, his voice pointed as a knife. 'You can start building another pyre.'

Scar smirked. Virri saw it. She saw Kenna's face darken at the thought of another day amongst the dead and dying too and his smirk deepened. *Do they* want *her to catch it?*

Wouldn't be surprised.

'I will need firewood too,' Virri said. 'To make charcoal, for smelting the metal. Where could I get some of those faggots?'

She expected them to say "cut some yourself", had practised asking for an axe – hoped Aric might even lend her her own father's axe . . .

No such luck. Aric just shrugged. 'Fine. I'll get some sent to you.'

So much for that plan.

The two women said nothing but passed each other a resigned look. They walked on after their armed guards.

There were a few other people up and about in camp. Two female pilgrims were picking through the remains of the pyre, chanting prayers as they found pieces of Firon's charred bones and placing them in a mourning pot. Maka was sat on a log outside the guest-lodge, waxing up her bow string. She smiled and waved when she saw them walking. *Now was that a wave at me, or him?* Scar nodded back to her

– he certainly thought it was aimed at him. Virri realised with a jolt to her stomach that the wrist-guard he was wearing was Maka's. The one they had brought with them from Duck Camp.

Oh no, Maka . . . you haven't, have you?

'Did my stepdaughter give you that wrist-guard or did you just take it?'

'It was a gift . . . in exchange for something I gave her.'

Oh no.

'What was that?'

His face split into a wolfish laugh. 'Well, aren't you nosy? Are all Pales as nosy as you? It's between me and her.'

'There should be a good deal more space between you and her – you're older, you should know better.'

'Don't get your arse in a sweat. It was a carving, if you must know. I happen to be good at carving.' He patted his upper-left shirt as if to mean his heart. 'Not that it's anything to you, you nosy bitch.'

'There's no need to be rude. Maka is my kin. It's my right to worry for her.'

He sniggered. 'Well I don't remember my own mother being so fussed about my maidenhood, and she was full-on blood mother to me.'

They had reached the birch wood. The yellow leaves were shivering in the breeze, yellow against a grey sky. She regretted leaving her cape in the house.

'How is the Sun-Speaker this morning? Is he still meditating at the Great Circle?'

It was a reasonable question, but she could not keep the touch of snark out of her voice. Scar grunted.

'You don't really care.'

Why do you *care*? She thought it but bit her tongue. He was strong, healthy, no religious zealot as far as she could tell. He could crush Sulo's skull with one hand, if he wanted, by the look of him. Why did they all follow Sulo?

When they got to the lean-to by the river Ruc was already there, crouching under the awning, trying to light a fire.

He looked up with a wave as they came up past the stump, his thin face breaking in a cheery grin.

Well at least Ruc doesn't hate my guts.

Virri and Ruc were busy all morning, grinding more ore and searching the riverbank for decent clay-rich mud to build the furnace from. By the time two guards arrived with the firewood they had worked up quite a sweat, despite the cool wind rattling the lean-to roof. Virri watched with surprise as the long-faced boy guard tumbled out part-burnt wood from a sack.

'Aric said you're gonna make charcoal,' he said. 'That's just part-burnt wood, right? He said it should speed things up.'

It might . . . depends how much 'oomph' is left in the wood.

'It might.' Something else occurred to her. 'Did this come from yesterday's pyre?'

'Yes.' The boy shrugged. 'Don't get the shivers. The Sun-Speaker said it's just wood by now.'

Virri sighed. *Fine.* 'Did you bring any food for us?'

Even Scar looked up in expectation at that. He had been sat by the river carving a penis out of chalk all morning and she'd been trying to ignore him but now he came over. As the boy guard brought a squashed loaf of bread wrapped in dock leaves from out of his shirt Scar's face fell.

'Is that it?' He jabbed a thumb at the loaf. 'For me too?'

The boy shrugged but Virri thought she saw a little more colour in his cheeks. 'That's all I was given.'

Scar shoved the carving back in his shirt and tore the loaf into three. 'Look, it's not enough. These two aren't too holy to eat and I'm sure as shit not. We're not short of food back at camp. What the Sun?'

Both guards took a step back, their hands up.

'Look, it's not our fault,' the other guard said.

Scar's eyebrows flew up. 'Well one of you could swap with me, so I can come back to camp this afternoon.'

'No, we can't,' the boy-guard said. 'We're both on path-guarding duty this afternoon. We were told to hurry back.'

'You could go back with them,' Virri murmured. 'I won't run off.'

Scar laughed. 'Yeah right. Nice try.'

'No, really. I wouldn't get Ruc into trouble.'

The two guards had taken the moment of distraction as their chance to slope off. Scar regarded their departing backs with undisguised contempt.

'You have your bow with you, why not hunt?' Virri continued. 'You could bring down a bird – Maka can do it.'

'Do you think I'm stupid?'

'No, honestly. I won't run off. We've got a lot to do this afternoon, we're going to be busy, and I'm not going to risk Ruc getting on the Sun-Speaker's bad side.'

Scar pursed his lips, looking out upon the wavering birch. The other two guards were well away now, but there weren't any birds either, not in the immediate clearing. She could hear his stomach gurgling.

'Go on,' she said. 'There's bound to be a wood pigeon or two, there usually are. The wind is just rattling them.'

He sighed, looking down at the bread.

'What's stopping you?' she goaded. 'Afraid of the Hunter's ghost, watching from the woods?'

Scar fixed her with a flint-sharp look, just for a heartbeat, but it was there. She felt a chill run up her spine.

You were one of the killers, weren't you?

He made a face and strode off into the trees.

Virri turned back to Ruc, who was giving her a wary look.

'I wasn't lying, Ruc. I'm not running away.'

'W – we were going to melt the ore tomorrow.'

Virri reached over to the pile of charred wood and felt a chunk. It was dry at least. 'We can get it done today, if this fuel works out.' She nodded to the glowering clouds. 'The weather could be even worse tomorrow.'

Ruc didn't look convinced, and she realised he could think she would just make a run for it, during the night. *I might, to be fair . . .*

They got on with it all afternoon, while Scar skirted around hunting birds. The wind risked the ore powder blowing away, so Virri kept it in her bag until they were good and ready. Ruc got on with digging the shallow pit while she mixed up the mud mixture.

'This isn't a great mixture,' she said as they began to build. 'It needs grog, and more bits. This furnace'll only last a few days, but if I show you the basics of what to do then you can build a better one in camp.'

Ruc bit his lip. 'You're talking as if you won't be here,' he said, casting a glance over his shoulder. Scar was striding back towards them, a magpie hanging limp in his left hand.

Mmm, roast magpie . . . delicious.

She held her tongue – again – and turned back to Ruc.

'Slip of the tongue,' she said. 'I meant we can.'

She built the furnace walls while Scar plucked and gutted the bird and roasted it over their original fire. He was interested, despite himself, she could tell, and when he had eaten the bird and begun carving the chalk penis again he did not return to the riverside but stayed right there. She felt her cheeks reddening, her muscles tensing up. Poor young Ruc looked just as uncomfortable.

'I think he fancies you,' Ruc whispered, when Scar had finally left them for a piss.

Virri snorted. 'No, it's my stepdaughter he's after. Do you know her?'

Ruc shook his head. 'Well you'd better watch it. Don't get near him drunk.'

When he's drunk, or me? I wouldn't touch him drunk or sober.

'Come on, concentrate. I'm about to put the ore into the crucible. Keep up the bellows.'

She took the chance of Scar's absence to sprinkle a generous pinch of copper ore into the furnace flames, getting a good burst of green fire and a delighted gasp from Ruc, but when the guard strode back across they were serious again. She poured the ground ore into the crucible. With each breath of the bellows its glow brightened.

'Will you get this done before nightfall?' Scar asked. 'Weather's getting worse.'

He was right. The sky wasn't grey any more, it was black. The wind whipped more clouds by the moment. Soon the light from the crucible would be the sole light around.

'We should just do it, if we work hard,' Virri said. 'You're doing well, Ruc. Keep at it. I'll just get the mould then I'll take a turn at the bellows.'

She got up to go to her bag and a sudden gust of wind sent her skirt up in a flurry. She grabbed it down, wary of Scar's gaze.

The wind did more. It bent the birch. Its strength bowed the trees' crowns like pushing a supplicant to the ground. As the young trees sprang back a pole from the lean-to roof slipped out of place and fell, hard into the furnace. Virri yelped as the furnace wall crumbled. The glowing crucible, so firm, now tumbled out like a loose stone down a mountainside.

Young Ruc did the worst thing imaginable.

He caught it.

20.

'Ruc! No!'

The boy's scream howled through the trees. He leapt backwards, his left hand held out in front of him as if it belonged outside of his body. For a blink it was on fire. The smell of burning flesh hit so strong Virri felt her stomach hurl.

'Oh Sun, oh gods, oh no oh no.'

She raced to him, yanking him away from the spill, but it was too late, way too late. Molten copper was passing through the flesh of his palm like a hot stone dropped in butter. *Burns burns – water*! The cooling pot had been dashed over when the roof pole fell. The water was all out. 'The river!'

Scar had stood stock still from the moment it happened, his hands clamped over his mouth, but her shout woke him out of it. They both grabbed a shoulder each and propelled the boy over to the river's edge, plunging his whole left arm down under the water. Ruc's scream reverberated through Virri's whole body. She held him to her.

'Don't look at it, Ruc, don't look,' she said . . .but the boy could not help himself. He raised his hand. It was ragged, blackened around the hole apart from a patch of white. *Oh by Sun, is that bone*? Around the black it was red, red to the wrist. 'Put it back in the water, back in the water, let it cool.'

Ruc obeyed, but the agony was too much. He buried his head in her chest, sobbing out in bursts. She felt him start to shake.

Scar had seen the wound and this one glimpse was making him look sick. 'We need to get him back to camp,' he said.

Virri nodded. 'Water isn't going to be enough for this. We need to get to Kenna.'

'Let's go then.'

They took one side of Ruc each, his ragged left hand clutched under his right upper arm, determined to steer him along, but the plan soon broke down. Ruc was shaking, and every step was turning into a stumble. As they eased him down onto a fallen tree a moment to get better grip she felt his bare right arm. He felt cold.

Virri and Scar's eyes met.

'You run ahead,' Scar said. 'Get the Moon-Speaker, get ready.'

'And what are you – '

He put Ruc across his shoulders and stood, easy as breathing.

Right. Perfect.

She set off, haring through the trees. Scar wasn't too far behind her at first, but the load took its toll and she reached camp ahead. Most pilgrims were still at work on the new path, as were their guards. Camp was dead quiet. The new pyre, unfinished, stood bleak and alone at the centre of the yard.

'Kenna!'

There was no answer but listening hard she heard the hacking cough coming from the south-side house. She charged that way.

'Kenna!'

Kenna came to the doorway, but Babca appeared too, sidling round from the back of the house.

'What? What is it?' Babca barked. 'Why are you away from your guard?'

Virri blanked her, turning straight to her friend. 'Please – help! Ruc is injured, badly. He's on his way. It's a burn, a really bad burn, right through his hand. Oh Gods, please help!'

Kenna gripped her by the shoulders. 'Calm down. Of course I'll help. Where is he now?'

'Coming in behind me, fast, maybe a hundred paces?' She leant over, gasping, clutching her knees.

'Right, let's get to the house. You get some hot water on, I'll get my herbs – '

'No you won't by Sun!'

Virri and Kenna turned to the guard open mouthed.

'You were in the middle of a Moon Goddess prayer ceremony,' Babca continued. 'One you've been begging me to do, all day. Finish it.'

Kenna threw up her hands. 'It can wait. The boy needs help *now.*'

'They'll be here in moments!' Virri insisted. 'Come, quickly!'

'I said no. Go back and finish the prayer.'

The Moon-Speaker's face was a storm brewing by the moment. 'No. I won't.'

Babca stepped out in front.

Kenna pushed past her.

'Come, Virri,' Kenna said, easy as if they were headed in for dinner. They walked, fast, Virri cringing inside with every step.

They're going to kill us.

She dared a glance over her shoulder and saw Babca draw out the knife from her belt. Babca didn't have her bow on her, for once, thank Sun and Moon, but . . .

'Aric!'

Aric appeared at Babca's shout, also from behind the sick house. He was holding his bow. He notched an arrow before he even spoke.

'Are they trying to escape?' he said, eyes glittering.

'No!' Virri yelled. 'We are trying to help someone injured! She – ' her thumb jabbed towards the young guard, ' – is being downright insane!'

Babca's fists clenched but she stayed put. 'They are defying me,' she said, low as distant thunder.

Aric raised the bow. 'Do as she has told you to.'

Kenna rolled her eyes again. 'No! Are you both mad? The boy needs help *now.*'

'A prayer for the dying is more important,' Babca seethed. 'A healer, an elder, outranks any child.'

'Outranks?' Kenna screeched. '*Outranks*? That's complete bollocks. Trust you to come out with something like – '

'Look!' Virri cut in. 'They're here!'

Scar had reached the camp, Ruc still across his shoulders. He eased the boy to the ground as Virri ran to them. Everyone else followed.

'Let me see his hand,' Kenna said.

'No!' Babca erupted. 'I said *no*. Are you deaf? Get back to the sick house this instant.'

Scar stared up at the others, baffled. 'What's going on?'

Aric raised an eyebrow. 'The Moon-Speaker is defying us . . . must be a day when the sun rises. She insists on seeing to this boy when she has been ordered to return to the sick house.'

'The boy has a chance – the elder doesn't!' Kenna yelled. 'You must let me help him.'

Scar looked to his comrades, mouth agape. 'She's right. Look at him! He's passed out from the pain, for Sun's sake.'

'That's not the point,' Babca snapped.

'Stay out of it, Jek,' Aric said, with a shake of the head.

'Stay out of it? Are you having a laugh? I just carried the lad all this way. Look at the colour of him.'

Kenna had taken their moment of distraction to crouch and examine Ruc's hand, but Babca now spotted her. She yanked the older woman back by the hair, throwing Kenna backwards to the dirt. Virri screamed.

Scar leapt to his feet. 'Hey!'

Babca turned to him with a snarl. 'We *said* stay out of it!'

He raised his hands, compliant, but the scowl on his face told otherwise. 'Babca, calm down, for Sun's sake.' The scowl curled into a sneer. 'Everyone knows you're in charge, you don't need to act like a complete bitch.'

Spark to the tinder. Virri held her breath. It felt like everyone held their breath. Babca lashed out with the knife but Scar was too quick. As he leapt backwards his own hand sprang to the knife at his belt.

Aric's arrow flew.

Scar gasped as the arrow sliced through his right shoulder. He fell back onto his arse, but he was alive. Virri cowered, protecting Ruc with her body. Scar was using his left hand, pushing himself back to his feet. His left hand reached for his knife, now on the ground, but Aric had notched another arrow.

'Don't even think it,' Aric warned.

The first arrow was sticking out of Scar's shoulder. He reached across as if to pull it out, but Kenna caught his hand.

'No – it needs to be taken out cleanly.'

Babca laughed. A sick laugh that shook her head feathers. 'You can forget about that. Do you think either of you is going to live after this?' She nodded over her left shoulder. 'The work party's coming back. So's the Sun-Speaker. Let's see what the Sun-Speaker wants to do with the both of you.'

She settled into a smile, a stone-empty smile, flax-flower eyes as cold as ever.

Kenna looked to Virri. Her own eyes were huge, her jaw tight with stress. Virri could hear her breathing. Big, deep breaths as if she was about to swim underwater. *Is she about to run*? As soon as Kenna's eyes moved to the knife upon the earth Virri knew what Kenna was going to do. She screamed out but it was pointless. She was too far away to stop her. Nothing now would stop her. Kenna snatched up the knife.

'Mother Moon take me,' she said, and plunged it into her throat.

21.

There was a flash of shock across Babca's face but she hardened again in an instant. Babca and Aric hauled Scar up by an arm each and turned towards the Sun-Speaker's house. Scar was still alive, but his head was dropping. Blood was streaming down his right arm.

Virri was left there, shaking, crying in the dirt, one hand hanging onto Ruc's body. She could feel him breathing, at least. Kenna's eyes were staring out, dead. Her blood was pooling into a slick on the ground.

'Save the boy, if you can,' was Babca's parting shot as they walked away.

Virri had no words, no defiant comeback, but she tried to control the shaking, biting down on her bottom lip to steady herself.

The work party was coming back into camp. Screaming started as soon as they saw the bodies and in a heartbeat she was surrounded by people. There were so many people talking and shouting at once it was like crows in a tree . . . but one question stood out stark.

'What did you do?!'

'Me?!' she yelled back. '*I* didn't do this! Help me, for Sun's sake, please . . .'

A woman left the pack and came forward, crouching beside her and gripping her shoulder. 'Just breathe, in and out, breathe.'

It might have been well intentioned but Virri felt like hitting her. 'He's still alive! Ruc's still alive! Please, I have to help him. Help me – help me get him to Kenna's house. I can't lift him by myself.'

Ruc was carried to the house by a good dozen people, grasping a bit of clothing or a limb each. Virri scrambled ahead, pushing open the door flap and urging them to lay Ruc down upon her bed. Someone threw a bunch of tinder onto the embers for light and sat down to start building a decent fire. Ruc's left hand flopped down as the light flared and there were gasps as people saw how bad it was. There was swelling now, on top of everything else.

'Is anyone here a healer?' Virri asked, pitching her voice high over the swarming questions. She knew in her heart what the answer would be.

'Where is Maka? Has anyone seen Maka?'

The young man building the fire looked to her. 'It's her initiation tonight, into the guard. She'll be at the Circle.'

Virri's heart chilled.

'She isn't a healer, anyway,' someone else said. 'We need the Sun-Speaker.'

There was a flurry of agreement, the room erupting into crow-caws again.

'No!' Virri cried. 'He won't help. He isn't a healer! I need someone who knows what they're doing, not just a mouth on legs.'

With her outburst the house started to empty out, people saying they would take care of Kenna's body, check on the sick house, start preparing the evening meal . . . Virri wasn't sorry to see them go, in truth. She busied herself trying to make Ruc warm, comfortable, raising his swollen hand onto a pad of bedding on his chest, putting on pebbles for boiling water. Kenna had said to boil water. Did she mean to clean the wound? Made sense. She'd said about herbs too. Virri hunted through Kenna's supplies frantic as a dog, but truth was Kenna didn't have many herbs in the house, just a few bits she'd managed to bring with her from the Mother Circle . . . and Virri didn't know what she was looking for.

Kenna . . . Kenna, help me. . .

She felt her lower lip start to tremble again, her nose sting with the strain of coming tears.

No! No, Ruc needs me.

She continued rooting through Kenna's things and spotted a twist of dried yellowy-white flowers loosely wrapped in a piece of leather. Yarrow flowers, by the look of it. Wasn't yarrow good for more or less anything?

'Ruc?'

Virri snapped round. She was not as alone as she'd thought. The little girl she'd seen with Ruc before was still there – or had snuck back in, more likely. The girl was tucked into the shadows on the far side of the house, but Virri could see the tears from here.

'I – I'm doing my best for him,' Virri said, realising how weak it sounded. She tossed the yarrow into the hot water to steep and slumped back beside Ruc. He didn't feel cold anymore, so that was something, but his breathing didn't sound quite right . . . and it was weird he hadn't woken back up yet. Not good. She felt his forehead.

Red hot.

Virri looked across to the girl and a full-on sob rang out.

Oh Sun and Moon . . . she can see it in my face.

'You can come over and sit with him,' Virri said. 'This isn't the sort of fever you can catch, and I don't bite.'

The girl came forward, holding Ruc's other hand while Virri dabbed at the wound with a cloth soaked in yarrow water. It was useless and she knew it, but better than doing nothing. What would Kenna have done, if she'd been given the chance? Maybe there was nothing that could be done. *Pray*. Yes, Kenna would have prayed. For all Kenna's words about healing skills she would have still prayed. Her faith in Mother Moon was strong. Virri had seen the Moonstone among Kenna's things while she looked for the herbs. As she got up to get it, she thought she heard her name mentioned from outside.

'I'm just going to see what's going on,' she said, to the girl, and went to stand aside of the door flap a moment, keeping well in shadow.

It was dark by now. The pyre remained unlit but it looked like Kenna's body had been moved. There were people over by the Sun-Speaker's lodge, guards and pilgrims, their voices high with emotion, but she couldn't make out most of the words. She couldn't see Maka. Scar wasn't visible either – was he even still alive? Gold-Braid was there, though, and Babca. It looked like they were arguing.

Further out, coming up from the direction of the Circle, she could see Sulo's skeletal frame charging towards everyone, ghostly in his linen-white, Aric at his heels. His arms were flapping about as he yelled.

The wind blew, testing her hold on the door flap, and she took a step back, but what was the point? They all knew where she was. As soon as Virri saw Babca and Sulo talking, the chief-of-guard's pointing finger cast her way, Virri's heart fell.

That's it then.

She looked back towards Ruc. His breathing could be heard from here at the doorway. It had a rasp to it now.

'I'm so sorry Ruc. I'm so sorry.'

Sulo had his head in his hands. She heard him say Ruc's name too. His cry that followed was loud as a wolf's howl. At a word from him Aric and the long-faced guard left the crowd and started heading her way.

'They – they are coming for me,' Virri said. 'I won't be able to look after him any longer. I'm sorry.'

The girl looked back at her wide-eyed. 'You're going?'

'I don't want to, but the guards are coming for me. I don't have a choice.'

A tear rolled from the child's chin and dropped upon her friend. 'If you're gone, what should I do?'

What indeed? Virri pulled at her braids, taking in a big breath. What could the poor kid do? She herself was useless. They needed a healer, someone skilled and trained, and the only one anywhere near was dying in the sick house.

Dying . . . but not dead yet.

The thought went through her like a blade. If the old healer could tell them what to do, maybe Ruc did have a chance. Fever didn't always result in death.

She snatched another look through the door flap. They were near.

'Hide now, keep to the shadows,' she said, in a low voice. 'When they've taken me, try to find my stepdaughter, Maka – do you know her?'

The girl nodded. 'The new girl-guard.'

'Yes. She was at the Circle, last I heard, but she might be on her way back by now. Tell her what happened and tell her to ask the healer, in the sick-house, what to do for Ruc.'

If the healer is still conscious then there's a chance.

'Hide now, go on, hide.'

The girl scuttled to the side of the house, disappearing into the deep shadow beyond the fire.

'Who were you talking to?' were Aric's first words as he pushed through the flap.

'The boy,' she said, without hesitation. 'I was praying for the boy.'

Aric snorted. 'I would let the Sun-Speaker do that. The Sun turned from you long ago.'

Your opinion. Worth less than chaff. Not worth an answer. 'Is the Sun-Speaker coming here? Ruc needs a healer, urgently. I have done what I can but if someone could speak with the healer in the sick-house perhaps she could tell us what treatment could wor–'

Aric hit her. It was a hard back-hand swing across her face, much like her stepson's moons ago, but here there was another man to catch her and grip her by the elbows in case he wanted to hit her again.

'Enough!' Aric spat. 'Enough from you.'

They dragged her through the doorway and out into the open. She would not have risked a look back towards the girl and there was no chance to anyway. They were moving so fast her feet sometimes left the ground. The moon was up, the yard deserted, but she could hear people inside the houses. *Should I scream? Would anyone help me?* She had to try. She planted her heels in the dirt, opening her mouth to shriek, but Aric's blade was at her throat in an instant.

'Silence!' he hissed. 'Or you'll bleed to death out here, like your friend.'

'What difference does it make?' she hurled back. Aric nodded to the boy-guard and she was thrown off her feet again, slung between them like a sack, shouting and wriggling away – but no-one came out. When they threw her to the ground it was at the centre of the ancestor forest, the crowd of poles blocking the view to anyone outside. Cloud-break moonlight picked out the fresh soil covering the child's grave, just to the side of her. Her hands and knees were slimed with rotted offerings. There was a powerful smell of rotting meat.

'Get up,' Aric ordered.

She obeyed, given she was in the process of getting up any way. As she rose she saw they were not alone. Scar's body lay to the left, three feathered arrows sticking out from him now. Her sharp intake of breath brought a smirk to Aric's face.

'He was your friend! Your comrade!' she yelled. 'Have you no shame?!'

Aric turned to the boy-guard with a laugh. 'Maybe we should have gagged her.'

She thought the boy looked uncomfortable – maybe she imagined it, but it seemed worth carrying on her protests. Her heart beat loud in her chest but she willed herself on. 'Where is the Sun-Speaker?' she asked, head high. 'If I am to be judged then he should be the one to do it. I *demand* to see the Sun-Speaker.'

'You are in no position to demand anything.' Aric took his bow down from his shoulder and notched an arrow. The boy-guard did the same. She clenched her fists, her whole body tensing, but stayed still. The opening among the poles wasn't huge but it gave them ample time to bring her down before she could run to the cover of the 'forest'. No-one had bothered to take the knife from her belt, but it was useless by this point. She had never practised throwing knives and even a god-sent lucky strike would only deal with one of them. *Did they leave it so I might kill myself? No. No, I will not do as Kenna did.*

'Take off your hair-glinters,' Aric ordered.

'No.'

'We'll just take them from your body after.'

'You'll just have to take them from my body after, then.'

Aric was still laughing as he raised the bow. He was somewhat to the right and ahead of her, the boy-guard more to the left. She imagined the first arrow would go straight for the left side of her rib cage, the next more to the right. The first would probably kill her.

Father, Mother, ancestors, I am sorry I was not more worthy of you.

Give me strength now.

As a bow string twang she flinched despite herself but felt no thud. She opened her eyes – and saw Aric falling.

22.

Aric was falling clutching at his throat – the arrow had gone straight through. The noise bubbling out from him was a gurgling choke. Virri was so transfixed she did not notice the boy-guard release his own arrow until it sliced through the flesh of her right arm.

'Run!'

Maka's voice. *Maka*? The shape emerging from among the poles behind the guards was Maka. She was swinging something at the boy-guard's head. Was that a joint of meat? It smashed into the boy's right temple. Now he collapsed too.

'Maka?!'

'Quiet!' Maka hissed. She grasped Virri's other arm and started running, towards the south side poles, away from camp. 'We haven't much time.'

'Maka?'

Maka cast her a quick glance. 'You're in shock. Just shut up, follow me.'

Virri obeyed. In a heartbeat they were out of the poles and racing down, down towards the river. Virri could feel warm blood seeping down her arm, making her hand sticky. The scene in front of her suddenly blurred.

'Keep it together, now,' Maka warned, gripping her other arm again. Virri took in some big breaths. She could smell water. Her feet slipped underneath her and she bashed into something wooden. 'Get in,' Maka whispered. Virri felt herself manhandled into the boat, sinking to the floor. Maka seemed to be hacking away at a rope with her knife.

'What – wha – '

'Shhh! We'll only get away with this if they don't spot us. Curse this knot!'

Maka's angry whisper was drowned out by yells, yells coming from up at the ancestor forest. Virri thought she heard a woman's scream.

Babca.

'I need your knife.' Maka reached down and took it from Virri's belt. She sliced away at the rope again. Now they were floating. 'Keep well down,' Maka ordered.

Virri couldn't have stood up if she'd wanted to. Her legs had turned to pulp. The only bit of her that felt warm was her blood-washed arm and the patch of her belly where Maka's reassuring hand rested. The yells grew distant, the sky span.

All turned to blackness.

'Should we hide it?'

Maka's voice. Somewhere behind her. Virri felt warmer. Strong sunlight was warming her body.

'I don't think so. Better to turn it over, make it look like you drowned.'

A man's voice. Young, by the sound of it. Virri couldn't see him either, only blurry blue above. She tried to push herself up. *Reeds*? Reeds were beneath her.

'Look, she's coming round.' The man's voice again. She didn't recognise it.

'I don't think so,' Maka said. 'Not really. Will you help me carry her?'

'Of course.'

Strong hands under her arms, a lurch, and the blue blurred nearer.

All was darkness once more.

When Virri stirred again it was to the smell of woodsmoke. She could hear the wood pop and crackle. She felt warm – too warm, almost. Something heavy lay on top of her. An animal smell. As she opened her eyes it was to see Maka smiling at her from across the fire.

'That's a good sight to see. Are you feeling better?'

Virri pushed back the cover and winced. *Better . . . I'm not sure.* Her left hand flew to her right upper arm, but she just felt leather.

'You lost a lot of blood,' Maka went on. 'I've strapped it up for you.'

'You – you saved me.'

Maka laughed. 'Well that's a turn up, isn't it? Never done that before.'

Did I sound incredulous? She hadn't meant to, but given Maka had gone over to them, pot-fire-soup-and-spoon, it seemed a valid enough point to make . . . *maybe not now, though.* She eased herself into a straighter position and looked around her. The heavy cover turned out to be a bear skin, dark brown and huge. There was a bag, too, that she didn't recognise as belonging to either of them, hanging in the tree behind Maka. The fire did not throw much light, but it looked like there were trees all around. Tall trees, more oak and ash than birch. She couldn't see the man, the boat or the river.

'Who were you speaking with, earlier? I heard you speaking with a man, about hiding the boat.'

'That was Huerin. He helped us.'

'Huerin?'

'Huerrrr-in. You rumble the bit in the middle, "like a bee, passing".' She shrugged. 'So he says.'

'Is he a guard, too? Did you run away together?'

'No – oh no. I never met him until today – when the boat ran aground. He'd been watching us from the bank half the night and came to help straight away.'

Some sense at Virri's inner core trembled with those words. 'Can we trust him?'

Maka shrugged again. 'Dunno. He's been all right so far.' She flicked a look over her shoulder. 'Shh – he's coming back.'

A rustling through the undergrowth did presage his entrance but Virri could not see anything yet besides dark and trees. His shadowy shape when once he emerged seemed huge and he was not much smaller when he stepped into the circle of light. He was tall, taller than either of them, but no older than Maka from what she could see. He was clad from neck to toe in deer-skin clothes that moved fluidly with him, patches, tatters, dirt and all. Raven feathers mingled with the straight, blue-black hair hanging long, past his shoulders. His skin was as brown as his clothes, darker than her own, but his eyes – eyes that met her own now in a direct, if concerned, stare – were pale, blue as the earlier sky. Sharp and blue. He smiled as he approached but there was something unnerving her.

'I know you,' Virri said. 'I've seen you before.'

He nodded. 'Yes. When I took you from the funeral barge, earlier. I thought you were waking up.'

No. Before.

Huerin took the bow from his shoulder and a dead mallard too. He unstrapped the quiver from his hip, crouched down beside the fire and started to pluck the bird without another word.

Is he going to tell us anything, without us asking? Doesn't seem like it.

'Why were you watching us from the bank?' she pressed.

'I wasn't. I was after trout.'

'Do you know who we are?'

'No . . . well, yes, I suppose I do now.'

'Do your people trade with the folk up at Old Camp?'

The man paused in his plucking a blink at that. She thought she saw a wry smile. 'No.'

Right. How far had they floated? A whole day had passed, it was night again, so a whole day or near enough . . . but even so with the Great Circle upriver there must be *some* parley between the peoples, surely? She peered at him again while his gaze was down on the duck. He was thin, but not starving-thin like Sulo. Pale eyes or not there was no trace of gold or copper on him, nor wool nor linen either.

'Do you actually live out here on your own?'

'Yes,' he said.

'For how long?'

Huerin tipped his head to one side. 'Oh . . . about seven years now.'

His face was open, no sign of annoyance, but his answer shocked her.

'Seven *years*?'

'Yes.'

Maka was giving her a 'leave it' look but she felt she must push on. 'What happened to your people?'

Huerin put the duck down, placing another piece of wood on the fire. 'There were only four of us to start with,' he said. 'When Mother married Father her people shunned her.'

'Why?'

He looked at Virri again. 'Father was as pale as you, paler if anything. He was born here on the Isle, but his parents had come from across the sea. Father, Mother, my sister, our cattle, and me, that was it.'

'And?'

'Mother grew sick, my tenth winter. When it became clear she wasn't getting any better Father said he would go to the Great Circle for help. Mother was too sick to move, and I was becoming ill too, so Father found a good spot for us to wait a few days and set off.' Huerin let out a sigh. 'He never came back. He'd told us not to move, told my sister to look after us both, so we waited, and waited and waited. Mother died, and he still didn't return. Well . . . eventually my sister felt she had to go and look for him.'

Maka was frowning. 'Then she didn't come back either.'

He nodded. 'I thought I would die, that first year, but the sickness passed, I got better. I knew how to find food and hide. I was ten years old, not a baby.'

Maka passed Virri a look. 'Do you know what happened to your sister, Huerin?' Maka asked.

He was looking down, poking at the fire, and did not see the glance that passed between them. Virri felt a jolt to her stomach. The blue eyes, straight black hair, height, build, light brown skin, even the corvid feathers. She realised where she had seen him before. It wasn't *him*, as such.

'Babca!' Virri burst out. 'Babca is your sister.'

Huerin looked back at her in astonishment. 'You know her?'

Oh by Sun and Moon . . .

'Yes,' Virri admitted. 'We both do.'

He turned to Maka but the grave set to her face panicked him immediately. 'She is still alive, isn't she?' he asked. 'I saw her, the eve after summer solstice, she was all right then.'

Right. My turn to panic.

'You said you didn't trade with the people up at the Circle. Do you worship there, then?'

'No! Oh no. I mean, these people killed my father, took my sister prisoner . . . no. I never get too near, I only saw her in the distance. But I always thought if I could just get her out on her own then maybe I could rescue her.' He looked back at them with such innocent hope it eased Virri's heart, a touch. 'I mean . . . if you could escape, then maybe so could she. Babca *is* still alive, isn't she?'

Virri had to resist the urge to cast Maka another glance. 'Um, yes.'

Huerin's face lit up in a smile.

Oh Sun and Moon, how do we tell him?

23.

'I – I think I know what happened to your father, Huerin,' Virri said. 'The old Moon-Speaker told me, not that long ago, about a boat-comer man who was murdered inside the Circle. They wanted to kill my uncle, Charn, but he fled, so they killed the first boat-comer who crossed their path. The sacrilege he was accused of was a complete lie.'

Huerin nodded. 'I didn't know about your uncle, but yes, I knew the thing about him disrespecting the sacred circle – driving his cattle into it, they said – was nonsense. I mean, people say you can't piss straight round here without hitting something sacred, but Father wasn't stupid. The cattle were left with us. Some returning pilgrims I met a year or two later, downriver, told me the tale. I gave up my last hope he was still alive, then.'

He put some more wood on the fire and carried on preparing the duck. Maka was biting her lip, as if she might be thinking of telling him about Babca's true status, but if so she must have thought better of it. *Should I?* Virri wasn't sure it would be such a good idea. She was wounded, in no condition to run if he turned on them, and they needed his hospitality – which had been willingly given, so far, it seemed.

'One of the men who killed him was killed in his turn, today,' she said, instead. 'I didn't like him, personally, but I have to admit he did try to help me, he tried to help me save the life of a young boy who was injured in an accident, and his murder made as little sense as that of your father.'

Huerin sighed. 'I suppose I should be pleased he's dead, but I don't know I am.'

He watched with curiosity as Maka's head bowed and she appeared to wipe away a tear, but he said nothing.

'Do you look very much like your father?' Virri asked. 'Now you've grown?'

Huerin shrugged. 'I suppose I do. My skin and hair are darker, like Mother. She used to say he was the son of the Moon and he loved the darkness. I have his eyes, I was told.'

Virri smiled. 'His height and build, no doubt, as well. I think sometimes when you've got near the Circle you have been seen. You must be the one they call the Hunter's ghost.'

The lad's jaw went slack. 'They saw me? I should have been more careful.'

Virri sat further up, straightening her back, and gave her wounded arm a rub. Her cheek, where Aric had hit her, was throbbing too. 'Let's just eat and then get some sleep. I think I need some proper sleep, not just being "out", if you know what I mean.'

Huerin nodded. 'I'll get more food, and some healing herbs, tomorrow, when it's light. We're all safe here, for now.'

Despite his words about how safe they were and her own on the need for sleep Virri found little rest that night. All three of them huddled beneath the bearskin, she in the middle, so she was plenty warm enough and her wound, whilst a constant presence, was not painful or inflamed, but each time she felt she was slipping into doze thoughts of Ruc, Kenna, even Scar, floated to the fore. Regrets piled up like leaves in a ditch. All the moments when she could have fought back, grabbed her knife, saved her friends. Ruc would never have been hurt if she had called a halt to their day's work a mere smidgeon earlier. When she did manage to push the thoughts away the sounds of the wood did their work. There must have been twenty different owls. Trees groaned in the wind. Every creak and snuffle sent a bolt of panic through her soul. She could swear she heard a wolf howling somewhere in the distance. Dawn was breaking before she sank into anything approaching true sleep.

When Huerin got up, put his raven feathers, bow and quiver on, and fetched his bag from its hook up in the tree, she noticed but was too hazed to care. It was only later, when she woke up to find the morning sun had warmed the wood and he still was not back, that alarm built in her chest.

'He said he would fetch food, it's fine,' Maka admonished, as soon as Virri spoke.

'Aren't you worried he is walking to the Circle, to swap us in for his sister?'

'No, I'm not. Are you mad? He hates them more than we do.'

More than you, maybe.

'Besides,' Maka went on, 'I think we're a lot further downriver than you think we are. We drifted a long way. It would take him all day to get up to the Circle.'

Well, he's not back yet . . . that's no argument.

Maka peered at her, lips pursed. 'Maybe I should have a look at that wound.'

Virri took an instinctive step back and then blushed, bringing a smile to Maka's face. 'It's all right,' Maka said. 'I won't be heavy handed. But if we leave it too long it could fester.'

Virri assented, albeit with reluctance. They sat on a fallen oak, using the break in the trees for good light, and began to peel off the strip of leather Maka had tied round the hole. It was caked with dried blood and Virri could feel the little cracks and tears as it was pulled, gently-gently, away. A bit of fresh blood seeped out, but not too bad. Virri flexed her fist open and shut and bent and re-bent her elbow. There was sharp pain, but not throbbing pain, and the rest of the arm did not look puffed or reddened.

'I've been lucky.'

Maka nodded. 'I thought that. A bit to the left and it would have been in your chest. Do you think you should leave it open, let the air get to it a bit? Or cover it up with leaves? I don't think we should put the bit of leather back.'

Virri turned to the blood-streaked strip now laying on the ground and raised her eyebrows. 'No, indeed. Your dress must have enough skirt left in it for some modesty, too.'

Maka grinned. 'Let's have a hunt about, collect some firewood, if you're up to it. If we see some decent leaves, great.'

It seemed a good idea to show willing, rather than allow Huerin to do everything, to Virri's mind as well, though she said nothing. Virri collected up sticks with her good arm and piled them in Maka's arms as they explored. They soon found the river again – far too soon, for the ease of Virri's heart. A shiver ran up when she realised how close they were.

'Do you really think they will find us?' Maka asked, looking out over the water. The upturned funeral boat was there, the current banging it into a stand of sedge at the opposite bank.

'Yes, I do.' They sank down upon the bough of a side-swept willow. A pair of damsel flies fled away. 'You killed Aric,' Virri went on. 'Babca isn't going to forgive you for that. If anything, you are more the target than me now. I think she'll hunt us day and night.'

'They killed Jek, they tried to kill you, I have nothing to apologise for.'

Those were Maka's words, but Virri could see the slight tremble in her flesh. She almost reached out to her but thought better of it.

'We have to tell him about Babca,' Maka said. 'If they do find us, he will be in danger too.'

Virri nodded. 'I know. Let's try to find a way to do it, today – but softly. If he really doesn't know then he could tip over the edge.' She sighed. 'And if he does know, but is denying it to himself, and us, well, that could wind up the same.'

'I'll try to get him talking again. He seemed less touchy, with me, before you were awake. Maybe 'cause we're the same age.'

Maybe more than that. How many long-legged girls would have landed in his path in the last seven years? Virri felt her eyebrows rising but turned her head so Maka couldn't see. There was no energy in her for an argument. She felt thirsty and scooped up a palm full of the water below them.

'Let's get this firewood back to camp, get out of sight. If Babca paddles by and we're just sat here, we'll be kicking ourselves.'

Huerin was back when they returned, reviving the fire. A large, dead, pike fish lay beside him on a mesh of twigs. There were blackberries and hazelnuts too, laid out on dock leaves, and bulrush stems, ready for cooking.

'I half-thought you'd gone,' he said, with a smile.

You and me both. She chose to just smile. 'Would you rather we did go? We don't want to drag you into our troubles.'

Huerin shrugged. 'I'm glad of the company, to be honest. Besides, it will be cold tonight. You two don't even have enough clothes to survive once the frosts start.'

It was true. One of the regrets piling up in Virri's mind overnight had been the loss of her things. The cape Tayoc had given her was in Kenna's house. Her goat-skin bag, bellows, axe mould and beaded ore-bag were still out in the birch wood, under the lean-to, unless someone had gone to look and brought them back to camp. Either way she would never see any of them again. If she hadn't been wearing her hair-glinters and the earrings Elo had made her then they would have gone too. Maka didn't have her cape, either. None of the regret overnight had been hung on their chances of survival, come to think of it, but he was right.

A wry smile was playing about Maka's lips. Her eyes turned to the bearskin, now rolled up and stowed in a fork of the nearest tree. 'You killed a bear. Maybe so could we.'

Huerin laughed. 'Hardly. It died and I skinned it. I was only ten – she'd have had me for breakfast.'

'Honestly, though – I can hunt. I could help you.' Maka flicked a look towards her own bow. 'I'm good with a bow.'

'I don't doubt it,' he said, 'but you'd have to work quickly to be ready for a frost tonight. No-one is *that* good.'

Well, there's a lad who's never flirted in his life . . . Maka looked a bit affronted, to her eye, but Huerin seemed unperturbed. His gaze turned to Virri's wounded arm. 'I think it's too soon to leave your wound open like that. I got some heal-herbs,' he nodded to his bag, stowed up in the tree again. 'Let me sort it out for you once we've eaten. I'll get some water boiling.'

Virri had yet to see a pot of any kind among Huerin's few possessions, but he had an animal stomach he kept for boiling purposes. A selection of leaves and bark were also drawn out of the bag, more dock leaves and what looked like comfrey.

'Comfrey,' Huerin confirmed with a nod. Once they had eaten the pike and bulrush nibs he levelled out the embers of the fire and set up a hanging frame with hazel rods, keeping the boil-bag well above the flames but directly over the heat. 'Won't take long,' he said. 'I should clean the injury before I put the comfrey on.'

Virri went along with it content enough. He seemed to know what he was doing. 'Did your father teach you all this?'

Huerin shook his head. 'No, Mother. She might have been Moon-Speaker, one day, if she hadn't died. It was very unlike her to get sick.'

Another loss to lung-fever. She couldn't be sure without asking but given his father had been a boat comer it was no doubt what his mother's people would have thought, if they hadn't already exiled her. Her marriage to an outsider might have put a cold dunk on her wish to be Moon-Speaker, too, long before death intervened.

How is he not more bitter? He didn't seem to be, but then maybe he just hid it well.

Huerin mushed up the comfrey leaves and bound them onto Virri's wound with dock leaves, strapping them in place with long strips of willow bark.

'Try not to touch it the rest of the day,' he warned. 'And I'll re-do it tonight before bed.'

Virri nodded. 'Thank you.'

He shrugged. 'I'll just go wash, while the sun is high, and then we should get on the move. I never stay more than one night in the same place.'

Why? They're not after you, they're after us.

'All right,' Virri said, despite the tingle of disquiet rising in her stomach. 'We'll damp down the fire and cover it up.'

He left. On reflection the long pause of silence before either of the two women spoke would have been downright suspicious if he'd noticed it, but Virri reflected all too late. She caught herself listening for his footsteps in the leaves.

'What? What is it?' Maka asked. 'You've got that "run away" look on your face.'

'Oh, I know – maybe I'm jumping at nothing, but I've got that feeling . . . don't you find him odd?'

'He's been nothing but generous to us. Being on his own for so long just makes him a bit. . .' Maka shrugged. 'Well, a bit of a loner.'

Virri sucked in a good breath. 'What if it's more than that?'

'I think just 'cause he looks like Babca it's rattling you.'

'No, no it isn't only that. . . I mean, now he's gone for a wash? Back to the river? Doesn't that seem suspicious? He doesn't look like the type that'd be worried about cleanliness.'

'Oh come on, now you're just being *mean*.'

Virri threw up her hands. 'Isn't it just that you will side with *anyone* who isn't me?'

Her sudden movement snapped one of the willow strips and one of the dock leaves round her wound now flopped outwards. Maka rolled her eyes.

'Now look what you've done. Go on at me for the next twenty years for almost becoming a guard if you want but for Sun's sake stop flailing your arms about.' She got up and went to the bag in the tree. 'He had some more bark. I'll sort it out.'

Maka reached into the bag and her face changed from clouds of annoyance to shock, in an instant, like a flash of lightning.

Virri's blood ran cold. 'What? What is it?'

The girl pulled out her hand from the bag and in her hand, hanging out from under the curve of her palm, was a skull.

A small, fine-boned, distinctly feminine skull.

24.

Instinct ignited Maka's muscles. She dropped the skull, leaping backwards with a yelp.

'What are you doing?!'

Huerin was charging back towards them. His yell sent another bolt through Virri's shattered nerves. She scrambled to her feet and headed to Maka's side. Maka reached for her bow and Virri bared her knife, but Huerin was way ahead of them. He was looking at them through the sight of a notched arrow, the aim switching from Maka to Virri every few blinks. His hair was dripping wet, his clothes in disarray, but his stance with the bow was perfect, practised. She had no scrap of doubt he was dead on target.

'*What* are you doing?' he repeated.

'What are *we* doing?' Virri yelled back. 'What are you doing? How many women have you murdered out here in the woods?!'

'What?!'

He took a step back, the arrow came down, but Virri's heart was still thumping.

Huerin was shaking his head. 'How can you even think this?'

Maka jabbed a thumb towards the skull. 'Explain this then.'

'I have only been kind to you,' Huerin said. It looked like there were tears in his eyes. 'I shared my food.'

'Yep, and I'm listening,' Maka snapped back. 'Explain.'

'There – there's no time – '

'Tell us!'

His head was still shaking. He took another step backwards. His eyes met Virri's. 'It's – it's my mother,' he said.

Oh no.

O Sun and Moon forgive me.

'I couldn't put her with her people . . . I couldn't put her with Father. . .'

Virri felt sick. She turned away, clutching at Maka's elbow. Maka looked like she wanted the ground to swallow her up.

'I'm so sorry, Huerin. I'm so sorry,' Virri said. 'I – I don't know what's wrong with me. I – I can't –'

'Your nerves are blown,' Maka interrupted. 'They've been scraped too thin for moons now.' She turned back to Huerin. He was watching them, bow still in hand. 'Can you forgive us?' she asked. 'Or should we just go?'

Huerin opened his mouth to speak and then shut it again. He put the bow over his shoulder and the arrow back in its quiver. 'We should all go,' he said. 'None of us has time for this.'

'What do you mean?' Maka cried. 'Are they coming?'

Huerin nodded. 'There were people upriver, sniffing about, that's why I came back so soon.' The skull went back into the bag. 'They hadn't found the boat yet.'

'Did they see you?!'

'Don't think so.' The bearskin was rolled and tied to the outside of the bag, which he now threw over his shoulder, and with that he was ready. Virri looked around in desperation. They had not dampened the fire nor hidden it, not even started. 'There's no time for that,' he said. 'Not now. Let's go.'

Maka slung on her own bow and quiver and the two of them set off through the undergrowth like deer. Virri ran behind them, heart pounding. Fear gave her strength . . . at first. It didn't take long for their night camp place to be well out of sight, but it wasn't long before she tired, either. The trees began to spin. She felt the rough bark against her cheek and palm as she slumped into the nearest one.

'We have to stop!' came Maka's hiss.

Virri felt the two come up either side of her, helping her along, up and down and through, until she was urged to sit. They stayed either side of her, alert and upright while she slumped. Everything was spinning now. Her stomach heaved.

'Maybe you should just leave me,' she whispered.

Maka snorted. 'What? Are you kidding me? Just shut up. Be quiet.'

Virri took in big breaths, trying to clear the fog from her eyes. She could smell leaves, damp leaves. As she turned her head there was a strong smell of scat, maybe fox. Her sight was steadying but she couldn't see much anyway. The day's light did not penetrate much down here. They appeared to be beneath a tree, a fallen tree. She could see roots hanging by the light of the opening they had come down.

She felt Maka tense beside her. *I hear it too.* Footfalls. A crunching of leaves. A man's voice? Two men. They were getting louder.

'She was right,' one was saying, 'there would have been kites and crows, if there'd been bodies.'

'Fire could have been anybody,' said the other. *Gold-Braid*?

'Probably them, though.'

There was a pause while the footfalls went off to the right, but before Virri could relax the men circled back.

'Should've brought a dog,' the other said. 'We could have borrowed Old Bucktooth's.'

'Wouldn't have stayed in the boat, unless we'd tied it down,' Gold-Braid replied, 'and then it would have barked enough to wake the dead.'

'Seems like they heard us coming anyway.'

The two men silenced as another voice rang out in the distance. A woman's voice.

Babca.

Oh no.

Huerin was as quiet and still as she was, but she could see he was trying to ease his knife out of its sheath on his hip without making a sound.

Doesn't he recognise her voice? Probably not, given the years they had been apart, but what if one of them said her name? No, no – they won't. How often do people actually say someone's name when they're talking to them? Virri could feel her heartbeat climbing again. What if he recognises her? The gap might be big enough to see her through – depended on where she stood. One of the others might say her name. *Stay calm, stay calm, keep still.*

Footsteps were approaching through the undergrowth. It sounded like the two men stood and waited for her to reach them.

'Anything?' Gold-Braid said.

'There are footprints pretty much everywhere from the river,' Babca replied, 'but yes, the strongest ones lead this way.'

Oh no.

Virri risked another glance at Huerin. He hadn't moved. Maybe he hadn't recognised her voice. . .

'We should go on inland, then,' Gold-Braid said. 'We might catch up with them.'

'They can't have got that far – the hearth was still warm. Keep looking.' Virri thought she heard the woman tut. 'You are always about the giving up – so lazy. Come on.'

They heard someone – presumably Babca - stomping off through the undergrowth. Only one person moved, though, at first, by the sound of it. *We should stay where we are.* Another set off, also to the right. *Thank Sun. They're going – they're going, and they haven't said her name.* Virri still held her breath though. One remained standing there. Had he heard them?

She heard a stick snap.

'Not everyone's got such a thorn in their arse as you, Babca,' Gold-Braid muttered, as if to himself.

Huerin's sharp intake of breath was loud as a thunderclap to Virri's ears. She winced, screwing up her face, expecting Gold-Braid to rip open their hiding place at once. She could feel Maka trembling beside her.

Sun and Moon, don't let Huerin give us away, please, I beg of you.

Gold-Braid hawked up some spit and they heard the spit fall to the ground. At last he started to walk away.

Don't sigh. Don't make a sound.

Huerin had had a tight grip of his knife, by the looks of it, but now he eased it, raising his left hand.

I think he just means 'wait'. I agree.

They emerged from the hidey-hole only when nothing at all could be heard apart from the forest itself. Huerin went first, as he was nearest the opening and there was no other way. Maka followed, helping Virri out. In getting out they caused a clod of earth to break off and the opening now looked enormous. She realised how lucky they had been.

Huerin scrambled up onto the sloping trunk of the fallen tree and peered around. 'I think we're safe,' he whispered, as he slid back down. 'But we can't risk going in the same direction as them – we might be better off doubling back.'

The two women stared at him as if he'd run to madness. 'Are – aren't you going to ask us about Babca?' Virri ventured, keeping her voice low.

Huerin threw his bow and the bag back over his shoulders, raising his hands but not meeting their eyes. 'Now, right now, no I'm not. Let's move.'

Given her own nerves were tight spun to snapping Virri was grateful.

They covered a lot of ground that day, or so it felt to Virri. The other two were careful not to rush her and send her weakened body into collapse again but they did walk until late afternoon, heading upriver and then north and east inland, over logs, through brooks, and fighting undergrowth every step of the way. She was glad to stop. Huerin took them to somewhere he had camped before, deep in a natural dell, surrounded by sentinel oaks staring down. The earth smelled rich here, ancient and full. There were insects on every surface, including themselves, once they'd stopped moving. It felt like an island of the old wild wood, spared the axe for generation after generation thanks to its steep sides and now allowed to re-spread.

'Dare we light a fire?' Maka said. 'We're going to be eaten alive without one.'

Huerin nodded. 'We should be all right. Even if they back-track they're not likely to venture this far east – I was careful with the trail we left this time.' He looked to Virri. 'Are you well enough to collect firewood and light a fire while we hunt?' he asked. 'We need food badly, and you need rest most of all.'

'Yes.'

He turned to Maka. 'Right then, let's hunt while we've still got light. You go north, I'll go south. Just bring back anything you can find.'

It was a good plan, but Virri felt the weight of loneliness settle on her as soon as the two youngsters disappeared into the darkening wood. Her arm had a dull, gnawing ache and she didn't relish the prospect of hauling back armfuls of firewood. Would the others find anything to eat, out here? She couldn't see a single animal even though it felt like a thousand eyes were watching her. The birds had stopped singing. There could be a lynx padding through the trees, hunting them – hunting her – for all she knew. She picked up a few sticks, dismayed by the damp feel to them. It hadn't rained for days but that didn't make a difference to a wood like this. Every branch and chunk of wood on the ground felt sodden, saturated. Some were empty shells, burrowed out by insects, crumbling to nothing as she touched them. Their chances of a decent fire tonight dwindled by the moment.

Virri felt tears welling up. She sank down upon a rotten old stump and wiped her filthy hands across her face.

Father, Mother, if you see me now, forgive me for my weakness. I think I will be with you soon.

A tear slid to her mouth and the salt water was welcome, so hungry had she become.

If you see a young boy, called Ruc, help him find his parents.

This was no good. She had been feeling sorry for herself all day and it wasn't helping anyone. She got up, continuing her search for sticks and finding much the same, but forced herself to persevere. There would be better wood, somewhere. Food, too. She couldn't see so much as a blackberry among these old, mature trees and hoped the others were doing better. She turned west, towards the brightest light, the symbolism not lost on her, but it seemed the best way to go.

There was indeed relief when she reached the clearing. A giant oak had fallen, probably in the spring winds, taking a couple of its sons and daughters with it. The late afternoon sunshine was flooding in here. She leaned up against the old tree and let the warmth penetrate her exhausted flesh. The tear trails dried. She spotted a great branch, whitened and dead from lightning, part hidden by the remains of the great tree's crown.

I can use that.

She got up and began the work of breaking off chunks of the dead, dry wood and soon had as much of a pile as she could carry. She'd seen something else, though, and went to have a look. It was the red hawthorn berries that first caught her eye but once there she could see rose-hips too, scarlet and tempting. Deep among them, bulbous and flaky, a wasp nest hung.

Tinder. Perfect tinder.

It was late in the season. She couldn't see or hear any wasps. Virri gave it an experimental poke with a fingernail and whipped her hand back.

All clear.

She broke it off, ready to drop it at first sound of buzz, and turned back to the berries. She needed something . . . Her string skirt was no good for this sort of thing. Her shirt was too short to scoop into a gather.

I could take it off . . . tie up the sleeves and neck.

'You've done well!'

Huerin's shout shook her out of her skin. He was loping across the clearing, something cupped in his hands.

'I don't have anything to put it all in,' she said.

'I can help with that.' He placed the two young puff-ball mushrooms down onto a branch and took the bag off his shoulder for a rummage. The birch bark container he brought out was about the size of two fists and already had some nettles at the bottom. 'We can fit some in here. Maybe put some direct into the boil-bag-stomach if I manage to keep it upright.' He shrugged, with a wry smile. 'It doesn't look like I'm getting any deer. I saw three roe but they were too far away even for a shot.'

Virri smiled. 'Well, we've both found something, we won't go hungry. And Maka might have caught something – she's a good hunter.'

'You're proud of her, aren't you?'

She almost laughed. *Some of the time.* 'Did she tell you? That I'm not her actual mother?'

He nodded. 'I would have guessed, anyway. You are such a boat-comer, like Father was. She would have been more a half-and-half, like me.'

Virri settled on the branch, careful not to knock the puffballs. 'When I was married some people said it was impossible, and that's why Elo and I had no children of our own. You and your sister show the nonsense of that.'

He nodded, sitting too. 'Do you want to tell me what you know about her? Now? I promise I won't boil over. I – I think I might have guessed some of it.'

Virri sighed. *I wondered if you had.* 'Well, as it was told to me, she arrived at the Great Circle when she was about thirteen years old – from what you told us it sounds like she left you in the woods, came looking for your father, and ended up straight there.' He nodded. 'The Sun-Speaker took her in, raised her as an orphan. She is like a daughter to him, although they are too close in age for that. She is the chief of his guard.'

Huerin took in a good breath. 'Was she *ever* a prisoner?'

'No, not in any normal sense.'

'What do you mean?'

'Well, she has all the freedom she could possibly want, while she acts as the Sun-Speaker's right hand, but I don't know what would happen if she *did* rebel against him. He is Sun-Speaker, his power has long roots. And the way the guards are gathered and moulded is sly, it weaves into their sense of who they are – or so I saw, with Maka.' He flicked her a shocked look and she nodded. 'You could say she has imprisoned herself.'

Huerin picked a burr from his clothes and threw it into the bushes. 'Do you think she knows that they killed our father?'

'I can't see how she could not. I was not there at the time but from what the Moon-Speaker told me rumours started floating straight after, there are still tales now, and she spends her days with the very people who did it.'

'The sacrilege he was accused of – the Sun-Speaker will have convinced her that that was true?'

Virri nodded. 'I expect so. He is a strange man – no more holy than any stone or leaf as far as I'm concerned, but I can see how he would be impressive, to someone so young.'

He nodded, staring down at his knees.

'Mother was dead, Father was dead and disgraced, I was dying – or she thought I was. She probably doesn't even know I'm alive.' He looked up, blue eyes glistening. 'I could still get her back.'

25.

Virri would have welcomed a chance to talk with Maka alone about Huerin's naïve belief, but the opportunity did not present itself. She and Huerin walked back together, he hauling the firewood and she toting the bag. She kept thinking of how she could try to dissuade him from approaching his sister and talked herself out of it every time. It was his right, after all, however unwise.

They found Maka already back at camp, cleaning her arrows. Two pigeons lay dead beside her.

'We'll eat well tonight,' Virri said, with a smile.

'You two successful too?'

Virri nodded to the bag in her arms. 'We've got mushrooms, nettles, berries – with the pigeon bones too we could make a good broth.'

'We'll need water too, then. I saw a pool, not far.' Maka tossed her head backwards to the north. 'Gimme the boil bag, I'll go fetch it.'

She scooted off, fast as a thrush. She didn't look back once but Huerin watched her go.

'Is she afraid of me, now?' he asked, softly.

Virri sat down, getting the bits and pieces out of the bag. 'I don't think so. She's not afraid of much, to be honest. But she might not know how to talk with you.'

'I'm the same person I was yesterday.'

She shrugged. 'It's awkward. Your sister murdered a friend of Maka's only days ago, tried to have me executed, but before that they were pally with each other, very much alike . . . We'd been worrying how to tell you about Babca, before it all came spilling out.'

'She will be able to help me, then, to bring Babca back.'

Um . . . 'Well as I said, they were friendly, but they're enemies now . . .'

'But that is all the Sun-Speaker's doing – he is the poison that spreads. If I could get her away – '

Virri had to stifle a laugh. 'What, are you going to try to abduct her? Not easy!'

You hadn't even managed to speak to her alone in seven years.

'Not easy, but not impossible, not with help. I'm not alone any more.'

Oh Sun and Moon.

A full belly and sheer exhaustion knocked Virri out for the night, all the hooting and snuffling and worries in the land notwithstanding. Her arm was healing, Huerin said, by morn it could be left open to dry out and scab, but for the night he packed it and wrapped it in leaves again. Birch, the last few green birch leaves he could find, this time, under the dock – they could find no comfrey. Even birch were few in this stretch of the wood. Virri wondered if they should take turns to sleep, leaving one of them to keep watch, but in the end was glad of a full night. No assailants came near. The bearskin kept them warm.

Dawn woke her in a din of birds. With great care she managed to extract herself from the bearskin without waking Maka or Huerin but regretted her exit immediately. Cold plunged round her like jumping in a river. Her breath was leaving in clouds. *Fire. Need a fire.* She got on with it, using the last of the wasp nest tinder, but, without her fire-stones – *another thing lost for good*! – it took a while.

Maka stirred at the first resounding pop from the wood. Huerin slept on.

'Maka?' Virri whispered. 'Come help me get more wood.'

'What?' It came out as a sleepy slur.

'Come, quick – I don't want to go on my own. I heard a wolf.'

The girl was pushing herself up, but she didn't look keen.

'Looks like we've got enough.'

'No, not for the cold today.'

Maka groaned.

'Come on. My arm's hurting.'

They headed off towards the clearing, cold speeding them on, Virri only revealing her true concern once they were well out of Huerin's earshot.

'They'll kill him,' was Maka's first pronouncement, once she'd heard all. She flopped down on a stump. 'We can't let him try it.'

'You don't think they'd try to recruit him?'

Maka shook her head. 'That's the thing about this daft plan – there's no room for that. He'll get caught trying to separate her off and that'll be it.'

Virri shivered. The sight of Kenna and Scar dead upon the ground flew across her mind. 'We realised who he was. Babca might, too, if she got a clear sight of him.'

'Oh I expect so, but what promise is there it will make a difference? I was with her for days, talking long into the night, sometimes. I told her all about Elyc, what happened back home – she never mentioned her brother once. Nothing about her life before the Circle at all, not a word.'

'He thinks we will help him.'

Maka rolled her eyes. 'No way.'

Blunt as ever. 'Don't you like him, at all? He likes you, I think.'

Maka flinched like a sprung snare. 'Oh no – another one?'

Virri threw up her hands. 'Oh I like him well enough, he's all right. But if he goes haring off to the Circle that'll be the end of him. He should come with *us*, not the other way round.'

Huerin looked a tad wary, Virri thought, when they returned carrying the wood.

'Do you want to stay here, the morning?' he asked. 'I thought we should get walking, while the weather holds out.'

Virri looked to the sky. The round patch above the dell was blue, icy blue but blue. 'Is the weather getting worse?'

He nodded over to the west. 'Fish-flake sky, over beyond the trees. I reckon it will be raining by nightfall.'

Great.

'We want to get going too, but it's so cold! We thought we should get more,' Maka gabbled.

He didn't look convinced.

May as well go for it. 'We always planned to go south-west, to try to find my uncle,' Virri said. 'If we can get there without following the course of the river then I hope we should be safe.'

She looked to Maka for support, without thinking, and Maka nodded away, making it worse. Huerin's lips thinned.

'The river goes due south, more or less,' he said. 'You could follow it to the mouth and then just follow the coast west. Easy, fool proof, but it's not the shortest way, if you want to avoid my sister.'

Ouch.

'You should come with us,' Maka blurted.

Huerin dropped his gaze, looking to the fire. Maka and Virri stood still and waited for him to speak again. Virri felt her heart rate climbing. The spit and crackle of the fire seemed unnaturally loud.

'I'll set you on the right path,' he said, at last . . . and left it there.

They were out of the old wild wood by mid-morning and into a more open forest of young birch and bracken. It was a weave of golds and coppers at such a time of year and beautiful, if Virri had been in better heart. Every birch swaying brought Ruc's young face to her mind. The silence of the other two did not help.

'Have you been through here before, Huerin?' she asked, near noon, to break the ice, then kicked herself straight away.

'Yes. Dozens of times.'

Of course. Still, she plunged on.

'The trees look young, like near the Great Circle. Were these planted on purpose, for the red and white mushrooms, too?'

Both the youngsters threw her a look. Complete bafflement.

'This was cattle pasture,' Huerin said, 'when my mother was young. Her people held herds here, summers after summers.'

'Why'd they move?' Maka asked. 'Was the grazing not good?'

He shrugged. 'Don't know. I've not seen hide nor hair of any of them in years.'

They had been climbing a slight rise, through the trees, but now, as they began the decline, they fell back into silence. Virri allowed the younger two to get in front, watching the little glances Huerin cast towards her stepdaughter as they walked.

Oh Elo, I wish you were here.

'Virri? You all right?'

Maka was looking back towards her with a concerned frown.

'Yes.'

'Don't slow down too much – you'll get cold.'

Huerin turned back himself, pushing his hair out of his eyes. 'We'll stop soon, find some food, but not here, it's too open.'

No sooner had he spoken than they all heard it – feet? Hooves? Something was heading towards them. Huerin raised his hand for 'halt' or 'silence', but he needn't have bothered – both women froze. Virri's mind was racing, shouting 'Hide! Hide! Hide!' – but where? Nowt but skinny birch trees around. The bracken was no more than knee deep. Knee deep was something. Maka must have been thinking the same. 'Drop,' she hissed.

The three of them crouched down, the two youngsters easing their bows down off their shoulders. The footfalls were getting louder, coming in from the left. Virri peered that way, over Huerin's shoulder. He was notching an arrow. *Would he really shoot his sister? I don't think so.* She realised her mistake as soon as she caught her first sight of the incomers through the trees.

Deer.

At least four red deer were charging towards them. The stag's antlers were what she saw first. The hinds were a patch of leaping red-brown behind him.

She felt Maka moving to her right and realised she too was notching an arrow. She had pulled the string back before Huerin turned. He shook his head, his eyes wild, putting his own bow down and Maka followed him, though Virri could see the confusion on her face.

Virri turned back left just at the moment the deer blurred past – and then she saw what Huerin had seen. The deer were flying from a pack of wolves. The next colours flashing past were moonlight and grey.

Oh Sun . . .

For one breath she could smell them.

As the sound passed right she felt all three of them ease. Maka was first to voice.

'I could have got one! They couldn't have got any nearer!'

Only a slight twitch of Huerin's eyebrows hinted ire. 'Leave the wolves to their kill,' he said. 'That's a feisty pack, I know them of old. They don't like people. We can go out for deer later.'

Maka pursed her lips.

Virri pushed herself up, realising she was trembling. *He's right, Maka.* 'How do you know them, Huerin?'

He fumbled putting the arrow back in his quiver and she thought he might be trembling too. 'They are the ones who took our cattle, one by one,' he said, 'the first winter I was alone.'

Virri swallowed. *We have to get out of here before winter* was Virri's first thought at Huerin's words, though she kept quiet.

Maka's take on his wolf story was quite different, as she found out later. Huerin had left camp to hunt while Maka dallied, loosening and re-tying up her hair, for a chance to speak.

'He's just trying to make us feel guilty,' Maka said.

Huerin had long gone but Virri still cast a glance over her shoulder before speaking. 'I *will* feel guilty,' she whispered, 'if we end up leaving him here all alone.'

Maka rolled her eyes. 'Why? He was doing just fine until we piled in.' She threw on her bow and quiver. 'I won't be long. Stay out of sight.'

"Stay out of sight". Virri almost laughed. It was only just after noon, there was daylight aplenty yet. The landscape of open scrubby woodland continued, with sightlines crowded but not closed off like in the deep woodland of the night before. They had crossed the Sacred River around noon – watching and waiting for safety's sake like deer before they did. There had been no sign of Babca or the others since the brush yesterday but if they were still roaming up and down the river in their search then the river wasn't far away. It was spitting with rain by now but not windy. As soon as they lit a fire the smoke would go up like a pole.

Virri sighed and sat down, pulling off her sodden shoes and letting her feet air. Their camp was centred around an ancient yew, once a red seed clinging to a sliver between rocks but spared the axe these thousand years by luck, or indifference, or maybe for the bows it could provide, and now huge. Maka probably meant she should stay beneath its spread. She could, if the rain came, but for now she wanted to be useful – and to be seen to be useful.

Her arm remained painful but not as bad. If anything, the cold whipping round her was worse. She started to gather fuel for a fire, eyes searching all the while for food and ears alive to any threat. The cold seemed to deepen as she neared the river. Mindful of the threat of being seen she turned back into the scrub. As she climbed the slight rise back towards the yew, she spotted some blackberries to the left and headed that way. They were on the turn by now, there were only four decent ones near the top of the tangle, so she ate them straight off and got back to collecting the wood. As she picked up one promising fallen branch it was not as loose as it appeared. It took a bit of a wrench to free, and she paid for it in her bad arm with a wince.

Gold, at her feet, caught her eye. Her left hand flew to the hair-glinters on her braids but no, they were still there. She crouched, scraping away the soil with one end of the stick. The object was free in a blink. It was small, no longer than the palm of her hand.

Squashed, muddy, but unmistakable. A perfect spiral twist of purest gold, once one of a pair.

Uncle Charn used to wear them on his ears.

26.

'Are you all right?'

Maka was calling her. Virri turned and saw the two youngsters coming up the bank themselves, Maka carrying Huerin's bow for him as well as her own, while Huerin held the carcase of a beaver over his shoulder.

'Yes!'

She was on her hands and knees, scraping away at the dirt. She had made a fair hole by the time they arrived but found nothing else. No bones, thank Sun.

They must think I'm after roots. 'Sorry, I got firewood, but then I found this.' She held the gold twist out to them in the palm of her filthy hand. 'It belonged to my Uncle Charn. I recognise it.'

Maka was frowning as she peered down at her. 'Did you think you'd find more?'

'I thought I might find his body.'

Huerin put the beaver down and reached out to help Virri up from the mud. 'Come, come down to the river and wash all this off. You'll open up your wound and be hot-high with fever if you're not careful.'

She obeyed, handing Maka the gold twist for safe keeping and leaving the girl to deal with the fire. They crouched by the river side and Virri started to wash.

'I understand,' Huerin said. 'The rest of him could have been there – you had to check.'

'The Moon-Speaker told me he was running for his life, when he left the Circle. He might have been wounded, or sick.' She sighed, swishing away more mud from her hands. 'And to find this here, after all this time, what are the chances?'

Huerin looked across at the far bank. 'It isn't so strange. This is one of the best crossing points for the Sacred River, especially from the direction of the Great Circle. Either he knew that already or he just found it the safest place to cross.'

Virri could imagine her tall uncle wading through, checking over his shoulder all the while. Perhaps it was dark? He could have got tangled in brambles and not noticed the earring fall.

If it's such a well-known crossing, shouldn't we be camping further away? She searched Huerin's face for treachery – not for the first time – and found none. She sighed. He was right to seek camp before the rain poured and hunger got the better of them. For all they knew Babca and the others had returned to the Circle empty-handed. One could hope.

'If my uncle got away free, so could we,' she said, with a smile, and the young man smiled back. 'This sign of him gives me hope.'

'I hope you find your kin, Virri.'

Her smile widened. A thought shot into her mind and, for once, she spoke it out loud. 'You are kind, Huerin. I wish you *would* come with us. I, for one, would gladly have you as my son-in-law.'

He blushed to his ears, as red as his nut-brown face could go. 'You noticed?'

'I notice a lot of things.'

Huerin took in a big breath. 'I suppose it doesn't matter, under the circumstances,' he said. 'Once you've gone south-west, I'll probably never see either of you again.'

Virri's heart fell.

Beaver, it turned out, tasted a lot like beef. Virri wasn't sure she had ever had it before. Perhaps it was through hunger, but she enjoyed it. The fire was welcome, too, to drive the chill from her bones, but once the promised rain came they had to retreat further under the yew's spread and pull the bearskin over them lest they freeze. The darkness came a little quicker each night.

As they broke camp in the morning the conversation she'd had with Huerin at the water side came back to her mind, watching the two youngsters skirt round each other.

Huerin had skinned the beaver, the afternoon before, while Virri put together a quick drying-frame of birch sticks and Maka built the fire. In case of wolves, or even a bear, smelling the fresh scraped pelt Huerin had put the frame high in a different tree overnight, not the yew, on the side the smoke tended towards. Virri saw Maka watching him as Huerin stretched to get the frame down. He noticed, too.

'You made a good job of that,' Maka said.

Now, did she mean it? Or had he just caught her looking at his behind?

It looked like he blushed again. He did smile. 'Just about got it done while the light held.'

Maka nodded. 'What will you make with it?'

'I was going to make a hat for you both, so you don't freeze – there's enough there, but it will take at least six days to dry properly, and we'll have parted by then.'

More guilt sowing. Virri expected to see annoyance on Maka's face but if anything her eyes widened with sheer surprise. 'Are we so close to the path?' Maka asked.

He shrugged. 'Tomorrow, maybe even today. It's not really a path, as such.'

The girl shrugged in her turn. 'I suppose whatever takes us south-west.'

'I'll give the pelt to you, when we part ways. You could finish it off.'

'Oh, that's kind. You can have two of my arrows, if you like.'

'Aw, thank you. They are very good.'

Maka smiled. 'It's the flint, from up at The Holes. Where's the best flint round here? Is there any?'

'Oh yes. I could show you. 'Yet another shrug. 'If we had time.'

'Never mind then.'

'There's pink flint, not that far away – to the east. It's beautiful, like a sunrise sky.'

Maka's eyes widened. 'Sounds fantastic! Have you made any tools with it?'

He shook his head. 'Seems wrong, somehow. But it's worth seeing.'
'It's east, though?'
'Yes.'
'Never mind then.'
Virri concentrated on covering up the remains of their hearth, biting her tongue.

Their walk for the day was more north and west than straight west. Virri wasn't sure if it was to avoid too well-trodden a route in case of their pursuers or a delaying tactic on Huerin's part because he didn't want them to leave – either way, she went along with it. Maka's head seemed off with the clouds all day. The walking was easy, thank Sun. Cold air but no more rain. They got lucky regarding food. A stand of once coppiced but now straggly hazels in a valley bottom gave them a midday snack and they had kept the last of the roast beaver, well wrapped up.
As the sun sped towards its rest they were coming out of scrubby grassland and towards something Virri began to recognise as a sacred site. The curves of banks and ditches lay ahead. It was quiet, as far as she could tell, but she looked to Huerin in concern.
'We should go around, I think,' Virri said, keeping her voice low.
Huerin shook his head. 'There'll be no-one here at this time of year.'
'You know it well?'
'I've been a few times, when I'm sure it'll be quiet. This place is sacred to my mother's people.'
Virri gaped at him in alarm. His mother and Babca's mother are one and the same. Maka looked spooked too, easing her bow off her shoulder, but Huerin walked on. There *was* no-one there, to be fair – or at least no-one they could see. The grasses and weeds were tall but not long enough to provide much cover. The single standing stone among the cluster of circular ditches was lit up aglow in the

setting sun. It was too slender for anyone to hide behind. The only sound was a distant cawing of crows.

'Why are we here, Huerin?' Virri asked. 'Why have you brought us here?'

He took in a good breath. 'Because this is the border,' he said. 'This is as far as I go.'

Maka had been somewhat tangent to them but now she swung round. 'Here? Now?'

Huerin remained calm. 'I'll camp with you tonight – there's a stream just north, we can camp there – but then, in the morning, I'll start back.'

'To the Circle?!'

'Yes.'

Maka looked to the sky and stamped her foot. 'This is madness!'

Huerin's face was a pond of calm, but his eyes flashed.

'I am free to go wherever I want, as much as you are.'

Virri got herself between the two of them, holding up her hands. 'Come, we haven't got much daylight left. Let's get settled, get a fire going. We can talk around the fire. Plenty of time to talk around a fire.'

Maka snorted.

Huerin's gaze dropped to his shoes. 'Just one thing first.'

Virri nodded. 'All right.'

Huerin had been making a beeline for the standing stone and now he completed the journey in a few of his long strides. It had a carved sun circle on it, about thigh-high to him. He stood in front of it, took the raven feathers down from his head and touched the carving with the point ends of the feathers. Across, round, back, round in a decreasing spiral, back across to the other side. Virri and Maka watched, stone-still themselves. He took his bag off and dropped to his knees. His mother's skull was taken out, placed between his two palms and, gently, touched upon the carving. Across, round, back, round in a decreasing spiral, back across to the other side. He put the skull back in the bag, closed his eyes a breath and then stood up.

'We can camp for the night now,' he said. 'Follow me.'

Their camp by the chalk stream proved the most comfortable of those they shared together. Fitting, given it was to be their last. Huerin settled them on a soft grassy bank beside a short pebble 'beach' while he searched the upper branches of the surrounding willows and alders. His mysterious hunt was solved when he brought down a conical fish trap, looking a little tatty from who-knows-how-long hidden in a tree's head, but nothing he couldn't fix with a few new willow whips woven in. 'Trout for breakfast,' he said with a smile, 'Supper if we're lucky.' He went upstream to place it while Virri built the fire and Maka set off with her bow. The last of the beaver meat went inside the trap but they had hazel nuts to tide them over until the promised trout arrived. Maka brought down a gadwall in the last of the light. The stream's water was so pure and clear they all drank deep and took their chance to have a good, if chilly, wash. It was only as they warmed up round the hearth that the mood soured again.

'I'll cut the bear-skin in half,' Huerin said, his gaze deep in the flames, 'when we part in the morning. Do you think it will work better lengthways or across?'

Maka shook her head. 'You shouldn't do that. You don't need to.'

He looked up at her, disbelief plain in his face. 'You're both going to freeze. You're in summer clothes – a fire each night isn't going to be enough. Another moon and we could have sleet and snow.'

'I'll have hunted bigger animals by then, we'll make some more.'

'Hunted, skinned, dried, scraped and sewn, all the two of you alone?' He nodded up to the beaver pelt, hung high in a tree again. 'With scavengers on the prowl?'

'Well come with us then,' Maka snapped. 'It's you who's leaving.'

Huerin's lips thinned but he did not respond.

'I've lost all my copper making things, but I can make baskets,' Virri said, looking between them both. 'If we find people, we could trade.'

Maka sneered. 'Pah. Once they've seen those gold glinters on your hair that's all they'll want.'

Huerin looked back to the fire. 'If you don't find your kin,' he said, his voice catching, 'would you come back and find me? You've seen the places I go.'

'It'll be too late, the Sun-Speaker's guards will have killed you,' Maka returned. 'I'm sorry, but by throwing in your lot with us your days of hiding out near the Circle are over. Wake up.'

'I can't abandon her.'

Maka snorted. '*She* abandoned *you*. Years ago.'

The tears were coming. 'How can you be so rude to me? We are friends, aren't we?'

'I'm not being rude. I'm trying to save your life. You don't know her, you don't know her any more. I know her better than you do and there's not a speck of unselfish feeling left in Babca, not for anyone but the Sun-Speaker, anyway. If he said spit on a grave she'd say "which one?". I *am* your friend and I say come with us. Give this madness up, I beg you.'

Huerin shook his head, wiping away a tear. 'No.'

27.

Every night they had been together Virri had slept in the middle but, that last night, she made a point of getting up for a pee early on so she could get back in at the side and let them snuggle together. The plan worked a treat, she awoke to find them nestled like pups by a hearth . . . but what good would it do? At dawn none of the stubbornness had gone.

Huerin cut the bearskin in two as he had said, opting for across the middle. The sadness in his face as he handed it over tested Virri's heart. Maka was no better as she selected two of her best arrows and passed them to him. Nevertheless, part they did. The two women watched as Huerin walked east, out of sight, tears streaking down Virri's face, Maka's fists clenched. Virri berated the girl, inside, at her coldness, but Maka's first sentence when she spoke came out strangled and choked. She had to forgive her.

'What shall we do now?' Maka said. 'Do we walk on west today?'

Do you mean 'should we give him a chance to change his mind'?

Virri shook her head. 'I think we should stay here, at least a day or two. Huerin won't mind if we use his fish-trap, as long as we hide it where it was again when we leave. It will give us a chance to make our own, and I can make one with straps that can double as a back-basket for me.' She nodded towards upstream. 'The stream seems to run west, so we can follow it as far as it goes, fishing as we go. Rushing won't do us any favours. This is a good place, and we should prepare.'

Maka nodded, pressing her lips together. 'It's a good plan. All right.'

Two days turned into three. There were grayling, trout and crayfish to eat, nettle-tops, pignuts and water-mint. It gave them a chance to make the basket-trap, to reinforce their well-worn shoes and for Virri's arm to finish healing. Maka didn't find much flint but enough to knap out a few new arrowheads, mounting them on ash shafts and fletching with the gadwall feathers. The nights were frosty but the days bright and fine. By the afternoon of the third day the beaver pelt felt dry enough to make the two hats. The gadwall bones proved too brittle to make a strong needle, but they punched holes in the pelt with an arrow point and Virri gave up two strings of her skirt to thread through, to create a drawstring, good enough for now. There was, thank Sun, no sign of their pursuers, but Huerin didn't return either. It felt like they were the last two people in the world.

The fourth day dawned heavy with cloud. Just two crayfish were caught in the trap. It was time to leave.

A cool wind whistled through the willow as they were stowing Huerin's fish-trap, stinging Virri's eyes to water, and she was surprised to catch her stepdaughter looking at her with open sympathy.

'He might make it back here one day alive,' Maka said. 'We have to hope.'

'Yes.'

They started walking, the half-bearskin rolled long-ways and stored inside the willow basket-trap on Virri's back, the beaver hats on their heads, turning into the wind. Virri could not help but think that Huerin was right. They were going to freeze.

'If we're lucky we'll find a village, before too long,' she said.

Maka's eyebrows went up. 'Given what we've run from, are you sure that's what you want?'

'You think Babca and the others might have got ahead of us?'

'Well, maybe, but pilgrims will have been leaving to go home, won't they, now the leaves have turned? Word about us will be getting out one way or the other.'

She was right. Virri felt a chill run up her back. 'We'll never find my uncle if we avoid people for evermore, though. I was thinking I could show people the earring – it's distinctive, they might remember.'

'They'll just want it.'

Well, we can't simply avoid people until we reach the sea.

They did find a fellow human late in the afternoon, though not in the manner Virri had thought they would. The stream did not run west – or anywhere – for long, it turned out. By afternoon it was petering out into little but soggy wetland. Virri was padding about looking for somewhere drier to camp down for the night, thinking how there might have been watercress, earlier in the year, when she came upon bones resting on wet grass. Not a whole skeleton. A left arm, shoulder and part of the ribcage, clearly human.

She did not scream. Perhaps it was her silent stillness that brought Maka over.

'Do you think it's your Uncle Charn?' Maka asked, softly.

Virri took a deep breath and leant down to pick up the upper arm bone. She held it to her own. 'No. This person was smaller than me and Charn was built like a pine.' She placed it back down, gentle and precise. 'If we find the rest, we should give them a decent burial.'

They did find much of the rest, scattered like seed. Disgust in the pit of Virri's stomach smelled some weird ritual here but, when they found distinct gnawing on the hip bone's curve, she realised her mistake and was glad she had stayed silent. Scraps of cow-leather clothing and a neat, plaited belt with beads, untouched, gave them more clues.

'Do you think she was killed by wolves?' Maka asked.

Virri sighed. 'No. I think she probably died first, and the animals got to her after.' She swung her hand out to the surrounding landscape. 'There's a reason Huerin hasn't seen his mother's people in a few years and the trees are re-growing. If she was the last to die, there would have been no-one left to bury her.'

The girl shivered. 'Lung-fever.'

Virri thought of poor Kalo, up at their own ancestor tomb. If his mother went first then he would have to join others, Elyc's group or another, or face the same fate.

'There's a soft bit in the stream bank we went past not long ago,' she said. 'We can put all the bones we've found there and pull the soil down on top.'

Maka shook her head. 'This isn't shameful – it's the old way, returning to the circle with the help of the animals. We don't need to do anything.'

'How can you say that? You won't catch lung-fever from rain-washed year-old bones, I reckon – and even if so then it's too late, we've handled them.'

'That's not what I'm saying. I just mean we don't need to back-track and bury her, like she is a boat-comer, she's not. And we'll have used all the light left in the day for this and not found a camp or food or made a fire.'

Virri agreed, though it stuck in her craw. In the morning, as they were leaving, she tied the plaited belt to a hawthorn branch nearest the bulk of the bones.

Supper the next night proved another spark to argument. They had not made the mistake again of leaving it too late to camp. Virri got them settled and Maka set off to hunt. What Maka brought back was almost too big for her to carry.

'A boar!' she puffed, dropping it down beside the hearth and wiping the sweat from her face. 'We'll eat for days now on this. We can start dryi-'

'That's not a boar. It's a pig.'

'Eh?'

Virri pointed down at the pig. 'It's a pig, someone's pig. Look at it.'

Both women stared down at the animal. The curve of its back – not as curved as it should have been. The tusks . . .

feeble. The simple fact she was *capable* of carrying it on her own.

'Well it's too late now,' Maka said. 'Best we can do is skin it, butcher it, hide the waste and hope no-one turns up.'

She had removed the arrows, no doubt at the kill site, but the holes were clear as day. Virri cast a desperate look around their chosen camp. It was a slight dell in open grassland. A few shrubs and trees. It seemed so open now. She had already got the fire going. Darkness would be upon them soon, but a meat-smoking fire would stand out – and not only by sight. 'If they're nearby, they'll smell it.'

Maka threw out her hands. 'What else can we do? First you say there's no-one around, they're all dead, now we're in fear of eating the ghosts' pig.'

Virri could see what the girl was getting at, the pig could have gone wild, moons or even years ago, but they couldn't be sure. 'We've walked all day, we could be in another people's land by now.'

'I'm sure we are – maybe they should have kept better watch on their pig.'

'Maka!'

'Well . . . you have so much fear in you!'

'Fear is useful! Fear will give you long life!'

'So will food and clothing!'

Maka prevailed, again. Virri didn't have much other choice.

Butchering and smoking a whole hog out there, the two of them alone, was not easy. It didn't rain, thank Sun. It was too cold for flies, thank Sun, but nonetheless it took them the entire night. For a few glorious moments the sky was glowing pinks and reds. While the light was still with them Maka got the pig skinned and Virri scrambled the terrain gathering sticks and branches. They ended up with two fires. One, for the smoking, up against the steepest wall of the dell, with the bearskin and the pig's own skin held up on sticks as windbreaks and fronds of gorse and juniper to direct the smoke. The other fire was for light. They were working too hard to get cold. Once the skin was off and scraped Maka sliced the meat into thin slivers for Virri to suspend over a makeshift rack of green sticks. Their hands grew sticky with blood and fat. Any piece of meat that fell to the fire could be whipped out hot and eaten. Hunger was sated twenty times over, but thirst grew a torment. Their eyes dried, their throats parched. The smoke worried Virri most of all. The scoop of the dell might hide the light of the fires if they were lucky but the great plume of pig-laden smoke . . . *oh Mother Moon protect us*. They were too busy to sleep – the smoking fire had to be kept going, the meat had to be turned, but she would have been too tense to sleep, anyway.

When dawn broke they were done. They were filthy, their eyes had great bags beneath, but they'd done it . . . and no-one had disturbed them, either.

'Now we need to leave,' Virri said. 'I know we're tired but if there are people hereabouts then the sun will bring them.'

Maka nodded. They took the bearskin off its sticks and rolled it, tying it with Maka's hair thong. Virri's basket would have to hold all the meat. The pigskin was stiff and warped from all the heat and smoke overnight, but salvageable, so that came with them too. Everything they owned reeked of smoke.

'No-one would be able to tell it's their pig by this point,' Maka said, waving a hand over the diminished carcase. 'I reckon we get walking, just leave the bones out. The birds are waking up, they'll pick it clean.'

She was right. They could hear magpies clacking. Two blunt-tailed buzzards were circling to the east. Virri pulled on the loaded back-basket, wincing. 'I thought I heard foxes, in the night, but nothing bigger, thank Sun.'

'Oh there were wolves too. I didn't like to say anything.'

Virri caught the mischievous look on the girl's face and grinned.

They got walking. The blood red dawn which greeted them as they packed up was giving over to glowering, slate-coloured cloud. Hold off, Sky-Father, please, Virri prayed, with a look back to where the sun should be.

'They might not have heard about us,' she said. 'I think when we find a village we should risk it – at least to ask if they know Charn. We can be careful.'

Maka nodded. 'I know. I would be glad to have a night inside myself, if they turn out to be friendly. It seems a long time since I slept under a roof.'

Virri smiled. 'I feel like I've forgotten the taste of bread.'

'We could do with a good wash too.' Maka chuckled. 'In warm water – can you imagine? Now my hair's loose I can feel the crud on it. Under my nails too.'

'Your toe nails?'

She laughed. 'Yes, them as well. That hog was a night and a half.'

They started to see signs of people, sure enough, before too long. The day before, as they walked, they had spotted another enormous sacred site to the north, deserted on an ordinary autumn day. Today brought a string of treeless hills on the chalk, green with rich grass and studded with cow pats. There was a line of ox skulls, mounted on spiked poles, as they forded a river. Perhaps to aid crossing . . . perhaps not. At noon Virri could swear she heard singing, but it was distant. They saw no actual people until mid-afternoon. Coming down a steep slope they heard more voices, chanting this time, to see a ring of people over in an ash grove to the right. The chanting stopped dead as the ring of people saw them.

'Hey!' Maka called, waving. 'Greetings to you!'

There was no response. No verbal response, at least. They had all been looking down, perhaps into a pit? Now they were bolt straight and looking their way. One of them, tall and thin, was wearing antlers, it looked like.

'Are we near camp?!' Maka continued. 'Shall we carry on west?'

Virri could feel her heart starting to thump. 'Maka, leave it.'

'Eh? You wanted to find people.'

'This looks like ceremony – a funeral, maybe. We – we should leave them be.'

Maka turned back towards the grove and even this small gesture brought a reaction. They started hissing, hissing through their teeth.

Sun and Moon protect us.

The antler man raised his right arm, shaking something. The snake-like hissing intensified.

'Maybe it's a man-only thing,' Maka reasoned.

I don't care. 'Keep walking.'

The upward slope was lung-burst steep, but a cliff-face would not have slowed Virri's walking then. She kept Maka ahead to drive her on. As soon as they reached the downward stretch Virri had to force herself not to run like a hare. Don't show weakness, don't show weakness, she kept telling herself, but it was only when there was good clear distance between them and the others, she felt her heart ease.

Late afternoon brought rain, as expected, cold and near hail hard. The village should have been a welcome sight when they came upon it but given what they had been through earlier Virri could not help but see it through wary eyes. Five steep-pitched houses crouched at the base of a hill, with a tomb at the top and a river below. Greasy smoke was curling down the valley. They could hear someone chopping wood, as yet unseen, and a baby crying. A bank of gorse and blackthorn branches, at least as tall as Virri, surrounded the houses.

The only villager outside the enclosure must have seen them at the same moment they spotted him – a boy, down the valley with a herd of cattle, set off at a run, urging the animals forward with cries and a long stick.

'Easy, lad!' Maka shouted. 'We're not here to hurt you!' She raised her bow, crossways and empty, to make the point. If anything he sped up. His squeals and the moans of the cattle had brought two men to the barrier and now a gap opened up to admit the boy and the herd. It was closed again as soon as the last cow's tail cleared the span.

'Very friendly,' Maka muttered. 'Reminds me of Laracida's lot.'

'Hmm . . . y'know . . . I reckon this will be even worse.'

Maka choked back a laugh. 'We could keep going, if you like,' she said, in a high voice. '. . . Gonna be dark soon.'

Virri shook her head. Rainwater was starting to drip down her neck. 'Nah, let's do it.'

They walked forward. Three men had appeared behind the thorns by the time they were within a bowshot. None had bows, not that they could see, but the first one had his stone axe. The big beardy fellow to his left had a club, an actual club, up against his shoulder.

Great . . . just great.

Axe-man was first to speak. A voice about as soft as his face. 'What d'you want?'

28.

Maka left the talking to Virri this time. Virri was pleased, at first. She stepped forward with a wide smile and the open hands of peace. 'Greetings to you,' she said. 'We are simple travellers, going south-west in search of my uncle. Can we ask for the kindness of your hospitality for one night?'

Stone.

She broadened her smile, tipping her head to one side. 'It will be dark soon . . . and with the rain.'

Granite stone.

'If y'think you're coming in here,' Axe-Man growled, 'you're on a path to nothin'.'

Virri felt her temper rising. 'Shelter only then, we do not ask for food.'

The club-wielding one now opened his mouth. 'You're a Pale,' he said.

Well fan me down, fellow's got eyes. 'Yes.'

Everyone behind the thorn laughed.

'What's that got to do with it?' Maka snapped.

'We've had enough of a crop of fever here this year, without adding to it,' the third man said. 'Keep walking, if you know what's good for you.'

Another laugh, this one definitely nowt but a cruel titter.

'At the very least you can give me news of my uncle, if you have it. He might have passed this way, seven or eight years ago now. Charn is his name. He was very well-respected, up at the Great Circle.'

Axe-Man's eyebrows twitched. 'Don't know him.'

A woman had come to a doorway behind the others, listening in. 'Old Uffa would know, if anyone does,' she said.

Club-Man grinned. 'She probably tupped him, back in the day, knowing her.'

I'd be surprised.

'Where is this Uffa?' Maka asked.

Axe-Man tossed his chin sideways. 'South. Near the hazels. Follow the bleating of the goat.'

'Far?' Maka pushed.

'No.'

Virri noticed the club one looking her stepdaughter up and down during this exchange. 'You're no Pale,' he leered. 'And I reckon there's a decent arse beneath all that dirt. *You* can stay, if you want.'

'Well you can sod right off.'

Virri didn't know whether to cheer or cringe at Maka's words. Fortunately, it only dissolved to another vulgar laugh.

'We'll get going, then,' Virri said.

The third man was not laughing with the others. His gaze was trained onto the glinters on Virri's braids. She wished she'd tucked her hair up under her hat. *Too late now.* 'What's in the basket?' he asked.

'Just some smoked meat for our journey. We have a long way to go.'

His face was impassive. 'Show me.'

She eased the basket off her shoulders, resisting the urge to throw Maka a look. Any delay or reluctance could prompt suspicion. She lifted the woven flap as soon as it was ahead of her. The scent of smoked pork wafted out. He took a cursory glance and waved it away.

She pulled the basket back on and they started to edge away. 'If you ever come to our village, we'll be sure to give you as warm a welcome,' was Maka's parting shot. They jeered, but they let them go. Virri had to be thankful for that.

The walk south was swift and not just from shock and anger. The rain was getting harder, and the light almost gone. They didn't have a hope of seeing these hazels, but the goat proved more useful. The poor thing was bleating louder than the wailing babe behind them. They were heading downhill and getting faster, at risk of their ankles. Cold and wet notwithstanding it was good to get the evil village out of sight. Uffa's place was no better when they found it, though. The skinny goat was tethered to one oak, the shelter, such as it was, centred round another. Hazel branches formed a partial cone about a bleak fire and a hunched-up woman, bundled in layers. Someone else, a child, from the size, was lying beside her.

'We can't ask her for help,' Maka whispered. 'She's worse off than we are.'

The woman looked up. It didn't look like she'd heard the words, but she had been alerted, at least. One eye was permanently closed, the other rheumy as cloud. Her face was wet, but whether from tears or drips from the roof was hard to tell.

Sky-God, have pity.

'Uffa,' Virri said, moving forward. 'We are Virri and Maka, from Duck Camp in the far east. We journey south-west and mean you no harm.'

'You here to take my milk-goat from me?' Uffa cried. 'May as well kill us quick as slow! She'll be through that tether by mornin' anyhow.'

It was true. It appeared a decent honeysuckle rope, but the goat had gnawed a good chunk and stripped a great swathe of the oak's bark, too.

'We're not here to steal your goat,' Maka barked. 'I'll sort that rope out. Gimme one flaming branch from your fire, and I'll sort the lot out.'

The woman's jaw dropped but she obeyed, fishing a torch out with a rag to protect her bony hand and passing it out to the girl.

'Virri,' Maka said, 'Give her some meat and bank that fire up.'

The girl gave the rolled bearskin, her bow and quiver to Virri, took the branch and disappeared into the brush wood, her torch the sole glow in the gloom. Virri took her basket off and unwrapped a leaf bundle of smoked pork.

'Here. Eat as much as you want.'

Uffa's one eye widened. 'I'll wake the boy.'

Virri nodded. She got on with sorting out the fire while Uffa roused the child. He looked about three, maybe four, with big eyes in a thin face, a snub nose and dark curls, all caked in dirt. Snot was running into his mouth, glistening in the growing light from the fire.

'Your son?' Virri asked.

Uffa shook her head. 'Grand-son.'

I have to ask. 'Why are you two out here, Uffa?'

The old woman wiped a rag across the boy's face. 'My daughter and her babe died. They say he's got it too. And they never liked me.'

Oh Mother Moon. Virri cast a desperate look about her. The 'roof' was barely big enough to shelter these two, let alone her and Maka as well. They would be forced to sleep tight. It was too late to go anywhere else. The rain wasn't stopping. Maka would never have come within ten bowshots of either of them if she'd known, but she hadn't known. Neither of them had.

'I know how that feels,' Virri said. She unwrapped another bundle of meat and forced herself to smile.

It felt a lifetime before Maka came back. Virri's mind was spinning hard the whole time, trying to think of excuses to leave, reasons to stop the girl coming back into the camp, but nothing would take. The rain, if anything, was getting harder. Wandering off into the night would be suicide . . . but staying might be too. The boy ate some ripped up meat with enthusiasm but paid for it straight away with a spasm of coughing. Uffa tried to get him to drink from a bowl, holding it up to his lips, and he did ease, after a while. His little hands were shaking. Virri felt her sense of pity being eclipsed by fear every moment, but there was nothing she could do.

She could ask about Charn, though. That was why they had sought the woman out in the first place. Uffa seemed happy to help, perhaps grateful for conversation. She had done her own stint locally, some twenty-odd years before, but she knew of Kenna from her daughter's stint at the Mother Circle a few years ago and was sad to hear of the

Moon-Speaker's death. Charn, the actual name, did not mean anything to her, but Virri's description lit a spark.

'You're too far north and east,' Uffa said. 'He was goin' south, towards the sea, when I last saw 'im, but he'd come from the west.'

Virri's heart leapt. 'You've seen him more than once?'

Uffa nodded. 'Yes. When the old head-man was alive he'd trade with westers every summer, boat-comers, anyone.' She pointed up the hill. 'Up at the old ancestor place.'

'When was the last time you saw him? Do you remember? Last summer?'

The boy started coughing again and Uffa rubbed his back. 'No, two years ago – no, three.'

It's something. Alive and well three years ago is better than seven or eight.

'Did he seem to be all right?'

Uffa barked out a laugh, revealing her terrible teeth. 'Oh aye. He had everyone watching him mould the gold with open mouths and what with being quite 'andsome, like, despite being long in the tooth, all the girls were after 'im. What was it you called him?'

'Charn.'

She pressed her lips together, shaking her head. 'No, that's not what they called 'im. I can't remember . . . but it wasn't that.'

Could it be someone else? But Uffa had seen him working gold – and his age, his height, the earrings, the audience gathered round – it was more likely to be Charn than another. He must have changed his name, as she thought he might.

'Y'daughter's coming back,' Uffa said.

She was right, Maka was striding towards them, her arms laden with hang-ups and snap-offs, big branches trailing behind like a tail.

'I wish Huerin was still with us,' Maka puffed. 'We could have got even more.'

'You did well, in these conditions.'

'Ha! Yes, the torch went out almost immediately and I've bust my knife, but there's a wooded gully not far, thank Moon.' Maka eased the load to the ground and unwound a length of honeysuckle from the tangle.

'You can have my knife. You'll inherit it soon enough anyway,' Virri said and passed it out from under the roof. Maka flicked her a puzzled look, water dripping down her face. 'Here, I'll come and help you with that goat.'

'No, no – you've almost dried out. Stay there. I'll handle it.'

'You'll need help, it's no problem.'

The puzzlement turned to a frown. 'It's crazy – stay in the dry. Build the fire up some more – I'll need drying when I'm done.'

She turned away and Virri sighed. She was conscious Uffa was watching all this. *So much for a chance to talk to Maka alone . . . but if I don't warn her, will she be angry?* The boy was slumped at his grand-mother's side, not coughing at the moment. *I'll try to make sure she is furthest from him.*

Maka got on with her work, splicing in a reinforcement to the rope, swearing at the dark and wet. She moved the goat and its rope to a drier spot with better cover and retied it to a higher fork, then turned to Uffa's shelter. The longest branch she'd dragged back was now denuded of its tricky side shoots, Virri's copper knife catching the firelight as Maka's swift, deft hands moved. Maka settled one end of it into a fork of the oak above the existing shelter, the other end resting on the earth a good two paces outside, and then got to work piling on the rest of the branches, making sure they were evenly spread.

'I'll tie it all in in the morning,' she said, wiping the water from her face. 'As long as we've no high winds tonight it'll be fine.'

Uffa looked up at the girl with tears filling her rheumy eye once more. 'Mother Moon bless you, girl.'

Maka smiled and gave her a nod.

'Come in and dry out now,' Virri said, and moved the bow, quiver and basket so that the only space was on her right side. Maka didn't appear to spot the ruse, she ducked in and sat cross-legged, rubbing her red hands over the fire.

They settled into as comfortable a night as possible. It was only in the pre-dawn, when the rain had stopped and old Uffa left the shelter to go for a pee, that Virri and Maka got a chance to talk alone.

'She has helped us, she knew of my uncle, but the boy has lung-fever,' Virri whispered. 'I'm so sorry, I tried find a way to tell you.'

'I know,' Maka whispered back. 'I guessed all along.'

'You guessed?'

'Why else would they be banished out here?' Maka turned over, plucking a twig from her back. 'It's all right. We couldn't just leave them.'

Mother Moon bless this girl indeed.

Instinct was screaming to leave at first light, thanks to the lung-fever and the sounds of the village men, calling out to each other and at the cattle, only just out of sight. It was better walking weather than the day before. The day dawned grey and dreary but dry. If they had been alone they would have got walking without delay, but Uffa and the boy's plight held them, without either needing to say a word. Maka got on with weaving in the strengthened roof while Virri fetched water for them all and released the goat for grazing, the boy coughing throughout. Uffa put some of the smoked meat on to boil in one of her rough, char-bottom pots, to soften it up, promising them a good breakfast. She took her own good time – and who could blame her?

By mid-morning they managed to prise themselves away, heading due south to avoid going within view of the village. Uffa and the child watched them out of sight. They left about half of the remaining smoked meat with her and the pig skin to finish working. Uffa, for her part, gave them one of her striped pots. It was a standard parting between travellers, from the outside, but the pall of death hung above like mist.

A morning of hard walking felt good. Virri's ankle twinge came back, perhaps due to the downhill scurry through mud and leaves the eve before, but not so bad it would slow her down. The open woodland they were walking through was blissfully free of people. They stopped at a clean stream early in the afternoon, for a snack, a drink and a chance to wash their face and hands. It was not a bright place, rimmed by oaks and ash, but the yellow leaves gave it cheer.

'Maybe we should camp here today,' Maka said, taking Virri's own thoughts into her mouth.

'I thought the same – if we're far enough from the village.'

Maka shrugged. 'Difficult to say, could still be their territory for all we know. But we haven't had a good night's sleep in two days and this,' she swung her hand out round, 'this could be as good as it gets.' She frowned. 'You looked to be limping, too.'

Virri sighed. 'Little bit. How about you? You all right? You look tired.'

She laughed, pushing her long hair out of her eyes. 'Knackered! And moon time's not helping.'

They stayed, spending the afternoon gathering firewood and moss, clearing a stick-free spot beneath the biggest oak where they could bed down when the time came. Uffa's pot meant they could boil up some of the stream's good clean water for a dose of nettle tea. They gathered but didn't hunt. Maka's bow needed care, after a few too many cycles of wet and dry, so she was reluctant to use it until she'd got hold of some beeswax. They were tempted to try out their fish trap, with the stream so near, but the smoked meat had to be stored up high in case of bears and the basket was the easiest means to do this. Supper was thus much the same as breakfast, but at least they didn't go hungry.

Last night's rain clouds had cleared, and it proved a chilly night. With the bearskin over their lower halves, their hats still on and their top halves nearest the fire they managed to get warm enough to sleep. Exhaustion took them deep.

Virri awoke, well after dawn, to see a stag looking down at them from a slight ridge behind the row of oaks. He was exhausted, bloodied, a broken tine. Did he know the bow was out of use? She froze, spellbound, but the mere opening of her eyes had broken the spell and he took off, a rustle in the undergrowth the only sign he had been there at all. She eased herself to her feet, creaking and clicking like a boat in a gale, put the rest of the bearskin over Maka and started tending the fire. The sky, where she could see it, was icy blue. There would be frost crisping the fields this morning, outside of the wood. She went down to the stream to refill the pot and start off some broth, wishing her skirt was longer, or she'd never lost the cape, grateful for the hat.

Sun and Moon look after you, Huerin.

When she returned to the fire Maka still wasn't up. As she knelt by the hearth to put the pot on to warm she saw Maka's eyes were open.

'You all right? Not like you to lay in.'

Maka looked back with naked fear pleading in her eyes. Her voice, when it came out, was a rasp.

'My throat feels like it's on fire.'

29.

Virri's blood ran cold.

Oh no. Oh no. Maka . . .

'J-just thirsty?'

Maka pushed herself up a bit, flinching, and shook her head. 'No.'

Stay calm. Don't panic her.

'I'll put this water on to warm and you can drink that – cold water will hurt but warm will feel good.'

Maka nodded. Her sharp-boned face, made thinner by a season of walking and hard-won food, now looked puffy, the glands in the neck swollen like she'd swallowed whole eggs. She wasn't pallid. If anything there was redness in her brown skin.

'Do you feel hot?'

She shook her head again. 'Not yet . . . but this is how it started with Father isn't it?'

Yes. It hadn't killed him, the splinter did that, but only because he'd been weakened like a bug-eaten branch.

'Yes.'

'We need to move,' Maka said.

'Really? Don't you think you should rest?'

Maka pushed herself to her feet. 'No. By tomorrow or the next day I might be too bad to move, and this place doesn't have enough shelter, if it rains. It was good enough for one night, but the trees are too big. You'll have to walk further and further to find firewood each day and then what happens if you get sick too?'

She was right. There was nothing Virri could build a shelter with, not without an axe and not on her own. She could imagine the stream swelling in rain, the banks becoming mudslides. They got going, Virri insisting Maka wear the bearskin like a cape against the morning's chill, though it meant she had to hold it. Virri took the basket –

lighter now so much of the meat had gone – and Maka's bow and quiver besides. It made for awkward walking, but Maka couldn't go fast anyway. They headed south, or roughly south and west at least, always choosing the downward slope, the easiest path, at Virri's insistence. Charn could be just about anywhere so what difference did it make, for now? The wood seemed to go on forever but in truth by noon they were seeing signs of people again. A few axe-chopped stumps. A snatch of sheep's wool caught on a blackthorn. Once they were out in the open again, they could see smoke rising from a settlement in the distance.

'Should we approach?' Virri asked. 'It didn't go so well last time . . . and now you're sick.'

Maka shook her head. 'We can't take it to them. I can't do that with an easy heart.'

'No. But we could ask for supplies at the gate – do a trade at a distance.'

Maka frowned. 'What do we have to trade?'

It's time.

'There's my hair-glinters.'

'Virri no! After all this time.' She winced, tucking her chin down to her chest.

'We need warm clothes, the beeswax, more food, some firestones would be good – the gold could buy us all that. Maybe even heal-herbs if they have any. It's time.'

Maka leant back, resting on a stump. 'Use your uncle's earring then, not the glinters your father made you.'

Virri gasped. 'I didn't even think of that – besides, I was going to show it to people to see if they recognise it.'

'Uffa knew who you meant without ever seeing it, didn't she? He stands out like a cow in the pig pen from everything you've told me.'

'You're right.'

They tidied themselves up a bit before nearing the houses, Maka pulling her hair back with the leather thong, now it was available again, removing the unsewn beaver skin hats for the time being and cleaning off the night's mud with a brook they found. Virri got the earring from the basket, restored its shape a little and buffed it up with her sleeve. They resolved that Maka would hang back and Virri do the talking again.

It was another squalid-looking place squatting at the base of a hill with a tomb at the top, but this one didn't just have a ring of thorn, it had a full-on palisade. Dogs started barking as soon as they were within a few bow shots; big, angry-sounding dogs with lungs like a bear. This started off the sheep. A woman, collecting water at a stream outside, dropped her pot and sprinted for the gate.

'Oh brilliant,' Maka muttered.

'Remember what we'd faced the day we left home. They could have been raided again and again, down here near the sea.'

Maka didn't argue the point, but even Virri didn't believe her own words. Two women? In broad daylight? The welcome wasn't getting any warmer, though. Three men and a woman had appeared behind the palisade with bows. The water-woman and a few others, including children, were there too. No-one smiled. No-one came out of the gate to greet them. There were whispers. She heard 'boat-comers' more than once.

'Hold the bow up cross-ways,' Maka rasped.

Virri tried to do so, getting into a bit of a tangle, but it was too late, anyway. 'No nearer!' a man shouted.

'We've come to trade!' Virri cried. 'We're not coming in – we're just offering you a trade at the gate.'

She had stepped forward without thinking but now the villagers erupted. She heard 'Spreaders' for the first time, but it was repeated. 'He said no nearer!' someone else yelled.

'This is ridiculous,' she said, out loud.

Bows were drawn.

Maka was reaching for her arm. 'Come, Virri, let's go. We're in range.'

Something thudded to the ground behind them. Virri rounded, expecting to see an arrow in the turf, but there was a cracked pebble – a pot boiler.

They ran, west, towards some hawthorn, stones raining down. Maka held the bearskin up over her head. Yells of 'Spreaders!' rang out, louder than the dogs. There were arrows too, not aimed to kill, maybe, but enough to drive them on.

When they were out of sight and out of range they stopped a blink to catch breath.

'They were throwing pot-boilers at us!' Maka spluttered. It came out a squeak and Virri couldn't be sure if it was the illness or pure indignation. Perhaps a bit of both.

'Come, let's go a little further and find somewhere to bed down for the night,' Virri soothed. The girl's shoulders seemed so low. She gave her a brief hug.

She felt hot now. Hot as a baking stone.

Camp for the night was not much better than the night before but served its purpose. Virri found them a dry gully, a rocky scar across some old pastureland, dotted with juniper and gorse. It would be a nightmare come rain but given the night brought biting winds the gully sheltered them from the worst. She picked a spot wide enough for them to bed down, with a broad gorse above on the windward side, wrapped Maka with the bearskin and scurried out to hunt for firewood. She didn't find much, but gorse burns like first love given half a chance and thank Sun there was plenty of that. She chose not the windbreak shrub nearest them but another and hacked armfuls off with her copper knife, ravaging her hands. Water proved more difficult. A pond – little more than a puddle – had formed in a natural mossy dip, given the rain of two days before, and it would have to do. It was dark and she was shivering by the time she was warming the water by the fire.

'How are you feeling now?'

Maka winced, swallowing as if to pop her ears. 'My throat's easing but now my head's thumping.'

'Have some of the warm water again before I put the pork in to stew, it'll do you good.'

'I don't think I can eat.'

'You must, you have to keep up your strength.'

Maka shook her head. 'No, just the water. Anything else will go down like knives.'

'Just the broth then, not the meat.'

'All right.' Maka pulled herself nearer the fire, her knees up to her chest and feet as close to the hearth as she could get them without setting her shoes alight. 'You're going to have to get under the bearskin too,' she said. 'I know it's icky with me being so sick, but the cold will kill sooner.'

Virri nodded. 'It's all right.'

Maka twisted a smile. 'Advantages of being a boat-comer.'

'There are some.' Virri managed a smile back.

Doesn't mean I can't catch it though.

Maka looked appalling by first light, sweat-beaded, blood-shot eyes, puffed like a bladder. When Virri suggested they get going she half expected Maka to say she couldn't, but the girl dragged herself to her feet.

The wind had not let up much and now filthy, greenish clouds were gathering. Virri took them on a vague south-west route again, keeping to lowlands, with a mind not to progress as such but to camp again as soon as they found somewhere with decent shelter. She might just as well have hunted for copper. The landscape was more open scrubby grassland, no tree higher than a gorse. They saw an old camp site near noon, hearth scars where cattle herders must have dwelt a while in the summer, but there was nothing left there they could use. Maka was walking slower and slower. As the clouded sun dipped below its peak and the first spits of sleet assaulted her bare flesh Virri lost all hope. She bent down to pull a thorn from her shoe so Maka could not see her eyes filling with tears.

'There's someone coming.'

Virri got up with a start. Maka was right, but for now the person was a distant figure on the horizon, she couldn't even tell if it was a man or a woman.

'We can't risk me passing the fever to them,' Maka warned.

'I know, but we have to ask their help. Come on.'

They moved forward, directly towards the person. He or she didn't try to evade. As the distance narrowed it became clear the figure was a man. He had an unstrung bow and seemed to be wearing a pack, perhaps a back-basket like Virri's own. He held a stick or staff in one hand like an older person might but was walking fast.

'At least it's not Sulo,' Virri muttered, 'too much muscle on his bones.' Maka didn't hear. She was crouching in the lea of the nearest broom bush, wrapping the bearskin round her as tight as it would go. She was breathing through her mouth now, as if her sinuses were closing off.

Oh Father Sun and Mother Moon, don't let this latest person be another selfish swine.

'Stay there,' she called to the man. 'There's fever! We don't want to put you in danger – we just want to talk!'

The man duly stopped. He was indeed wearing a pack, made of hazel hoops she thought. He was broad and tall, with a long face made longer by a pointed, greying beard. A lynx fur hat gave him more height.

'I'll come a bit nearer,' he called back, tapping his left ear. There was a twang to his voice which seemed familiar, though she knew for definite she'd never seen him before. He was no boat-comer in looks but the upturned pot sticking out of the top of the pack looked as fine a boat-comer crock as you could find.

'All right! I'll come to the gorse, you come to that rock,' she said and pointed.

'I am Barin, of Axe Lake Camp, son of Creya and Barinol,' he said and Virri suddenly realised why his accent sparked her memory – he was a northerner. It was like her sister's husband's voice, as she recalled.

She hesitated when she should have introduced them both and Barin looked from Maka to her and back again. 'You are Virri and Maka of Duck Camp, aren't you?' Virri's jaw dropped, and he grinned. 'There was a lass just got back from her stint,' he said, nodding behind him, 'where I stopped off yesterday. I heard all about you.'

'Well, it's too late to deny it now.'

Barin shrugged. 'You've no need to fear me; I'll not go prattling to the Circle. Moon-Speaker might as well have died by the Sun-Speaker's own hand, if I've sifted that big-mouthed tale from yesterday right. He might impress these youngsters but I'm not green as grass.'

Interesting.

'Do you return north now?'

Barin nodded. 'I want to get home before the winter sets in.'

'I could tell you the whole truth of what happened at the Circle, and I'd welcome the true account spreading in the north but,' she sighed, 'I think we need to find shelter, now, before dark. I don't think we'll make it through the night if not.' She tipped her head towards Maka, still crouched on the ground and met his gaze. He knew. 'Do you – do you know anywhere?'

Barin bit his lip. 'Your best chance is the beach. I know it sounds like madness but there's a cave, in the black cliff – you're not that far. I stayed there myself a night on my way down in the spring. It's high enough not to fill with the tide.'

And a storm? It did sound like madness, but she didn't want to appear ungrateful . . . and nothing better presented itself.

'Do you have food?' Barin asked.

Virri wiped her hand across her face. 'Some. Maka was a good hunter, but now she's sick, and the bow needs beeswax.'

He nodded. 'I can help with that.' He shuffled the backpack down and rummaged. 'I use a mix of beeswax and pine resin, you can have a chunk of mine.' He looked back up at her. 'Here, have this too.'

He placed the chunk of wax on the rock and a sealskin as well, tightly rolled, then stepped back away.

Virri took the gold earring from her belt and placed it on the ground before her.

'No, no,' he said. 'I didn't mean for trade – you can have them.'

'But the skin alone – '

He stopped her with a wave of his hand. 'It was meant for my missus, but my missus'd give it you herself if she was here.'

'Thank you, Barin. Sun and Moon bless your path.'

He grinned again. 'It's an uphill slog to get home but worth it when I'm back in the lakes.'

'I remember it well – I spent a few years in the north as a youngster.' She hesitated – was it worth asking? Perhaps better not to know. 'Do – you don't happen to know a woman who looks like me, do you? A bit older. Her name is Innsia. She has a husband from Crag Cove Camp, Daco, and they had a boy, eleven years old now, Insso.'

He thought for a moment then gave a sad shake of the head. 'No, sorry, but people are plentiful as the stars in the north.' He closed the pack and put it back on his shoulders. 'I should get going, if I'm to make my next stop before dark. You should too – head straight south for the cliff then west until you see the way down.' He met her gaze one last time. 'I meet lots of traders, through the year. If I meet your folks, I'll be sure to tell them you are all right.'

Virri watched him, out of sight, a steady pacing figure in the afternoon gloom, then put her own pack back on and turned to get Maka up. She looked frozen, holding the bearskin so tight around her the whites of her knuckles showed through. There was a bubble now to her breathing, a wet rasp.

All right? Is that what I am?

30.

Virri found the cave without too much trouble, thank the gods. The way down – a green, slippery scar where a gushing brook tumbled to the sea – would have been a death trap in the dark but they made it in time. The cave in the 'black cliff' itself necessitated a short climb upwards. She stayed behind Maka, in case she slipped. It was a small cave, no cavern, not much bigger than an upturned boat. Easy to heat, if damp for now. She could see the remains of a campfire near the cave mouth and a small stack of driftwood further back. The floor of the cave was littered with stones but there was a barer patch towards the left wall, as if Barin had cleared it to sleep.

Bless you Barin.

'You sit here,' she said, settling Maka on the barest patch behind the hearth. 'I'll nip back and fill our pot with water.'

Maka said nothing. Virri might have hoped Maka would have got the fire-bow going, at least offered – she would normally – but the girl was silent, the half bearskin round her like a cone. There was a shine of sweat on her forehead, but she was shivering. Virri removed the girl's sodden shoes and wrapped her feet in the sealskin.

'I won't be long, then I'll start the fire, but I have to do the climb while it's still light.'

She unpacked their crock and hurried down. The sun was setting. The black cliff and its nearest hill loomed over the beach. More sea-sick clouds were rolling in, back-lit by the falling sun. *Help me Sun, keep me strong.* The wind billowed round her, her clothes so flimsy she might as well have been naked. It was a strange beach, neither fully sand nor shingle, with some big stones in the mix, so she had to pick her way through, in the failing light, to get to the waterfall and then back again, trying not to spill any. When she saw the chunk of driftwood rolling in with the surf it was too good to miss, but it meant two climbs. It was only when she was back in the cave, puffed out and working on the fire-bow, that it occurred to her she hadn't asked Barin one word about Charn.

'Shit.'

Maka coughed. 'Sorry I can't do it . . .'

'No, no, it wasn't the fire-bow. I'll get it done. You just rest now, keep warm. Once I've got the fire going, I'll warm the water, then get the broth on. You'll feel a bit better once you're warm.'

The clouds opened. Sleet started shooting past the cave entrance, spitting into the beach below.

'I'll be all right,' Maka said.

'Course you will. You, you're the strongest person I know.'

The laugh came out a cough.

The next days passed as in a dream. Virri did not even count them. Sometimes Maka seemed worse, sometimes there was a spark of hope. Dawn and dusk could bring a complete reversal. She tried not to hope too much. Her days were busy. There was not enough driftwood to rely on this alone so, if the weather was dry, she walked in search of firewood. There was a headland to the west with a scrub of trees. Beyond an eddy caught and often provided her with bits, but they needed drying in the pile at the back of the cave. She never let it get too low, or the sun go down without a stock of heather and gorse for tinder, in case the embers died whilst she slept. The smoked pork ran out after the first night, so she had to search for food too. The waves were too fierce to risk the fish trap, so she did not try it. Often great flocks of birds would pass over her head, but she did not try the bow either. It would waste arrows. She unstrung it and put it at the back of the cave, away from the searing heat of the fire. At low tide she would put her back-basket on and hunt in her own way. There were razor clams to lure out with salt-water, crabs under rocks, winkles by the hundred, seaweed and gorse-flowers for greens. Some seaweeds, she found, were more delicious than others. They'd be rope thin, but they wouldn't starve. All around were also strange creatures – animals turned to stone. Most were long and thin like burins, some rounded and spiralling like sun circles. The ones on the beach itself were hard as granite, those in the cliff soft like clay. Virri could not help but stop to examine each one but had to resist bringing them back, loading the basket with things they could not use.

Each time she returned there was the slight hesitation, the moment of dread, before she came through the cave mouth, the breath of relief at the first sign Maka was still alive, even if it was a hacking cough.

At night Maka would cough worse than in the day. Exhaustion alone lulled Virri to sleep. More often than not it was coughing which woke her at dawn, coughing and the soft swish of the waves.

The day Virri ventured furthest from the cave was the day she regretted it. How the gods laugh. Dawn had been bright, almost warm – warm for autumn. She had peeled off her shoes and washed her disgusting feet in the surf, licked by little eddying breezes coming off the sea. By mid-morning she had to hold onto her hat. By noon she could barely stay upright, and she turned back. She was so far away by then that the steep hill was disappearing into cloud. Fat, black clouds building above the sea. The waves were no gentle swish now.

It was a relief to be climbing the slope up to the cave, mid-afternoon, tired as she was. Only half-way up, gulls screaming above her head, she noticed there was no coughing.

Oh no. No!

She hurried the rest of the climb, falling through the entrance. Maka was lying on her side. There was no visible movement. The fire had gone out, in the strength of the wind.

'Maka!'

Virri fell to her knees beside her, yanking on her shoulder.

There was breathing. *Thank Sun*! There was breathing, but it sounded rough. She helped Maka back up into a sitting position, wrapping the bearskin back round her. The girl's eyelids were flickering, but she did not seem able to focus on anything. Virri rubbed her back.

'Just breathe, don't try to cough for now. Lean on your knees. Let me get the fire going again and I'll warm the water.'

Maka slumped to the side, towards the floor.

'No, no, no – not until you've had some water.'

Virri positioned herself to bolster Maka as she teased the fire back into life with handfuls of tinder and lots of puff. She shoved the pot of water as far into the embers as she dared, growling 'Don't you dare crack on me.' Warm water was all the medicine she had. *What else can I try, Kenna*? Elo had seemed to rally a bit with infused blackberry leaf – but who knows? Besides, there was none here. *Come on Maka, come on*. There was a wet gurgle to her breathing. Virri rubbed her back again.

'Cough! Now! Spit!'

The girl obeyed, her face crumpling with disgust, but the next breath sounded clearer.

'Right, now some water.'

Virri supported her with one arm while scooping warm water to her lips in an empty shell with the other hand. Drink-rub-cough-spit, drink-rub-cough-spit – this was the pattern until the girl was breathing easier. Only then did Virri allow her to lie down, on her side, with both the bearskin and the seal pelt over her. Virri put both the beaver hats over Maka's feet.

I must not let the fire go out again.

Outside the waves were so loud they were more like thunder. The wind was shaking little scatters of stones from the entrance. *What if the cave roof gives*? Virri knew she would never get out in time, let alone drag Maka out too.

They would be crushed in a moment, squashed down until they were themselves turned to stone.

'Ma – mama.'

Maka's eyelids were flickering again. *She must be starting to dream.*

'No, it's only me.'

Maka reached out from under the bearskin and gripped her hand.

The day dawned grey, but calmer. Virri watched the first gleams of daylight on the sea with sore, sleepless eyes, but an easier feeling in her heart. Maka's breathing had grown steadier. She was sleeping now, on her side. Virri could hear a crackle to each breath. Three times further during the night she had had to support the girl and rub and thump her back whilst she coughed. It sounded like she was about to wake up to cough again – but not as bad. Not as bad, thank Sun, thank Mother Moon.

I think I might have done it, Elo.

Maka coughed, waking herself up. Virri went back to her side.

It was three more days before Maka was closer to her usual herself. Virri came back from one of her forays to find the girl sat at the cave mouth, oiling up her bow with the chunk of resin-wax.

'What are you doing?! Get back in the warm!'

Maka's hollow face cracked in a smile. 'I need some air.'

Virri scrambled up the slope and dumped down the driftwood. 'Seriously, you're not all better yet – don't tempt the gods.'

'I know. I remember Father.'

Virri left it there, but inside she soared at the sight of the fire well-tended, the girl sitting up and talking. She still watched her like a hawk all day but by nightfall her heart was calmed. They slept well.

The next morning Maka spoke of restarting their journey, and with that she went too far.

'No,' Virri said. 'No – it's too soon. You need rest. You should treat your lungs as if they're made of spider webs.'

'They feel like they're made of clay at the moment.'

'Exactly.'

Maka's face fell. Virri could understand. 'Come down to the beach, though. Help me find clams. It will test the strength of your legs.'

That raised a shaky smile. 'The beach it is.'

They spent the morning down below, hunting in the sandiest stretches for the tell-tale holes, Uffa's pot filled with seawater at the ready. They found a good chunk of pine too.

'Have you ever seen a boat while you're out here?' Maka asked, while they were dragging the branch up the beach.

'No, not one. I suppose it's late in the season for journeys.' She shrugged. 'But I've not seen a single person up on the cliff either. You are the only person I've laid eyes on since Barin.'

'Are you losing hope of finding your uncle?'

Virri thought about it a moment. 'No, I wouldn't say that. We'll find people again once we go back inland, I dare say.'

The girl whipped an emerging razor-clam out of the sand and chucked it into the basket. 'I had a lot of hope Huerin would change his mind, and catch up with us,' she said, 'but I've lost my hope now. I think he would be here by now.'

'Oh Maka . . .'

She waved it away. 'It's all right. I'll be all right. He might succeed, y'know . . . I mean, he'd survived this long.' She bent low, pouring salt-water into another notched sand-hole. Her hair flopped down beside her face. 'Is it bad to wash your hair in salt water?' she asked, getting up. 'Does it make it fall out?'

'Um . . . I don't think it will fall out, but it's not good.'

'I should cut it then. I feel so filthy.'

You're definitely feeling better.

They started west again two days later, heading inland a bit in the morning to get away from the worst of the sea winds. Virri turned for a last sight of the cave as they departed. It was a stinking hole by then, so much phlegm streaked down the cliff below even the gulls were avoiding them – or so it felt – but it had saved their lives. The last night they had eaten everything they could gather, used up the firewood to warm the cave and then stripped off to clean themselves as best they could. They warmed fresh water in their pot and rubbed themselves down with bunches of seaweed, cleaning under their nails with edges of shell. Maka went ahead with cutting her hair, against Virri's better judgement, sawing off great chunks to throw in the fire, but it did look cleaner. The bearskin was fashioned into a proper cape for Maka, with punched through holes using an arrowhead again and her leather hair thong threaded through, now it was no longer needed. Virri did much the same with the sealskin, making a short cape, using the second half of the thong. With the hats too it did feel as if they might survive the next bout of bad weather.

'We need to find shelter, though, every night,' Virri said, as they packed. 'You can't risk the fever returning.'

Maka nodded. 'We'll have to keep asking people, whether they are friendly or not. We don't even know how much further west we have to go.'

'Yes. We'll have to ask everyone we meet about Charn. It was a good sign Uffa knowing about him.'

They did not see another human being, though, that first day back walking. There were hearth scars, cow-pats, areas of cleared brush, so people had been around. They found shelter in an abandoned house, disappearing season by season into brambles and ivy, but still better than facing the cold night air.

The next day dawned bright and autumn sunshine right till noon sped their feet. When they entered a lowland, soggy and reedy, a planked pathway offered a way forward.

'If we follow this, we're bound to find people,' Maka said. 'Do I look fully better? Really? I don't want to frighten anyone.'

Her scrappy hair still took some getting used to, and they could both do with a bit more flesh on their bones, but Virri reassured her. They stopped a while on the sun-warmed planking, took off their shoes and let their feet dry. The air was filled with the sound of birds.

'I should hunt,' Maka murmured.

'Are you feeling up to it?'

The girl shrugged. 'I'm up to trying, but I can't promise I'll hit anything.' She smiled. 'At least the ground is familiar. It kind of reminds me of home.'

Yes. Virri watched her prowl up and down the path, bow ready, with a growing sense of pride. Nothing was brought down, though. As the sun dipped towards its slumber Maka's arms were tiring and she called a halt to it.

'We can eat bull-rush nibs,' Virri said, pulling on her shoes. 'We might even find something else, yet. Let's walk on a bit further, before it gets dark – we could even find the village.'

Maka was only half-listening. Her eyes were focussed over Virri's shoulder, towards the path behind them.

'Someone's coming.'

31.

Virri had been looking west, towards the low sun, and was still squinting a bit as she turned. She could see nothing but reeds and alder. No human at all.

'Are you sure?'

Maka was notching an arrow.

'They could be friendly,' Virri warned. 'Maybe just going towards the village like us.'

'Yes, but if they're not friendly we've only one direction we can run.' She tipped her head towards the expanse of reeds and raised her eyebrows. She was right. They would have to stay on the track, wherever it led.

'I still haven't seen anyone – do you think it was a man or a woman?'

'All I saw was the top of a bow. There! Where the track curves, the stand of rushes – I saw a flash of black.'

'Black? You don't think it's Babca?'

'I didn't say that,' Maka insisted, but her hold on the bow had strengthened, the stance between her feet an archer's poise.

Sun and Moon protect us. She's still recovering. . .

'We should go,' Virri murmured. 'Get to the village ahead if we can. There's a chance they wouldn't side with Babca . . .'

Maka was still peering east. In an instant her face brightened. The bow went down.

'Huerin!' she cried.

'Huerin, really?'

Maka ran forward and now Virri saw him. He was running too, and they swept together into a happy squealing mass, like two children. Virri felt a lump come to her throat. He looked unharmed, not that she could see much of him. There was a dead goose over his shoulder, so she helped that to the ground, smiling. They were embraced so tight

Maka's face had disappeared into his raven feathers. She felt bad to separate them, but sooner or later someone had to speak.

'It's so good to see you Huerin! How are you? Let me see you.'

The two youngsters parted a step and Huerin turned to her with a sheepish smile.

'It's good to see you too, Virri.'

He did appear unharmed, not so much as a bruise. 'Did you manage to follow us all along? You've done well to find us otherwise.'

Huerin shook his head. 'I did go all the way back to the Circle, but I changed my mind and doubled back quite soon. I've always been a day or two behind, I think, until today.'

Maka's grin was fading. 'Were we so easy to track?'

'Oh yes – the others must have just given up, a child could have done it, but then for a few days the trail went dark.'

'Maka was sick, with lung fever, we had to stop. We were in a cave, in a cliff.'

Huerin looked to Maka, and she nodded. 'I'm all right now. I do look all right, don't I?'

He took a moment, too long a moment. 'Nothing a moon of nettle tea and bone marrow won't cure.'

Virri burst out laughing and Maka followed, giving him the gentlest of punches. 'Someone needs to teach you to flirt, lad,' Virri said, ' . . . but you're right.'

Maka shrugged, a wry smile playing about her lips. 'Well! While we're here chatting, the sun is busy going down. Shall we find a camp, like the old days?'

They carried on along the wooden track and came to a river proper, where the track was more a bridge. The river valley itself offered little but yet more reeds, golden in the dusk light, but soon after they found an island, where alder and willow had made a stand, and this islet became camp for the night. Virri and Huerin wove together a basic shelter of willow and rushes whilst Maka built the fire. Huerin's goose was a feast. It felt warmer, with the three of them, and not just because of the fire.

'You said you left the Circle quickly,' Virri said, while Huerin was gutting the greylag. 'Did they chase you off?'

He shook his head. 'No. They never knew I was there.'

What changed your mind then? Virri bit her tongue but Maka, returning with their pot full of water, went for it.

Huerin sighed. 'I feel a coward, and a failure to my parents, but I thought about everything you'd said about my sister, both of you, and then I saw something with my own eyes to knock the wind from me.' He threw the stomach aside. 'I hid, in one of the old pits, to the north of camp, hoping she would come past – and she did, after a bit, but she wasn't alone. There were a whole bunch of men round her, joking and laughing. A child came up to Babca and asked for some bread – bread! – and Babca hit the girl so hard round the head the child fell. The others laughed and Babca dragged the girl up by her hair.' He shook his head. Tears were glistening his eyes. 'That's not my sister. Not anymore.'

Virri remembered the little girl who had sat with her by Ruc's side. 'Did the child get away?'

'Yes. As soon as Babca's hold loosened she ran off to someone else, someone I couldn't see. The whole lot of them moved off down to camp and I just sat there, until the sun went down, shaking. I kept thinking about what I should do – what I could do – but there was nothing that wouldn't be suicide.' He sighed. 'I thought about all you'd said, and I turned back.'

Maka reached over and held his shoulder. 'We're glad you did.'

They talked long into the night and slept late. Virri was the first to wake, to find the sun high and the last wisps of night mist burning off at the edges. As she stretched, pulling herself into a standing position, she felt eyes on her. She turned to see two young men watching from a pair of dug-out canoes on the upriver side of the island. One looked about twenty, the other younger.

'Mornin',' the elder said.

'Good morning.'

'You're a boat-comer.'

Great . . . 'Yes.'

'What you doing on our sacred island?' the younger one said, scowling.

Oh no. 'Um, well – '

The older lad turned and gave the boy a light slap round the head. 'Ignore him,' he said, to Virri, 'He's messing with you. We are Avan and Wyc, sons of Woryc and Avana, of Otter Bend Camp. What's your name?'

Virri hesitated, a mere heartbeat, but a crease of a frown appeared on Avan's forehead. *I'm going to have to tell the truth*. 'I am Virri, widow of Elo, of Duck Camp.' She gestured behind her. 'These sleeping are Maka, daughter of Elo, my stepdaughter, and Huerin, our friend,' she thought for a breath, 'also of Duck Camp.'

It was mostly true. . .

'Have either of you been to do your stint, lately?' she asked. 'At the Great Circle, or the Mother Circle?'

'No. Why?'

'There – there's trouble there – lung-fever . . . and other things. . .'

'Do any of *you* have lung-fever?'

She shook her head. 'But my stepdaughter only recently survived it. Huerin and I both survived it as children.'

Avan's eyebrows lifted. 'Does that mean you can't have it again?'

'No – but it doesn't seem so bad if you get it more than once, it's like the first time is most likely to be deadly.' *And in my people maybe not even then . . .* She sensed Maka and Huerin waking up behind her, saw the younger boy look to his brother in warning. 'We mean no harm,' Virri said. 'We just want to journey west, to see if we can find my uncle, who might have passed this way a few years ago.'

Avan nodded. 'What's his name?'

'I know him as Charn, but we believe he changed his name after fleeing for his life. If you've met him, you might remember him. He's a gold-worker, a master at it, and a boat-comer like me, but tall, and older. He must be about five-and-forty by now. He used to wear a long gold earring in both ears.'

The two lads looked to each-other. 'The gold man!' Wyc cried. Virri's heart soared.

'Yes, he definitely passed here,' Avan agreed.

'When?!'

'Late last winter.' Avan shrugged. 'Maybe early spring. I saw him at the Summer Solstice meet down at Big Herd too.'

Virri felt her grin was spreading beyond her face. 'Thank you! Until you said these words, I was not even sure he was alive this long. What was the name you called him by?'

Avan smiled. 'To all of us he was "the gold man". You need to talk with the elders, I think. Mother will want to talk with you, come to that.' He looked about the island. 'How did you get here? I don't see any boat.'

Virri nodded up towards the walkway. 'We climbed down from the path and waded through the reeds.'

'Go back the same way then, and carry on west,' he pointed with the paddle. 'Not far. When it forks take the right fork and you'll meet my mother. She'll give you food.'

'Thank you. Thank you, Avan.'

He pushed off the dug-out with the top edge of his paddle and they started to drift out in the current. 'No matter,' he called. 'Tell her what you told me about the fever.'

The right fork brought them to a huddle of rush-topped houses as he said it would, where a woman and child were enjoying the afternoon sunshine on a plank platform outside the main house. The woman had a knapping cloth on her lap and was roughing out a tool of some kind. The infant was making little piles of the flakes. Both adult and child looked up as the three strangers approached and Virri saw caution in the woman's eyes. Still, it made a change from outright hostility.

'Good morning!' Virri called, with a cheery wave. 'We met Avan and Wyc on the river, they told us to come and talk with you!'

These words secured their welcome and they were beckoned onto the platform while the woman, Avana, fetched cups of sharp-sweet drinking yoghurt and little honey cakes from inside the house. She was all smiles and nods during the introductions, but Virri sensed remaining caution in her, her eyes flicking in curiosity from Huerin to Virri to Maka and back again. Black hair, brown hair, straw hair; brown skin, sun-red skin, somewhere-in-between; two types of arrows, a copper knife and boat-comer gold, but the terrible beaver-hats. When they all sat down to eat she came straight out with it.

'Pardon me saying, but you are an unusual group, even for travellers. Is Duck Camp a boat-comer village?'

Maka's smile almost twisted into a smirk, but she controlled it. 'No. I am the only one born of Duck Camp. It's in the far east of the Isle, but not unlike here. The others, well, they can tell you themselves.'

'My Father came from the mountains in the far south, in the land across the sea,' Virri said. 'Mother was from the flat wheat-lands to the south-west if you cross the sea. I have lived on the Isle since I was a young girl, but I only moved to Duck Camp when I married.'

Huerin looked down, running a thumb nail down the grain of a plank. 'And I am a half-and-half. My father was a boat-comer, by blood, but my mother came from the Stag-and-Doe camps peoples, not so far east of here.'

Avana looked to him with sympathy. 'I've not seen any of them in a while . . .'

Huerin shook his head. 'No. I think I am the only one now.'

No Huerin, you have a new family now. 'Has this village been touched by lung-fever?' Virri asked, to change the subject, then wondered if she should have.

Avana sighed. 'Sadly yes. My husband drowned, may the ancestors meet him, but the other deaths we suffered last winter were all lung-fever. Did Avan tell you what happened with his girl? No?' An even bigger sigh. 'He went to the Mother Circle to do his stint last year, didn't meet anyone he fancied, then met a lass on the walk back, as these things happen. She'd done her stint at the Great Circle and probably caught the fever there. Avan went to pick her up for the wedding at first shoots of spring as agreed and found she'd died – half her village wiped out.'

'I am sorry to hear that. It will be much the same this year, I fear. Lung-fever is rife at the Circle – two healers dead and dying in just the short time we were there, a lad called Heryc spreading it unknown back to his village in the east. We managed to avoid catching it until after we left, then Maka only just survived.'

Avana looked to Maka and back to Virri. 'You nursed her through it?'

'Yes. And my own husband, early this year, though he died of another fever after. I am no healer, but I suppose what I learned with Elo helped me with Maka.'

'What worked?'

Virri shook her head. 'I can't say, for certain. Blackberry leaf tea seemed to ease Elo, a bit, but I didn't have any of that with Maka – I'd say the main thing is to get the phlegm out. Don't let the person just lay flat all the time like you might with a wound fever. Help them to cough – I was thumping her back.'

Maka nodded. 'She was brilliant.'

Virri smiled. 'I would ask the Moon-Speaker what she thought was best, if I could have my time again, but too late now. Avan should know, actually, as he did his stint at the Mother Circle, and he would know her. The Moon-Speaker has died – by her own hand, but at the Sun-Speaker's doing.'

'No!'

Avana listened with open mouth as Virri relayed the tale, Maka and Huerin adding in their own threads. At the end she sat back on her haunches, cuddling her youngest son to her.

'You know, I'm shocked,' she said, 'but not as shocked as I would have been a year or two ago. . . There was a reason Woryc and I encouraged Avan to do his stint at the Mother. Nothing like the story you've just told me, but little hints, y'know.'

Virri nodded. 'If it's safe to do so, tell others, spread the word.'

'Oh I will. The Moon-Speaker was well loved, round here.'

Gods keep you, Kenna.

'And – ' she hesitated, 'Avan mentioned you might know of my uncle? He called him "The Gold Man".'

'Oh yes.' Avana's eyebrows lifted. 'I thought it must be him when you were telling what happened. He stands out. I can't say I know him well but yes, he has been to the Big Herd meet a few times – he's friendly with all the leaders down west, even right down to the Horn lands, so I've heard.'

Virri grinned. 'So he's well?'

'Healthy as your best ox, as far as I last heard. You have a long journey still ahead of you, though – he's moved around, I can't say exactly where he is. And the high hills of the west are no place to be wandering about at this time of year.' She waved her hand out to the welcome autumn sunshine. 'This might not last the afternoon. If you miss the settlement you're aiming for by nightfall then it's all rock-rolled hills and wind-twisty trees.' She sighed. 'Aim for the village nearest Maiden's Rock, in the first leg – I'll put you on the right track, then ask again.'

'Thank you.'

'It's nothing, I'm glad to help, but I think you'd be better off waiting for spring.'

Virri cast a look to the others. *Normally I'd agree with her, but we've come this far . . .*

'And my uncle's name? I knew him as Charn but when he went into hiding he changed it – not surprising considering the Sun-Speaker tried to have him killed. It will be a lot easier to find him if we know his new name.'

Avana thought for a moment. 'I did hear what they called him . . . it wasn't one of our names, what was it now? "Noctso", that was it. Noctso.'

Virri's grin widened. In her father's born language it was clear: Night Sun.

32.

They left the next morning, having been persuaded – without too much effort needed, on Avana's part – to stay for a big meal and then the night. Virri was grateful to see Maka fall asleep early, lulled by a full belly and the warmth of a proper house. Avana asked many more questions about the fever and the evil doings at the Great Circle and Virri was happy to answer them. The boys were interested too, though as much in her boat-comer metals, it must be said. As they prepared to leave Virri wondered if she would offend their generosity if she gave them the gold earring but, given Avana was a widow like herself, she decided she should. They set off on their journey with packs full of food and a rolled ox hide.

The trail proved hard, though. Avana had been honest about the land. They were out of the river valley and into hills within their first morning of walking west. It felt colder. The highlands were grazed short and offered little shelter. They headed down to the trees and scrub of the vales and dells each day, not long after noon, lest they get caught out. Every cattle-boy and shepherd they found got asked about Charn, 'Noctso', the 'Gold-Man' and at least half of them knew exactly who he was. *Where* was the problem. Yes, he'd been to the Solstice meet, moons ago. Yes, he'd over-wintered in the Horn lands, further south-west, more than once. No, he didn't always. No, they hadn't seen him lately. The people of Maiden Rock Camp, whom they reached on the third day, said he'd last been seen with a group of other boat-comers, all set to sail to the West Isle.

Mid-way through the eighth day, the skies greying above them, Virri stopped.

'I think we need to give up. Find somewhere to over-winter and try again. We can go to this Big Herd meet they all talk about.'

Maka had been striding ahead but now she turned. 'That's not for more than six moons – are you sure?' She plucked a strand of bracken for no reason and chucked it over her shoulder. 'I mean, I know you're worried about me, but I'm all right. I feel as good as new now.'

Huerin spread out his hands. 'With the three of us I think we can live out here on the land all winter if needs be. We can build a good shelter, if we pick a quiet spot.'

Maka nodded. 'The people down here haven't been so unfriendly in any case. Not so far.'

'That's just because the lung-fever hasn't hit them too badly yet . . . give them another winter and it'll be different. And, if people head to the Great Circle for the mid-winter pilgrimage, they'll hear Sulo's counter-tale to ours. I don't think we should be on our own.' Virri took in a good breath. 'As we can't find my uncle and his friends, we need to find another group that might take us in. We could do worse than going back to Avana.'

The two youngsters huffed and hawed, spouting reasoned objections and rocking back and forth on their heels. Virri understood. It was hard to give up, hard to back-track, making eight days walk for nothing. What if Charn was behind the next hillcrest? He could be. A sail to the West Isle didn't necessarily mean for good. Maybe he hadn't gone at all. Maybe he'd been and come back. Maka's own past willingness to give up and settle at the Great Circle now made her the chief zealot for continuing. Huerin could see both sides, she was sure, but he was reluctant to undermine his one true love. Virri understood it all.

At high noon a decision was reached: they would camp tonight and, if the day dawned fair, they would continue; rain or worse would mean turning back.

Virri watched the sun going down as they pitched camp, torn in her own heart. The sun was tumbling in a festival of ripe pinks and furnace reds. It boded fair travelling – but bed for the night was another rough camp, nestled between gorse bushes in a dell to keep out the night's cold, the ox hide beneath them to save their own hides from thorns.

Maka did seem better but how long could she herself stand all this? *Did your bones ache like this, Father? You journeyed so far and never said.* She sat and massaged her ankles, wishing the sun was strong enough for the warmth to penetrate them.

Day dawned fair, on balance, as it turned out. Thick frost coated everything outside of their gorse nook when they got up and stretched but the sky was an unbroken expanse of blue. Continuing had to be the winner. They set off at a brisk pace, their loads light because Avana's provisions had gone by then and the glorious day firing their feet. The landscape stretched on, rich grassland studded with outcrops of grey rock and the odd twisted tree. Maka climbed one of these rocky knolls as the sun reached its daily peak.

'I think I see smoke, that way,' she said, pointing north-west. 'Let's head over there.'

Virri shielded her eyes. 'Just smoke?'

Maka shrugged. 'It's probably coming from a house roof but it's too far, I can't tell.'

'How about food?' Huerin asked. 'Does it look promising, that way? We could do with a river or a stream, too, before the day is out.' He climbed up on the pile of rock beside her and scanned around.

'That's a brook down there,' Maka said, pointing. 'That line of hawthorn. We'll cross it, so that's fi–'

'Someone's coming up behind us.'

Virri and Maka both spun round to look the same way as Huerin. He was right. In the distance a blob was moving. Very much following the course they themselves had taken through the morning. Virri thought she could make out two faces, but there was something strange. Animals with them, perhaps. *More cattle-boys*?

'No!'

Maka's exhortation made Virri jump. 'What?'

Maka's grin split her face. 'You remember telling me about horses? I think these people are *on* them.'

Huerin and Maka took a hand each and drag-lifted Virri up onto the tor. Soon she was grinning with joy herself. The man on the left horse was unmistakable.

'Charn! Uncle Charn!'

The two horsemen waved back and Virri hugged her two youngsters with a squeal. The three scrambled down and ran to meet Charn and his companion. Charn was on a brown horse, mid-brown like roe deer in summer. His companion's horse was paler, with a creamy white mane and feet. Another horse, brown like Charn's, followed them, bearing packs. Charn looked well – amazingly well for a man of his age. His teeth were spoonbill white as he beamed at them. Both men were dressed in thick woollen clothes against the cold, but Charn's love of decoration and skills with gold still stood out. He wore a tassel trim to his cloak, a pin fastening it of pure gold, a gold twist in both ears, an arm-ring worn low, near the wrist, of leather embellished with gold. His smiling companion – though as native to the Isle as Maka, by the looks of things – wore no fewer than four hair-glinters on his four black braids, catching the light.

'Virri!' Charn held out his arms. 'At last!'

Virri ran to him and embraced him as he slipped down from his horse. 'At last? Have *you* been looking for *me*?'

'Yes! We stopped in with the folk at Maiden Rock Camp on our way back three days ago and we've been tracking you ever since.'

Virri laughed. '*We've* been looking for *you* for moons on end! They told us you were planning to sail to the West Isle.'

'So we did, we've been there most of the summer, but we've come back before the seas get too rough. Cotro and I left the rest of our party at Maiden Rock while we searched for you.' He hugged her tighter. 'How are you, niece? Are you all right? The things they said . . .'

Virri buried her head in his shoulder, the smell of his woollen cloak filling her nose. *Just like Father. Thank you, Sun and Moon.*

'There's a lot of stories for the telling,' she said, muffled through the cloak, happy as the sun at dawn.

They camped right there by the rocks for the night, multiple introductions and the tales of years apart taking up the whole of the afternoon. Charn and Cotro had smoked beef and pork, all the way from the West Isle no less, in their pack-horse panniers, plus dried juniper berries, skinny carrots and herbs. It boiled up to a good stew to talk over while the horses themselves munched.

Cotro intrigued Virri from the start. He appeared around the same age as Charn, with streaks of grey striping his dark hair when he took off his hat and a fine crop of smiling crow's feet about both eyes. All the same there was a youthful sheen about him. He and Charn had been together for over two years, they told her, travelling about, but he originally came from deep within the Horn Lands, in the far south-west. There his wife, son and other kin, he said, still reside.

Virri flicked a sharp look at her uncle, when Cotro said this. She couldn't stop herself.

Cotro saw, and smiled. 'Former wife, I should have said. She is happy with her new man now, and my children are grown and in their own homes.' He laughed – a big bursting laugh like a popping log on a fire. 'When your uncle first visited our place, I tried to get him interested in wedding my eldest daughter.'

Charn blushed. 'In truth I was looking for a new strange metal I have found in those parts and had no intention of walking off with any of the family. Life takes strange turns sometimes.'

'And your daughter?' Maka asked.

'She is wed to a different boat-comer, a big strapping fellow from the West Isle – and gleeful she is too,' Cotro said, with a grin. 'That's one of the reasons we went there, after Solstice, to see her.'

Huerin was frowning, but more in puzzlement than anger, Virri felt. 'You actually wanted your daughter to wed a boat-comer?' he asked.

Cotro's grin broadened. 'Yes! All people were created equal, in my mind, just as they should be.'

'That's not what the Sun-Speaker spouts, day after day, to the pilgrims at the Circle,' Virri said.

'Sulo's cant is poison,' Cotro dismissed, with a snort. 'He was always like it. Blame, blame, envy, blame. We need to see the deeper knowledge which surrounds us. Does the blackbird envy the owl because he can fly at night? Do the bluebells blame the trees in leaf for blocking their light?'

Charn had been looking at Huerin, one eyebrow raised. 'Your father would not have been killed, I think, if I had not fled for my life. Do you not blame me?'

Huerin shook his head. 'No. My anger has always been aimed at the Sun-Speaker, and still is – for my sister, as well as Father.'

Charn looked to Virri. 'There are a growing band of people who level their anger at Sulo, I think. Maybe it's about time we all did something about it.'

Virri saw Maka throw a look of naked horror at Huerin.

The young man himself was staring into the fire.

Cotro was up first, at dawn, to welcome in the new day with a meditation sat on some sun-caught rock. As was his wont, apparently. Virri waited until Charn himself had left camp, to tend the horses, then followed him. She waited until Maka and Huerin were out of earshot before she opened her mouth.

'Did you mean what you said? About us doing something about Sulo?'

Charn turned. 'Yes. I think it's time. Do you doubt me?'

'No, no – it's not that.' She cast a look over her shoulder. 'It's just Maka and I only just about convinced Huerin out of a mad plan – we thought we were heading to safety, when we found you.'

He smiled. 'Well, you might still be right. Safety is a slippery fish. Is it safe to be in hiding for the rest of your life? I've had my fill of it, and I think I need to turn and fight before my age catches up with me. From everything you've told me Sulo is at his weakest *now* – imposing terror is not strength. You were right to convince young Huerin not to go it alone, I would have done too, but together we have a real chance.'

The brown packhorse nuzzled her back and she turned to give him a scratch. 'I want to avenge them too – Father, Kenna, Ruc, all of them – but there are not enough of us.'

Charn shook his head. 'Not just us. You haven't met the rest of our party.'

'Are they people like us?'

'You mean what they call boat-comers? Yes, but not from our own homeland. Closer to your mother's, I think. I'd never met them until I came down here.'

A cold wind blew, and she pulled the sealskin further across her chest. 'Do you trust them?'

Charn pursed his lips. 'Yes and no. Maybe. Perhaps it's too early to say.'

Fantastic. He must have gathered the thought from her face and laughed, which made her laugh too.

'That's a good answer,' she said.

'Well, as Cotro would say "You can trust a wolf to be a wolf, don't trust them not to bite your hand".' He threw the loose bit of his enormous cloak around her shoulders. 'Come on, let's go back and get a fire going, have some breakfast.'

They started walking back and saw Maka and Huerin already had smoke rising. 'Are those two a couple?' Charn asked.

'Yes . . . well, I hope so. I'm not sure they know what to do about it – well she probably does, but he spent those seven years all alone. I fear he is a bit lost.'

Charn sighed. 'Perhaps get them to firm it up a bit, before we get back to Maiden Rock.'

'Why?'

'All our companions are men . . . and I think Cotro and I are the only ones content with each other. Best to be on the safe side.'

Virri shivered. *Maybe going back with them isn't such a good idea.* Something else then occurred to her about what he'd said. 'I am quite safe, then? At my advanced age?'

Charn grinned those brilliant teeth. 'More than her. She has the bow, the knife, all the sass of the young. You, you have the wisdom that comes with years.'

Virri smiled. *Well recovered, Uncle.*

Virri spent the rest of the day wondering how, by Sun or Moon, she could broach such a subject without causing uproar with Maka – or Huerin, come to that. She hung at the back as they walked, the two youngsters being fascinated by the horses and both Charn and Cotro happy to oblige. It was slow walking. An icy cut-you-in-half wind blew all day. They camped as soon as they saw a decent spot, where a stand of hawthorn by a stream offered some respite against the wind. Charn and Cotro had a tent, pieced together from patches of leather, so they would be all right. They got on with pitching it while Huerin and Maka set the fire and Virri picked some dry hawthorn berries to add to the day's stew.

When the tent was up Charn went back to the packhorse. 'Here,' he said, throwing a rolled wolf pelt to Huerin. 'The tent's only big enough for us oldies, you two spring lambs'll just have to snuggle up by the fire.'

Huerin caught the pelt with the look of a stunned fish, but there was no outburst of anger. Virri's gaze swung to Maka, setting the boil bag over their fire. A smile played about her lips. 'Thanks,' she said, and got on with the meal.

Virri was grateful to have a place inside the tent that night. The wind had not let up. Even the shaggy horses, left to roam, sidled themselves up against the hawthorn. A hot meal inside their bellies had the two older men snoring before too long but Virri lay awake, listening to the wind, and alert to any cry for help. She could hear the two youngsters talking as they cleared away the supper things and banked the fire. She heard the familiar flick-unroll-flap of the ox hide being laid out, then it went quiet for a while.

'Are you warm enough?' Huerin asked, in a low voice.

'I'm all right, under here,' Maka whispered back. 'I think this is two wolves sewn together, and you feel burning.'

A nervous laugh. 'I never felt the cold much, and I have better clothes than you. When we get to the village, I'll ask to borrow a needle and thread and sort out that hat for you.'

Now Maka laughed. 'I *can* sew, you know.'

'Really?'

'Yes, *really*.'

A pause – was that a punch? Or a kiss? Maybe both.

Virri heard Maka speak next. 'The stars seem brighter when it's cold.'

'Yes, I think they are. Do you have names for them too, with your people?'

'Yes. You see that one, up there – the one with a knife hanging at his belt? We called him the Hunter, you know, long before I ever knew about you, or your father.'

'We call him the Hunter too.'

'And the Seven Sisters? Over there?'

'Yes – though with my people it is six and one.' There was a pause. Virri could imagine Maka's puzzled look. 'You see how one star is fainter? The other six are the daughters of Mother Moon, but the seventh is the daughter of the Goshawk Woman.'

'I don't know this tale.'

'Well, the Goshawk Woman was the first of my mother's people.'

'A goshawk?'

'She was not always a goshawk, sometimes she would be a woman – she could be whatever she wanted – but in the winter she chose to be a goshawk and she would dance across the sky. The Hunter would watch her all day and pine alone in his place in the sky all night. The Goshawk Woman was not afraid of him, but she loved him not. She married another. Years passed. The woman grew old, her brow grew white. The Hunter did not age, in the sky. When the woman's daughter had grown the Hunter watched the daughter dance in the sky all winter by day and pined in his lonely place all night. The daughter knew she was watched, and she was afraid. "Don't be afraid," the Goshawk Woman said, "for we can hide better than he." They turned into deer for a year and hid in the woods. By night he could still see them. They were salmon in the river for a summer, but the winter came, and he found them, so they turned themselves into clever crows and by their blackness they hid, five long years. The Goshawk Woman thought she had triumphed, she became bold . . . but the moon shone very bright one night and the Hunter saw them. He snatched her daughter away into the sky. The Goshawk Woman screamed and yelled out to Mother Moon. "Why? Why have you betrayed me Mother Moon?" The Moon turned her back, for she loved the Hunter her son, but the mother and daughter's cries softened her heart. She plucked the girl away and set her among her own daughters, where the Hunter can still see her, but never touch her.'

'And the Goshawk Woman?'

'She is in the sky too. You see, the one right over there? Like a diving bird in flight?'

'Oh yes!'

They were silent a moment.

'You know,' Huerin whispered, 'the others, I think they deliberately left us alone together tonight.'

'Oh yes. Definitely.'

'Are – are you all right with that?'

'Fine with me.'

'Then with me also.'

Virri smiled and turned over, her back to the tent wall. She let her eyes grow heavy and drifted to contented sleep.

33.

It was good to see Maka and Huerin clasping hands as they walked onward the next day. Virri felt a lightness in her own step, as if Elo still walked beside her. The weather improved too. The wind had brought clouds, keeping warmth in like a blanket, easing their parched skin. By late afternoon, though, it was brewing for rain, and they were relieved to see the familiar outline of Maiden Rock in the distance, but as they neared a grim smell drifted towards them on the damp breeze. Kites circled and dived. A funeral platform on wooden poles, new since their visit only days before, greeted them on the west side of the settlement.

'We should skirt round,' Cotro said, in a low voice. 'Come in the other way.'

Charn nodded and steered his own horse right. The packhorse followed.

'Was anyone sick?' Virri asked. 'When you two were here? They didn't say so to us.'

'Yes,' Cotro said. 'Two children, when we were here last, but they were keeping them out of sight.'

Virri saw the flicker of concern cross Maka's face. 'It couldn't have been you,' Virri said. 'You were fine long before we got here.'

'Don't feel bad in any case,' Charn said. 'There are more woes than lung-fever to stalk the land.'

He had said something about hunting out their companions as they'd neared the village but as it turned out no 'hunting' was required. The boat-comers were camped outside the settlement, beside a wide pond the villagers came to for water, within sight but not within the shadow of any house. They had tents too, like Charn and Cotro's, but Virri still marked it as odd.

'Do you worry about passing them the fever?' she asked the main man, as they were introduced.

He looked back at her in complete bafflement, a fleeting glimpse of doubt crossing his confident facade. Then the gate closed again.

'No. Just don't want to outstay our welcome.' He held out his right hand. 'Laracon, son of Laracon. Call me Larac, everyone does.'

Larac? Could it be? He was the right sort of age. Older than Virri, but not by much. His wheatsheaf of hair was turning from gold to white, but not all of it yet. Maybe forty. Instead of girlish puppy fat he was solid muscle, tall, broad and built out of oak, but there was something about the nose and brow.

'Do you have a grown daughter, called Laracida?'

He laughed. 'I do! This world is not as wide as I thought it to be.'

Virri smiled. 'We "Pales" stand out.'

Larac's grin broadened. His left canine was missing, rather giving him the smile of an old dog. It suited him. 'Not so much anymore, though, eh? We'll be plentiful as sand on the beach the way things are going.'

Virri threw an awkward glance at Maka and found herself watched. The two sons had just been introduced to her, but Maka's attention was more Virri's way.

He said it, not me.

'Come! Sit by the fire!' Larac said, taking Virri by the elbow. 'There's beef roasting and bread on the stone . . . no beer, but we've travelled light.'

She was grateful for a seat, to be honest, if a little narked by the amused look she saw in her uncle's face and the wary one on her stepdaughter's. Larac passed her a fur to put over her knees and placed himself beside her. The sons, meanwhile, remained on their feet, making a show of admiring Maka's bow. One was big, as big as his father, but with thinner flaxen hair in a knot at the back. His brother was younger, tall, slight and ghost pale, with a crop of fox-red curls at the top. All of them were dressed much alike, in tunics of dark and light wool woven in squares, belts with jet sliders and capes of dense wool, but it was the father who carried it best. The one boy was starting to slide to fat, the other straight up and down like milk pouring from a crock.

Larac had seen her looking at them. 'Come, lads, sit. Introduce yourselves to the Noctso's niece.'

They obeyed, the elder, bigger one, giving her a smile and a nod. His eyes, already small, disappeared into his chubby face. 'I am Larac too,' he said, 'but you can call me Pig. Everyone does.' He gave his young brother a slap on the back. 'This one is Weddi. He doesn't look much but he's sharp as a dagger.'

Weddi had a mouth full of beef by that point and looked back at her with a sheepish nod.

Well I'll take your word for it.

'Our other brother's up there,' Pig continued, tipping his head towards a stand of tortured oaks on a hillock. 'He's got the runs.'

Larac laughed. 'You didn't need to tell them that.'

'You have a big family,' Virri said, by way of compliment, and the man turned back to her with another warm smile.

'Aye. Orcos is my nephew really, the boys' cousin, but my sister died young, so he's been with us since he was a babe. He's a good lad.' He gave her a dish and gestured for her to eat. 'The Noctso was telling us you were among the very first of our people to come to this isle.'

'Yes. I was a young girl then, so I've lived here longer than I ever lived in my father's homeland. Mother was a boat-comer too, though her people were from further east. We were welcomed, by the old Sun-Speaker. Father and Uncle Charn were great friends with him. Our knowledge of making the metals was respected, not simply exploited, like now.'

'And you can work metal yourself?'

'Yes.' She followed up this assertion with a wary sideways glance, remembering what Laracida had said about his views on women working metal, but he was giving her an appreciative smile now.

What is going on with him? Surely he's not after me?

'Huerin's father was a boat-comer too,' she said. 'His people must have been here as early as us, if not earlier.'

Huerin had been sat at the edge of the campfire's circle, she suspected a little uneasy at being among so many people, and now she felt a pang of guilt at bringing him in to change the subject, but Huerin nodded.

'Father was born here, on the Isle,' he said. 'He'd had no trouble from the old Sun-Speaker, nor had his parents, but the new one killed him.'

Larac's lips thinned, shaking his head. 'Everything I hear about this "Sun-Speaker" stings my craw. And you survived out on your own, in the cold, a full seven years?' Huerin nodded and Larac tipped his head back and guffawed. 'By Sun, you must be tougher than you look, boy!'

Virri's heart leapt, but Huerin took it well, unperturbed as a rock in a gale. She saw Maka giving him a supportive smile.

Larac leant back, placing his palms on his knees. 'So, everyone here has some feud with this Sun-Speaker that wants lancing.'

'Except you,' Virri said. 'He hasn't done anything to you and yours.'

Larac smiled. 'Sounds like a matter of time, from what you've all said. You should know as well as me – mould it while the metal is hot.'

The predicted rain came at about midnight. Virri was tucked up in Charn and Cotro's tent again by that point, Maka and Huerin happy despite – or perhaps because of – some teasing to make their own arrangements. As they'd got up to leave the fireside Larac had come straight out and said it.

'You two wed then?'

The two youngsters had looked to each other, to Virri and then back to each other. 'Not yet,' Huerin said at last.

Virri looked to Maka's reaction and was relieved to see no panic on her face. 'What is the marriage rite among your people, Huerin?' Virri asked, nodding to her stepdaughter.

'If we were back at Duck Bill Hill you would cross the sacred river together and back again then build your house, but we can scarce do that.'

Huerin took in a good breath. 'I need to offer you a feather,' he said to Maka. 'If you accept it, it's done.'

Maka didn't hesitate. 'I would accept it.'

Virri beamed.

Larac watched the three of them with open mouth. 'By Sun and Sky, if you've just made that up lad, you're the cleverest man alive. I had to drive fifty head of cattle three days across a filthy swamp t'my father-in-law before I got anywhere.'

'I didn't make it up.'

Maka shrugged. 'Our traditions are different.'

Larac slapped his left knee. 'There you go lads,' he said to the three of them – Orcos having re-joined the party by this point. 'If we can find some un-hitched women it won't only be your sister who's wed before the year is out – easy as milking a goat.'

Virri had to fight down a laugh at the look of sheer disgust on Maka's face but to be fair the girl didn't say anything.

'I think you should send for your daughter, Larac,' Virri said. 'All was not well there, when we left Windy Chalk camp.'

Larac had cast his eyes to the stars, picking a burr off his tunic. 'Ah well . . . she's promised to the lad. I'll not renege on it now.'

Her betrothed might not survive, neither might the other one, was Virri's first thought, but she kept her thoughts to herself. Later, though, lying in the bedroll, listening to the soft rain patter upon the tent, their conversations with Larac so far rolled about in her head.

He plans to use us.

As soon as Cotro left for his meditation at dawn Virri shook her uncle awake. He listened to her whispered concerns, patiently enough, while he combed his hair.

'You're absolutely right,' he said, at the end, 'but are we not also using *him*? We want revenge on Sulo, I want to be Sun-Speaker, we all want to live here free of persecution – Larac can help us achieve all that.'

'You really think he won't just want to be Sun-Speaker himself?'

Charn laughed. 'No. We went over this together, him and me, when we were on the West Isle. He is ambitious, no doubt, he would gladly be a leader here, much as he is in his own homeland, but the life of the spirit is dry as ash to him – surely you got that impression yourself?'

Virri snorted. 'So he would invent a new role for himself? In a foreign land? Just how many cuckoos will fit in one nest?'

'You simply don't like him, I think.' He threw her a sneaky side-eye. 'He is *very* keen on you though.'

'I don't believe it.'

'I don't mean as a potential wife – though that could well be part of it – I mean as part of the plan. I believe they will want you to be Moon-Speaker.'

'Me?!'

Charn laughed. Any notion of her whispering had gone up in smoke, but he kept his own voice low. 'Is it so surprising? You are my kinswoman, a 'boat-comer', you've lived here a long time, you knew the previous Moon-Speaker, you have experience and wisdom on your side . . . You would be a great Moon-Speaker.'

Virri rolled her eyes. 'I did know Kenna – I know I'm not a pale shadow to her. I'm no healer, for a start . . . And I'm not holy, not by any stretch.' She gestured to the tent flap. 'Your Cotro is holier than the rest of us put together from what I've seen.'

'Well, holiness and leadership are no easy bedfellows, I've found. He wouldn't want it – and the Moon-Speaker has been a woman for generations on end, in any case.' He sighed and reached over to hug her. 'Just think it over, for now. Don't throw the idea out before it's even fledged.'

Virri nodded, though inside she was all a-tumble.

Me?

34.

When Charn and Virri left the tent they found Pig and Orcos already up and sat by the fire, sharing a side of smoked pork. It didn't look like they'd heard anything. Larac was down by the pool, shaving his face with slow, careful movements. There was a definite twinkle in his eyes as he nodded over to her.

Mother Moon give me strength.

'Here, sit, have some breakfast,' Pig said, gesturing to a free log. 'Father said we'll be leaving soon.'

Did he now?

Virri was grateful enough to sit by the fire. She pulled her sealskin cape closer about her. There was a heavy dampness in the air, every spider's web in the bushes glistening with dew. Orcos looked pinched and wan, curled under his cloak, as cold as she was.

'Are you feeling any better? Do you think you will be well enough to get going today?'

Orcos looked back with a laugh in his rain-grey eyes. 'Oh, I'll be all right. I've had worse from the beer.' He took off his felt hat to give his head a scratch and she saw he had darker hair than the others, mid-brown like an otter. It made him look all the paler. He was dressed much like his cousins but, as he shifted, she saw a bone flute thrust through the loop of his belt.

'You are musical?'

Pig's mouth set into a grim line. 'He's a bloody nightmare.'

Orcos lay back along the length of the log and laughed.

'You two are the same age, aren't you?'

Pig nodded, passing her a strip of the pork. 'Barely a moon between us. Twenty years next harvest.'

Charn had gone to check on the horses but now Larac was coming back towards the fire he headed back too. Larac was dabbing at a slight cut on the side of his chin.

'My son spoke a little out of turn,' Larac said, looking to Virri. 'We'll only leave here today if your party and ours agree.'

'And we have a workable plan,' Charn added.

'Absolutely.' Larac sat, choosing the log opposite Virri this time rather than next to her. *This time he wants to watch my face. Did* he *hear us, earlier?*

Virri could see Weddi was walking over from the direction of the village, carrying a small sack, maybe of grain, but there was still no sign of Maka or Huerin, or Cotro, come to that. 'We should wait for the others,' Virri said.

Larac smiled. 'Agreed. Never a good plan made on an empty stomach, anyway.'

Cotro returned within moments, sauntering back with a sprig of rowan berries tucked behind one ear. Virri saw a few raised eyebrows but to be fair nobody said anything. By the time Maka and Huerin came back to camp everyone else had finished breakfast and they had to face a bit of whistling and joshing themselves, but they took it in good heart, or ignored it, at least.

Once the circle was complete Larac wasted no more time.

'We'd heard rumours. We skirted round the Great Circle on our own way west,' he said, 'so I've never been there. If we're going to take down this "Sun-Speaker" then what do you all think? Is the site well defended?'

Charn shook his head. 'I wouldn't say so. It's never been built with defence in mind. There are the stones themselves, pits and ditches that could be used for cover, the few buildings of Old Camp, the odd fence, but no wall or palisade to speak of anywhere.'

Larac nodded, chewing on his bottom lip. 'So, once we're in, we're in . . . but from what everyone's told me the land is very exposed there, the guard would see us coming.'

'Yes.' Maka gripped her own bow tight. 'They're good archers – as good as we are.'

Pig looked to his father. 'A night attack then. Catch them napping.'

'Agreed.' Larac turned to Huerin. 'You've padded in and out a few times by night, by the sounds of it.'

'Yes. I can take us on the easiest route.'

Oh Huerin.

'How many guards are there?' Larac asked Maka.

'There are about thirty, all told.' Maka weighed up with her hands. 'But Jek, one of their best, they killed, and Aric, the chief-of-guard's favourite, I killed. I hit Yarlo in the head, too, when we escaped, he could have died. At least two are usually stationed up at the Mother Circle, to wait for anyone coming in . . . so maybe twenty-five.'

'There is dissent though, among the guard, from what you've all said.'

Virri and Maka both nodded.

'I reckon we can probably halve that number, then,' Larac said. 'They've seen one of their number murdered in cold blood – for nothing, really – another of their best fighters killed . . . They won't necessarily go out in a fury, they'll make excuses – trouble at home, help with the harvest or whatever – and then not come back. It didn't sound like your Sun-Speaker had a means of dealing with that sort of thing.'

'No-one devout will want to rile the Sun-Speaker,' Cotro said.

Larac's lips set into a line. 'We'll see.'

'I saw about ten guards with my sister when I was back there,' Huerin added.

Maka's eyes were wide. 'It's still at least two more than us.' She threw a shaky glance at Virri. 'And – and, well, not all of us are fighters.'

Virri chuckled. 'That's fair. I've never won a fight in my life.' She looked into Larac's eyes. 'And I won't be the only one. We should remember there will be people at the Circle who are wholly innocent – the orphans, for a start.'

'I hadn't forgotten.' Larac tipped his head to one side. 'I think there's a danger this Sulo will use one or all of them as a shield, to be honest. Our task will be to separate him from them – from everyone – quickly. Once we're in, you can get to them.'

There was sincerity in his sharp, pale eyes. Virri gave him a nod. *Reality might be more chaotic, though.*

Charn was toying with one of the tassels on his cloak hem, a frown growing between his brows. 'Do you know where the Sun-Speaker usually sleeps, these days, Maka? Is he always alone?'

Maka waggled her hand in the so-so gesture. 'Not always in the same place – in his house, most nights, but out among the stones more than once whilst I was there; among the grass and stars on summer nights, I'm told, if the mood takes him. Sometimes they say he doesn't sleep at all. The guards – at least Babca – always know where he is, though, and keep an arm's length watch.'

Larac took in a big breath. 'We could do with someone on the inside, I think, who could give some sort of signal.' He turned back to Maka. 'Do you reckon if you were to go and pretend to plead forgiveness, they might take you back?'

'No!'

The cry came from Virri and Huerin in unison and everyone laughed, not least Maka.

'So much for that then', Larac said, with a grin. 'How about if me or one of the boys ventures in saying we want to trade?' He tipped his head towards his own horses. 'We've got a packhorse load of copper from the West Isle.'

Virri shook her head. 'It's too risky.'

'Look what happened to my father,' Huerin said.

Cotro scanned about the circle. 'It should be me. I'm not known to the Sun-Speaker as trouble – it's nearly twenty years since I last visited the Great Circle – but I have every right to be there. I could say I've come early for the mid-winter festival.' He turned to Charn with a sad look. 'I could say I've come early because I want to atone, or seek purification, or something.'

Charn looked aghast but Larac reacted with an enthusiastic clap.

'Perfect.'

They all left mid-morning, but not together. As far as the folk of Maiden Rock Camp were concerned two groups had met, parleyed and parted. There had been debate on whether they should tell the truth or not. They decided to be honest about the death of the Moon-Speaker with anyone they met, to spread discontent with Sulo, but not to reveal the actual plan, or that there was a plan at all. Sure, people might have joined them to help, if they knew, but if any word got back to Sulo it was over. Virri and Maka's tale on the way down had been that they were looking for Virri's kinsman – well, they'd found him, so the whole group were now heading back towards Huerin's homeland, to seek his kin, should anyone ask. Larac's party were 'heading for home' too, seeking a rendezvous with a boat on the south coast, if pressed. They would travel along the coast then head inland at the last moment, where the sacred river meets the sea, both groups merging at Huerin's ancestor stone, if everything went to plan.

If everything went to plan.

Virri found herself chewing at her nails as the sun went down. 'What's wrong with me?' she said, with a titter, to Maka, walking beside her. 'I shook this habit years ago – you'd think after everything we've been through this past year I would have already started if I was going to.'

Maka shrugged. 'It's different. You were running away before, now we're going on the attack. It's a different sort of nerves.'

'I suppose you're right.' She cast a glance back to where the three men lagged behind, hooking some debris off one of the horses' hooves. 'Are we really going to do this?' she whispered. 'I don't think your Huerin is any more a warrior than I am, when it comes down to it – he's never hurt anyone, as far as I can tell.'

Maka shook her head. 'No . . . but his need for vengeance has brewed too long, he needs to let it out. I think he'll get there.'

'Neither are Charn and Cotro.'

'Did you see the others, though? Getting ready, when we left this morning?' She let out a whistle. 'Those weapons!'

She was right. It wasn't only bows and quivers full of arrows. An array of knives, both flint and copper, were being strapped on. Pig had rearranged his arrows in the quiver before mounting up and Virri saw the points on them. No doubt they'd done a bit of hunting for food, while they travelled, but those were man-killing points, for sure, flared like swallow wings. He'd seen her looking and grinned.

'It could still all go wrong.' She tossed another look over her shoulder. 'If we fail, if Sulo guesses what's up, then Sulo's response will be hard as granite.'

Maka's eyebrows lifted. 'Yes, and if Cotro rats out on us, too.' She plucked a stray fern from their path and swept up again.

'You're suspicious of him? I'm not sure about the whole "at one with the animals, spirit-spirit-blah" do-da myself but he hasn't actually done anything to deserve our suspicion . . .'

Maka laughed. 'No, it's not that. It's just he's the only one who hasn't got an actual thorn in his shoe about Sulo and yet he agreed to go in so readily . . .'

Yes. 'His loyalty to my uncle though. . .'

'I dunno, I'll keep an eye.'

'He could have the same qualms about you,' Virri warned. 'You're the one who used to be a guard. Be careful – don't be so suspicious you push him into it.'

'Oh I know – he's probably fine, it's just there lies the risk . . .'

When he's alone, inside the Circle. 'You're not wrong.'

Short days and cold weather notwithstanding it was an easier journey back east than the trip west had been. The two groups had shared dried meat stores before they parted so there was little need to hunt and no need to trade. If they met people by chance they stuck to the plan and told them about Kenna. Everywhere they went there was disquiet about the Moon-Speaker's death. Virri started to feel a touch more confidence in their plan, though not a single person they spoke to proposed any move on Sulo themselves. Prayers to Kenna's memory were much easier and safer.

It was pouring the afternoon they arrived back at Huerin's sun stone, dark before its time. All was quiet.

'I thought we would get here first,' Huerin said as he loped across the ditches to the centre. 'I explained the spot well, but coming along the coast must take longer, even with the horses.'

Maka threw Virri a look. 'Let's hope it's just that,' she muttered.

Charn and Cotro were dismounting. 'Where's best to camp, while we wait?' Charn asked.

Huerin tipped his head north. 'Up at my river camp. Not far. We'll probably hear them, when they arrive, but I can keep nipping to check.'

Huerin hurried on, as if hoping to get to the stone before the sun sank. As he reached it Virri saw him crouch and touch something in the ground, but the light was so poor she could not see what it was until she had caught up with him.

A black feather. Speared into the ground so that it stood pine-straight, even in the wind.

Virri heard Huerin's sharp intake of breath.

'Babca. Babca has been here,' he said.

35.

Maka was first to speak. 'Is it so surprising?' she said. 'This is your sacred ancestor place so it must be hers too.'

Huerin shook his head. 'In all the years we've been parted I've never seen her here. Never seen any sign – '

'What sign *is* this though?' Maka gestured to the feather and Huerin threw up his hands.

'This? This isn't anything. No tradition of ours, not stuck in the ground.'

Virri turned back to her uncle and Cotro. 'We need to be careful. We should have a good look around before the light goes entirely.'

Maka's eyebrows shot further up her head. 'What are we looking for? Babca crouching in a ditch?'

Virri sighed. 'No. Any other sign of people having been here, recently – footprints, hoof-prints, blood, arrowheads, anything.'

Huerin was still crouched by the stone and now he looked up to her in horror. 'You think the others got here first and Babca's guards have killed them?'

'I don't know, but I think we have to rule that out.'

Charn and Cotro tethered their own horses and all five of them searched as Virri had said, every ditch and bump and into the surrounding land, as far as the light allowed them. They did find what could be a footprint in the mud to the north of the site, but that could have been Babca herself. There was nothing else.

'I don't think there's been a fight here,' Charn said as they came back together by the stone. 'I doubt they've got here yet at all.'

Virri shrugged. 'It doesn't look like it, but until they come riding over the horizon, we can't be sure.'

Charn reached over and hugged her round her shoulders. 'You're right, but everyone's tired, and wet. We need to camp and get a fire going.'

Cotro was wringing water out of his braids. 'I'll get the tent up. It's going to be snug, but I think we'd all better sleep in there tonight.'

Huerin shook his head. 'No, I'll keep watch. If she's been here once, then she could come back at any time.'

'No Huerin.' Virri took his arm. 'You need rest too. We'll all take turns.'

Maka was nodding along – the two older men . . . not so much.

Virri took the second watch, taking over from Huerin. It was a relief to get out of the stuffy tent, tired as she was. She picked her way to where Huerin sat, scared of turning an ankle in the dark. There wasn't much of a moon or stars. It felt like midnight but, given the time of year, was probably earlier. At least the rain had stopped.

'All quiet,' Huerin whispered, as she neared. He was sat upon a fallen willow, high enough to see in every direction, clothes pulled high against the cold. She could see his breath coming out in puffs. 'The others think I'm mad, don't they?'

She settled down beside him. 'You're right to be careful. They don't know her – we do.'

He sighed.

'Have you been thinking of what the feather could mean?' she asked.

'Yes . . . but I'm still not sure.'

'Do you think it could have been left as a sign solely for you?'

Huerin turned to look at her. 'But she doesn't know I'm even alive.'

Virri pulled her own cape closer to her against the damp night air. 'I don't think we can be sure of that, can we? I told you there were tales of 'the Hunter's ghost' at camp, so we know you were occasionally seen. That last time, when you parted ways with us and went back to the Circle, maybe you were seen then.'

He shook his head. 'Maybe she just wanted to get away for a few days, on her own.'

'Why here, though?'

'We used to come here, as children, with Mother and Father, every mid-winter – but not at the Solstice, in case mother's kin turned on her again. We would come just before.' He swept his hand out to the late autumn gloom. 'Effectively she's done the same.'

'Do you think the others might have kicked her out?'

'I don't know. It seems unlikely. But I know it's where I would come, if I was troubled, or lonely – and often have.' He tapped the bag by his side. 'I had a mind to bury Mother's skull here, when I returned. I'm not so sure now.'

Not so sure of his sister's turn to badness, either, I think.

She shivered and Huerin turned back to her. 'You get back to bed,' he said. 'I can watch the whole night. It was my dopey idea, and your teeth are chattering.'

'No, no. I'm all right – you go snuggle up to Maka. We all need to keep up our strength.'

They argued a little longer, but she prevailed. She watched him lope back towards the tent with a heavy heart. He was never going to confront his sister, if it came to it. He might never forgive the one who did it, either, if she was killed. Virri pulled the cape tighter, trying to get a more comfortable seat upon the gnarly willow and failing. Maybe she should have accepted the young man's kind offer.

Sun and Moon protect you, Huerin.

The night stretched out. So black, without a star. It was difficult to know when she should swap with Maka, as planned. As she walked up and down to keep her blood moving it occurred to her that if Babca – or anyone – was approaching the breath puffs would be visible, clear as day.

This is pointless.

She felt a fool, but it was too late. She couldn't give up and go back to bed now. If they were all asleep at dawn and guards did show up, then she would be kicking herself.

I'll tough it out until the first glimmers of the Sun.

Virri felt like shit the next day, not to put too fine a point on it. Tired, grouchy, aching like fury from the ankles up. What was Maka's phrase? "Rough as a crock of sick"? Well, that. The one high point was Larac's lot turning up, safe and sound. They rode in fresh and smiling, horse hooves splashing up the dew, breath clouds steaming, none the worse for nine days travel along the coast. Virri felt relief lift a weight from her.

'Did anyone see you turn inland?' Charn asked.

Larac shook his head. 'No. The last people we saw were down on the coast, a day ago. We told them about the ship, as planned. All is well.'

Given how eye-catching – intimidating, even – they were, his confidence seemed over-sold, but Virri had no strength in her for an argument. As Larac slid down from his horse he was looking at her with concern.

'You all right?'

Maka answered for her. 'She was supposed to get me, to take over the watch, but she did the whole night. And now she's paying for it.'

'You needed your sleep – all the fighters do,' Virri snapped. 'This isn't going to be easy.'

Larac frowned. 'No, and we want *you* to live through it as well.'

Maybe Charn was right, about them wanting me to be Moon-speaker...

'Do we attack tonight?' Huerin asked. 'It's still a long way.'

'No. I'm thinking early the next morning, maybe even the one after that.' Larac's eyebrows twitched. 'We want *us* to be fresh, to catch them napping, not the other way round.' He swept his arm about the sacred site. 'This was an ideal place to meet, your directions were good, but it's too open for us to linger. Is there somewhere nearer, but hidden, where we can rest up and bide our time?'

Huerin nodded. 'Yes, in the old wood.' He glanced to Virri and Maka. 'There are other reasons we should get out of here too.'

Larac was dismissive about the threat of Babca's presence at the stone, at least to their faces. The fact she had known the place as a child and appeared to have visited it alone to him was a good sign. She was uncertain, troubled – maybe thrown out, as they had also considered. The feather could mean anything. The only downside, as Larac's party saw it, was the thought of rogue guards wandering out from the Circle camp, stumbling upon their attack band and haring it back home to blab. The move to Huerin's place in the wood was made without delay and there was a watch set again, as soon as they stopped, throughout the day and night, everyone taking turns.

Virri managed to stay awake through her own next watch, but it was a struggle, sitting quiet, still and alone in a pleasant patch of wintry sunshine, the sounds of the others a gentle patter through the trees. When Orcos came to swap with her she caught herself planning a nap before dinner and felt suddenly ancient. He was looking replete with youth and health, the colour back in his cheeks.

'Pa said to go and see him, once you're done,' he said. 'He's over there.' He tipped his head south, further into the trees, away from the others. Virri felt a jolt run through her. She was about to ask 'what does he want?' but bit her tongue, lest her naïveté prompt laughter. *Surely not*? She smoothed down her braids without thinking about it and this alone brought a laugh to Orcos's face.

'Aw, stop preening, you look great.'

Virri threw him a glare but there was such a sunny look to him she softened. He swung himself up onto an oak branch and got himself comfortable as she left.

'Don't fall asleep,' she warned, but put a laugh into her own voice.

Larac was not alone, when she found him, in the glade in the woods. Weddi was there too.

What is this? By Sun and Moon . . . was I not nervous enough?

'What's going on?'

Larac smiled. 'I'm worried about you. You said, at our first meeting "I've never won a fight in my life" – well, come tomorrow, that needs to change.'

Virri's eyebrows shot up. 'You want me to stay out of it? It's my battle as much as anyone else's.'

'I agree. That's why you need to learn how to defend yourself. Dumb luck only gets anyone so far.'

Charming. 'In one day?'

'The basics, yes.'

'All right.'

He slapped his thighs and got up. 'Weddi, the stick.' The boy handed him an oak branch, about the width of her wrist at one end, perhaps her thumb at the other, denuded of side-shoots. 'You wear a knife,' he said, gesturing to the copper blade at her belt, 'but if anyone gets close enough for you to use that, chances are you're already dead. Don't turn your nose up at a humble stick.' He swished it through the air a couple of times for effect. 'Weddi, come at me with a knife.'

The boy obeyed, holding the blade strong in his right hand and lunging forward at speed. Virri had the impression Larac was careful not to hurt him, but the stick moved so fast she could barely see it. Weddi had to duck, crouch and – within a few blinks – retreat.

'It's light, so you can carry it all day and still fight.' Larac threw the stick to her. 'You try.'

Weddi was on the attack again so fast Virri had no chance to object. She whipped the stick up to protect her neck before she had a chance to think about it too. He lunged left, she dodged right, bringing the stick down towards his head.

'Good!' Larac yelled. 'It's lengthening your arm – that's good. Again.'

Weddi tossed his blade to his left hand and swept it in a swift upper cut towards her belly. She brought the stick down to clop him on the hand, this time not stopping short. The knife fell to the ground.

Virri felt her cheeks redden up. She glanced to Larac in apology, but Weddi was grinning as he rubbed his hand.

'That was good,' Larac said. 'You can use the ends – why not? Again.'

They continued to practice, until Virri was puffed out, red and sweating. *Maybe he doesn't fancy me.* When she was about fit to drop, he got rid of the stick and taught her how to throw an attacker. An attacker from behind, an attacker from the side . . . Poor young Weddi was thrown about like chaff, but he took it without complaint. She could see his father's logic – youthful and green-boned as he was, she and the boy were about the same size. Whether all this would make any difference against Babca, Gold-Braid and the like . . . well, it couldn't hurt.

The sun had dipped and Larac just suggested they call a halt and return to camp when they heard Orcos's flute. It was short peeps, similar to a bird, but distinctive enough.

'Quiet,' Larac ordered.

The three of them padded through the trees, coming up to the oak where Orcos had been sat, but now he was on his feet, hidden behind the trunk, his bow poised.

'Someone's down there,' he whispered, nodding to the trees down the slope. It was mid-afternoon and the trees were disappearing into darkness, but he was right. They could hear someone moving. Footsteps. Voices.

They were moving west, towards camp.

Larac brought his finger to his lips and the four of them crept down the slope for a closer look, moving diagonally west, to intercept. They settled behind a fallen tree and Orcos notched an arrow, loosening another in the quiver ready.

Virri could feel her heart pounding in her chest. She had been tired, now she was exhausted. A real fight, today, might be too much. With a bit of luck, if it was only two guards, Orcos might bring them both down – but what if there were others, skulking quiet, as they were themselves? She peeked above the trunk as the voices neared.

As the two appeared Virri was not the only one to sigh with relief. Two children. One, a little girl, the other a skinny boy. He had one sleeve hanging empty.

'Ruc!'

36.

Virri broke cover and ran to Ruc with open arms without thinking, to begin with, that he might not want to hug her. It was a relief to feel him hug her back, if strange to feel the absence of his left arm.

'The healer said it was the only way to save me,' he said, as they parted, peeling back the sleeve to show his scarred stump. 'Old Kahil just about got it done then collapsed and died that night. Everyone said it was the Sun's own gift I didn't die of lung fever too.'

'Thank the gods, thank the gods – I thought you were surely dead. Did you come out here looking for me? How did you know?'

He shook his head. 'No – we ran away, two days ago, but we don't have any place to go. We just couldn't stand it anymore.'

The men were coming out of cover, and she saw fear spring to his eyes. The small girl retreated a step, part hidden behind Ruc.

'It's all right, these are my friends.' She placed a steadying hand on Ruc's shoulder and turned to face the others. 'I know them. This is Ruc, who worked with me, and –' She realised she had no idea what the girl's name was. She had never known. 'The girl is one of the orphans from Old Camp also.'

'Ziwa,' Ruc supplied. She carried on clinging to him, shivering. There was no fear in her eyes, as such, more a listless gloom.

'What's wrong with her?' Orcos asked. 'Is she sick?'

Ruc shook his head. 'Starving.'

Virri and Larac's eyes met. 'Let's get back to camp,' Larac said. 'Weddi, you take the next watch.'

Orcos handed Larac his bow and gathered the girl up, carrying her all the way back to the camp.

They didn't press the children too much, at first, keen to get some hot stew down them and wrap them up. Ruc was a torrent of information nonetheless, between mouthfuls. They had survived the cold of their first night away from camp hidden in the birch wood, he said, huddled beneath one of the skins taken from the ruins of the smelting shelter. No-one had come looking for them, as far as they could tell. When dawn came, they had skirted about, avoiding anywhere Sulo or the guards were likely to be, but were forced to keep moving in a hunt for berries – or any food.

'We're the last two of the orphans left,' Ruc said. 'Now the pilgrims have gone home, and the healers are dead no-one cares about us. Another two of us died of lung-fever since you left.'

Virri remembered what he had once said of Sulo: "Father in all but bones". 'What about the Sun-Speaker?'

Ruc shook his head with a grimace. 'He grieves and howls every time someone dies, but he doesn't do anything to stop it.' He looked over to where Ziwa slept, her belly now full, by Orcos's side. 'I think she would have been next.'

Maka and Huerin walked back into the camp, Huerin bearing a pair of trout on a twist of twine, chatting and smiling with each other. They stopped dead when they saw the two children, but Ruc's reaction was worse. He froze, his eyes fixed on Huerin.

'I am her brother,' Huerin said.

Maka smiled. 'You might know him as "the Hunter's ghost", but he's very much alive.'

Ruc looked to Virri. 'It's all right,' she said. 'No-one here will hurt you.'

Huerin crouched down so he was eye to eye with the boy. 'Have you come from Old Camp?' he asked, softly. 'Can you tell me any news of my sister?'

Again, Ruc glanced to Virri for reassurance. 'He knows she is the Chief of Guard,' she explained. 'We know that she left the Circle and went south, too, not long ago. Did she return?'

The boy nodded. 'She came back. She and the Sun-Speaker argued so loud everyone heard it, then she stormed off, maybe ten days ago, but she came back.'

'What did they argue about?' Huerin asked.

'The mushrooms and honey are running out, but he refuses to eat anything else. She begged him to eat.' Ruc grimaced again, his eyes turning to Ziwa. 'I wonder if he thinks the lung-fever comes in food, he seems to hate it so much.'

Charn and Cotro turned to each other, raising eyebrows. 'I've heard of this sort of thing before,' Charn said. 'Holiness through denial.'

'The Sun puts the fire in his veins, as he sees it, I expect,' Cotro added.

Pig snorted. 'The Sun will have the last laugh then. He's on a path to death.'

Huerin had sat back, his face clouded. 'She is afraid he will die and leave her all alone.'

Larac and Virri's eyes met. *You see it too, don't you? He won't kill his sister in a thousand years.*

'We stick with the plan,' Larac said. 'Tomorrow, we move to the closer camp, Cotro heads in, and the following morning we make our move. Now the children are in, they stay in.'

Virri put her arm about Ruc, with a smile. 'Fine with us.'

There was a hard frost the next night, but not where they camped. The spring, and the alder-fringed pool seeping out from it, felt warmer than they had a right to at that time of year. The trees which surrounded them, hid them, should have been a comfort, but there was eeriness in the quiet, the little wisps of mist curling out, the spellbound fix of the air like something in a tale. 'Pink Flint Camp', as Huerin called it, set Virri chewing on her nails again.

Cotro loved it. When Huerin showed them the flint, rosy-pink like a good sunset, she thought she saw tears in his eyes. If he did intend to betray them then there was no sign of it. As he walked off to complete his task in the afternoon, his own bag over his shoulder but without his horse, he looked tiny and exposed against the expanse of frostbitten grass, but there was a fire of purpose in his step. Charn watched him out of sight.

'The plan is a good one,' Virri said, taking her uncle's arm. 'He is brave to do it.'

Charn smiled at her, but there was a wobble to his voice as he spoke. 'He *is* brave. People don't think our kind can be, but he always has been.'

'Best come back from the edge of the wood, though – we can't blow everything now.'

'No, indeed. Just one last thing.' He took his two gold earrings out, clutched them in his right hand, kissed them and turned his eyes skywards. 'Sun, protect him for me please, even as you slumber. As I was ever your servant.'

'Mother Moon watch him also,' Virri whispered, and Charn glanced to her with another smile.

'You see? It's not just about ambition.' He put the earrings back in. 'Come, let's get some rest, while we can. Once darkness falls we can risk a fire.'

Rest would have been a good idea, had Virri been able to settle. She had her chance, as did everyone else, but in between Larac kept them busy. Food was prepared, weapons checked, sharpened and cleaned. They were close to Old Camp – a short walk – so the watches had to be kept up, on both sides of the camp, to be sure. He planned to leave the horses out of sight, for ease of stealth, when they made their move, so he spent some time with the two children, familiarising them with these strange creatures, so they could 'keep guard' while the adults attacked. He got a good layout of the site, in his mind, from Ruc as the two of them chatted, too, Virri thought, watching his industry with an appreciative eye.

As the first gleam of dawn appeared in the east they set off, quiet and steady. Huerin took them north-west, avoiding the river and its bends, heading for the slight ridge that would take them in towards Old Camp. They moved 'as a snake' to avoid too much silhouette, Huerin at the head, but as they started climbing the ridge Maka was by Virri's side a moment. 'Stay close to me, and Huerin, when the fighting starts,' Maka whispered.

'I will.'

They crested the ridge, the cold morning wind catching Maka's ravaged hair. Virri dropped back. The Circle and the new sacred path shone out behind them, the last of the starlight brightening the stone and chalk. Clouds were building, to the east, keeping the dawn dark. There was, as predicted, no-one out on the path, no glimpse of any movement among the stones themselves.

Thank you, Sun.

They scrambled along the back of the ridge, keeping their heads down. Huerin seemed to be aiming straight for the stone known as 'the stone-on-its-own', a great lump of stone which appeared to have always been there, without the help of human hand, but before they reached it Huerin ducked them down into a hollow.

'We can watch, from here, for Cotro's signal,' he whispered.

He was right. The west side of the settlement lay before them, still dark, but the lines becoming sharper. Tendrils of smoke rose from the roofs of some of the houses. Nothing from the 'sick house', Virri noticed, nor the house she had once shared with Kenna, as far as she could see. They could hear a few bleats from the sheep pen over on the other side but no other sounds.

The weak winter sun was rising by the moment, clouds notwithstanding. Someone would be up and about before too long.

Come on, Cotro.

He appeared, bundled against the cold, braids loose in the wind. Virri heard her uncle sigh with relief. Cotro passed an anxious look behind him and then moved forward, picking his spot, looking out towards the stone-on-its-own. It looked as if they could see him, but he couldn't see them. *So far, so good.*

Cotro climbed up on something, perhaps a rock, passed another furtive glance back, and then held up both hands, all his fingers spread bar one thumb.

Nine guards. *Still a lot.*

He put his hands down and then raised the left alone, the middle finger and thumb pinched together.

'The guard house,' Larac muttered. 'Could be worse. Get ready.'

That was the signal to tell them where Sulo was, so they were not expecting anything else, but then Cotro put his hands down and lifted them, as if to make another signal. Was it to change his mind? Perhaps he'd made a mistake with the signal? Virri tightened her hold on her stick. When the shout rang out it made her flinch.

'Oi! What are you doing?!'

Gold-Braid. Gold-Braid's voice. At first they couldn't see him, but he stormed over to Cotro soon enough. Cotro was yanked down from the rock, the guard towering above.

'*What* are you doing?!'

Cotro flustered an answer. Virri caught the word 'meditation'.

Gold-Braid threw his left arm east. 'The Sun's that way!'

Oh no . . .

'Son,' Larac growled, 'Do it now'.

Pig stood, breaking cover, but his bow was ready and drawn. Virri saw Gold-Braid's eyes snap straight to him.

We're too far!

Virri yelped, and she was not the only one, but the arrow went strong and straight – straight to the guard's heart. He fell, silenced, the words of warning still on his lips . . . but the damage had been done. Somewhere behind him came the woman's scream.

'Now! Go!' Larac yelled. 'Before they have a chance!'

37.

Larac and Pig were at the front, the others not far behind. As they leapt the small outer ditch Babca came into sight. She was in the guard house doorway, shouting. It didn't look like she was armed yet, but she was yelling for weapons. Pig stopped running and aimed but she saw it and ducked inside. The arrow hit the doorpost.

Babca's yelling had disturbed the rest of the camp. Virri saw a shadow figure appear in the guest house doorway, the line of a bow bending.

'Hey!'

The bow twang and instinct threw her left, the arrow swatted right with a whip of her stick. Huerin saw where she was looking and loosed his own arrow. The guard slumped to the threshold.

'There could be more in there! You three check!' Larac yelled, pointing to Maka too. He and his boys were piling into the guard house. From the bow strings – and the cries – it sounded like they were making short work of it. Virri looked to Huerin's face and saw cold horror, but he did not disobey. He readied another arrow and surged onward, Maka right beside him. Neither shot again, though. Virri peered into the house between them. There was someone there, a woman crouching, shaking, her knees tucked to her chest. The rest of the house was empty.

'We should help the others,' Maka said, but taking another look at the woman she broke the dead guard's bow over her knee, to be sure. Huerin divided the arrows from the man's quiver between the two of them. It was still on the ground, where he hadn't had the chance to belt it on yet.

Virri turned to see how her uncle was getting on. Cotro had dropped to the ground as Gold-Braid fell and Charn was helping him up, but Charn's gaze now shot to the guard house.

'The back! They're getting out!'

Maka and Huerin charged forward, Virri behind. Charn was right. She saw three people running from the back – Sulo, Babca and another. Maka shot but her arrow went wide. Huerin's did too, on the other side. They ran forward and re-aimed. Orcos was emerging from the back of the house, and he shot at the same time as the other two. His arrow glanced the third – old Bucktooth? – but Bucktooth kept running, only the flinch telling them it had touched him. Maka and Huerin's fell short.

'Keep going!' Larac urged. He was coming through the gap. Maka, Huerin and Orcos all obeyed, but as they re-strung and aimed the three hunted kept running, dodging between the houses.

'They're heading for the river!' Maka yelled.

Babca was, maybe Bucktooth too, but at Maka's shout he split from Babca, turning south, towards the ancestor forest – a crazy move. Larac aimed as soon as he had a clear shot and Bucktooth fell long before he reached the poles, an arrow between his shoulder blades. He pushed himself up and tried to carry on running but Larac's second arrow finished him. Maka took a shot at Babca but Babca ducked down behind the sheep pen. The arrow hit a wattle. Virri saw Huerin jump up onto a fence for a clear aim. He went so far as drawing – then remembered himself.

'Sulo!' Virri cried. 'Where is he?! They are drawing you away!'

She spun around, half-expecting to see Sulo at her back with a knife, but her cry had been true – he was no-where to be seen. Larac's boys had been running up behind her but now they spread out, hunting between the houses, Charn and Cotro joining them.

Babca took the chance at Virri's shout. She shot from the pen down towards the river. Maka and Huerin hared down behind her, Maka loosing another arrow. This one hit her in the right calf.

'Give up, Babca!' Maka yelled.

Babca was felled like a tree as the arrow struck but now she turned with a snarl, throwing herself up from the dirt. She staggered backward towards the river, right foot high.

Maka strung another arrow and re-aimed but did not shoot. 'Give up,' she said again.

Huerin moved forward, his bow now over his shoulder and his hands held out. 'Babca, don't you know me?'

Babca's eyes were moving from Maka to Huerin to Virri to Larac and back. She must have looked at him a dozen times, but she never fixed on him.

'It's me, Huerin, your brother.'

He took a step forward. She took a step back.

'Huerin,' he said again. 'Huerin, your brother.'

Another lurch back. She was near the river now but there was no escape that way, no boat within reach. It wasn't deep or fast enough there for her to drown herself.

Go on Huerin, you'll reach her.

'Babca, it's me. We won't hurt you.'

Maka had lowered her own bow and Larac took their lead in this but now Babca's gaze had settled on Huerin, Virri wasn't sure she noticed. There was no spark of recognition in Babca's eyes that she could see. She did open her mouth to speak though.

'He left me. He left me.'

Huerin moved forward again. 'He was killed, he couldn't help it,' he said, his voice choked up.

Babca stepped back again, her feet now in the water.

'Huerin, I think she means Sulo,' Virri said and Babca's gaze snapped to her. Virri's stomach turned to ice.

'He left me,' Babca said again.

She pulled a blade from under her shirt and Larac and Maka's bows came straight back up. Virri's muscles tensed to push Huerin out of danger . . . but they were all wrong.

Babca turned the blade inward and plunged it into her neck.

Huerin's cry of pain cut through the air. He threw himself forward, wrenching the knife from her hand, both of them landing in the water. He managed to pull it out, but it didn't help. Blood erupted out, showering them both, so much it stained the river water where they were.

Maka and Virri had leapt forward to help him but there was nothing they could do. Babca's eyes were closed. If she was not dead already, she would be within a few breaths. As they stood there rigid, with hands clasped over their mouths, Larac was the one who grasped the moment. He threw his bow down, ran forward into the water and held onto Huerin's shoulders.

'Let her go,' he whispered. 'Let her go. Let the sacred river wash her.'

Larac repeated it, holding onto Huerin in two strong arms – and Huerin complied, to Virri's surprise. Babca floated out a bit, into cleaner water, and Larac took the chance to draw Huerin away a little, out of the blood. The lad turned with another howl and sobbed into the older man's shoulder. Larac rubbed his back.

'Your father and mother will meet her, and show her the way,' Larac whispered.

Virri sensed people coming up behind and turned to see Larac's boys, looking worried. Pig was bleeding from his left hand, holding it to his chest, but it didn't look too bad. They looked more crestfallen than anything. Charn and Cotro too, bringing up the rear.

'We didn't find him,' Charn spoke, for all of them.

'How far out did you go?'

Charn threw out his hands. 'Right round the site, in every building, young Orcos went over to the great Stones, Weddi and Pig into the Ancestor Forest and downriver a bit . . .' He sighed. 'There's no sign. Nothing. It's like the gods snatched him up.'

Virri frowned. *Less of that, I think.*

Maka and Larac were helping Huerin up onto the bank. 'What about the pits?' Maka asked. 'Did you check the pits? Huerin has hidden in them in the past himself.'

Charn raised his eyebrows. 'All the pits we could find. Perhaps there are more.'

Virri wiped the sweat from her brow. Her heart-rate was coming back down, but despair was setting in. The sun was well up by now. She remembered how open the landscape was around the Circle – how it had put off her own thoughts of making a run for it while she and Kenna were captive. Sulo was skinny, sure, but a full grown man. How had he managed to pull it off?

'I think he's still here,' she said. 'I think we should look again.'

No-one disagreed – no other ideas were forthcoming – so they fanned out again. She tried the guest house first, but it was now empty as the others had said, and the same went for Sulo's own. The guard house was full of bodies, so she did not linger there – only long enough to see the 'hole' they had escaped from. It was a full-on door frame, on the inside, but small, as if built for a children's game, or a dog. A pile of sheepskins appeared to have been pushed aside to reveal it in their moment of need.

Clever.

She left, heading to the house she and Kenna had shared next. There were no bodies there, thank Sun. Indeed, it had scarce changed. The daylight through the wattle settled on the dresser and there was a new crock there, though, in pride of place.

Kenna's ash.

She approached it, to be certain, pleased that someone had held her in enough respect to collect it, then something else caught her eye, tucked down the side. Her own goatskin bag.

'Found anything?'

Virri flinched, but it was only Orcos, at the doorway.

'It's my own things. Someone must have brought them from the ruins of the shelter.'

Orcos smiled. 'Your lad Ruc, maybe. Is it all there?'

She picked it up, the weight alone bringing a smile to her face. Yes, it was all there – Father's second-best polishing stone, her hand-carved mould, the beloved bellows, the beaded ore bag. She turned back to him with tears springing to her eyes and his smile broadened.

'Come on, Pa's called a meeting.'

She slung the bag over her shoulder and followed him. Everyone else was in the centre yard, near the pyre place. In the distance she could see Ruc and Ziwa leading the small herd of horses across the grass, Weddi running out to give them a hand. Huerin and Maka were sat side by side on a woodpile. Charn waved to her, grinning, an axe held up in his other hand.

'Look what I found.'

Yes!

Virri hurried over. It was her father's axe all right, mismatched pattern on the handle and all.

'It was through the belt of another guard,' Charn explained. 'After the death of the guard you talked about, he must have taken it.'

'Aric, yes.'

Charn offered it to her.

Should I? Charn was Father's brother, and an axe seemed like a manly thing to wield . . . but he would be Sun-Speaker, one day, Gods-willing, he'd have treasures enough . . . She took it, keeping her stick, but tucking the copper axe through her skirt waist band.

Larac coughed. He had his hands on his hips, in the centre of the ring.

'Somehow, we've managed to lose him,' he started, with a roll of his eyes, 'but everything else went more or less as planned. From what you've told me – ' his gaze shot to Maka, ' – there are guards up at what you call the Mother Circle too. He'll try to get there, then. We need to pursue him but hold onto this too in case there's an attempt to retake it. We need to decide who stays here and who goes, quick, before he gets too far.'

His gaze turned to Virri. 'The children will have to stay here,' was all he said, not “and you will have to stay with them”, but nevertheless she nettled.

'I know the Mother Circle, better than almost anyone else here,' she said. 'I should be in the pursuit group.'

Pig raised his left hand. It had stopped bleeding but was gashed across the palm. 'This isn't too bad, but I need to keep it clean. I can still use my bow, though, if I need to – I can defend the children.'

Larac assented, to both of them, though he looked a bit narked. He turned to Maka and Huerin. 'How about you two? Would you rather stay here?'

'No, we're coming,' Huerin said, his tone dark. Maka cast him a quick glance.

'I feel bad, about the escape hole,' she said. 'We should definitely keep up the chase.'

Larac's eyebrows shot up. 'Did the hole even exist while you were still here?'

'I really don't know,' Maka said. 'If it did the rest never shared it with me.'

Larac tipped his head to one side.

'Besides,' Maka gabbled on, 'Huerin is a brilliant tracker – if anyone can track Sulo, it's him.'

Orcos caught Larac's eye. 'With two good archers coming with you, I think I should stay here and back up Pig.'

Larac nodded. 'Agreed.'

Cotro looked around to everyone. 'I think there should be someone else here to explain to any locals who happen to turn up – and begin the clean-up, to be honest. If any pilgrim walks into that guard house full of bodies. . . '

Larac nodded again. 'All right, everyone else, let's go.'

Virri had enough time to pass her bag to Ruc for safekeeping before they headed off, but only just. Ruc confirmed there had been no sight of the Sun-Speaker to the south, Huerin picked up the trail to the north and they were off. It was cold, not like the summer, but she was reminded of the reverse journey, tortured by Babca and Aric, moons ago, as her cheeks burned and lungs strained. Now they were all 'Are you all right?', 'Do you need a rest?'

every ten bloody paces, but whether they respected her decision to tag along was another matter.

Well, it's my father's rib he wears as an earring.

Huerin had found the start of the trail, a hollow in the side of a pit, obscured by a self-set hazel, room enough for a slight man to hunker down and wait to make his run. There was nowt about the spirit-world to Sulo's disappearance – he had left his supporters to die. The danger now was that he could get to the Mother Circle before them. Footprints Huerin found in the birch wood suggested he was heading straight north, up through it, so they did the same, Huerin and Larac up front, Maka and Weddi guarding the flanks, Virri and Charn somewhat to the rear.

By noon they were long since back out in open grassland, getting more and more tired . . . and they still hadn't found him.

'What do you think? Have we lost him?' Larac asked of Huerin, stretching a cramp out of his left leg against a rock. 'Perhaps he set footprints in that birch wood and then doubled back, up through the river shallows, and is now laying low.'

Huerin shook his head. 'I checked the shallows. The north-heading prints looked genuine to me.'

Larac ran his hand through his hair and puffed out his cheeks. Weddi turned to his father with a raised eyebrow. 'I thought this Sun-Speaker's supposed to be half-starved and weak,' he said.

'Maybe that's his public face,' Charn said. 'He could be stuffing himself when no-one's looking.'

'No, he is skin and bone,' Virri said. 'I think it's fear giving flight to his feet.'

Maka sighed. 'Should we split up?' She flashed a guilty glance at Virri. 'The faster of us trying to head him off, like a hunt?'

'No. We should stay together,' Larac said and Huerin nodded.

'I haven't lost the trail,' he said. 'We could be catching him up, for all we know.'

Huerin made a point of sharing the clues out loud from then on – a patch of flattened grass, a snapped stalk, a dislodged stone. Virri wasn't convinced and she wasn't sure anyone else was either, but they were covering ground at a blistering pace. The clouds were getting lower, as the sun dipped. There would be rain, or worse, before nightfall. Her old ankle injury was nagging louder by the moment.

As the first flake of snow fell Huerin turned to them with a grim set to his mouth.

'Blood.'

Weddi frowned. 'But we haven't wounded him.'

'His feet have started bleeding.'

Virri felt a shiver run up. *So . . . he's barefoot.* He'd probably been in bed when they attacked, it made sense. After everything he'd done to her and hers a swell of pity still rose.

No!

She scrambled to keep up with the others. Now the tracking was so easy the speed went up another notch. Her chest was tightening. The air went down like knives. Her head was down and gasping when Huerin's shout rang out, but she knew what it was – they had Sulo in sight.

He hadn't quite made it to the Mother Circle, but he wasn't far off. She could see Moon-Speak Hill up ahead, its chalk white starting to disappear into the landscape as the snow settled. Sulo's linen robe might have blended too, if he had gone to ground, but he was moving, fast. She sensed he knew they were behind him. He looked over his shoulder and made a sudden move right.

This time Maka didn't look to Virri for permission – she just took off. Huerin too, sprinting, she to Sulo's left, he to the right, Larac and Weddi not far behind.

'We can't let him get to the Mother Circle,' Charn wheezed. 'We should let them get on with it.'

She turned. He looked as bad as she felt.

Virri waved it away, clutching at her knees. 'They'll catch him . . . but I worry for *them.*'

She gulped in more air and pressed on. Sulo had changed direction again like a hare, but the pack were closing on him. The old Moon-Speaker tomb loomed behind him. He was running out of places to run. Larac stopped and aimed, and his arrow fell short, but not by much. Huerin took a shot himself, forcing Sulo backwards, towards the tomb, but great flat stones met Sulo at the forecourt. It was the bolt hole of the tomb's mouth or nothing. Maka took the chance to run up the tomb's side, aiming down from above, stopping Sulo from entering in. He froze.

She looked to Huerin.

Huerin aimed. There was no hesitation this time. Sulo's fate was no different from any deer or beast. Huerin's first arrow was straight through his heart. As Virri sped to them she saw Sulo fall to his knees. The look on his face was sheer astonishment – not fear, despite the sweat streaking down, the blood on his feet. Huge eyes, staring at his adopted daughter with a man's face, in the instant before they glazed.

Maka loosed an arrow that went into the back of his neck, Larac and Weddi's went through his stomach, but it was over. Sulo slumped to the stone.

Virri took a huge breath and heard Huerin do the same. She tucked the axe back into her belt and moved forward. The earring was clear to see, as he'd slumped to the other side. She leant down and snatched it out, clutching it to her chest, her hands shaking.

'Perhaps my father and yours will rest easier now,' she said, to Huerin. He nodded, a slight tremble visible in his own flesh. Maka was scrambling down the side of the tomb and came over to hug him. They looked down on Sulo's body, so small and motionless now. Snowflakes were melting on his hands and head but on the folds of his robe they were already starting to lay.

'What do you want us to do?' Larac asked. 'Should we drag him into the tomb?'

The cry of 'no' came back from Virri, Maka, Huerin, even Charn.

'This is the old Moon-Speaker tomb,' Virri explained. 'The first of the Moon-Speakers and their families are buried here, from long, long ago. Given he caused the death of the latest one it's the last place he should rest.'

Larac looked to the skies. 'Well, it's not over yet – we need to deal with the guards at the Mother Circle and we need to get shelter, soon.'

'Leave it to the animals to deal with him,' Maka said. 'It's the old way. It still shows him respect as Sun-Speaker.'

Larac looked to Virri and she nodded. 'Fine by us,' he said. 'Let's go. Stay alert.'

38.

Virri wasn't sure she had it in her for another chase let alone a battle and thank the gods they didn't need one – the 'guards' had long gone. The Mother Circle and its ramshackle camp were stone silent as they crept near, not so much as a sparrow disturbing the snow as it settled. No smoke was rising. When they checked the hearth in the Moon-Speaker tent the embers were cold, finger-deep down.

'Long gone,' Larac said, a somewhat smug twist to his mouth.

'They could come back,' Virri said. 'We should keep up the watches.'

'No, they've scarpered. Home for the winter. We should rest up, keep warm, see if we can find something to eat, head back in the morning.'

'One or both of them might have worried they had lung-fever,' Maka muttered, picking through the crocks in the tent. 'There's no food here and no healing herbs – they packed before they set off.'

She was right. There was enough firewood for the night and a few furs and skins beyond what made up the tent, but that was about it. The other tents were the same. Weddi and Maka got a couple of fires going and set water to warm while the others searched about but the best anyone found was a few grains.

Virri found herself wandering out towards the great stones as the sun made its final dip. She could hear wolves howling in the distance and yelping to each other. She shivered, pulling her sealskin closer.

Wolves to the south. Near the old Moon-Speakers' tomb.

'Virri?'

Charn was looking at her, from over a ditch.

'Come back, get by the fire,' he said. 'Huerin has said he'll go find food.'

'I'm not sure he should – none of us should be alone.'

Charn smiled. 'The wolves are busy down there, he'll be all right.' He held out his hand and helped her over the gap. 'You're freezing! Definitely come in.'

She agreed, though she cast another look over her shoulder as they walked. The white landscape was becoming bleaker and bleaker beneath the darkening sky.

'Do you think he is really hunting?' Charn whispered.

'What do you mean?'

'Well, maybe he's heading out to help the wolves desecrate Sulo's body . . . I wouldn't blame him.'

Virri sighed. 'No. I think he probably just wants some time to be alone. He's a good lad, he will find food if he can.'

Huerin came back long before midnight, a dead goat, of all things, across his shoulders. Virri and Maka left the warmth of the tent to help him skin and butcher it. His eyes looked a bit red, but he was otherwise unchanged. Maka and Huerin got on with it and Virri held the light.

'Who do you think this might belong to?' Virri asked, quietly.

Huerin shrugged. 'There was a whole herd of them, upriver a bit, running wild on a night like this. Either they got out or someone let them loose.'

Maka looked up to Virri. 'Would the Moon-Speaker have had her own herd?'

'Probably . . . she didn't mention them to me, but we had so much to talk about in the short time we had. She wouldn't begrudge us one.'

'It's us or the wolves,' Huerin said, prompting another glance passed between the two women.

Huerin saw it and smiled. 'I'm all right, don't worry.'

'I think we've all had a rough time of late,' Virri muttered.

'What's been going on in there?' Huerin whispered. 'Do we have a plan for tomorrow?'

Maka raised her eyebrows. 'Well the plan is still to head straight back to the Great Circle tomorrow, unless there's a blizzard, to make sure Charn is dug in as Sun-Speaker before Solstice . . . there's more though . . .'

'They want me to be the new Moon-Speaker,' Virri finished for her.

Huerin had been cutting fillet strips but now he put the blade down and gaped.

'I'm really not sure,' Virri said. 'I wanted to see what you two feel about it first.'

'I think you'd be perfect,' Huerin said, and Maka nodded along. 'What do *you* want, though?'

Virri swapped the torch to her other hand and sighed. 'I'm tempted . . . I mean, we need a new home. My uncle will be just a day or two's walk south. I like it here, I know it quite well . . .'

'But you're not sure you can do it, are you?' Maka cut in.

'No...'

'No – you've only walked across the whole isle, saved my life, stood up to a tyrant, taught dozens of people how to work metal, taken in two orphans.' She winked to Huerin. 'You're a bit useless really, aren't you?'

Huerin grinned and Virri couldn't help but grin with them. 'We'll see. Let's go back in the warm and get this lot cooked.'

They should have been exhausted. Virri thought the food would bring their eyelids down at last, but there remained a crackle running round the tent, nerves jumpy as fleas. When Virri admitted out loud that she was thinking about accepting the Moon-Speaker role it sent another wave of excitement rippling round. Larac lit up like tinder.

'I will have a lot to learn,' she said, smoothing out her skirt strings and sitting a little straighter. 'I won't have anyone saying I am not worthy of it. It's going to be a busy winter.'

Charn smiled at her. 'That's a good attitude to have. I will be doing the same.'

'I can help,' Huerin said. 'With the healing knowledge and the gathering of herbs – there's nothing much here now.'

Charn shook his head. 'It's almost like starting from scratch, I think, here and at the Great Circle. That's a good thing.'

'You need both,' Larac said. 'A continuation of the old traditions, where they are good, and a fresh start where not.'

Charn looked to Virri again. 'Did you say the Moonstone is at the Great Circle?'

'Yes. Kenna must have had it on her when she was taken. It was among her things.'

'We'll need that then. We need to have the whole ritual ready, too, before Solstice – before any pilgrims turn up, ideally.'

Larac was frowning. 'This Moonstone, is there any equivalent for the Sun?'

'No, not traditionally, but there should be, I think. Cotro has something in mind.'

Does it matter? It's just a stone.

Virri rubbed her eyes. 'I'm all spun round – how long have we actually got until Solstice?'

'Ten days,' Maka said, then glanced to Huerin. 'No, twelve.'

'Twelve,' he confirmed.

Larac threw a cheeky gap-toothed smile Virri's way. 'Bags of time, then.'

The walk back to the Great Circle was more sedate than the breakneck chase of the day before, but not by much. The plan was to leave at dawn. They had been forced to spread out into three tents to sleep, the Moon-Speaker's tent not being big enough for so many . . . and it was uncomfortable in another way. Virri woke with a chill around her, having been wary of snuggling too near Larac in the night.

Clouds were gathering again in the east as she stretched the cramp out of her legs and watched the sun rise. The land was clean and sparkling, bathed in pink light. The stones stood out, as if warmer than the snow-covered ground around them.

Kenna must have left this tent and seen this view, thousands of times.

'Rest now, Kenna,' she whispered. 'I will make sure the people remember you.'

They arrived back at the Great Circle long after dark, given the time of year, dawn departure or not. Sun be thanked the clouds had held off from depositing more snow and the snow they did have brightened the later part of the journey. It could have been worse. The sight of the campfire was welcome, though, as they approached Old Camp.

Ruc, Ziwa, Pig, Orcos and Cotro all got up to welcome them in but there was another, a woman. Virri near jumped backwards when she realised who she was. The woman from the guest-house, yesterday.

'It's a three day walk to her home village,' Pig said. 'On her own . . . we couldn't do it to her.'

Larac nodded, unperturbed, but Virri's sense of caution flared, and she saw it too in Maka's face.

'Where were you?' Maka asked. 'When we were hunting round the camp for Sulo, yesterday? You weren't still in the guest house.'

The woman looked back at her, brown eyes steady. 'I ran into the guard-house and laid down among the bodies.'

Virri shivered. *I went in there. When I looked at the escape hole she must have been there.*

'What's to stop you just knifing us all in our sleep?' she asked.

The woman's jaw dropped. 'I – I wouldn't . . . I'm not vengeful. I do understand.'

Orcos spooned out a bowl of mutton stew and handed it to Virri. 'She could have last night, if she'd wanted. It's all right. Rest.'

Cotro flicked Virri a look. 'Her name is Prya, of Split River Camp, in the west. She is the first of many Solstice pilgrims here. . . We must start tying knots of peace.'

Virri forced herself to smile.

'What have you done, with the bodies?' Huerin asked, in a low voice.

Orcos handed him a bowl of stew. 'We held a pyre for everyone, last night, apart from your sister, and released the ash into the sacred river today. Your sister is laying in the sick house, untouched. We waited to see what you would want.'

'I don't want to see her,' Huerin said, straight out. 'Not again. Please, just give her a respectful funeral as you see fit.'

'We will,' Pig said, with a nod and kind eyes.

'Your Father was a boat-comer,' Cotro said. 'They wondered if they should give her a boat-comer grave.'

There was the barest of nods from Huerin. 'It's fine. He must be here somewhere himself.'

Oh Huerin. Maka put her bow down, crossed the yard and hugged her arms around him.

Virri sat her weary bottom down next to Ruc and started eating the stew.

'This is good,' she said, to Orcos.

He grinned. 'Not just a pretty face.'

A bit inappropriate, young Orcos.

'I've put your bag back in the Moon-Speaker's old house,' Ruc whispered. 'We slept there last night. Is that all right?'

Virri turned to him. 'Of course. After the Solstice – perhaps in spring – I will travel to the real Moon-Speaker's home, at the Mother Circle, for I am to be the new Moon-Speaker. Do you want to come with me?'

Now it was Ruc's turn to grin.

Virri slept until near noon the next day. She'd half expected the children to have her up at the crack of dawn, as Elyc and Maka used to do, but they must have been tired themselves. Having said that, Ziwa was full of energy once she was up, helping Virri to wash, untangle and re-braid her hair. Ruc looked on in amusement as he prepared them some breakfast.

'You're getting good at working with one hand,' Virri said. 'That was quick.'

Ruc shrugged with a little smile. 'I didn't get much choice. The Sun-Speaker never spoke to me again, once it was clear I would survive. No-one would help me but Ziwa.'

Virri took the cup of nettle tea he handed to her and smiled to the little girl. 'It's good you look after each other. We should all do more of that, I think.' She sighed, turning back to Ruc. 'You won't hold it against us, how the Sun-Speaker died?'

'I won't . . . I'm not sure about the others, though . . . y'know, the pilgrims.'

No, indeed.

'Do you have a plan for today?' Ruc asked.

She did, though it didn't further their take-over one bit. 'I must visit my father's grave,' she said. 'Come with me, if you like.'

There was snow flaking down again when Virri and the children set off. She made sure they were well wrapped up and wore her own beaver skin hat. She saw the Moonstone again as she rummaged around for something to use as a cape for Ziwa and slipped it into her bag.

'What's that?' the girl asked, so Virri showed her. It was a circular, rounded stone, greyish-white. The white parts seemed to glow. She suspected it had a bit of quartz veined through it.

'If I do become Moon-Speaker then I will hold it in my cupped hands, as I talk to the Moon from the top of Moon-Speak Hill.'

Ziwa reached out to touch the stone with her forefinger and Virri let her. 'Will you really be naked?' she asked.

Virri laughed. 'That's the tradition. On warmer nights than this will be, I hope.'

Snow or not Orcos and Pig were sweating, shirts off, as they dug a grave for Babca with antler picks and shoulder-bone shovels on the outskirts of the site. The two lads waved. It wasn't 'on the way' by any stretch but Virri felt she should go over for a chat.

Babca's body lay a few paces away. They had put a blanket over, but her crow feathers peeked out at one end.

'Ground's rock hard,' Pig said, with a roll of his eyes, 'but we should just about get it done by sundown.'

'Do you wish you'd gone for a pyre after all?'

'No . . . She was a boat-comer, by her father's blood at least, and we promised Huerin.'

Orcos wiped the sweat from his brow, smiling. 'Where you three headed?'

'I'm going to visit my father and foster-brother's graves.'

His face clouded. 'I'm sorry . . . Your mother, is she still alive?'

'No, she died in the far north, where my elder sister married. I am hoping my sister and her family are still all right.' She smiled, to try to ease his discomfort. 'Perhaps, when I am Moon-Speaker, I shall see them again.' Snow continued flaking down. 'We should let you get on, before you freeze, and get on ourselves.'

It was a short walk to the grave site but on such a cold day it felt longer. She remembered her mother's anger at the distance from the Great Circle, out of sight of the great stones, but for now Virri was grateful. It took a while to find the exact spot, what with the snow cover and the lack of a high-domed barrow. Ruc and Ziwa helped her define the edges, tracing out the circle in the snow. She'd half expected Sulo and his cronies to have destroyed it in their search for gold, but the edges were sound. They must have dug straight down through the middle, breaking open the wooden roof.

'Did you bring any offerings?' Ruc asked.

'Not as such. I was hoping to put something back.' She took the earring out of her bag and showed it to him. 'You remember it? Sulo had it made from one of my father's ribs.'

Ruc looked from her to the grave and back again.

'The ground's too hard, isn't it?' She sighed. 'And if I leave it on top scavengers will have it.'

'Why not just keep it?' Ruc said, with a quizzical look on his thin little face. 'It's not the same as an enemy having it.'

Yes.

Ruc wasn't a boat-comer, nor Ziwa. Maka would say the same.

She nodded and walked to the centre of the grave. She touched the rib to the ground and then raised it to her chest, holding it tight in both hands and looking westwards, towards the sun. A weak and wintry sun, but reliable as always.

'You see me, Father? You see I am all right? I'm all right now. I have a new home, a new family, and my old kin too. If you and Mother and brother can see me, from the other side, I want you to know I am content. I'm home again . . . and I won't be weak anymore.'

She touched the rib to the grave once more and then put it back in her bag.

39.

Larac called Virri and Charn to a meeting the next morning. 'Nothing to worry about,' in his words. 'Just we three elders to walk the site and have a chat.'

Elders. Virri could not help but smile.

It was a crisp, bright morning, the snow tripping over itself to melt. She decided to forego the hat and went for her wooden earrings and gold hair-glinters instead, giving the seal-skin cape a brush and rearranging the items in her bag so that it sat better on her hip.

'You look nice,' Larac said, as she walked up to the two of them. She felt the blood rushing to her cheeks.

'Well, it's good to be settled.'

Charn nodded with a smile. 'I second that. Where shall we start?'

'Well you two know the site a lot better than me,' Larac said, '. . . I'd like to know a lot more. Where would *you* start?'

'The Great Circle itself,' Charn said. 'We should start and end there. In Sulo's time very few have been allowed within the circle, so it has been shoved to the side, in people's minds, but it is the sacred core. It has been for generations.'

'Fine.'

They set off, following the unfinished sacred path. The tools had been cleared away but there were piles of chalk hither and thither and it ended at an abrupt stop. 'Do you two think we should finish this, or leave it as it is?' Larac asked.

Charn turned to Virri. 'I think we should finish it,' she said. She remembered young Cam's words, moons ago, "I can move stones about all day long, but I don't want to be treated like shit", or something like that. 'It's not the work that people objected to, it's all the other stuff. When pilgrims come to do their stints next summer we could get the path finished. We just need to treat them with respect, and be part of it.'

'It would show we bear no malice to Sulo, too.' Charn shrugged. 'Whether we do or no, the pilgrims who were supportive of him don't need to see it.'

Larac nodded. 'Agreed.'

They had reached the First Stones and paused a moment to take in the scene. The great stones glowed in the morning light. A sparrow hawk was weaving at break-neck speed between the uprights in pursuit of a tit or such like. Nothing else stirred.

'You said Sulo kept most people out of the inner circle,' Larac began, 'Are you sure you'd want to change that?'

Charn sighed. 'I think it should be something people look forward to, say if they only go inside on the Solstice nights themselves, or at the end of their stint, apart from when they re-enter in time as the spirit torch alone. Like . . . like a taste, or a glimpse, of the other world, to keep them hungry, but not shut out entirely.'

'Makes sense.' Larac pointed to the inner circle. 'Are the stones two different colours? Am I seeing things? Or is it a trick of the light?'

'They are different,' Virri said. 'The darker ones sound different too, almost hollow - though they're heavy enough! They are said to 'sing'. The old Sun-Speaker, the one who was friends with Father, used to play them like drums.'

Larac smiled. 'That would be a sight to behold.'

Charn chuckled. 'I'm not sure I have his ear for music, but I could try.'

They carried on downwards, passing the Wait Stone and into the Circle. There was shade straight off, but also an eerie quiet.

'The old Sun-Speaker said the dark stones were far older than the others,' Charn continued, his voice lower. 'They were brought from the west, where the Sun sleeps.'

Larac ran his hand over one of them, daring an experimental tap. The noise sang out as Virri had described and they exchanged a smile. 'Perhaps I should do my own "stint", if I am to marry again,' he said. 'I don't want to flout the traditions.'

'Surely you've done enough?' she said – without thinking, then turned away, which was probably worse. 'There have never been any carvings on the stones,' she blurted, to change the subject. She pointed to a flat expanse on one of the giant uprights. 'Yet I've seen carving on stones elsewhere – the stone at Huerin's sacred place for one.'

Larac frowned. 'And what you call the Ancestor Forest is covered in them.'

'That's different though,' Charn said. 'Each one represents a people, a home territory.'

The frown had not left Larac's face. 'Do our people have poles there?'

Charn looked to Virri. 'Not that I've seen,' he said.

She nodded. 'We always tried to tread with a light step. Father thought it was safer.'

Now Larac's eyebrows shot up. 'Bit late for that.'

He had a point.

'We should start a new tradition,' he continued. 'Leave the people their poles, if they want, but we carve our symbols here.'

'What would our people's symbol be?'

Charn gestured to the axe at her belt. 'Could do worse than an axe.'

Really? Father's axe or no it still seemed a bit . . . well . . . aggressive.

Someone in the distance caught her eye. 'Uncle, is that your Cotro waving?'

Charn peered east and then slapped himself in the forehead. 'I forgot the stone! I was going to bring the stone for you both to look at.'

'It's all right,' Larac said. 'Nip back. We'll wait.'

There was a long moment of silence when Charn had walked away. She sensed Larac was looking for a spot for them both to sit but there was nowhere bar the cold wet ground. Ultimately he smiled. 'Let's leave the circle and stand in the sun, while we wait,' he said.

They did so and she felt an inexplicable relief once they were out in the open. She looked about for something to point to, to explain, to get the conversation going again, but Larac set off first.

'Have I done something wrong?' he said. 'Because you aren't entirely comfortable with me, are you?'

Oh by Sun. What do I say?

'I – I'm worried. For years and years there has been a Sun-Speaker and a Moon-Speaker and that's it, no other leader or role. How are you and my uncle going to share it, without problems?'

Larac laughed. 'Well all right, there's that too – but it's not what I meant.'

Virri sucked in a good breath. *Oh Sun and Moon.* 'No, I suppose not. But – but you are widowed too . . . you must know what it is like. My Elo has been gone less than a year . . .'

Did he blush? He looked away, but she could have sworn he blushed.

'When will it have been a year?' he asked, after a moment.

'Spring. Late spring.'

Cotro's stone proved a useful distraction, when Charn returned, Cotro in tow. It was a warm golden-brown in colour, not as impressive at first sight as either copper or gold, but there was something odd about it, the pattern of little flecks more like the grain of wood than stone.

'I found it when I was a boy,' Cotro said, 'eroding out of a cliff. It looks like it was once alive, don't you think? But it's stone all right, as if Father Sun preserved it forever.'

Virri remembered the animals turned to stone near the beach cave where she and Maka had sheltered. 'I think you're right.'

Larac turned it over in his hand. 'What would you actually do with it, though? Hang it round your neck? It's heavy.'

'The Moonstone is held in the Moon-Speaker's hands as she talks from Moon-Speak Hill,' Charn said, with a look to Virri. She nodded.

Larac pursed his lips. 'You might want your hands freer, though. How about putting it on the top of a staff, or baton, more like an axe?'

Aggressive, again. Virri caught herself thinking it and felt the blood rush to her cheeks once more – this time with a pang of guilt, given they had taken the site by force. She hesitated to answer.

'What do you think, Virri?' Charn pressed.

'The Moonstone should stay as it is,' she said. 'Held in the hands.'

'Fine,' Larac said, with a wave of his hands. 'Fine with me.'

She saw Charn and Cotro throw each-other a look. Larac was facing her and possibly didn't, but she saw. *If they aren't thinking 'what's up with those two?' then I was born this summer.* She steered the conversation elsewhere again. She had until late spring to think about it . . . and she didn't feel like sharing.

They returned to Old Camp at around noon to find Maka and Huerin missing. Virri felt panic welling up, irrational as it was. 'They said they'll be back by supper,' Ruc blurted, with one glance at her face.

'Hunting? There's no real need.'

'They didn't say.'

'Do you know where they went?'

'East. No more than that.'

Virri set the children gathering firewood and busied herself with the sick house for the afternoon, throwing out anything that was best burnt and scrubbing out the rest, propping open the door to let fresh air and winter sunshine in. She half expected Larac to come seeking her, or to send one of his boys, so it was a surprise when Prya poked her head around the door.

Be friendly.

'You sent a boy with one hand collecting firewood,' Prya said.

'It's safer for them than in here, at least until I've finished. I didn't expect them to get that much.' The woman looked unconvinced. 'It's not safe for you either. You're more vulnerable to it than me.'

Now Prya looked nettled. 'Well I know that.'

'Was there something, that you wanted?'

The words came out before Virri had a chance to rethink. *Oh by Sun . . .*

'No not really.' The voice was bright but the expression stony. She turned to leave. 'Oh, Cotro said he'd cook tonight.'

Virri stood and watched her walking back towards the yard. There must have been *something* she'd wanted. Maybe she'd wanted to make friends. Now their hostility had slipped down another notch. She remembered what Cotro had said about the need for tying knots of peace. If she was to become Moon-Speaker she had to do better than this. *I should go after her.* Every instinct was screaming no – Prya had been pretty rude herself, and she still didn't know what to say – but willpower got her out the door. She caught up with ease and had to feign being more puffed out than she was.

'Prya, wait. Look, I'm sorry we seem to have got off on the wrong path. I really am just trying to keep everyone safe.'

'Huh, well . . . so was the Sun-Speaker.'

Ouch. There it is. Virri rounded on Prya a little, so she could look into her eyes. 'You said you understood. You understood what we did. If that's not true, then why are you still here? A three day walk on your own in winter is still better than staying with people you consider murderers.'

The pout and glare slipped from Prya's face. She dropped her gaze. 'He had it coming. I see that ... but, but he was going to help me. I don't want to go back empty-handed.'

'What do you mean?!'

This met with a roll of the eyes. 'Well I was here to do a stint, wasn't I? I've got a three-year-old back at Split-River and the father in a tomb. You must know what it's like . . . at least a bit.'

If I am to be Moon-Speaker, then I must deal with problems like this. Kenna would have done.

She smiled at Prya, patting her on the shoulder. 'The other pilgrims will be here soon for Solstice. We'll make sure you meet everyone – you'll get your fresh start.'

'I don't care if he's a boat-comer.'

'Yes, well, my own marriage was happy, and Huerin's parents, Ruc's mother and her man too –'

'Is Larac married?'

Virri's spine chilled. 'He – he's widowed, like us.'

Prya frowned. 'Really? He must have been very young.'

The blood was flying to Virri's cheeks. *By Sun – am I jealous*? 'Oh – oh! You mean Pig. The *younger* Larac.'

'Yes.'

'Yes. No. He's not widowed. He's never been wed that I know of.'

'Do you mean his father's unwed too?'

'Yes.'

Prya's mind was smelting that. Virri could see it on her face. *Oh by Sun and Moon . . . what do I do*?

Over by the campfire she could see Maka and Huerin were back. The others were stood up, greeting them.

'Let's head back, have supper. I'll talk to Larac – I won't promise anything, but I'll see what I can do.'

The day's light was fading but even from here Virri could see Maka was now wearing at least one black feather from the back of her hat. She sped up to greet them both and everyone else backed off a bit to let her get to them.

'You two! So that's where you've been!'

Maka beamed. 'My hair is too short for now to wear them any other way.' She took the hat off to show her. 'Huerin sorted the shape out for me too, look.'

Virri hugged the lad, standing there with a sheepish smile. 'Aw, you said you would. Where did you actually go?'

'Not far,' he said.

Maka cast a glance behind her. The others had retreated to the campfire, but all eyes were on them. Orcos had pulled the flute from his belt and struck up a cheerful tune.

Larac was on his way back, arms outstretched. 'Just for a bit of peace,' she whispered. 'We've got kind of used to being out on our own.'

Indeed. Virri lowered her own voice. 'I think once the Solstice meet is over, I want to go straight up to the Mother Circle, not wait for spring.'

Maka raised her eyebrows, but any other response was cut off by Larac's arrival, yanking the three into a big bear hug.

'You should have told us you were getting wed today! We would have made tonight's meal a feast!'

'With what?' Charn said with a laugh. 'We've barely got enough for Solstice.'

'Oh, we'd have managed.' Larac flung his hand outwards as if to include the vast bounty of the land. 'Come, sit by the fire. Cotro has a good stew for us at least.'

'A stew is a feast if you're in love,' Cotro said.

Prya had sat herself down nearest Pig and Virri found herself aiming for the stump opposite so she could keep an eye on her while Cotro doled out the supper. Ruc and Ziwa soon settled themselves either side of her. Ziwa was looking a lot better, fuller in her cheeks, thank Sun and Moon. She fought the temptation to help Ruc, seeing him clamp the bowl between his knees so he could free his one hand for the spoon.

'Did you make plans, for the Solstice celebration?' Ruc asked.

'We did, sort of . . . we might change them yet.'

'It's just . . .'

'Yes?'

'I had an idea.'

'Go on.'

'You remember what you showed me, with the green fire? That would be amazing – especially if you could make it even bigger.'

She saw Larac's ears prick up. 'I know what he means. We could do it,' he said, meeting her gaze. 'We've got enough copper ore to powder some down.'

Virri hesitated. 'It – it is a good idea. Every time I have taught anyone, I've always made green fire, everyone loves it . . . but, but don't we want to move away from Sulo's stance? Less tricks, more solid service?'

Charn shook his head. 'Day to day you're absolutely right, but on Solstice night itself we need spectacle. He wasn't wrong about everything.'

Maka nodded to Virri. 'I see what you mean, but think – it would be good for the people to see you in a different light. The way you were treated before – that needs to be wiped away.'

Wiped away. That's a good way to put it.

She smiled at Ruc. 'It's a fine idea. We'll do it.'

The stew was soon gone, and awkward silence descended a moment round the campfire, until Prya piped up.

'It's dark so early at this time of year, too early to go to bed yet. Shall we tell stories?'

Larac shrugged. 'We could.'

'Well as we have newly-weds among us, perhaps our own tales of first love?'

She grinned, but Larac's face fell. 'If you want to have us all in tears and them with us – three of us are widowed, including yourself.'

Young Weddi made a face. 'And some of us wouldn't have any story.' He nodded over to Ruc and Ziwa and smiled.

Prya's face twisted into petulant irc and silence descended again.

'I wish we had some beer,' said Pig, with a sigh like a dying breath.

Orcos laughed 'We do. I found some, earlier.'

'You did?'

'Yes – in the guard-house. It's in our type of crocks but ones we'd use for milk – I suppose to hide it.'

Cotro shook his head. 'Probably just unaware.'

This is not going well . . . beer might help.

Virri slapped her thighs and stood. 'I'll go get it – I need to stretch my legs.'

'I'll come with you,' Orcos said. 'It'll be heavy.'

They were up at the guard-house within a few short strides. Away from the campfire the cold and dark hit them. The house itself was fit only for ghosts. Orcos pegged back the door flap to let in a sliver of light.

'Maybe we should strip anything else useful out of here tomorrow and then raze it to the ground,' Orcos muttered. 'They're over here, by the dresser – don't trip on the hearth pit.'

'Listen, while I've got you on your own – '

Orcos laughed and Virri couldn't help but laugh too.

'Nothing like that! It's just, you know Prya?'

'. . .Yes.'

'Well, she asked me for my help earlier. She – she was here for a stint . . . to find a husband.'

Even in the gloom it looked like Orcos's eyes went round.

'And ... she has shown an interest, in your family . . . do you know if it might be returned?'

This time the laugh left Orcos almost like a bark. 'Oh by Sun – did she actually admit it then? Because she's been fawning over Pig like a pup who wants a belly rub pretty much since we got here.'

Not the most complimentary way to put it. 'Does Pig . . .?'

'No.' He shook his head. 'He doesn't. She won't be wedding any of us. Father wouldn't allow it. Not even a runt like me. It was bad enough our sister was wed to a chief of a tiny mud-hole, but at least he was a chief, and didn't have a string of past women behind him.'

Virri frowned. 'She can't help being a widow.'

'It's not that – where was she, when you first met her? Bedded up with one of the guards.' He shook his head again. 'Father wouldn't have it.'

Neither would you, by the sound of it.

She raised her hands. 'All right, I understand. I just promised I'd ask . . . and, well, we have to be careful – we have to make friends here.'

Orcos raised an eyebrow. 'Do we? Really?'

40.

Orcos had returned to his usual, jovial self within moments, but his 'Do we, really?' chilled Virri to the bone. She told herself, after, that it was the cock-sure speech of vigour and youth . . . but his words proved prescient. By Solstice Eve a paltry eleven people had arrived for the celebration, and three of those were boat-comers, "having a look", before they went back to the West Isle. Virri remembered hundreds of pilgrims coming to the winter Solstice in her youth. There were never as many people as in the summer, thanks to the weather as much as anything, but hundreds. Every person who did come this year had a tale of fever along with their tribute. There were people bringing the ash and bones of kin who'd died earlier in the year and some coming fresh from grief because they had nowhere else to go.

Charn, or Larac, but mostly Charn, made sure one or either of them was always there to greet the pilgrims as they dribbled in each day. Virri welcomed the travellers once she met them, later, but most of the time she was able to get on with other things. Ore had to be powdered for Ruc's idea to go ahead, and in quantity. The pilgrims had to be fed and housed, few though they were. For now they were obliged to use the current buildings, but she checked and cleaned each one. Arrowheads from the attack could be dug out of the wood, blood patches on the floors chalk-packed over. The last scraps of Sulo's mushrooms she found were thrown on a fire, out of sight of the others.

Virri was busy fencing in the growing stockade of tribute piglets for the night on the evening the last man arrived, and she didn't notice another arrival until Maka came to find her. Her and no other.

'He wants to see *me*?'

Maka nodded.

'How does he know me? Did he say?'

'He asked to see the Moon-Speaker. Huerin is talking to him now, telling him what happened.' Maka helped Virri over the mud at the gate and tied the wattle shut. 'He knew the last one – quite well by the sound of it.'

'And he still wants to talk to me?'

'Yes. He wasn't rude about it, but he wouldn't say a thing to Larac or Charn.'

They walked back up to camp, the setting sun turning the clouds pink above the Great Circle. Larac and his boys were taking care of their horses and chatting with the three new boat-comer men – comparing scars, by the sound of it.

'Y'know,' Maka said, as an aside to Virri, 'The men who attacked Duck Camp – would you know them, if you saw them again?'

'Oh yes. It's not them.'

'Well that's something, then.'

The three newcomers had their copper knives out and were showing the others, laughing and joking as they stabbed at the air.

'Don't you ever wonder, though,' Maka muttered, 'If we might have jumped from the hornets' nest straight into the mouth of a bear?'

Virri laughed. 'Yes – but that would be a good way to sum up life, would it not?' The party of men up ahead had spotted them, and they were met with a cheery wave. *Thank Sun they are on our side.* 'Where is this man for me to talk to?'

'I put him in your house. Huerin is giving him some hawthorn tea.'

The man had been sat by Huerin's side, his hands wrapped around a warm cup, but he jumped to his feet as soon as the two women entered. He was old – older than Virri, at least – with slate grey hair pulled back into a tight braid and a spare, wiry frame. His left eyelid was slumped, and scarred, but his remaining eye settled on Virri like a deer on an incoming arrow.

'You are a boat-comer as well!'

'Yes, yes I am.' Virri took in a big breath and held out her hand. 'Virri, of Duck Camp, in the far east of the Isle. Widow of Elo. I was a friend of Kenna's.'

The man threw Huerin a look and the young man nodded.

'This is Firrad, of Sun Rest Camp in the far west,' Huerin said.

Sun Rest Camp . . . sounds familiar. 'Where the singing stones came from?'

Firrad gaped. 'That's right.'

'I - I've never been there,' Virri admitted, 'But Kenna, or the old Sun-Speaker, must have told me.' She smiled at him. 'I spent much of my girlhood here, at the Circle.'

'And you knew the Moon-Speaker from then?'

'Yes. Before she was even Moon-Speaker.'

'I have just been hearing what happened to her – ' He shivered and bowed his head.

Virri nodded. 'Yes. I witnessed a lot of it. She will be remembered, and respected, from now on. Thank Sun and Moon she is with her ancestors now.' She looked towards the urn on the dresser, and he followed her gaze. Although he had not shaken her hand he was calm again and she was wary of setting him off, but she had to know. She sat down on the opposite side of the hearth. 'How did you know Kenna?'

He sat back down himself and sighed. 'I did my stint here, almost thirty years ago, and I met her before she was Moon-Speaker, too.'

'You were sweethearts?'

'No, I wed someone else, but we were friends, and we remained friends. I sent young people from our camp to do their tribute at the Mother Circle, and sick people too, as I knew her skill as a healer. I would hear her news, and she mine, every year until this one. My youngest son set off to do his stint the spring before last, happy as a lamb,' his voice cracked, 'and came back running with sickness. He only lasted another three days.'

'Did he go to the Mother Circle?'

'He was supposed to, but he fell in with some others who were heading here. He spent the whole summer listening to every word they spouted off.' He shook his head. 'The things he said. The disrespect.'

Maka passed Virri a look. 'Did he become one of the guards?'

Firrad shrugged. 'I'm not sure. Taw definitely said he *intended* to come back here, but the fever thought otherwise. All that autumn and winter it spread amongst us and we fell like leaves.'

'You got it too?' Maka asked.

'No.' He threw out his hands. 'I don't know why. I'd nursed Taw day and night, with him raving and cursing at me, but it passed me by. My eldest son, two of my grandchildren, my nephew, his wife, their baby, they all died. People began to suspect . . . They said because I had always favoured the Moon over the Sun we were now cursed. I was cursed to see my family die.'

Virri saw the tremble in him. The tears welling in the one good eye. 'They threw you out, didn't they?'

He nodded. 'I thought I would go to Kenna – and I get there, to the Mother Circle, and find no-one there. I thought she had probably died of fever too – and now I hear all this. I am surrounded by boat-comers – it's as if what Taw said has come true.'

'If Sulo told your son that our people are the enemy then it's because he was determined to make it so. My father lived in peace under the old Sun-Speaker's roof for years.' She nodded to Huerin. 'Huerin's father, too, was as innocent as Kenna.'

'And the fever?'

She sighed. 'We don't know why it has less effect on us any more than you do. There's no tiny hint it has *anything* to do with worship of the Sun or Moon. We worship both with respect, as everyone does. We always have.'

'I am not a boat-comer,' Maka said, 'and I survived it. She treated me.'

Firrad knocked back his tea. The tremble was still there, but his expression had softened.

Should I extend a hand? Exile to exile?

'Stay. Celebrate Solstice with us. Come with me to the Mother Circle after, and we can lay Kenna's ash to rest together.'

Firrad peered into her eyes a moment.

'All right.'

Virri woke early on the morning of Solstice Eve and crept about the house trying not to disturb everyone else as she got herself ready. Ziwa woke up, but she succeeded with the others. Virri raised her finger to her lips in a 'shhh' and beckoned the girl out with her for a walk. The hard sunlight shafting through the gaps hinted there had been more snow overnight. She wrapped the girl up warm. There was still much to be done, but first a walk, on such an auspicious morning.

Their shoes crunched on the snow as they left the house. The covering was a good handspan deep, but now the bruise-green clouds were retreating east on a stiff cold breeze. 'We won't go far,' Virri whispered. 'Let's just find a good juniper branch for tonight's fire while the others are sleeping.'

Ziwa embraced the task and Virri was happy to let her scamper about while the strengthening sun warmed through to her bones. The Circle looked glorious, near hot-white in its gleam.

Here's hoping for weather like this tomorrow.

'How about this one?' Ziwa asked.

The branch was perfect: deep glossy green, bristling, laden with dew-sparkled berries.

'Excellent – well done. Mind your fingers, though, let me do it.'

She reached for her knife then remembered. The axe would be better for this. One deft movement and the branch was off, the rest of the bush unharmed. Ziwa grinned.

'I remember doing this with my father when I was little,' Virri said, but the child's attention had swung to something else.

'What's that?'

Virri turned and followed the girl's point. There was something slumped at the base of the outer ring of stones. Slumped but moving.

Mad as it was Virri's first thought was that Sulo had survived everything, cold, arrows and wolves, and dragged himself here. She pictured him pulling himself across the snow, arrows out of his back like a hedgehog.

Don't be so stupid. It can't be him.

'It could be a pilgrim . . . someone who's got sick or injured on the way.' *Sick.* 'You stay here – let me check.'

The girl obeyed, to begin with at least, but by the time Virri had run halfway she could see it was no human, sick or otherwise, and perhaps her demeanour changed. Ziwa soon caught her up.

'It's a dog!'

'Could still be dangerous, though,' Virri warned. 'Stay behind me.'

He let out a tumbling high-pitched whine as they got nearer but there was no growling, and no foam at his mouth, either so Virri's heart eased. Crusted blood at his right haunch showed up livid against his overall grey. Pus oozed. It looked like a bite.

'Wolves have got him,' Ziwa said.

'I think if it was wolves there'd not be much left. More likely a badger. You stay back.' Virri eased herself forward, keeping her hands away from her weapons. 'Easy boy, easy. Let me just take a look.'

He struggled up onto his three good legs with another burst of whine, but he didn't attempt to run away.

'That's it, good lad. I think you could walk on those three legs, if you need. You're hungry, aren't you? Cold and tired and hungry.'

He came forward with a weak sway of the tail at the softness of her voice.

'That's a good boy. You come back with us, and we'll get you some grub, good lad.'

The wag grew stronger. Virri took a few steps towards Old Camp and heartened when he came further forward.

'He belonged to one of the guards,' Ziwa said.

Well, let's not hold it against him.

'Do you know his name?'

Ziwa thought for a moment. 'Acci.'

The dog brightened at the sound of his name. They turned back towards Old Camp, Acci limping behind them. It was going to be a long way, at such a speed. They had made it maybe halfway when Virri heard hoof-beats behind her. Larac drew up, with bow and quiver over his shoulder and a puzzled look on his face.

'Are you all right?' he asked.

'Yes, I'm fine. It's the dog who is injured - we're taking him back to mine to sort him out.'

Larac took in the situation, slipped from his horse and lifted Ziwa, then the dog, onto its back. 'You keep patting him, keep him calm,' he said, to the girl, 'And we'll be fine.'

He led the horse, he and Virri up front, their pace much swifter. 'Do you honestly think you can heal the dog?' he whispered.

'I don't know. I want to try, at least.'

Larac's mouth settled into a line. 'Another stray for your pack.'

'What's that supposed to mean?'

'Well . . . this man you have taken into your house . . .'

'Firrad? He's a healer – or near enough. I will need healers.'

'You will. Is that all he is?'

'Yes! Well, and a friend of the old Moon-Speaker. He can help me.'

'Uh huh.' He cast a glance back. Ziwa was doing a good job, the dog quiet and still. 'Perhaps he and young Prya could start a new life together.'

Oh sure, that'll happen. 'Did Orcos tell you?'

'Orcos didn't need to tell me anything. I've got eyes.'

Two eyes. Was that a barb?

'Jealousy doesn't suit you, Larac.'

'I never met a man or woman yet it did look good on. Nevertheless, it exists, like sky and clouds.'

Help me, Elo. She thought it, but she sensed she was on her own. *Shall I say what I think?*

Yes.

'I think you need to decide,' she said. 'Do you want me to be Moon-Speaker, with my own responsibilities, my own household, or do you want me to be your wife, while you are ruler here? Because those are two things that have never gone together, not in any known memory, nor in my own mind.'

She braced herself for a flash of anger, she expected it, but he looked more crestfallen. She thought of how he had taught her to defend herself, his kindness with the dog right now.

'Perhaps we can start a new tradition,' he said, voice low and even. 'I'm all for tradition, but sometimes you need to start afresh.'

'Perhaps we can.'

Virri stewed on it for the rest of the day and decided she had to tell Maka about Larac. She took the chance while they were in the house alone, getting ready for the feast, somewhat late, having been delayed by tending to the dog. Acci had let Huerin bathe his wound in some herb-steeped warm water without so much as a whimper, but the attempt at a bandage had been short-lived. The dog had gulped down a mess of left-over stew and an entire crock of water and curled himself by the hearth, where he now snoozed.

'Huerin said he reckons he'll be all right,' Maka said, pulling on her shoes. 'We'd best get going.'

'Yes, yes I think he will too – but there is something I need to talk about with you, on your own.'

Maka stopped in her tracks, eyebrows soaring. 'About Larac?'

'Um, yes.'

'Well, I've seen the way he's been looking at you, and with him wanting you to be Moon-Speaker . . . it didn't take much to thread the needle, y'know.'

Virri stood and brushed the dog hair off her skirt. 'How – how do you feel about that?' She realised she had been looking down and made a point of raising her chin. 'I am still in mourning for your father – I've told him he has to wait.'

Maka nodded. 'It's all right – I don't expect you to be alone forever. The worst thing about it as I see it is that I'll be – what? Step-sister? Half-sister? – to that dopey cow. But at least she's on the other side of the Isle.'

'Step-sister.' Virri pulled on the seal skin cape. 'And let's not get ahead of ourselves . . . it's not even a formal betrothal. I have until late spring, as I said.' She tightened her hair-glinters onto her braids with a quick pinch. 'And . . . well . . . you could try being a little *nicer*, if you are to be family.'

Maka rolled her eyes and grinned. 'Let's see how it goes.'

They went to the doorway and pulled the flap back. There was a cheer as they were spotted. The men had got the feast fire going in the yard earlier and the smell of roasting hog hit them at once. Virri's mind was sent back to their 'stolen' pig and the night of drying. She gave Maka a quick hug round her waist and received a squeeze in return.

'We did all right, didn't we?'

Maka nodded. 'We certainly did.'

Charn, resplendent in every bit of gold he owned, was lifting Ziwa shoulder-high so she, the youngest, could place the juniper branch atop the feast fire.

Ruc waved to Virri. 'Everything's ready! We're just waiting for the moon to come out from behind the clouds.'

The clouds scudded east, and moonlight burst out. The new Moon-Speaker stepped over the threshold towards her people and smiled.

Acknowledgements

I continue to be sincerely grateful to everyone who has supported me in my writing life: Mum, Dad and Mikel for their support and enthusiasm; Ann at Pendown for all her help and advice; my old friends at Norwich Writer's Circle (though I now live elsewhere), and all my friends across the world who have encouraged and helped me.
Learning to smelt copper was great fun, not least with the methods of the ancient world. I couldn't have done it without helpful courses I attended at Berrycroft Hub in Oxfordshire, under the tutelage of Dr James Dilley, and with New British Art in Carmarthenshire.
I also did an introductory course in archery in preparation for this novel, thanks to a lifelong learning initiative run by Cornwall County Council, while I was living in Cornwall. It wasn't free, but it was affordable, and I applaud their broad thinking and commitment to adult education.
Thank you so much to Richard Pearson at PenguinBoy Graphic Design in St Albans www.penguinboy.net for his work on the excellent cover.
Gratitude must go, too, to the teams of archaeologists, who have worked for over a century to reveal the lives of our ancestors, bit by bit.
Any mistakes are, of course, my own.

Printed in Dunstable, United Kingdom

70357741R00170